I0733348

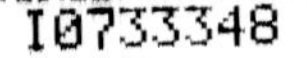

Damaged KINGDOM

MJ CROUCH

DAMAGED KINGDOM: GILDED EMPIRE

Chapter 1
Mari

I always knew I would die young.

No matter what I did or where I went, I couldn't shake this notion that old age wasn't in the cards for me. It lingered in the back of my mind as I had lunch with school friends as a teen and echoed in each fake smile I offered my allies. I would never know a peaceful or happy life, never grow old. I would die early, in my prime.

Knowing it my whole life meant I'd had time to accept it. That was why I wasn't shocked when Cash left me alone to die. Cold and bleeding on the floor of the warehouse, with ribs that were desperate for a fucking break, I felt it. That inevitability. Fate was a hard press on my chest, forcing me to acknowledge the end with every tight breath.

This is it. There was no doubt about it. Everything had fallen into place exactly how I'd always thought it would. But for the first time, it didn't feel right. The Mari destined to meet her maker early wasn't me. I had too much to live for to go so soon.

It hit me like a sledgehammer as warm blood seeped through my fingers before dropping to the ground like sands through an hourglass. I didn't want to die. I had too much to do to succumb. I had to survive.

Once again, I was grateful for the damn tracker. Sooner or later, it would guide my men to me. I just had to make it until they arrived. I could do that. While I did, I'd try to save myself.

Grief had shackled me for long enough. It was time to let the real Mari out again. The woman who'd taken the city and rebuilt it the way she wanted. She wasn't the type to lie around and wait. She was a woman of action. I never wanted to forget her again. I wasn't a damsel waiting for saving. I was a motherfucking queen, and I would claw my way home from hell if I had to.

Peering around the neglected warehouse, I grimaced at the state of it. The lights overhead were too bright and my head too foggy to make much out, but I could see dirt-covered floors and windows, while random reels of what looked like rusted wire lay discarded in the corners. That wasn't even counting the dark mystery piles in shadowed corners that my eyes couldn't quite make out.

Note to self, get a tetanus shot when you get home.

Squinting harder, I saw a door in the same direction Cash had left from and smiled. If I could get out there, the tracker would work better than it would inside the building. I was fairly certain the walls weren't thick enough to stop it from working, but it would give Grey a better chance of finding me in time.

Plan in place, all I had to do was figure out how to get across the floor. My arms were still locked together, the metal cuffs digging into my skin with every movement. They latched my palms together, so I couldn't do too much with them. I couldn't walk either, not without risking even more injury.

"Thank god for leg day," I murmured, wincing at the pain just whispering created. Pressing my legs to the floor underneath me, I shoved myself forward, trying to keep my core stable so I didn't make my injuries worse. I had no other option, especially with my ribs still damaged from the first time Cash had ambushed me, but I tried to be as gentle with myself as I could. The last thing I needed was to end up with a hole in my lung because I got too cocky.

Every movement was agony, pure and simple, and I had to stop often.

Greyson won't leave you here, I reminded myself every time. *He'll come. He always comes, and this time, Dominic will be with him. They'll be here soon. They're coming for you.*

Except, I didn't think they would. Or could. The longer it took, the harder it was to move, and the more my heart sank. Was Greyson even okay? Had Dominic even made it out? If Cash had been telling the truth, they both could've burned. And then there was Nate. Was he panicking inside my home after we didn't return on time, or was it the first place Cash looked after he left? Did I damn Nate's soul the first time we met?

I didn't know, but I vowed to find out. And if anyone had hurt my men, I was going to survive long enough to make them wish they'd never met us.

Even though I mostly used my thighs to do the work, my fingers dug into whatever crevices and cracks they could find to help me on my way. Every inch felt like a mile, but I didn't give up. Still, the longer it took, the harder it was to move.

Time hung in suspended moments I couldn't measure as I grew cold enough that my fingers stiffened and shook against the concrete as I tried to find a handhold. My nails were broken and bleeding, absolutely ravaged from my attempts to help heave my body forward. To find help. To survive.

Black sharpened at the edges of my vision, and weakness weighed down my limbs like heavy boulders.

A break, I promised myself. *Another short break and then I'll get back to it. I'll get out and find the guys.*

I didn't know how long I passed out, but I woke dizzy and exhausted, with no clue how I was still alive. A glance at the smeared blood trail behind me told me it was a miracle I'd survived this long, but my time was running out. If I didn't get out soon, I wouldn't make it at all.

No more breaks, I commanded myself. *It's do or die.* Literally.

I was so focused on what I was doing that the scuff of shoes and the quick tap of footsteps startled me. Listening harder, hope brightened in my chest. At first, I was sure it was Greyson or Dominic, maybe both. The longer I listened, the more I realized how wrong I was. The tread was too heavy for anything my men wore. Ignoring the despair, I assumed it was Cash coming to gloat. He was just the type of asshole to do it.

I'm going to make him pay, I swore. *I'll use every last bit of strength to give him something to remember me by. However he grabbed me, I'll make it work.* Even a single scar on his pretty little face would be worth the effort.

"Back to watch me die, Cash? How clichéd of you." Pain was evident in my voice, but there was no point hiding it. I hurt. I ached. I was dying. We both knew it, even if I loathed the idea.

I'd just decided to live, but my mind wanted what my body didn't have the energy to offer. It was bullshit.

Silence was Cash's only answer.

Not wanting to die on the floor, I hauled myself to my knees, breathing through the vertigo that threatened to flatten me again. My limbs were so weak, I shook hard enough for anyone to see, and my teeth were chattering.

"You're a coward, Cash. Even if I die, I'm going to haunt you until you're begging for death." With no affinity for brujería, I wasn't sure how to make it happen, but I hoped intention would do the trick. Maybe my ancestors would put the work in motion for me.

Amara always said I had a little magic in my family line. I had to hope she was right. If not, the world was a cruel place.

Lifting my head to spear Cash with a wish so fierce his grandchildren would feel my wrath, I expected the last face I saw to be an asshole. Instead, I looked up and saw an angel.

"Antoni."

The word was barely more than a breath on my lips, but it felt good to say out loud. The meaning of seeing him hit me, and I sucked in a breath. Amara always said angels carried the righteous to heaven themselves. I was neither righteous nor a true believer, so maybe he was really a fallen angel. Truthfully, I didn't mind either way, as long as I got my brother back.

Seeing him was bittersweet and beautiful. Even if I grieved what could have been true happiness for me, I was happy to see him. So damn happy. I'd missed him more than words.

He dropped to his knees at my side and mumbled low enough that I couldn't make out the words themselves. The tone told me he was swearing, though. Callused fingers brushed my hair from my face then worked on the manacles at my wrists. The soft whir of a Dremel, accompanied by pinpricks of what felt like burning, was the soundtrack just before the chains linking the cuffs together broke. My shoulders screamed at the unexpected release, but having my hands free tamped down some of the panic I'd refused to voice that lingered at the back of my throat.

"Thank you," I croaked, tipping my head back. I wanted to see Antoni, to refamiliarize myself with the face that had been at my side my whole life, but the lights were too bright and my vision too hazy. I cursed, annoyed that blood loss was getting to me.

"Time to go, *tesorita*."

In the back of my mind, I wondered why he called me that instead of the snarky *princessa* he'd always preferred, but as he lifted me into his arms, I found I didn't care. My twin was with me at the end. That was all that mattered.

Though he tried to be gentle, Antoni's movements sent agony rippling through my stomach, and I winced. "I thought dying was supposed to be less painful," I panted. "This shit hurts."

"I know," Antoni soothed, bundling me closer. "Breathe through it just a little longer."

Right. Because I was dying. It would all be over soon.

I let him carry me out of the warehouse until the cold brush of night air graced my skin. Every step, I felt myself slip closer and closer to the place where we would be united again for good. I welcomed it. I was so tired of being alone.

But was I alone?

No. I'd had Grey, always. The thought of him—of Dominic and Nate, too—sent more pangs through me, though they were of the emotional variety. I debated keeping my questions in, but I didn't want to. If I was going out, I wanted to go with nothing left to be answered. "Are they alive?"

Thankfully, I didn't have to explain. Antoni knew whom I meant. "Yes."

Relief bowled me over, and grateful tears ran from behind closed eyes, though I had no clue when I'd shut them. Barely there mist caressed my cheeks as the faintest sprinkle of rain fell. It felt cleansing. Like if I stayed in the mist for long enough, all the blood would wash away, and I would be clean again.

A beautiful lie.

"I miss them already," I admitted. It felt like a dirty secret, but Antoni was my vault. My home. He would hold my secrets for me until I was strong enough to carry them again.

Warm air coasted over my forehead, followed by the press of dry lips and an unshaved cheek. "It will all be okay. I promise."

And I believed him.

I tried thinking of all the things I wished I'd done, but regrets didn't matter. What mattered was what I had. I'd cleaned up the city, rebuilt it strong enough that I had faith it would withstand

Cash. I couldn't say I'd fallen in love, but I'd finally let myself take the love that had been offered to me time and time again. I'd had Greyson—and even Dominic—for a time. I'd had Nate close, and in those moments when it was just us, he'd seen me. I knew he had. I had family like Cameron and Rey, friends like Shara and Aislynn. They'd guided me, kept me on the path I wanted to stay on, helped me become the person I was.

For all the blood and death of my life, they made everything worth it.

With nothing more to do, no last words to say, I curled against the chest of my brother and waited for him to take me home.

Chapter 2
Nate

Thirty, thirty-one, thirty-two, thirty-three, thirty-four...

Once again, I paced the foyer, waiting for Mari and the others to get home. At first, I let the sound of my footsteps on the tile soothe my worries. But the longer they were gone, the less it worked. So, I counted. Forty steps to one end of the room, forty steps to the other. Over and over, and over again.

No matter how many times I did it, the tightness in my gut wouldn't ease.

It'd started about the time Mari had called to tell me they were planning to infiltrate Cash's den. This unrelenting twist of my stomach screamed at me: *something's wrong, something's wrong, something's wrong.*

Regrets wormed their way into my mind about the same time as visions of a bleeding Mari rushed through my head. I should've pushed harder to go with her, not taken no for an answer. My only excuse was I wasn't awake, and she'd already been out of the house when she'd let me know what was going down.

Never again, I vowed. It was Mari's choice, but I'd do my damnedest to make it happen. If she let me, I was going to be so far up her ass, she'd have to pry me off like a barnacle if she wanted space.

Raking a hand through my hair, I felt my fingers clenching at the strands as the urge to call her nagged at me until I couldn't take it anymore. The first glimpse of dawn crested the horizon as I pulled up her number and hit send.

Voice mail.

I did it again. Same thing. They were busy, I knew that, but I couldn't help myself as I did the same to Dominic, then Greyson. Hell, I even called Moore.

No one answered.

The unease twisted harder, like a wraith trapped beneath my skin. Something was wrong. Very, very wrong.

"Fuck it."

I ran for the living room, running my fingers over every nook and cranny to find the weapons cache I knew was there. I wasn't an idiot. This was a kingpin's home; there were guns everywhere, and I just had to find one. Then I could go find my girl.

Not your girl, the little voice in my head reminded me, but I shoved it aside as I kept looking.

I was on the second to last piece of furniture, a side table next to the window, when I felt the slight give of a hidden drawer. It took a minute, but I pried it open just as someone knocked on the front door. Knowing it could be Aces coming for the Marcosa seat of power while Mari was occupied, I prepared to do battle.

Running through the motions to arm myself was like riding a bike, and I stuffed my pockets with extra ammo before closing the hidden safe again. If it was one against a dozen, I doubted I'd survive, but at least I wouldn't let them take Mari's home without taking some of them with me.

If that was all I could do, I'd do it well.

Another knock brought the sound of tense footsteps from the back of the house as Amara went to answer. She caught sight of me, armed and admittedly semi-feral, and blanched. Holding up a hand, I motioned her back and away from the door. Once she realized I wasn't armed against *her*, she nodded and retreated to the kitchen, where I was sure she had her favorite toys stashed too. She wasn't the type to let someone trash a home that was just as much hers as it was Mari's.

Gun at my side, I opened the door a crack, surprised when instead of the pack of Aces ready to knock down the door and take what was Mari's, it was a girl.

A glance showed she wasn't much younger than me. Twenty-two at least, but she had that air of sadness about her that made people seem younger. More fragile. She twisted a bracelet around and around her wrist like it was her version of a worry stone. Gaunt cheeks and hollow eyes set into skin that looked unnaturally pale for her skin tone made me wonder when she'd last seen the sun. Even the clothes on her body didn't fit right, though they were stream-lined and expensive.

Honestly, she looked like shit. I could relate.

Apparently, she wasn't expecting me either because she stepped back, eyes darting around me like she was looking for anyone else. When she didn't find whoever it was, she squared her shoulders. "Is she here?"

My default setting was distrust, and something about her had me on edge. Tucking the gun into my pants casually, I crossed my arms and spread my feet, taking up more space in the doorway. "Who the hell are you?"

"Sabine." She said it like I should know who she was and deflated slightly when she realized I didn't. Nerves had her craning her neck around me, and I shifted to keep her line of sight on me and only me. With a raised eyebrow, I made it clear she wasn't getting past unless I let her. She nodded to herself, almost like she expected it. "Is she here?"

She. *Mari.* That was twice she'd asked, and the cramping in my gut was getting worse. I was going to need an entire roll of antacids by the time my girl got home.

"No, she's not."

She nodded, looking again like she'd expected it, and that set me on edge. I looked at the girl—Sabine—over again, closer this time. Tear tracks marred her face, and deep regret was heavy in her eyes. Something about it and the soul-sucking feeling of despair in the air make my jaw clench.

There were times when you were on a mission and everything seemed fine. Normal, even. Then your gut started screaming at you to get down, get out, get gone. You'd be a mile away when a bomb went off or found out later that someone got shot where you'd been standing, or you'd go to clean your weapon, only to find it primed to misfire. The subconscious saw more than the conscious mind could ever dream of, and it was an unspoken rule that if your instincts were screaming at you, you fucking listened.

After years of experience, my gut was well honed, and it said that whoever this Sabine was, she knew something about what had happened to Mari.

Yanking her inside, I slammed the door and locked it before I dragged her farther into the house. She hung limp in my grasp like a kitten with its scruff caught, and my teeth ground at the submissive move that screamed of guilt.

Only when we were in the living room did I drop her arm and step back. Deep breaths filled my lungs as I tried—and failed—to calm myself. Couldn't get information out of her if I lost my cool. "What did you do?"

"Nothing."

"Let me make one thing clear—I don't do lies. I may be new here, but I wasn't born yesterday. Mari hasn't come home yet, and I know you know why. So save us all time and tell me what happened."

"I didn't do anything," she insisted. "She should be here."

"But she isn't, so what the fuck did you do to her?"

"I didn't do anything."

"That's two lies," I said clearly. "Don't attempt a third. Tell me."

"I didn't—I can't—I'm sorry."

Fresh tears streamed down Sabine's face as she sobbed, and I knew I was right. I shoved her into the wall, one arm braced against her collarbone to hold her in place. I didn't hit women, but I didn't count them out either. *"What did you do?"*

She yelped at the darkness of my tone but shook her head, keeping silent. No matter how many times I asked, she refused to answer, and she wouldn't meet my eyes.

"What are you doing?" Amara rushed into the room and grabbed me by the bicep, trying to pull me off. "Get away from her! What the hell are you thinking, Nate?"

"She hurt Mari."

Amara stilled, staring at Sabine like she'd never seen her before, when I knew that wasn't true. No one walked up to a kingpin's house like that unless they were comfortable with them. Close, even. The protectiveness I saw when Amara interacted with Mari slid into something deeper, something darker. If I'd had any doubt that Mari was a good boss, friend, and person, it was gone. Amara was ready to disembowel Sabine on my word alone, all because she *could've* hurt Mari. That spoke volumes.

"You're going to answer his questions, or I'm going to pull the answers out of you in the most painful way I can imagine." Amara's promise rang through the air, and Sabine paled even further.

Before anything else could happen, the front door opened, and Dominic came in, practically carrying Greyson.

Grey looked awful. Blood dried along one side of his face, but it was the burn along his temple that told me he'd been grazed. A shot close enough for a burn that bad would've been damn near fatal. His hand was tight against his side, where blood leaked between his fingers, but it wasn't steady so I wasn't worried. All in all, he was lucky, though I could tell he didn't feel it when he looked around at the empty room and found a Mari-sized hole in the atmosphere waiting for him.

Meanwhile, Dominic's eyes lit up at the sight of the woman trapped below me, and he scoured the hall even as he moved farther into the living room. "Where is she? Is she okay?"

"No," I said. "She's not with you?"

Dominic's strides hitched on his way to toss Greyson on the couch, and that unease cramped my gut so tightly, I wanted to throw up. "No."

Then where the fuck was she?

Dominic moved carefully to settle Greyson before he strode over to our little friend. He laid a single finger under Sabine's chin and tipped her head up, up, up. "Where is she, Sabine?"

He said it softly. Hell, even the way he looked at her was gentle, but something about the way he stared at her told me nothing about him was anymore.

"I don't know," she whispered.

"You were the last person to see her," he countered, and my hold on her grew firmer. She was the last tether to Mari. The last sighting that wasn't one of these men. I didn't know them well, but I knew enough. They'd have never let her leave without them unless she was with someone they trusted.

They had trusted Sabine, and she had betrayed Mari. She'd betrayed the Marcosas, and in all likelihood, she'd die for it.

As if she realized it too, Sabine cried in earnest. Desperation coated every syllable out of her mouth. She wrapped a hand around

Dominic's wrist, clinging. Begging. "I really don't know. I brought her where I had to and—"

"*Had* to." My voice was thick with hate, but knowing something and hearing it were two different beasts. It was easy to hold out hope you were mistaken until you were given proof direct from a liar's mouth. "Someone told you to take her somewhere, and you did it."

Her nod made Dominic's fingers spasm, and he shifted his grip until his palm rested on the top of her throat, long fingers cresting her cheeks. Squeezing until I could see the imprint of her teeth against them, he kept her gaze trapped on him. "Who?"

Sabine said nothing, and my heart sank. He had her. That fucking psycho had her.

"Cash took her," Greyson said quietly. He knew it just like I did, but we had to be clear. Anything less was starting a war on hearsay, and that would put Mari's position in jeopardy. Even with the tension bleeding off all three of us, we had to be careful. We had to take the right steps, or things would get infinitely worse.

"Yes." Sabine's voice was barely audible, but it stole the air like she'd set off a bomb in the room.

"Tell me why I shouldn't slit your throat right here." Dominic squeezed until his fingers mottled, and Sabine's eyes watered. One look at him and all I could see was the same monster that had lurked inside another pair of eyes. Rage. Madness. I hadn't expected it, but I should have. Love had the ability to make monsters of men.

"Don't," Greyson croaked, sitting up with a grimace. Eyes semi-glazed, he was obviously in pain, but he didn't settle back. "Mari wouldn't want her to die. Not when she did it to protect her sister."

Dominic's fingers tightened, and Sabine squeaked in pain. "I don't give a shit about her sister; I care about our girl. *Where. Is. Mari?*"

"I don't know!" Sabine sobbed, though it was hard to hear with how tight Dominic held her. As if he realized it, he loosened his grip, and Sabine sighed in relief. "She handed me her keys and told me to run, so I did. I went back for you two, but you were already gone, and I didn't want to stick around so Cash could kill me. As soon as he cleared out, I came here. I don't know anything else."

He didn't like her answer, and I could see the madness festering. Ironically, that was the dark side of Dominic that matched Mari, like bookends made of the same wood. That man, once he found some control, would be the perfect warrior to protect her. He could have her and keep her safe too. He just needed to open his eyes and realize that black and white was an illusion. We were all shades of gray.

But until he realized that, Dominic wasn't like Mari. If he killed Sabine, it would take a piece of him that he'd never get back. The man Mari loved would be gone. I couldn't let that happen.

"Let her go, Dominic. Don't become a monster when it won't help anything."

For a minute, I didn't think it would work. Then the words penetrated the red haze of Dominic's mind, and he stumbled away from Sabine so fast, he nearly tripped over his own feet. "I didn't—"

No one said anything, and I could see the shame settling on his shoulders. Grey hobbled over, ignoring everyone but Dominic as he clapped a hand on the other man's shoulder. "It'll be okay."

Dominic nodded, eyes stuck to the window across the room and as far away from Sabine as he could get. For her part, she didn't look shaken; she looked...resigned. Like his actions were her penance.

Only when Dominic was settled did Greyson dig into his wallet and pull out a business card. "Call this number and ask for John. Tell him Mari sent you for Brittany. He'll get you to your sister, and you can get out of the city."

She reached for the card, only to struggle when Greyson refused to give it up. He yanked her closer, letting his frame dwarf her. "I think it's time you left the West Coast."

Sabine's eyes filled, but she nodded. Message received. "Thank you."

Greyson dropped his hand, letting her take the card and her personal space back. "You can show your gratitude by never coming back."

We all watched as she sprinted out of the house, nearly slipping on the tile in her haste. The door shut behind her, and I worried it shut behind our only lead too.

"Where does that leave us now? We have no way to track Mari," I reminded Grey.

"Yes, we do."

He hobbled to the office, with Dominic and me following close behind. A quick fingerprint scan and a passcode that had more numbers than I'd ever seen, and we were in. The lights flicked on, nearly blinding in their brightness, and all of us squinted.

"Get one of the tablets from the far table," Grey told Dominic before turning to me. "You, sit."

Right. Despite the desperate urge to find Mari, I wasn't one of her men, and I wasn't one of the family. That they let me into the inner sanctum was a show of trust I hadn't earned yet. But I would. I'd make sure of it.

I just had to hope my secrets wouldn't destroy us when I did.

After getting what Greyson needed, Dominic leaned against the table next to me, arms crossed and brow furrowed. I wanted to check on him, but we didn't have that type of relationship. I didn't know him, and I doubted he'd appreciate me seeing underneath the jovial playboy mask he wore so easily. So I kept my mouth shut as we watched Greyson plug in the tablet and pull up a map program that looked just like the GPS on my phone.

"The tracker," Dominic swore, lifting fully to his feet. I followed, eager to get closer and see what was happening. "I completely forgot about it."

"That's the point. She didn't want us to use it unless we had to," Grey said as he typed. "It's offline now, so I'm checking her last known location. If she's in a basement or something like that, the signal may not register."

A few more clicks and the sight of a blinking black dot greeted us. "What does that mean?" I asked.

"It means it's been offline for thirty minutes." Grey checked the map and his watch and frowned.

"How long have you been out of contact with her?"

"At least an hour. Maybe more," Dominic admitted. "I sent her off with Sabine and went back in for Greyson. The bastards started a fire around us, and this numbskull refused to leave without Mari's fucking painting. By the time we got out, the car was gone, so we thought Mari had come home. I didn't even think about the tracker."

"It's not a numbskull move if we can find Mari and avoid the fallout of a Kincaid meltdown. Trust me, they aren't pretty. Besides, you wouldn't have had access to the tracker to look," Greyson told him. "I'll fix that for you as soon as we get her back, though."

"Me too." Having her location was dangerous, but I was through wondering if she was coming home alive. I wanted eyes on her at all times.

Greyson snorted and ignored my request, not that I expected him to grant it. It was up to Mari. I'd just have to convince her it was necessary.

Suddenly, the dot flashed red and disappeared from the screen.

"What the hell?" Greyson sat up with a wince, while Dominic and I leaned in over each shoulder. "Get back, you fucking gargoyles."

Dominic snorted. "Mari used to love that show."

"She still does," Greyson corrected, but he was distracted. We all were. "I catch her watching it some nights when she can't sleep and working out doesn't help."

He zoomed out, found the dot, and zoomed back in on the map so we could see where it was. "What the hell?" Frowning, he did it again like that would change the dot's location.

Dominic tipped his head and squinted. "Is that—"

"Yeah," I answered. The question was, how the hell did she get there?

All three of us stared at the screen for a heartbeat before breaking into a run down the hall. It didn't matter if she'd hotwired a car to drive herself to Seattle General; it mattered that we'd found her. It mattered that she could be alive.

Don't hope, I told myself. *The fall is too painful to risk it.*

But I was pretty sure it didn't matter anymore. Looking back, I'd been falling since the day we met.

Chapter 3
Dominic

Everyone noticed when we burst into Seattle General. It could've been the blood coating Grey and me or Nate's scowl, but I had a feeling it was the dark aura of retribution trailing in our wake.

Our girl was in the hospital, and someone was going to die because of it.

"What name would she go under?" Nate asked, and I was impressed he'd even thought about it. Mari obviously wouldn't be under Marcosa; that would be too easy for her enemies to sniff out.

"Mine," Greyson answered. For once, I was bummed I'd kept the family name.

As we neared the information desk, I tried to don the friendly mask I wore in public. Normally, I could slip into it like a second skin, but now, the seams felt too tight, like it didn't quite fit anymore.

I didn't know if it was because I was worried about Mari or because of what I'd done to Sabine.

I'd nearly killed the girl, and I wouldn't have flinched. Oh, I would've hated myself for it later, but in the moment, that didn't matter. She crossed Mari. End of story.

Leaning my arms against the counter, I tried my hardest to fall into the role I'd perfected over the years. "We're looking for someone."

"Name," the woman behind the computer drolled.

"Marianna Andrews."

She didn't move, didn't so much as blink faster, but there was a twitch at the edge of her eye that told me she was about to lie. She typed something and dropped her lips into a fake frown. "I'm not seeing anyone by that name. Are you sure she's here and not at another hospital?"

Considering we have the GPS location to prove it...

Greyson stepped forward. "We're sure. Try again, please. She could be under Mari."

The woman's fingers didn't flinch on the keys. "As I said, she isn't in the system, and even if she were, I couldn't tell you anything. So, unless you're family—"

"Husband, husband, boy toy," I interrupted, pointing to myself, Greyson, and Nate in order. If Mari came to the hospital instead of going home, she was hurt. We didn't have time to play around. "Can you please just tell us where the fuck she is?"

To her credit, the woman didn't bat an eye, and after Grey fished out his ID that clearly showed he was an Andrews, she relented on getting a doctor to speak to us. With a wary eye and a scowl aimed directly at me, she waved us over to an empty seating area and went back to her computer.

Nate sat, leg bouncing, but it wasn't a nervous tic. His lips moved silently as he...counted? I didn't ask, though. It was none of my business how he coped with stress. Grey sat still and sharp in the chair, eyes on everyone, even as he made calls and sent texts. Meanwhile, I sat and stared at the wall and let the regrets eat me alive.

All I could think about was the worst outcome: that she'd died alone. Without us. That I'd never get the chance to fix things between us. That our breakup at the docks was the last time we'd actually spoken. It couldn't end like that. We couldn't be over.

I *had* to fix things, but that meant she had to be alive.

Eventually, a doctor stopped in front of us, and Greyson must've made introductions, but it was hard to hear over the heartbeat pounding in my ears. Grey nudged me, and I forced myself to focus on what the doctor was saying. "Your wife lost a lot of blood and sustained some nasty internal injuries to boot. We've given her a transfusion and fixed what we could, but she needs time to rest and heal."

I pointedly ignored the shiver down my spine when she called Mari my wife. It sounded good. Perfect, even. But we had a long way to go to get there. "She's alive, though?"

The doctor's face softened a fraction, and she smiled. She was older, with smile lines embedded into her face. She looked like she enjoyed her life and was happy. I wanted that. Not for me, necessarily, but for Mari. I wanted her to grow old enough to show her life on her skin in more than just scars. "She is."

Thank fuck. I drew in an intentionally slow breath and let it out, feeling the tension holding Grey, Nate, and me together loosen.

"We'll give her whatever she needs to heal *at home*." Confirmation that Mari was alive took the edge off my panic, but the walls still felt like they were closing in. All I could think about was how easy it would be for someone to sneak in and take her out. We needed to get her home and out of easy access as soon as possible.

Greyson shoulder checked me, pasting on a strained smile for the doctor. "What he's trying to say, Dr. Grant, is Mari's a figure who isn't safe in the open. We need to get her somewhere secure."

The woman—Dr. Grant, apparently—didn't budge an inch. In

fact, she crossed her arms and glared at us. "I'm aware who she is, but she's not going anywhere. Your wife just had *surgery*. She needs at least a few days to see if she'll even wake up on her own. After that, we'll have to make sure there's no chance of sepsis or any other infections. Move her, and risk her recovery."

Nate answered before Greyson or I could snap. "We'll figure it out. For now, we need to speak to your head of security and whoever runs the place. There are things we'll need to do before we let anyone near her again."

"You're not going to stop me from taking care of my patient." Dr. Grant leveled a glare my way, and I was actually impressed. How many people glared at someone in the mafia? The doc had a spine of steel.

"No," Nate replied patiently, "but we are going to do whatever it takes to make sure our girl is protected. That includes vetting and securing the best staff for her care and moving her to a private area that will ensure we can not only monitor her efficiently but will remove any danger from the rest of your patients. Does that work for you?"

Dr. Grant stared at us, and I wondered if she was trying to think of a way to throw us out that wouldn't have us breaking down the doors. Joke was on her; there was nothing she could do to keep us out. Finally, she nodded. "That's fine."

"Can we see her?" Grey rasped, and I could see the sweat beading against his temple. He was in pain, but with Mari out, we were the Marcosa leaders. Neither of us could afford to show any weakness.

The reminder that we were the only things standing between her and a coup from the other families straightened my back. If they needed to see strength, I'd be a fucking statue until Mari was ready to take over again.

"Third floor. I'll let the charge nurses know to extend visitors passes to all three of you, but she needs quiet." Dr. Grant's eyes were planted firmly on me, like I was the troublemaker. I didn't blame her.

"We'll be on our best behavior," I promised.

She didn't respond to that. "I'll send the people you need upstairs."

"Thank you," Nate said, shaking her hand. She did the same to Grey and me, and then the good doctor was gone.

"She's alive," I breathed, still a little awed. It didn't seem real after the night we'd had.

"She's alive," Grey agreed.

"Let's get to her, then."

Moving like we'd done it a thousand times, Nate and I boxed Grey in, giving him what little support we could offer in public under the guise of guiding him while he was on his phone.

"Moore and the others are coming up. They'll get the background checks done and clear out her current floor. Then they can find a way to separate her from everyone else."

Nate cleared his throat. "There's a private ward near the top of the building. It's older and slated for renovation soon, so it's probably available."

Grey side-eyed Nate. "How do you know that?"

Nate shrugged and leaned forward to punch the elevator button, only for it to open immediately. "I watch the news, just like everyone else."

Grey mulled it over while we stepped inside and hit the button for Mari's floor. He glanced at Nate again like he wasn't sure he believed him, but by the time the elevator stopped again, Moore and his crew were headed up to check it out and Nate was trying and failing to hide his smile.

Smacking him upside the head, I led us into the hallway. "Don't be so fucking smug."

"Of course not," he said with false solemnity. "It's a totally normal occurrence to know something Greyson doesn't."

For his part, Grey didn't interject. He straightened himself to his usual stick-up-the-ass posture and strode down the hall like he wasn't hurting at all.

"We're here for my wife, Mari Andrews."

The nurse's head popped up, eyes wide. "Right, Dr. Grant called up. She mentioned...multiple husbands."

The nurse, Deborah, took her time looking us over, and by the time she was done, I was sure she'd have no problem leading one of us to an empty closet or a break room.

Mari would absolutely ruin Nurse Deborah if she found her or any other staff hitting on us, and the fact that she thought it was okay to leer at a patient's partner? Gross.

Seeing it too, Grey's tone turned frosty. "That's correct. All three of us are her husbands. So, I'd appreciate it if you kept your tongue in your mouth and your eyes focused on our *wife*."

Nurse Deborah gave one slow, desperate blink, then it was gone, and she held up a stack of printed name tags. "Right. Room 344. End of the hallway, take a right. You can have two people in the room overnight."

"We'll all be staying until further notice." Before she could argue anymore, Grey snatched the visitors' passes from her, and as one, we moved down the hall, leaving a gaping nurse behind us.

Nate snickered the second we were out of earshot. "She's going to be a pain in the ass."

"She's inconsequential. I'm removing her from Mari's team the second I find the charge nurse." Grey waved the concern away.

"What if she is the charge nurse?" Nate asked.

"Then I'll go over her head until I get what I want."

There was a long pause before Nate muttered, "Rich people solutions."

"Damn right," Grey and I confirmed.

It took no time to find Mari's room. The door yawned open, and another nurse exited, one with a bright-blue tag on her lanyard. *Charge Nurse Erin.*

"You must be the husbands."

Again, Grey talked to her, but my mind was elsewhere.

The hallway looked so plain. White tile, white walls, blue trim. It was all so perfunctory. So why did it set my heart racing? Why did I feel like I was breaking apart just standing near it?

What if she's dead? What if they lied, and we go in and she's stopped breathing? What if she doesn't want to see me? I don't want to be here. I should leave. What if...

On and on, the thoughts whirled until I thought I'd puke, but I couldn't stop them. Couldn't move. Couldn't do anything but stare and wait. Eventually, the charge nurse left, and Grey turned to me and sighed. "It's normal to be anxious, but we've got to get in there."

That was Greyson. He saw the core of people, even when they didn't want them to. "I can't."

"You can, and you will," he promised. A look at Nate had them bookending me like we'd done for Grey, except they each had a firm grip on my arms this time.

"I'm not a flight risk," I snapped.

"No?" Grey's laugh was pointed, so I shut my mouth. I had considered leaving, but I wasn't *going* to. At least, I didn't think I was.

"I've replaced Deborah. From now on, Mari will have competent nurses who can do their jobs without their libidos causing a problem," he sneered as we crossed the threshold and paused. All that separated us from Mari was a blue-and-green curtain so thin I could practically see the shape of her already. "Christ, they need to upgrade this place."

Nate rolled his eyes. "The little people can't afford cashmere curtains, Your Highness."

"They could if a rich person donated them," Grey snarked as he yanked back the curtain and bared the bed to the world.

They were still talking, but all I could focus on was her.

Since I'd come home, I'd spent hours just watching Mari. I wanted to see that girl I knew, the one who came to me to fix her problems and sought shelter in my arms. But I hadn't found her. Even when grief stole the spark in her, she was still strong. Still a force all on her own.

Staring at her in that hospital bed, hair damp and limp around her pale, bruised face, I saw the girl I'd known. She was there in the stillness of Mari's body and the soft rise and fall of her chest underneath the world's thinnest blanket. She was there in the way her brutalized hands lay gently on her stomach, even as Grey moved to her side and picked one up. That stillness was the soft, delicate version of Mari, and suddenly, I wanted it gone.

I was a fool to think that girl would've survived. Mari was right; there was no room for softness in our world. Not where everyone else could see. I'd been wishing for an impossibility and hoping for a pipe dream. People grew and evolved. They changed. Mari had to even more than most in order to stay alive. I didn't understand it before, but I got it now.

She was soft where it counted. With us and her friends, her trusted people. She was soft with Jerron, even when she didn't have to be. She could've killed him the second she made him, but she didn't. She recognized the trappings of her life winding around him, and she got him out. Even her father wouldn't have saved the kid. He was a liability and a threat, and he would've been put down as one, but not Mari.

Despite knowing it could make her look weak, Mari led with her head and her heart. She led with compassion. It was why Moore and Tennessee were devoted to her, why Rey took a bullet to protect her. She was good. So fucking good, and I'd been so blind to it.

How could I have thought she was anything other than who she was meant to be? I'd seen for myself how easy it was to fall into darkness when the people you loved were in danger or hurt. Could I really blame her for doing exactly that?

Mari had made the right choice ending things between us. The realization hit me square in the chest. Even if she forgave me, I didn't deserve a third chance. Not anymore.

"Get over here," Grey snapped, eyes burning into mine. He was livid, and I knew the fine shake of his hands wasn't pain anymore. It was rage. "You don't get to bow out yet. I don't care what she said before, you'll be here until she kicks you out herself. Same to you."

His glare turned to Nate, who'd taken up a post by the door. The kid crossed his arms and lifted his chin, his feet firmly planted. "I'm not touching her until she's awake and can give me permission. Unlike you two, we aren't that close, and I'm not going to go any further until I have her consent."

The reason was sound, so Grey turned back to me. "She needs us to anchor her. She needs a reason to wake up. Give her one."

"Do I deserve to?" I didn't mean to say it, but once I did, there was no taking it back.

"That's not up to him. It's up to her," Nate answered, nodding at Mari. "It's her choice. Let her make it."

I made my way slowly to her bedside and stared down at the dark circles under her eyes and the bruises on her face. There was no part of me that wanted to touch her, but I had to. I had to feel her for myself. With trembling fingers, I brushed the hair off her forehead. She felt normal, like my Mari, and I bent down to lay my lips against her forehead. "Please wake up. Please."

Though it would've been nice for her to wake up then, she didn't. Not that hour or the next or the next. No matter how much we talked to her or kissed her palms, her wrists, her fingertips, she never stirred. Not when the nurses came in to check vitals or when Moore came by with food that none of us touched.

It was torture waiting, wondering, hoping, but it gave us time to prepare. Moore and Tennessee worked their magic and moved her to the abandoned ward, which apparently had lost its funding before renovation started. A hefty check from Grey and an exclusivity contract gave the Marcosa empire its very own place and Doc a new place to stitch us up. Twenty-four hours after her tracker had come back online, Mari opened her eyes.

We let the nurses in to check her over, and once they gave her the all clear, we shooed everyone out so it was just the four of us again.

"You're here." Mari's voice was low and ragged, and my hand spasmed around hers.

"Of course we are." Greyson gently traced his fingertips over her cheek.

"How'd you get in here?"

"Dominic told them we were your husbands," Grey deadpanned.

Mari froze in the middle of readjusting, eyes jerking to mine before laughing. "Of course you did."

That laugh was a shade of her normal one, but it was still a kick to the chest. When you don't know if you'll hear someone laugh again, you cherished the sound in any form it came.

"How did you get here?" I asked, curious. Nurse Erin had said Mari was nearly dead when they found her in the ER. They had no clue how she'd gotten inside.

"Antoni."

Grey's head snapped up. "What?"

"I thought I was dying and he was taking me to the afterlife. Instead, he brought me here."

She sounded so sure of herself that I immediately believed her. I mean, it made sense. In her last minutes, Mari had conjured the one person she missed the most—her brother. It was beautiful.

Grey looked away and cleared his throat. When he spoke, his voice was as rough as Mari's. "I wish I could've seen him."

A throat cleared. "Actually, I think she meant me."

As I whirled toward the voice, shock held me immobile for a single second at the sight of the man at the door. Then I was on my feet, gun in hand. "What the fuck are you doing here?"

Chapter 4
Mari

It was like staring at a ghost. Or maybe not a ghost, but the version of Antoni he would've become if he'd lived longer. The man in the doorway's hair was shorter than my brother's ever was, his eyes more guarded. He had none of the laugh lines that Antoni would've had, none of the joy. Had he always been like that, or had it been stolen from him like it'd been systematically stolen from me? I wasn't sure I wanted to find out.

The other Antoni watched me, calm as could be, and I wondered what he saw. Did he see a queen getting back to her feet or a woman who was tired? Did he see how much I craved safety for my people, or could he only make out my blood-soaked hands? Was I etched in grief, or did I just look normal to him?

Throughout my inspection, Dominic never wavered, never took his eyes off the man, and never lowered the gun. He stayed between us, and I knew that if my savior pulled a gun, Dominic would take the bullet. Just like Rey had, like Greyson would. I didn't want that. Whatever happened between us, I wanted him with me. Alive. I needed it like I needed air. "Enough, Dominic."

He just lifted his gun a fraction higher, an unspoken promise that he could do it for however long he had to. "Answer my question. What are you doing here?"

That cracked the calm façade, and the man glared at my ex. "I don't answer to you, boy. Best remember that and listen to her."

A fraction of a movement by the door showed Nate looking between the newcomer and me like he was trying to decide where he fit best. He glanced at me, and when I shook my head, he settled back in his position, more alert than I'd ever seen him. Dominic stepped forward, everything about him screaming aggression and angst. He was ready and willing to pull that trigger, regardless of the consequences.

I kind of liked seeing the bloodthirsty side of him. Too bad he hadn't shown me while we were together.

Don't think about it.

Since we needed answers more than we needed a pissing contest, I turned my attention to the man. The ghost. "You aren't my brother."

The man inclined his head in agreement. He didn't have to, though. Drugged or not, I knew my brother was dead. I'd carried his body home myself. But the way this man looked was uncanny and too similar to be a coincidence.

"You planning to spell this out for us, or should we start guessing?" Grey drawled from his spot next to me. He hadn't let go of my hand since I'd woken, and the grip he kept on me said I'd scared the absolute shit out of him.

"Rafael Osorio." The man leaned forward in a caricature of a bow. "Your uncle."

Not just my uncle, but my mother's *twin*. The resemblance to my own made more sense now.

Dominic ground his teeth, and it struck me that he'd known exactly who Rafael was the moment he stepped inside. Considering I didn't have a single memory of seeing even a picture of an Osorio, I was surprised. I'd always known Dominic was aware of the cartel— my father had told me as much when our parents were engaged— but my instincts said there was more going on than just a good memory. It felt intentional for my father to have told Dominic this over me. For the first time, I wondered just how close Dominic and my father had actually been before he'd left the city.

Had he been the second heir Mario was looking for?

Nate's whole body tensed at Rafael's announcement, his hand drifting to his side, where I spotted the barest hint of metal. Very few people knew about my mother's family, and half of them were in the room. The Osorios and the Wolf, my grandfather, were good at keeping noses out of their business. Greyson squeezed my hand, and I was aware he'd seen Nate's reaction too, and I knew we'd all need to have a talk later. Flashes of memory came to me. The cold of the floor, the ache in my fingers. Whispered words that barely registered over the pain. "You called me *tesorita*."

Little treasure. He'd said it with such fondness too, like he'd meant it. Odd for a man I didn't remember meeting.

Softness washed away some of the tension the face-off with Dominic had left in his expression. "It was my nickname for your mother when we were children. When she told me she was pregnant with you and your brother, I knew you'd be the same. But your mother died before she could make it back home."

Shock made my fingers spasm. I hadn't realized that she'd tried to leave Mario.

I must've said it out loud because Rafael nodded, the whole act reeking of bittersweetness and pain. As a remaining twin myself, I knew the feeling intimately. The knowledge that you weren't quite whole anymore. That the other piece of you was just gone. Snuffed out. It ate at you.

"Bianca wanted to raise you and your brother in Colombia. She meant to make you a princess."

"Mari was always a princess. Now she's a queen." Greyson's eyebrow lifted as he feigned relaxing, comfortable and confident in the hospital chair, but I could see otherwise. He favored his side, and the shadows of his eyes said he needed rest as much as I did. He was hurt, and the anxiety and rage that had forced me to keep moving slowly eked back into my system.

As if he felt it, Grey ran his thumb over my skin in slow, soothing movements. Rafael tracked it but said nothing.

"So you are." The hint of a smile crested his mouth, but it died soon after, as all the others had. It was like happiness didn't know how to survive on his lips anymore. I wondered if he felt as if grief colored the world differently as I did. "Your mother would be proud."

I had to trust him on that. Bianca Marcosa, formerly Osorio, was just as much a ghost in my life as my brother was. There had been no mention of her anywhere, no stories to be told, no pictures to see. My father had every trace of her removed from his presence the moment she died. At first, I'd thought it was grief, but I knew better now.

He'd only cared about her until he'd gotten what he wanted. When she was carrying us, he doted on her with whatever humanity he possessed. The second we were born, he had no use for her anymore. The only person who actively told us about Bianca was Amara, and even those moments had been rare and stolen.

"Why are you here, Rafael?"

"I came to help you."

Dominic scoffed, but we all ignored him. There was no time for temper tantrums with an Osorio in the room.

"You've been watching us." Admittedly, I believed in fate, karma, and justice, but unless the Osorios were watching me, there was no way Rafael should've gotten to me before the boys did. None.

"Since your second died."

Rey. The twinge of grief was still there, buried under my breastbone, but it didn't feel debilitating anymore. Instead, I just felt angry at myself. The loss of one of my most trusted people had shattered me, and I'd let it. Secure in the knowledge that we were at peace, I'd thrown myself into that ocean of pain like I had no responsibilities. I'd let Greyson shoulder the burden of an empire he didn't want because I was too hurt to see anything, and in the interim, Cash had come to play.

Never again, I vowed. I had to be stronger, to hold myself up when I felt like falling. Cash was a needed reminder that I didn't have the luxury of burying my head in the sand. I had to be present and survive, or everything would go down in flames with me.

"You know about our problem, then."

"Cassius Beckstrom, yes."

Dominic's finger twitched near the trigger, and I knew we needed to speed this along. Normally, I would've been more tactful, but I was beat. My head wavered, and my stomach ached where Cash had stabbed me; my fingertips burned, and I wanted to sleep for a month. We didn't have time for cryptic answers. "Explain to me why an uncle I've never met was skulking around my city while we're on the brink of war."

"Because you needed me." As if it was that simple. As if I should've guessed that on my own.

"And it had nothing to do with your father?" Dominic asked, still pointing the gun. "The Wolf didn't tell you to come here and ingratiate yourself to Mari for some half-baked alliance or easier access to her?"

Rafael looked at me like I'd taken Dominic back off his leash, but I was curious too. I could see the tic of frustration in his jaw when he answered.

"The Wolf isn't aware that I'm here. In fact, he'd probably kill me. He's been *explicit* in his instructions to stay away. So I'd appreciate it if you could keep it to yourselves."

Dominic finally lowered his weapon, though he didn't put it away. Nate's posture loosened too, though he kept his hand close to his weapon. You could never be too careful with an Osorio in the room.

With the tension much lower, Rafael settled against the doorframe.

"We'll keep your secret in exchange for a favor at a later date."

He grinned, and fuck, that smile was too close to Antoni's. "You're just like your mother, though less dangerous."

Considering she was dead and I wasn't, I didn't quite believe that. Admittedly, the fact that he thought I was a mouthpiece and not an actual threat irked me more than anything. "Who says I'm not already dangerous?"

"Black widows don't get stabbed by their lesser."

Dominic opened his mouth to snark at Rafael, and I cut him off. "You're right. I miscalculated Cash. I won't make that mistake again."

"How do you intend to do that? You don't have the intel to get you ahead."

"And you do." Not a question because I could see it in Rafael's face.

He lifted a shoulder. "I do. I'd be willing to share in exchange for a meeting."

I spread my hands to encompass the room. "Is this not a meeting? And one I gave you a promise I'd protect, at that."

"With my father."

I didn't want to meet the Wolf. I'd heard enough stories of him killing his own men for small infractions or disrespects, and I had no doubt that I wouldn't measure up to whatever pedestal he kept my mother on.

"Thought you said the Wolf didn't want you here?" Greyson asked.

"He doesn't, but it's in Mari's best interest to get his attention. Your little problem could be obliterated in a week if he gave the okay."

"Would he?"

"For anyone else, no. For you?" He shrugged again. "You look like Bianca. Meet him, and see if he'll help."

"You don't think we can beat him alone?"

"It's not your success that I worry about. It's the costs that would come with it," Rafael admitted. "You're the last link to Bianca and Antoni. I'd hate to lose you over something as small as this."

Spoken like the cartel. Only they'd think a territory war was small.

"I can't guarantee anything." My world was too out of sorts to agree to a meet with a cartel leader, family or not.

Rafael nodded, eyes glinting with mischief. "What if I made it worth your while?"

"How?" Nate asked. He'd been silent the whole time, taking everything in like it was his job. I wasn't sure if it was the military training in him or something more ingrained in his system, but I liked it.

"Agree to a meeting at a later date, and I'll get you all the intel we have on Cash. I can guarantee it's more than you have."

I knew it would be. Despite being hunted by the FBI, Cash was a fucking ghost. Greyson had nearly broken one of his laptops in a fit of rage when he'd tried. Whoever Cash was, he was very well hidden.

"Don't," Dominic warned. He edged closer until he could wrap a hand around my knee, though he kept his eyes firmly on Rafael. "We don't know what the Wolf—"

"Deal."

Dominic's hand tightened so much I hissed, the scrapes I'd

gotten from the floor smarting against his grip. Like he'd just realized what he'd done, he yanked away from me. I could feel Rafael's eyes on us, but he didn't comment. "The deal is struck," Rafael murmured as he stowed his hands in his pockets. I didn't know if he was trying to look harmless, but it didn't work. Osorios were notoriously ruthless. It was how my grandfather had survived fifty assassination attempts while maintaining a hold on the cartel that had lasted the entirety of his adult life. The man was a legend and a nightmare wrapped in one, and Rafael was his heir. There wasn't a chance in hell he'd ever look less than lethal. "It will take time to get the Wolf into the country and find an appropriate place to meet here. Likely, a few weeks."

Not enough time to help if shit hit the fan, but I already knew there would be no aid from the cartel anyway. Emmanuel Osorio would rather watch my father's world burn than spit to stave off the fire.

"When can we expect the information?"

"Soon."

Greyson met my gaze, the same thoughts running through his mind clear on his face. I was the leader of an entire city. How much more power did I need to root Cash out?

Rafael stepped forward, and all three men tensed. My uncle chuckled under his breath but kept moving until he could carefully grip my ankle over the hospital blanket. "Heal and be well, *tesorita*. I'll be in touch soon."

"What if we need to reach you?"

Rafael grinned, and it was a shark's smile, all teeth and terror. "I'll be around."

Right.

Nate and Dominic crowded Rafael until Moore and Tennessee took over escorting duties in the hallway. Now that Rafael was gone, I didn't want to stay in the hospital. All of the Marcosa powerhouses were in one room—minus Cameron—and I didn't like it. There were too many unknowns, too many things that didn't add up, and my gut was screaming that my allies weren't as loyal as I thought they were. I had to show them that I was still the queen, still the baddest bitch in this city, but to do that, I had to leave.

Before I could get too squirely about it all, Dominic spoke up. "I don't like this."

Of course he didn't. That didn't change the fact that it was happening.

"We need the information, and this is the only way to get it," I told him.

"That doesn't make it the right choice."

"No, it makes it the only one."

Dominic growled under his breath and turned to me. He was still handsome, still the man I'd loved as a boy and a friend as close to me as any other, but he had a weariness in his shoulders now. The blue under his eyes that spoke of a sleepless night and stress. He was worried for me. Even after we'd ended, he cared. I didn't know how to take that, so I pushed it aside for future Mari to look at later.

I'd almost lost them. I didn't care as much that I'd almost died; I cared that I'd almost lost them in the process. That my last memory of Greyson would be him bleeding out on the floor. Nate's voice on the phone. Dominic telling me he loved me.

"Mari?" Grey's voice pulled me back into the present. Into the hospital room. At the sight of all three of them, I felt the panic ease a little. "Are you okay?"

Clutching his hand in answer, I pulled him into bed with me. He tried to fight me, but a stern look and a semi-feral growl got him moving. I had no doubt that he was hurting, though he'd hidden it well, but he needed rest and so did I. When we struggled, Nate helped us, carefully arranging the blankets and fussing with the pillows until we were settled, with me carefully snuggled into Grey's side.

"Whatever else is going on, we can discuss later. Right now, we're *both* going to take some painkillers and take a nap." I twisted my head up, ignoring the ache behind my eyes. "Don't fight me."

Greyson's breath gusted over my face as he kissed my forehead. "I would never."

"Good. When we wake up, we're planning a prison break."

"Promises, promises."

Nate cleared his throat. "I'll be just outside the door if you need me."

I crooked a finger, though it hurt like a bitch. He leaned over me, and I found I liked the way it felt. So did the heart monitor, which everyone thankfully ignored. "You and I have a lot to discuss."

He obviously knew more than he was letting on about my family, and I needed to know what before we could move forward. If he was a danger to me, he had to go.

"Trust me, I'm aware." His eyes darkened as he ran his fingers over my cheek. "Sleep well, angel."

I was anything but an angel, but for Nate, I thought it might be nice to try. Especially when his ass looked that good in jeans.

Dominic shuffled on his feet as the door swung shut, leaving us all in silence. "I'm going to head to the house now that you're awake. We've got a ton of shit to deal with."

I knew he wanted an invitation to join us, but I couldn't give it to him. While I was glad he was okay, I didn't want him with me anymore. "Keep us posted."

The hurt on his face was swept away on a tide of determination that made me nervous. "I'll take care of it. You just heal."

Right, because that's what kingpins did when they got a boo-boo. Heal up in peace.

Dominic and Grey had a long, silent conversation that I didn't even try to decode. Frankly, I was too fucking tired. Especially when Dominic left and the nurse who took his place gave us both meds to take the edge off.

With the world getting fuzzy around the edges, Greyson pulled me tighter against him and buried his nose in my hair. "I'm so glad you're okay."

I didn't know how to say it back, to tell him how terrified I'd been, so I didn't. "I love you."

"I love you too." Those four words from the man I'd loved my whole life said everything.

I'd kill for you.

I'd die for you.

I'll protect you.

We'll make it.

"I know." I rested my head on his chest and let a huge yawn take me. We'd rest and recover, but we wouldn't be idle.

Cash started this war, and we needed to finish it.

Chapter 5
Mari

Dr. Grant was not an easy person to argue with. It took over an hour and promised monitoring at home by Doc to get her to sign my discharge papers. Though she was clear it was under *extreme* caution and against her wishes. I didn't care. I just wanted my own bed.

When we pulled into the garage, Dominic opened my door. His fingers twitched to help as I climbed out of the SUV, but he kept himself in check. "I have all the capos waiting in the dining room."

"Good. I need a shower first." I couldn't go into meeting Joaquin and the others with hospital all over me. They'd scent it like blood in the water.

The men tried—and failed—not to crowd me as we moved through the house. Dominic and Greyson were at my sides, and I felt Nate's watchful eye on my back with every step. Moore led the group, and Tennessee was the tail. Normally, it would've made me feel smothered, but all I felt was a possessive sort of cherished.

We were nearly to the stairs when the breathless yell echoed around us.

"Mari!"

Dominic slipped in front of me just as I saw the blur of pink braids, taking the brunt of the hug attack.

"What the fuck?" Shara snapped, pushing him away. They had a considerable height difference, but she stepped up like she was ready to unleash hell. All she cared about was that he was in her way. *The power of a 5'2" goddess.* "Move."

"No."

"Dominic," I warned softly.

"I'm not going to let her bowl you over like that." He didn't even look at me when he snapped at her. "She's hurt."

Ah, fuck.

Greyson and I shared a wince as wonderful, formidable Shara panicked. We *never* told Shara we were injured. It wasn't that we treated her with kid gloves, but the trauma of Antoni's death still haunted her. Knowing that her people were hurt sent her right off the deep end. Beyond that, I didn't want the rest of the house hearing him. The Marcosa mansion had ears, and not all of them were one hundred percent mine.

Slipping around him, she snatched my wrist to yank me closer and hissed. I'd forgotten that my hands looked like I'd been cosplaying a mummy.

"What the hell, Mari?" Her voice broke as she ran her hands softly over the gauze. It made me feel like shit. I hated scaring her.

"It's not as bad as it looks. I promise, Shara."

The glare said she didn't believe me, and I didn't blame her. I looked awful. "Where else are you hurt?"

Knowing if I didn't show her, she'd strip me down right there, I reached for the hem of my shirt. Dominic hummed in disagreement while Nate stalked closer to help me lift it.

"You're going to fuck up your shoulders if you do it," he murmured. They hadn't been dislocated, but it was a near thing. The pain made it easy to avoid thinking about the pads of Nate's fingers running over my skin again, though.

Shara circled me, taking in the myriad of bruises and small scrapes. My chest was wrapped to the point of overdone, but I needed the stabilization for my ribs to heal. Bonus points, it hid the stab wound on my stomach from sight. If she caught wind of that, she'd never leave me alone again, and I needed my space.

"See? I'm fine, Shara."

"No, you aren't. What the fuck is wrong with you?" Tears glossed her eyes, and she looked away from me with an incredulous sniff.

"Watch it," Dominic growled. Irritation prickled at me, but before I could shut him down, Nate did.

"You keep putting your foot in your mouth, and Mari's going to put hers in your ass."

"Shut up, fuckboy."

"No, you giant baby. Shara is Mari's sister. She's family." He didn't elaborate, and it meant everything to me that he understood.

Shara and I had lost something integral to ourselves when Antoni died. In order to survive, we'd clung to each other. We were more than family now. It earned her a little leeway in how she treated me. Dominic didn't have siblings, so he didn't understand that we could fight but he wasn't allowed to do the same. That was against the rules. It made me curious how Nate knew them. He didn't have siblings either.

"I'm sorry I scared you," I whispered, wrapping Shara in my arms. She shuddered before her head fell softly to my shoulder. The castor oil and cocoa butter scent of her washed over me, finally telling me that I was home. I was safe. It did more for me than a hundred guards on a hospital door ever could.

"You should be, you harpy."

I smiled at her sniping and twisted our hug to keep her tucked against me even though it fucking hurt, because that's what you did for family. "What're you doing here, anyway?"

"I brought them." Cameron walked into the room and took a single look at me before smirking. "You look like shit, cousin."

"She looks perfect, you asshole." Aislynn stepped out from behind my cousin, looking far more comfortable with him than she had before when she smacked him upside the head. He growled at her as she wrapped her arms around me in the faintest hug imaginable. "I'm glad you're okay."

"Ditto," Shara muttered irritably.

The smile hurt my face, but I didn't care. "Try to sound more sincere next time, yeah?"

Shara grumbled but didn't reply, so I turned back to Ash.

"Cameron's been *temporarily* staying at my place since the restaurant," she explained. "When you...went away, he brought Shara and me here."

She threw a solid glare at Cameron, who ignored it and her very pointed statement. The fact that my cousin had broken in to his future wife's house really didn't surprise me, and neither did Ash's response. She'd been suffocated by her father her whole life and preferred her space. No wonder she looked fit to kill Cameron already.

Her smile was sickly sweet when she said, "I'm returning him, by the way."

"Like fuck you are." Cameron's eyes narrowed as he twisted to look his fiancée in the eyes.

"Five bucks they don't make it to the wedding," Greyson murmured when they started bickering.

"Ten they don't make it to the engagement," Shara countered.

"Fifty she guts him in his sleep," Nate whispered behind us. He'd long since put my shirt down, but he'd stayed close enough for me to feel his heat at my back. I shouldn't have liked it like I did.

"Yeah, she is." I laughed, trying to disguise it as a cough when my cousin and Aislynn both glared at me. Trying to defuse the situation, I nodded to the stairs. "I need a shower, and then I'll meet everyone in the dining room."

Cameron glared at his fiancée. "We'll be waiting."

"I hope you rot on that floor tile, you insufferable ass," Aislynn muttered, sliding my arm through hers. The laugh hurt, but I welcomed the pain this time.

The two women got me upstairs and unwrapped in record time. The water stung my cuts and I could feel their eyes on me as they made sure I didn't take a fall on the slick tiles, but I didn't care. Nudity was normal for me, and a shower in my own home did a lot to soothe the minor aches. Plus, I didn't have to worry about the stitches because they were all under waterproof bandaging.

Dr. Grant really knew how to treat a lady.

Before I could shampoo my hair, Ash smacked my hands away from my head. Her expensive clothes were getting soaked but she didn't seem to mind, and I adored her for it. "You're going to bleed everywhere if you do it. Just stand there and look pretty."

"Technically, yes."

I thought of Rafael and wondered if I should tell Shara that he was in town. Thinking about her reaction if she ran into him by accident made the choice for me. "Shara, there's something you should know."

Her head jerked up from where she was posted at the edge of the large waterfall shower like a sentinel.

"Rafael Osorio is in town."

Those dark eyes widened, and I saw her knuckles blanch as she squeezed the towel in her fist. "Why is he here? Is the Wolf coming?"

"It's complicated, but we think he's a friend."

She stared at me, peeling me apart in that way of hers. "Is this about Gilded or me?"

"You."

While Ash went to town, I told them about the warehouse and the Antoni angel that wasn't really him, even offering to see if a meetup with Rafael was possible if she wanted it. Tears welled in Shara's eyes, and I could see her warring with herself. The probability that seeing him would hurt her more than she was already hurting was high, but grief was fickle. The chance to see who Antoni could've been was an opportunity she probably wouldn't pass up.

Not answering me yet, she changed the subject. "So, you and Cameron seem comfortable."

Ash yanked a little too hard on my hair, mumbling an apology when I grimaced. "He's infuriating."

"He's a flirt, but he's always been relatively harmless."

"He's an ass. He keeps trying to tell me what to do like I'm not a grown woman who's taken care of herself for years. Last night, he told me how to load the dishwasher. *My own fucking dishwasher.*"

"I'm guessing that wasn't the first argument between you two, then?" I turned off the faucet and carefully dried myself off. Every movement hurt, but fuck, it was good to be clean.

"No. He woke me up sneaking into my house at four a.m. for the third night in a row, and I went off on him. Told him he's not going to have a side piece unless I can too. It went downhill from there." I could imagine it did. For as charming as he was, my cousin was territorial at best. Aislynn's cheeks pinkened, and Shara and I shared a grin. We would know that blush anywhere. She was hiding something.

"What did he do, spank that ass for mouthing off?" I asked.

Shara smiled at her. "It's okay if you're into a little punishment with your pleasure." We howled when Ash's whole face turned red.

"Shut up."

While Shara needled Aislynn, they wrapped my ribs again and helped me into some clothes. The hands, I'd have to cover with gloves since the wrappings were too noticeable. Besides, I didn't need them on display, when the capos would view it as a sign of weakness that Cash had gotten that close.

While Ash brushed my hair, Shara left to go back to Antoni's room. My normally extroverted friend was in desperate need of some peace and quiet of her own, so I let her go without a fuss.

As Ash braided my hair, I checked in. "Are you sure you're good with my cousin? We can change the plan if we need to."

"I'm fine." She squeezed my arm gently, careful of my injuries. "We're just in transition."

"Let me know if that changes, okay?" I trusted my cousin with my whole heart, but if he wasn't good to her, I'd kill him myself. Family or not. Sometimes blood didn't mean shit.

✷ ✷ ✷

By the time I went downstairs, I was bone-tired and ready to crash for the night. Cameron was gone, but Nate, Greyson, Moore, and Tennessee had changed and returned while I showered.

"Everyone ready?"

Moore looked me over slowly before grunting and making his way down the hall. Tennessee chuckled under his breath at his partner's antics. "He's going to act like a bear with a sore paw for weeks because of this."

He would because he felt guilty. We'd have to talk later. I didn't have another emotional chat in me.

Waving Dominic and Greyson with me, I started down the hallway. I had to get my game face on. This wasn't just a touch base; it was the starting of a war council.

"Where should I go?"

I stopped, turning to Nate in confusion. "Wherever you normally go."

He nodded like he expected that, but instead of leaving, he straightened his spine and crossed his arms. "I'm staying with you."

"You're not." He couldn't.

"I am."

"That's not your choice," Grey said calmly. Dominic was silent at his side, but the tense way he held himself told me he'd go after Nate if I let him. He had too much anxious energy bubbling inside him, and I made a note to get him into the gym before he exploded *again*. "You two go ahead," I told them. "Nate and I need to chat."

Greyson immediately turned, yanking Dominic along with him so he couldn't argue. I waited until they were out of sight to turn back to Nate.

"What's this about?"

"I know we've got a lot to talk about and I'm neither a Marcosa nor your boyfriend, but I'm not letting you out of my sight."

The word *boyfriend* struck me hard and fast. Confusion mixed with a seedling of hope that I squashed before it could attempt to take root. I would *not* moon over Nate Black. "Where is this coming from? Correct me if I'm wrong, but you refused to join the family."

"I did, and I stand by that."

"Then why are we having this conversation?"

"Because I was at home alone while you were out nearly dying." The stark conviction he said it with pierced me in the chest. I'd scared Nate. I'd hurt him. *Christ*.

"That's why you want in."

"I want in because I never want to see you walk out that door without me at your back. I'm aware I have no right to ask this, but let me help." He stepped closer until our breaths mingled. "You saw my file. You know I've got the skills to protect you, but I'll show you if that's what you need. Just don't make me stay behind again. Don't shut me out."

I'd already promised I wouldn't, but I couldn't help needling him. I blamed the drugs.

"Is this what you do for friends, Nate?"

The second the words came out of my mouth, I knew I shouldn't have said them. I couldn't help it, though. The way he looked at me made me wonder if he was as uninterested as he'd originally said, or if things had changed once he moved in. Before, it was polite distance, but now, it was heat and turmoil and a little fear.

"No, but I don't want to be friends with you," he admitted.

"No?"

"I have my sights much higher."

Tilting my head, I smiled and tried not to show how much that frankness turned me on. Apparently broken ribs had nothing on my libido. "Rejection to friends to something more. Careful or you'll give a girl whiplash."

A ghost of a grin crossed his face, and he dipped even closer until every word brushed against my lips. I felt those small touches everywhere. "It took me a while to realize that having someone like you is a once-in-a-lifetime thing. Whatever the cost, I think you'll be more than worth it."

That sounded great, but... "Is this just sex, then?"

His eyes darkened, and he ran his thumb across my jaw so softly it made me shiver. "No, but that'll be nice too when you're ready."

I believed him. "I don't think I've had a man tell me no so many times."

"I'd promise to stop, but it would be a lie."

Pulling back, I looked him in the eye. I needed him to hear me. "Don't lie to me, Nate. I can handle almost anything as long as you talk to me, but if you lie, all bets are off. Deal?"

Something passed across his face, there and gone before I could figure out what it was. "Deal."

A cough down the hall reminded me I had places to be, but I couldn't let it go yet. Dominic's inability to accept who I was had caused more damage than expected. Not to mention, Nate had already changed his mind about me. What if he did it again? "I'm not going to change just because you're with me. I'm always going to be the Marcosa leader. I'm always going to rule. If that's a problem—"

"It's not." Nate's face was serious when he slid a hand into my hair and forced my eyes to his. "I don't want you to change. You're exactly who you need to be, angel."

"Okay. Come with me."

He jerked back, careful not to pull me with him. "Really?"

"Really. We need to talk later, but consider yourself on temporary probation. Do well, and I'll make you a full member." He already knew the consequences of doing poorly, so I didn't remind him.

The softness of his face morphed into indifference as he moved back to give me space. He looked serious and formidable. It was hot.

Striding down the hall firmly in *pretend my ribs aren't screaming at me* mode, I made it to the dining room just in time to hear Joaquin pissing and moaning about the wait.

"If she's not even going to show up on time, why should we?"

"Because that's your job," I snapped. All eyes jerked to me, but I ignored them as I walked myself to the head of the table with the rest of my men following behind. Moore and Tennessee took their places by the door, while Greyson and Dominic took theirs at the chairs closest to me.

"What's he doing here?" Joaquin jerked his head at Nate, who had followed me to the front of the room.

"He's with me. Let's sit." Daring my uncle to speak, I directed Nate next to Greyson, but he shook his head and took a position at my shoulder. Nate held the space like a bodyguard, while Grey held it like a partner. The difference was obvious, and I appreciated it more than I could say.

Sitting as carefully as I could, I rested my hands on the table.

"Thanks for being here. Let's get started with the warehouse. How did we do?"

"Kincaid's painting was rescued without damage," Grey said. I barely held in the breath of relief, not willing to show my uncles just how nervous I had been about the painting. A Kincaid meltdown was the last thing I needed. "I'll call tomorrow to arrange a pickup."

"I'll do it myself." I needed to put the damn thing in his hands myself, or I'd worry about something going wrong the whole time. The logistics of it would be a bitch, but that was a problem for later.

"What about casualties? I heard there was a fire."

Joaquin sat up straight. "Four dead, three more injured. Not including yourself." I waved him off, but his eyes stuck to my gloves with narrowed suspicion.

"My injuries aren't important. Let's make sure their families are compensated. We take care of our own."

Everyone nodded at that. "Did anyone hear from O'Bannon?"

Dominic's hands clenched on the table before he smoothed them out. "He called an hour after everything and said he got caught up with family stuff and didn't have his phone."

I didn't believe it. Sean was a territory leader, just like I was. We didn't go anywhere without our phones, and if we didn't have them, one of our closest people did. Besides, I knew Dominic. He'd have called everyone he had a contact for when he didn't get Sean directly.

The Irishman had chosen not to come, and I wanted to know why. If his version of a temper tantrum cost my men their lives, he owed me more than a pound of flesh.

Joaquin cleared his throat as if he was trying to be delicate. "There are rumors on the street that Cash gutted you. That you're dead."

Fuck. I knew he'd spread the word, but I didn't realize he'd do it so soon. Instead of reacting, I leaned back in my chair and smiled. "Do I look dead to you?"

Joaquin's eyes went back to my hands, and his voice held a world of skepticism. "Not at all."

"Curb the rumors before they get us into more trouble. There's enough going on right now."

"We'll put the word out on the street," Gabriele said, already typing into his phone. His crew typically did the night shift in the bars and clubs, so they were already out and about.

"Cash is still coming for us, so pay attention and don't go out alone. Pairs or more at all times. I don't want any more casualties right now. Anything else?" When everyone shook their heads, I dismissed the meeting. We had the painting and the families we needed to visit and take care of. There was always more to do, but for tonight, it was enough.

With a nod to the door, my capos filed out. Joaquin gave me another long look before he went, too. As soon as they were gone, Moore locked us in before checking the room for bugs again.

I wasn't worried about external bugs, but internal ones. My capos were loyal to me, but I didn't trust that their loyalty wouldn't shift the next time someone with a dick got the idea to take me out. So I kept them busy and comfortable while I watched their every move. Now that Cash was around, we were balancing on a tight wire, and I needed everything going my way.

Moore finished his search and found his place again. "We're clear."

"Good. I want eyes on Joaquin and his crew going forward. They've always been opportunistic, and I don't want them thinking now's the time for a coup."

Tennessee crossed his arms over his chest, nodding. "I'll handle it."

"Good. Now, let's talk Cash. He's going to assume I'll lie low and recover—if he thinks I'm alive at all. We'll use it to our advantage."

Dominic cocked his head. "How?"

"Eyes everywhere. The Aces will get bold if they think I'm gone. They'll assume the organization will be in tatters and everyone will be scrambling for power. They won't be as vigilant as they were before, so they'll give us more information. Locations, people, routines."

"What about the other leaders?" Greyson asked.

"We need to show everyone that any rumors they heard are just that—rumors. Marianna Marcosa is fine. Anyone saying otherwise is an incorrect idiot."

"How are you going to do that?" Nate asked.

Batting my eyelashes with all the false innocence I could muster, I grinned. "Poker, of course."

Chapter 6
Greyson

While Gilded was the first official neutral space in the city, it wasn't technically the only one. Hidden places where the denizens of Seattle did their work were owned by the city but were slated for our use only. They'd been gifts, a good-faith measure to Mari and her empire. It was an unusual situation, but we'd spent the first bloody few years of her reign cleaning up the streets and removing most of the gangs that were making it dangerous to walk alone at night. The city's political sphere couldn't actively condone our actions, but they were grateful, and the meeting zones were their show of appreciation. In the end, it'd worked out for everyone. The off-record buildings gave us more than a bit of freedom. The Cardinal was one of them.

The run-down hotel had been abandoned fifty years ago when the owners went bankrupt, and because of structural damages, it never resold. Until the city bought it for us, it had remained frozen in time. From the outside, it looked nothing like it used to. The shuttered windows were cracked and drooping, graffiti littered the once-pristine brick, and the sidewalk outside had craters that threatened the ankles of everyone who walked past. The inside was another matter entirely, but most people never made it that far, avoiding even glancing at it because it practically looked haunted. They didn't see what I did.

Micro cameras picking up every face on the street were surrounded by graffiti so thick the metal blended into the harsh colors of the paint nearby. The people drifting around the street who appeared dazed and out of touch with reality were actually watching everyone. Their only job was to report movement and keep the unsuspecting from stumbling upon something they shouldn't. People only saw what they wanted to, and we used that to our advantage.

I followed Mari through the opulent hallways—restored by the city and kept religiously clean by the housekeepers we employed—to the back of the building, where a hidden door took us to the basement. The upper floors had been renovated too, but they were a sort of haven in case the worst came to pass. A safe house for everyone to use, though no one ever did. It was too hard to fortify the building.

The three security checkpoints we had to pass through just to get through the door were slow and bothersome but were needed, considering who was waiting in the other room. Every two weeks, the leaders of Seattle sat down for a friendly poker game. The stakes were high, the gossip elite, and the drinks flowed freely and without judgment. More than once, the players had to be peeled off their chairs and forced into waiting cars by their sober seconds. Normally, it was one of Mari's favorite events, but with the opening of Gilded, she hadn't been able to go personally in months, so she'd sent envoys instead. Dominic and I had each taken a few turns. Hell, Moore had gone once, though he was immediately asked not to return because he was a cheat.

How a group of criminals couldn't handle cheating at a card game, I'd never understand.

Despite how much she enjoyed the game, we'd all tried to convince Mari to stay home. It was too soon after she'd been hurt, and she was barely walking straight, though I knew it hurt her to do even that. Even Moore and Tennessee had pleaded with her to send someone else, *anyone* else, but Mari overruled us.

"I'm injured, not dead. If I don't show my face, the rumors will gain more traction, and we don't have the time or resources to fight two uprisings. I appreciate the sentiment, but queens don't get days off, and if they did, I've used all mine up. Now, who's coming with me?"

Cameron was her first choice, but he was busy watching his father. Since Joaquin had no knowledge of her abduction, he'd assumed she'd been injured in the fire. None of us believed he was happy his niece had survived, so Tennessee's men had an around-the-clock watch on him in case he decided to do something stupid.

Dominic offered to take Cameron's place as escort, but Mari declined on the grounds that he would overcrowd her. Tennessee and Moore were vetoed for the same reason, and I agreed. Their natural overprotectiveness would just point a neon sign at Mari's injuries, and we couldn't do that. The game was a statement that no one could kill the Marcosa queen, and that didn't leave room for kissing boo-boos.

That left Nate and me. He was the better choice since I was still aching from my own injuries at the warehouse, but he was new, and while Mari had decided to trust him, she wasn't going to start that relationship in a room full of all the leaders. Not when she didn't know if Nate could play in our world and not when things weren't stable. Surprisingly, he'd agreed. He felt he didn't know enough about the players to be an effective bodyguard. He couldn't protect her against threats he didn't understand, so the others promised to get him up to speed while we were gone.

I walked in behind Mari, trailing my eyes along the black jumpsuit she wore. The front had a halter neck that normally showed her shoulders and back, but she wore a cropped jacket to cover the bruises that were still visible. The cut flattered the curve of her waist and hips, drawing the eye there first before it dipped to her hips. It usually flashed a hint of those mile-long legs as the slit up the sides moved when she did, but the bruises made that impossible. A disgruntled Gretchen had agreed to adjust the legs to be completely closed this time—after doubling her normal Mari fee. The fabric skimming over the muscles was just tight enough to show that Mari had them without giving the definition of any bandages she wore. It was the best we could do.

Even completely covered, she was stunning and sexy, and I was debating if I really hurt badly enough to forgo sex for a while. The only reason I didn't jump her on the way over was her own injuries, but the way her ass swayed in front of me, I was ready to rethink that decision.

I could just eat her out the whole time. She wouldn't have to do a thing. Just lie back and let me do my job.

Mari clicked her tongue, and I looked up to see her smirking at me.

"Put your tongue away. We're here."

I pressed in close, savoring the contact. I'd thought we'd lost her, and it had stung worse than death ever could. I kissed along her neck, enjoying the little squirm and soft sigh she tried to hide from me. "If you think I'll ever stop looking at you like you're the eighth wonder of the world, you're wrong. I'm grateful for you, *reina*, and the second you're cleared for it, I'm going to remind you just how much I want you."

Her pupils dilated, and she licked her lips. I loved when she looked at me like that, like she couldn't wait to rip my clothes off. I had no doubt that if it were any other time, if we were any other place, she'd do it. "What happens in the meantime?"

"I've got some ideas. What do you want to happen?"

She thought about it, playfully tapping her finger to her lip. Those black gloves were a necessity, but I liked seeing them on her. I wanted to see them wrapped around my cock, though I wasn't sure if it was a leather kink or just my infatuation with Mari.

"Show me how much you're missing me. Consider it my incentive to heal faster."

She wanted a show. The idea warmed me up, and I had to readjust my dick so I didn't walk into the room with a boner. When I was finished, I kissed the smirk off her lips, careful not to mess up her makeup. "I think I'll do just that."

She gave me another kiss with those deep red lips before she turned back to the door. I didn't even bother to check if the lipstick transferred; I liked the idea of her marking me. Watching the way she pulled herself up, stepping into the role of the Marcosa queen with little more than a single breath of warning, just added more fuel to the flames, and she knew it. *Little tease.*

The door opening snapped me back to the present as the sound of male laughter hit us. The basement was massive, though most of the room was blocked off by storage areas we hadn't been able to access. It'd been redone as well, so everything was high-end and luxurious, from the chairs everyone sat in to the bar the drinks were made on. Servers milled around the room with appetizers the guests could snack on and delivered drinks to the table where the others leaned over their cards.

"Got a seat for one more?"

The soft lilt of her voice cut through the easy conversation like soft butter, and the noise died down immediately. We'd planned our arrival perfectly, so that the usual suspects were already in their seats and playing when we showed up. As one, they turned to stare at Mari, and in turn, I watched them. Haru looked bored, as usual. He only came because he couldn't *not.* Kosas seemed pleased, though he did nothing more than nod in greeting.

Ajilon threw his head back to laugh before waving his hand at the chair beside him. "For you? Anything."

I walked ahead, pulling out the chair so she could sit, before taking up my position against the wall at her back. Through it all, Sean O'Bannon caught my attention. While everyone looked surprised and faintly confused, the Irishman looked both terrified and pissed. Ruddy cheeks and angry eyes met mine before they immediately looked away, like he could hide what I'd seen. I wondered if he worried that Mari was going to skin him for not showing up. It was a distinct possibility.

"We've just started, but we can deal you in," Two-Bit offered.

When I peered at him, I saw humor in his typically strained expression. He knew what Mari was doing, and he liked setting O'Bannon on edge. That, mixed with his knowledge of her cartel roots, had me reevaluating the gang leader. He knew too much for absolutely no reason. It made no sense.

"No, no." Mari waved them off as she ordered a drink and her chips before settling into her seat. "I'm fine to watch this round."

The first hand went quick, with Haru winning a few hundred thousand on a bluff that even I couldn't ferret out. While the others chatted and refilled their drinks, Sean typed furiously on his phone. Breaks were the only time when the devices were allowed near the table, despite the multitude of scramblers that were in this room. Since the game was meant to be a time when they could just relax together without all the politics and bullshit, the leaders often didn't talk shop, but that didn't mean they were stupid. Sometimes shit came up, and the last thing we needed was someone listening in or recording conversations when it did. It was the same reason all the servers had signed contracts—and leverage—to keep their mouths shut. Nothing left the room without Mari's say-so.

The dealer passed out the cards, and Mari angled hers so I could see. King of hearts and ten of hearts.

The others picked up their cards with calculating eyes as the first round of betting started. I could see each of them darting their gazes toward Mari, but they'd get nothing. My *reina* was a fortress.

I could practically feel the anticipation radiating from her and not just because of poker. Before Rey died, Mari's favorite thing had been the hunt. It eased some of the worry I'd had for her that that hunger had survived her grief. Maybe she was past the worst of it so we could rebuild what it had stolen.

Antoni hated when we played poker with Mari because Mario had spent her entire life teaching her how to read people. Men, in particular. Antoni could be as blank-faced as he wanted, and she still knew exactly when he was bluffing and how badly. It was likely also a touch of that twin connection they had, but it still pissed him off to no end. I'd always found it fascinating, though.

Especially since she had a knack for getting information while she played.

The first round of bets was quick, and the dealer continued. The flop was in Mari's favor with a nine of hearts, four of clubs, and a jack of diamonds. All she needed was two cards to win.

Ajilon and Kosas tittered, as they often did when they'd had too much to drink, but Mari kept her face in that bored impassiveness she excelled at while she rearranged her hand. "You've been quiet, O'Bannon. How have things been?"

He'd been avoiding eye contact so much that it took the Irishman a second to realize that Mari was talking to him.

"Fine. I've been settling things for my daughter's wedding." He sounded like he was chewing rocks, and I wondered how a man so easily ruled by his temper had created someone like Ash, who was commanded only by herself. A queen in the making, though none would rival my own.

"That's right," Kosas said with an easy grin to both him and Mari. "Congratulations are needed. You're going to be family soon."

"We're thrilled to have Aislynn. She's a gem." Mari's smile was real, as it always was when she spoke of her friends.

"Your cousin has already moved her out of my home. I don't like it." There was a warning there. He thought we'd overstepped ourselves by taking Ash early. Good thing he didn't know it was to protect her from *him*. Honestly, despite it being exactly what she didn't want, the marriage to Cameron had given us the leverage we needed to get her out. I knew it brought Mari comfort to have her friends close and protected again. I just had to hope Cameron would do right by Ash.

"It's not up to us. Aislynn is a big girl. She can make her own choices." Mari tossed her chips into the pot with a limp hand, and I saw the way Two-Bit's eyes darted to the gloves she wore. Thankfully, we'd had a late cold snap, so it wasn't entirely out of place, but the way he watched her with an awe he shouldn't know told me that, once again, he had more information than he should.

Did we have a mole for the Vipers, or did that annoying nurse spill? If so, she was dead. Fucking Deborah.

"It's not right for them to lie together before marriage," Sean snapped. The servers jolted, and the bartender lost his grip on a glass, dropping it against the bar top with a wince. Everyone waited with bated breath to see what would happen.

Mari cocked an eyebrow before setting her cards down and taking a long, languid sip of her drink. "I wasn't aware you were interested in abstinence until marriage, O'Bannon."

It was a well-placed taunt. Everyone knew Sean O'Bannon would fuck anything with two legs, just like we knew he'd never marry. He'd made it very clear when he'd thrown Aislynn's mother away after she'd delivered his final child.

"I'm not, but this isn't about me."

Mari hummed, not bothering to pick her cards back up. "No, it's about your grown daughter, who has a mind of her own."

"It's not right," Sean insisted.

"Enough." Her flippant wave of a hand pissed him off, but he held his anger for once, and the tension in the room broke. "It's the twenty-first century. If they want to live together before the wedding so they can get to know each other, that's all right by me. If they want to fuck every day, that's okay too. Women are in control of their bodies and their lives now. Even mafia princesses can have sex without Daddy's permission."

Sean's face darkened, but he kept his mouth shut while the dealer placed the turn down. Jack of hearts. *One more to go.*

The betting continued, with Kosas and Ajilon folding immediately before turning back to their hushed conversation. Haru and Mari entered their typical staring match until he finally folded as well.

"Of course it's okay with you. She's in your house," Sean growled as he doubled down.

Mari called and picked up her glass for another sip. I didn't even have to see her face to know she was smirking. "Something wrong with my house?"

"You mean besides all the men in it? No, not at all."

Sean seemed to realize his mistake, and the whole of him turned red. I wasn't sure if it was anger or embarrassment, though. He knew he had to play the good boy and heel, but he didn't want to. He also knew that he'd made a rookie mistake, and as he was one of the leaders with the longest tenure, it was fucking juvenile to watch.

"I meant no disrespect," he said through gritted teeth. "I only meant that I would've liked to keep her home longer. To keep her safe."

Because he had other plans for her. I didn't know what they were, but I had no doubt they were something to give him a leg up over Mari, and I didn't like it.

"You love her, I understand." Mari tapped her fingers on the table, the soft *thud, thud, thud* echoing in the space like gunfire.

"She's my daughter." He said that like it was an answer, when it wasn't. Not for Mari. Mari sat back in her chair as the final bets were placed, with Two-Bit folding rather than calling Sean's bluff.

"Daughters in this life are fascinating, aren't they? They can be your biggest asset or your biggest weakness, but most men aren't big enough to figure it out until they're gone. See, women have power and not just the kind we get from spreading our legs for men who have it. We have the ability to ensnare the hearts of those around us. To build or crush an army with a single blow. You think men are powerful because you held the cornerstone of our world for so long. You forget that to do it, you had to put us on our knees in the mud."

We waited until, finally, the hand was played.

Queen of hearts.

Sean had three kings. It would've won on any other hand, but not this one.

Before she showed her cards, Mari paused. Another sip, another sigh of pleasure at the drink. "Women were playthings and brood-mares. We weren't powerhouses in our own rights. We were property. Chattel. You called us *princess* to make us lesser than your princes. Lesser than your kings. Men like you and my father forget that wars were waged for women before, and they will be again. After all, princesses are made to become queens."

When she flipped her cards over, Sean realized what the rest of us had known for years.

There was a reason Mari had kept Seattle's throne when everyone had bet against her. She was a force of nature, and Sean O'Bannon was nothing but an object she had no problem removing from her path.

Chapter 7
Mari

Troy Kincaid's apartment was exactly what one expected from a rich bachelor. Floor-to-ceiling windows, heavy metal furniture and polished cement floors. Then came the paintings. Splashes of color and portraits of long-forgotten women lined his walls. I had to hand it to him; the fakes were impeccable, but the whole place was a modern nightmare.

The man himself waited for us on his living room couch, sipping a cup of coffee like he hadn't buzzed us into the building. Still, it was good to see a friendly face again.

"Mari Marcosa, I'm glad to see you in one piece." He met me halfway, leaning down for a polite kiss to the cheek. I had to lean up on my toes, and the stretch felt nice even as it hurt. My ribs were wrapped, and I'd even donned a brace to stabilize them while I moved around the city. Doctor's orders.

"Was that a concern?" I asked when he'd gotten his fill of me.

"With the rumors floating around that you were dead, I'll admit I was worried."

I wasn't surprised he'd heard Cash's toxic little whispers. For as much money as he had, Troy was a gossip hound. It was half the reason I kept him happy. I also wondered if I needed to use him more, sometimes he heard more than I did. Probably, but I didn't trust him enough for that.

"You should know better than to bet against me. Anyone who opens their mouth before they see my body on a slab in the morgue is an idiot."

Kincaid shocked me by grabbing my shoulder. Grey and I both tensed, but it wasn't an attack. It was...comforting? *What the fuck is that about?* "I've heard there's been trouble for you lately. Is there anything that I need to worry about?"

Wait. Was Kincaid *worried* about me? Despite being friendly for most of my adult life, Kincaid and I weren't what I considered friends. Maybe it was some unexpected loyalty to my father that had him caring for me. Still, I wasn't sure how to react. Patting his hand, I slipped out of his hold. "You have nothing to worry about. Even if there were problems, they wouldn't affect you."

Kincaid followed my lead, brushing off the concern with ease. "I'm glad to hear you say that. I expect nothing less from the Marcosa queen."

There was an awkward pause, and I wasn't sure how to fix it. Troy had managed to throw me off almost immediately, and I didn't like it.

"This isn't your usual type of painting." Grey stepped forward, bringing Troy's attention to the wooden crate behind him, and I was grateful. I needed a moment to get my head on straight again.

Troy smiled, all teeth and deadly intellect, as he motioned for his men to open the crate. "It isn't, but I've been looking for the right forgery for years. Every time I've found them, the artist gets picked up or killed. It's exhausting. This time, I put a guard around them the moment I saw their work. This isn't the first collaboration, and it won't be the last. Especially with how much it's going to fetch at auction."

He pulled out the painting, and while I was underwhelmed, I couldn't help but be proud that we've managed not only to get it back but to get it back in one piece. He had no idea the danger his precious painting had been in, yet there it was, standing against his wall like it was always meant to be there.

Another job well done for the Marcosa empire.

Troy unboxed it, checked over every single inch of it, making sure there was no damage. Once it was cleared, he nodded to one of his goons in the corner, who handed Moore a small briefcase. We weren't fools; we didn't do cash. Well, not *all* cash. The rest of our fee would be split between the Marcosa coffers and my own offshore account. Grey called it my rainy-day fund, in case we ever had to leave in a hurry. It was standard operating practice for anyone in the underworld to bank in a handful of other countries. The last thing we needed was the Feds freezing our accounts if they ever investigated.

With work done, Troy settled on the couch, and Grey and I moved toward the door.

"Sit with me."

Well, fuck. One of the worst parts about running a city was the fucking politics. If we walked out now, it would put our working relationship at risk, and Troy could use that against us. Since we were fighting to hold the city, we needed all the allies we could get. Which meant I had to indulge whatever softheartedness had crawled up Troy's ass.

Grey and I sat on the couch opposite Troy. He didn't bother offering us refreshments, knowing we wouldn't take them. It was another of my father's rules. Poison was too easy to slip into someone's beverage.

"I hear congratulations are in order." When I stared at him

blankly, Troy grinned. "Young Cameron finally found himself a bride."

Once again, I wondered if I'd been underutilizing Kincaid. His gossip network had to be massive if he knew about the engagement before we'd officially announced it. "How is it that you always seem to know what's going on in the city before everyone else?"

Troy smiled. "I have eyes and ears everywhere."

Grey's voice was markedly less friendly when he responded. "Best make sure those ears stay out of our business."

Troy heard the warning, though he didn't comment. "When's the wedding? It seems like this city could use a little bit of a pick-me-up."

I heard so much in the undercurrent of his words. *People are talking. The rumors are gaining traction. You're losing ground.*

I couldn't ignore our reality. Power came from perception, and if I wanted to regain what little bit Cash's rumors had stolen, I needed to reinvigorate the Marcosa image. We needed to celebrate our success, our prosperity. What better way to do that than with a wedding?

Especially when the last one we'd attempted was my brother's, and he didn't make it to the altar.

"Funny you should mention it. They've decided to move the date up."

It was a testament to our trust that Greyson didn't flinch with the lie.

Kincaid's face changed, and I saw a hint of approval. "Is that so? How exciting. Any *particular* reason they may be rushing for the rings?"

Grey stiffened beside me, and I realized Kincaid was asking about heirs.

The reminder sank in my stomach, and I had to swallow down bile. I knew Grey and I needed to talk about kids, but with things still up in the air with Nate and Dominic—not to mention Cash—it wasn't the right time. I wasn't sure if it ever would be.

Waving off Kincaid's attempt to gather intel, I smiled like we were in on some big secret. "Not that I know of. Aislynn is enamored with him and asked me to move the date up. Considering Cameron feels the same, I saw no reason to delay."

"Have they set a date yet?" Kincaid, like all the key players in the city, would expect an invite. To not allow them to come was an insult, one we couldn't afford.

"We're looking into options right now, but I'll let you know when we decide," Grey said smoothly.

"I'll be sure to clear my calendar. For what it's worth, I think it's a great idea. What better way to lift spirits than a wedding?"

I would've preferred safety to a party, but what did I know?

Apparently, that was all he wanted to know since he moved back to business immediately after. The artist he'd worked with had already completed their second commission, and he was ecstatic to get it into the city. After finalizing the arrival, Grey and I left.

Because he was amazing, he waited until Geneva pulled away from the building to ask. "I didn't know you were thinking about moving up the wedding."

"I wasn't," I admitted. "Something that Kincaid said got to me. Cash has been dragging the city down, and whether they know it or not, everyone can feel the tension. We need a little joy, a little excitement. Something to remind everyone that they've been prosperous with us. *Because* of us. Besides, what better way to show Cash we aren't cowed by his attempt to take me out than to throw a party?"

I expected Grey to agree with me as always, but he didn't.

"Do you have a better plan?"

We rarely ever saw things differently, and I was curious. While I ruled independently most of the time, I couldn't ignore the fact that

Grey was my most trusted adviser, and whether he liked it or not, he ruled at my side.

"No, the wedding makes sense." But something was bothering him. I looked at him, and it hit me almost immediately.

"You're worried."

I didn't recognize it at first because fear wasn't an emotion Greyson often showed, but it was there in the furrow of his brow and the tightness of his shoulders. When he didn't answer, I slid across the seat and climbed into his lap. Geneva didn't hesitate to roll up the privacy window, and I appreciated her more than ever for it.

Alone and separate from the world, I let myself soften away from the Marcosa queen I always had to be. Wrapping my fingers in his hair, I tugged his head up to sweep my lips against his. "Tell me what's wrong."

He leaned forward to deepen the kiss, but I kept myself out of reach. Grey and I were good at sex, but this felt like something he'd allowed to fester. I couldn't let that happen.

Realizing I wasn't dropping it, Grey wrapped his hands around my hips, keeping me pressed tight to him. "I almost lost you."

The strain on his face was painful to see. He looked wrecked, and it was all my fault.

"But you didn't."

"Don't do that," he snapped. "Don't pretend it's no big deal. You nearly died, *reina*. I just got you, and *you almost died*."

The crack in his voice told me more than words how much the thought of losing me gutted him. I understood his pain, but it was like the reality of the situation hadn't quite computed. I knew Cash had almost killed me, but it felt like a movie I'd watched. Like it was someone else's life entirely.

Grey's fingers clenched against me, almost to the point of pain, but I didn't move. He needed it to ground him, and after all he'd done, it was the least I could do. "I keep seeing you in that hospital bed, still and sleeping, while I'm wondering if you'll ever wake up again."

Christ.

This was more than just bad memories, and I didn't know how to fix any of it. How could I convince him I was fine when his brain reminded him of his worst nightmare over and over? How was I supposed to help when I was struggling with the same thing?

Framing his face with my hands, I did the only thing I could think of. I kissed him.

It was meant to be something soft and sweet, reassuring, but that wasn't enough for Grey. He hauled me as close as possible and ravished my mouth. His grip tightened, bruising as he kept me trapped against him. For a moment, I wondered if it would trigger something in me, but all I felt was safe.

As he took my mouth, Grey ran teasing circles across my thigh with his hand, having bypassed the skirt. Warmth flowed through me, but I tried not to think about it. This wasn't about sex. It was about comfort. But he was hard under my thighs and ass, and every move he made had him grinding against me. We both pulled back, gasping for air as he reached the junction of my thighs.

"Fuck." I didn't know what he was trying to do to me, but I was dying. I wanted his hands all over me even when I knew it wasn't the time.

"I keep dreaming that you're dead," he confessed, his words a haunted whisper against my lips. "I close my eyes, and I see you on the floor of that warehouse bleeding out. I can't reach you. I can't protect you. You're just dying there alone, and I have to watch."

My chest ached at the pain in his voice, but I couldn't fix it. Not on my own. Grey was the only one who could tell me what to do.

"How do I make it go away?" I asked him.

"I need you. Under me, on top of me, whatever. I just need to feel you, so I can prove to myself that you're alive."

My ribs were still sore, though the brace made it a little easier to function, but I didn't care. What was a little pain when Greyson was hurting so badly?

"Then take me."

Greyson shuddered underneath me, and for a moment, I thought he would deny us both. Because the truth was, I needed him too. Nightmares of him on the floor when the shot rang out still plagued my sleep. If it could ease both of our burdens, I was more than willing to deal with the discomfort that came with it.

"I don't want to hurt you." Grey took stinging bites across my jaw, my neck, and along my shoulder.

"I want you to." He jerked away, but I shushed him with another kiss. "I think we both need the reminder that I'm alive, because it still doesn't feel real."

Beyond everything else, I felt like I was still trapped in Cash's warehouse, praying that it might be over soon, even as I wanted to survive. I needed to *feel* something, and Grey was the only one who could give it to me.

My confession ripped a sound from his throat, and suddenly, I was falling. He trapped me underneath him across the wide expanse of the seat, careful to keep his weight off me with one hand while the other held my ribs gently. Dark eyes tracked my face, checking for any ounce of pain.

When he found none, a tendril of the tension in his shoulders disappeared. He trailed his hand on my side until he found the hem of my skirt again, this time pushing it up until nothing was between him and my pussy but the satin of my panties.

I thought he'd get right to it, that he'd rip them off me and fuck me into the seat, but he didn't. He kissed soft, slow paths across my skin in all the places I knew still held the memory of the warehouse. Scratches and bruises, bandages and scrapes. Every one got Grey's attention. The chaste kisses shouldn't have done anything, but it was Greyson. Any time he touched me, I wanted more.

"They're fading." He sounded surprised, like he hadn't been sure they'd ever go away. Maybe for him, they wouldn't.

"I'm glad. Will you fuck me now?" The moment reminded me so much of the club, of the first time we'd let ourselves enjoy each other that I thought he would make me wait until we got home, but he didn't. He pulled himself from his pants, giving his cock a long, languid stroke.

"I don't know if I can be gentle." He trailed his eyes over me again, biting his lip, and I had to swallow my groan. Poised above me with his cock hard and ready, Greyson Andrews looked like a god I wanted to worship.

"You don't hurt me, Greyson. You make me feel alive."

With a soft curse, Grey wrapped his hands around my thighs, pulled my panties to the side and plunged inside me. For a moment, the only sounds in the car were the faint hum of music from the front seat and our matching groans.

"Fuck. I've missed this." I didn't know who said it, but it didn't matter. We both felt it.

I expected Grey to fuck me hard and fast, some sort of claiming. Instead, every stroke went as deep as possible, like Greyson was trying to bury his way inside me so he could never be free. I tried to move my hips to meet him, but he didn't want that either.

With a dirty smirk, he smacked me on the clit, and the force bowed my back. "If I wanted your help, I'd ask for it. Now, lie back and take what I'm giving you."

I narrowed my eyes. "You're lucky I'm injured, or I'd make you pay for that statement."

He adjusted his hips and mine so his next stroke rolled over my G-spot. "I look forward to the day that you can, but for now, you're under my control."

I wasn't surprised when he built me up faster than expected. Even before we were together, Greyson knew what I needed almost better than I did. Of course that didn't change with sex. As I crested the first orgasm, my muscles clenched, and the first wave of pain hit me.

Sex with damaged ribs was going to hurt no matter what precautions we took, and it had. I'd welcomed the small aches as my body shuffled on the seat, but I hadn't realized it would get worse as I came. Greyson slowed his strokes, running his thumb over my clit to keep the orgasm rolling as his other hand soothed me.

"Breathe through it," he instructed. "It'll pass."

It would, but I liked that he reminded me. That he took care of me. Grey loved me without smothering my independence, and I'd never be able to explain how much it meant to me.

When it was over and my body melted into the seat, Greyson kissed me. "Can you handle more?"

"Honestly, I don't know, but I want to find out."

He stared at me as if he could see the hurt underneath my skin. Again, I thought he'd pull away, but he seemed to come to a different conclusion.

He adjusted himself so he had me pinned between his hips and the hand he tucked close to my shoulder. Then he pressed his other hand against my sternum, keeping me tight against the leather beneath us. It was enough pressure to keep me from moving too much and hurting myself.

"I'm going to hold you down and fuck you however hard I want, and you're going to tell me if it hurts too much or you need to stop."

Oh fuck. It was a command I'd gladly accept. "I will."

His hand pressed a little harder, and while my ribs protested, it didn't hurt too bad. "Good, because I want one more from you before we get home."

I barely had time to take a breath before he was pulling out to plunge back inside me.

I'd never been one for restraints, and after being tied up in Cash's warehouse, I didn't think I ever would be. But the feeling of Greyson's hand holding me, the pressure of his finger against my clit, the furious pace he set as he fucked me into the back seat, sent me flying in no time.

I clenched around him, crying out as I came. It was half pleasure, half pain, but a good kind of pain. A reminder that I was alive, that Grey was alive. That we had survived. It was the type of pain that broke and healed at the same time.

And when Greyson came after me, his fingers bruising my skin, I knew that connection that had bound us together for years was roaring between us, burning out the fear and leaving nothing but love in its wake. We had been broken, but we wouldn't shatter. And one day, Cash would be nothing but a blip in our memories.

With careful hands, Grey flipped us so he was lying down with me on his chest. He didn't pull out, and neither of us fixed our clothes. We just lay there and relaxed with soft touches wherever we could reach. We let that connection build between us again, stronger than ever. And with each heartbeat, I felt that shattered part of us heal a little more.

Chapter 8
Mari

Grey and I walked into the house to find a huge bouquet of rainbow flowers spilling over the foyer table and Dominic glaring at them like they were a ticking time bomb.

"Secret admirer?" I asked, ignoring the ache in my chest at the idea of Dominic moving on. Shitty of me, but he was mine.

Except he isn't.

"They're from Cash," he muttered, waving the little card around.

Grey straightened up, snatching it out of Dominic's hand to read aloud. "Little Queen, I'm so glad to hear you're still in the game. My apologies for any damage I caused. I do hope you have a speedy recovery. Round two is just around the corner, and I don't want you to miss it. Love, Cash."

He was apologizing for nearly killing me? Joke or not, I was starting to wonder if Cash really was a psychopath.

"He's taunting us," Dominic snarled.

I rolled my eyes. "Of course he is. Did you expect anything less?"

When Dominic said nothing, I brushed him and the bouquet off. "Have somebody grab a hazmat suit and take that thing out of here."

"What?"

"Bag it, trash it, and go sanitize the fuck out of yourself. I wouldn't put it past Cash to have poisoned the flowers or the card."

Dominic grimaced, looking at his hands. "I didn't think about that."

"Of course you didn't. You were letting jealousy override your brain cells. Get to it."

Before he could say anything else to irritate me, I headed farther into the house with Greyson at my side.

"Where are we going?"

"It's time to tell the lovebirds about their nuptials," I said, dread sinking in. Cameron would go along with things; he was a soldier. But I was worried about Aislynn. I felt like I was putting her into a corner, forcing her into a life that I'd promised her I would get her out of. I felt like I was no better than her father, and comparing myself to Sean O'Bannon put me in a shitty mood.

We weren't even to their doorstep before we heard the screaming.

"You can't tell me what to do, Cameron!"

"Actually, as your future husband, I can and I will. You are not going to dick around the city all day by yourself looking for one fucking flower. It's not going to happen."

The dull thump of something hitting the wall made me smile. "It's not a *flower*. It's the dye I need for my wedding dress, but of course, you don't care. This is just something for you to tick off your fucking checklist. Marry the Irish princess so my boss still loves me. *Check.*"

I heard venom there—and bitterness. Grey grabbed my hand as the unease blossomed. It felt like I was too close to ruining one of the few good things I had.

"Oh, for the love of *God*." Cameron's frustration told me this wasn't the first time they'd had the conversation, and again, guilt churned. "What do you want from me?"

"I want you to let me live my life! I didn't leave my father just to find another jailer."

"I'm not trying to cage you, Aislynn. I'm trying to keep you safe. You walking around the city for a fucking *flower* isn't an option."

"It's not just a flower," she growled. "This is art, you asshole."

"I don't care. You aren't going, so get one of your minions to do it. Call up a flying monkey or five to get it done, because let me be clear. If I find out you've gone against my instructions, I'll spank your ass so hard you won't sit for a month."

"If you touch me, I'll rip your dick off in your sleep."

"At least it'll get some action."

More throwing, more cursing that we couldn't quite hear.

"I may be an asshole, but you're stuck with me. Get used to it, babe."

"I'm not your fucking *babe*," Ash seethed, another dull thump hitting the wall.

"You going to open that, or are you hoping one of them kills the other?"

"My money's on Ash."

"Same."

I shared an amused glance with Greyson before knocking on the door. It swung open so hard it hit the wall, and both of them yelled. "What?!"

I stepped inside with raised eyebrows, and instantly, the tension level dissipated. Cameron cleared his throat. "My apologies, cousin. We were discussing something."

"Very passionately," I said. Aislynn's cheeks turned pink and I laughed. "It's fine, considering I'm going to put you in an even shittier mood."

Embarrassment very quickly turned to fear, and Ash paled. Cameron grabbed her immediately, seating her in a chair and softly rubbing her shoulder. A comforting gesture I didn't know my cousin had in him. "Don't freak out before she tells you what's happening."

"Fuck off, *Cameron*." Ash flung his hand off her. He rolled his eyes, looking at us for mercy, but there was no mercy to be had. His relationship with his wife was none of our business.

"There's been a development," I said, not wanting to drag things out. "We're moving the wedding up."

Despite not actually wanting to be in an arranged marriage, I knew Aislynn was looking forward to the wedding she was planning. The fact that I was cutting her timetable by more than half was going to sting.

"How soon?"

"Two weeks." Ash's knuckles whitened as she clenched her fists on her legs. Cameron swore softly under his breath. "I'm sorry, but there's no other way. We need to show the city that not only are we a united front, but we're healthy and safe. This is the easiest way to do it. A celebration like a wedding sends a message."

"And my marriage was always going to be a message." I heard the sadness in Aislynn's voice and I wished I could change it, but we were who we were. Maybe I was kidding to think I ever could have gotten her out of the city in the first place. A pipe dream for people who couldn't afford them.

"For what it's worth, I'm sorry. I know this isn't what you wanted."

Aislynn waved me off immediately. "It is what it is. There's nothing we can change, and I agreed. So, two weeks."

"Can you do it in that time?" She frowned, and I could practically see her ticking through her mental to-do list, crossing off some tasks because they just took too much time. "I'll give you whatever staff that you need to complete things. Whatever overtime you need paid, I'll pay for all of it. Just tell me where to sign."

A ghost of a smile tipped Ash's face, and just the sight of it sent relief tumbling through me. If she could smile at me, she didn't hate me, and if she didn't hate me, maybe this whole clusterfuck was still salvageable.

"Don't tempt me with a blank check, or I'll use it," she teased.

"Please do."

"If I simplify a couple of things, I should be fine," she said. "The dress is going to be the hardest thing, but since my team's already working on it, it shouldn't be too bad. I might have to hire a few seamstresses, and you'll definitely have to double Gretchen's wages." Ash grimaced, knowing the Irish battle-ax was going to absolutely gouge me, but for her and for Cameron and for the city, I would pay anything.

"Thank you for this."

"No problem. You're helping me too, remember? Speaking of, have you told my father yet?" Aislynn asked. Her nerves about O'Bannon were obvious, and I didn't like it. He'd never treated her with love or kindness, which was common for daughters, but I hated it regardless.

I'd lost enough family to know they should be cherished whenever possible, and Ash was a gem. She deserved every good thing in life, including to be treated with respect, courtesy, and love.

"I haven't, but I'll call him as soon as I'm done here," I promised.

"He's not going to be happy," she warned. "I wouldn't be surprised if he did something at the wedding to prove it too. This is a slight, and he's going to do whatever it takes to prevent this from going through."

"He can try," I said. "The contract is signed. You're officially ours, and he has no access to you. What's he going to do? Kidnap the bride?"

The joke fell flat when she paled a little further, and I felt like an absolute asshole. The last thing she needed was more worries. Before I could step up and correct myself, Cameron did it.

"No one is coming for you. Whether we're married or not, you're a Marcosa now. You're protected, and you will be safe. Do you understand me? I'm not going to let that Irish *fuck* touch you again."

Aislynn's smile was a little watery but no less real when she looked at him. "You realize I'm Irish too?"

"Maybe so. But at least you're tolerable."

"Tolerable," she laughed. "Just what every wife wants to hear from her husband."

"Do you want to hear what I really think?" he teased, and the watery smile firmed up a little.

"That would imply I cared."

"Oh, you care, sweetheart."

"I'm not your fucking sweetheart."

It was fascinating to see them interact. I wouldn't have put them together if I'd had any other choice, but I liked them. I wasn't sure if it was Cameron's natural inclination to find affection for the people closest to him or Aislynn's ability to make a friend out of everybody she met, but they suited each other well.

After a bit more conversation about the logistics, we left.

Cameron walked us out of their suite, uncharacteristically quiet. For my golden retriever cousin, it was almost unheard of for him to not have something to say, so I waited for him to tell me his concerns. He didn't disappoint.

"I was serious when I said the Irishman doesn't touch her."

"You're awfully protective of Aislynn." I took a page out of Troy's book, fishing for hints.

"She's my wife." I could tell just by looking at him that he meant it. Cameron was nothing but fierce protective energy. A groom protecting his bride. A husband fighting for his wife. Whether she knew it or not, Ash was lucky to have him in her corner. He would protect her to the end.

"We'll make sure of it," I promised. There was no other way.

The sound of annoyed muttering filtered through the doorway, and I grinned. "You better get back before she throws something else."

"Hopefully it's her shit this time. She's got a serious arm on her."

I snickered as Cameron disappeared back into the suite, and the arguing resumed as if we'd never interrupted.

"They'll be okay," Greyson said after a minute. He rubbed his fingertips against my palm as we walked to soothe some of my anxious energy. "We'll make sure of it."

I didn't have the same faith Grey did, so I just had to hope I wasn't screwing up their futures.

* * *

Two hours later, after I'd caught up on paperwork and anything else I could do to avoid O'Bannon, I acknowledged that procrastination wouldn't make my phone call more pleasant. Locking the door, I slipped out of my clothes and into the loungewear I had in the closet for when I worked late. Interruptions were the last thing I needed, and comfort was a necessity.

The little window in the corner of my office let just enough afternoon light filter in that it seemed a little dreamy and unreal. When things got tough or I didn't know what to do, I'd sit in my favorite chair and work through my problem, often with Grey close at hand. I hated to bring anything but good energy to the little space, but I needed the peace if I was going to argue with O'Bannon.

Forcing myself to dial, I settled into the chair and prayed for patience.

"Marcosa." Sean's voice was about as dry as sand in the desert. *That doesn't bode well.*

"O'Bannon. How are things lately?"

"Fine." Christ, short answers at the start. I could already feel the conversation dragging on for days.

Not willing to waste my whole day on the Irishman, I just went for it. "I'm calling with news. The wedding is being moved up."

"What?"

"Your daughter's wedding is being moved up. Two weeks from Friday."

There was nothing but silence, and then he exploded. "Is this a fucking joke? How am I supposed to get my family out on such short notice? What will people say about a quick wedding? This is because of *your cousin*. He wants her, and he's willing to make her look like a whore to get her."

I wished he were upset because it was his only daughter's wedding or even because he loved Aislynn enough to want it to be perfect, but that wasn't it. He was using the wedding the same way I was, as a show of power. In Sean's case, he needed the elders of the Irish mafia to see that he was stable and in control of his children. The same people who were still mad he hadn't been able to oust me early on in my reign didn't like it when women exercised their right to bodily autonomy. Pricks.

"I've already warned you to watch your tone when speaking of my cousin. Don't make me repeat myself. As for Aislynn, she's a grown woman, one who's already agreed with me."

"I can't get everyone out here on such short notice," he growled.

"Frankly, that's not my problem, but I'm willing to help. Charter a plane to bring them in, and I'll take care of the cost."

"And the prep? Arranged or not, I want this marriage to be something my daughter can look back on fondly."

Doubtful. The more likely scenario was he was worried Aislynn would whine about how much she'd hated her wedding, and he didn't want to hear it. If he truly thought that of his daughter, he didn't know her at all.

"I'll take care of that too. I'm hiring the best wedding planner in the city. Everything will be done to Ash's specifications."

He huffed, and I could hear the animosity in the small sound. "Of course you will. I thought this marriage was intended to make us partners."

"That was your mistake. This marriage was intended to make us allies, closer than just our truce. We're going to be family, but there is still only one Marcosa queen, and you're talking to her."

"So I'm just supposed to sit back while you toss money at things like it'll solve all your problems?"

"Won't it?"

"No." He paused, and when he spoke again, it was markedly more cheerful. I didn't like it, and I definitely didn't trust it. "Some things need a human touch. Your father understood that."

The reminder of my father's personal touch sent shivers down my spine. He was a brute in the worst sense of the word, apt to kill before asking questions. I obviously employed more self-control.

"I think you'll find I'm still very much hands on. My father was a lot of things, but a delegator wasn't one of them. It's why he died so soon. Had to have control over everything."

"Maybe that's what kept him alive for so long. He wasn't trusting the wrong people."

I had no doubt we weren't talking about the wedding anymore. This was something far more dangerous, and warning bells sounded in my head. "Are you the wrong people, Sean?"

A long pause and then a laugh that wasn't even attempting to be real. "Of course I'm not, Mari. Like you said, we're allies. *Family.* Isn't that right?"

He said it like he thought I was being paranoid, but I wasn't a fool. I could smell lies from a thousand miles away, and O'Bannon reeked of them.

"As I said, I'll take care of whatever needs to be done to make

Aislynn's big day everything she's dreamed of. Just let me know what I can do for you, as well. I always take care of my family."

"I'll let you know when to send the plane," Sean said before ending the call, and I knew I'd made another enemy of O'Bannon. We'd already been treading the line, but I knew he wouldn't let it go anymore. I just had to see if I could win him back before he did something we couldn't recover from.

Chapter 9
Mari

I prided myself on being a leader my people could interact with. One they weren't scared of. That was not to say I wasn't feared, but I didn't want to be my father. I didn't want my soldiers worried I'd kill them for speaking out of turn. So, I made myself accessible *and* approachable. Even though I had a private gym that I could and did use, I often sparred in the gym connected to the barracks. The building was still on my property, making it easy to stop by when I wanted to check on everyone, and I took advantage whenever I could. It gave me a better understanding of my people's strengths and weaknesses and allowed us to connect one-on-one.

As an added bonus, they got to see me fight too. Women were so often viewed as the face of an organization, not the muscle. It did my men good to be reminded not to underestimate me. I was just as vicious as they were, and I had more to prove.

I wasn't on display today, though. Nate was center stage in the ring with Tennessee, hands wrapped, body sweating as they ducked and weaved, throwing punches here and there. After reading his file, I knew he had skills, but words on a page didn't always equate to real-life experience. This time, they did.

Every move Nate made was calculated, smooth and two steps ahead of Tennessee. A feat, considering he was the reigning champion of the internal Marcosa Boxing Championship six years running. The fact that Nate had him sweating and panting, practically walking him around the ring like a show pony, spoke a lot for his abilities. Not to mention that he did it with a serious size difference. Tennessee was six inches taller and at least fifty pounds of muscle heavier, whereas Nate had a leaner figure. Not to say he wasn't built, but you couldn't see him from outer space like you could Tennessee.

Smaller or not, Nate fought smart and with enough passion that it felt like he had something to prove. I didn't even have to look around to know he was doing it, too. More than once, I caught my men pausing their workouts to watch the new guy fight. They cheered on Tennessee, heckling Nate every chance they could, but I also could see the respect building. It was exactly what we needed.

Moore stood next to me, barely more than a statue. He made comments here and there about their form or things they could adjust later, but that was it. There was no easy banter about his husband's muscles or the way Nate's back was distracting in the best ways. No mention of work or play. Nothing. He was a blank slate, and it bothered me.

He'd been quiet since the warehouse fire, and I knew I needed to talk to him. To check in and make sure he was okay. The problem was Moore preferred to take care of his own problems without involving anyone else, especially me. He was self-contained. That meant that in order to get him to answer me, I had to approach the situation delicately. I didn't want him to shut down on me, but I overthought every opening line I came up with. Finally, I knew I had to just go for it.

"How have things been?" I asked, immediately wincing. *Not even remotely subtle.* I blamed the painkillers Grey gave me. They made me a little loopy.

To his credit, Moore just laughed at me.

"I'm pissed as fuck that you got hurt," Moore admitted. "I should have been there. I don't know what the fuck Dominic was thinking, sending you off by yourself, but you never should have been alone."

"We all made mistakes that day," I said. "I knew Sabine was compromised, but I still went. The only thing that matters is that everyone made it out alive."

Moore snorted, and I knew he didn't agree with me. I also knew he wasn't going to say anything where others could hear. He really was the best.

"Admittedly, I probably would have done the same thing, but I would have made sure you weren't by yourself with her. I certainly wouldn't have trusted somebody that I knew had ulterior motives. Your boyfriend should've realized it wasn't a good move."

"Not my boyfriend." I didn't bother defending it more than that. Dominic's actions were his own, and if anyone should defend them, it needed to be him. Instead, I focused back on the ring just as Nate threw a right hook that caught Tennessee on the chin. Moore growled next to me. He was not a fan of his husband getting hurt.

"Are you sure you're okay?" I didn't look at him, and I wouldn't pry again. Moore was my employee second and my friend first, but I knew I had to walk a fine line with him. If I pushed him too far, he'd retreat so fast I'd never reach him again.

I had to be okay with whatever he wanted to tell me. If he wanted to answer, he would, and if he didn't, that was okay too.

"No," he admitted. "But I will be. As soon as we put that little pissant in the ground, I'll be good as new."

I smiled at Moore's ferocity, knowing it was part of the reason Tennessee had fallen in love with him years ago. They went from partners in work to partners in everything because Tennessee realized that he wanted someone whose fierceness was tempered by affection instead of a need to hurt. He got angry for me because he loved me. The difference mattered.

Resettling on the wall we leaned on, I bumped Moore with my shoulder. "What are we going to do when the drama is over? Take a vacation?"

Moore barked a laugh, and Tennessee's head jerked toward us just in time to get nailed with yet another punch. I winced as he swore the ceiling down. "Damn, that one's going to bruise."

"Good. Pay attention to the dude in front of you, you fucking idiot!" Moore yelled, turning back to me. "Hell yes, I'm taking a fucking vacation. Considering that one's about to put my man on his ass, I think your boys can protect you for a week while I go bake in the sun."

The idea of running off to an island sounded perfect. I was so jealous I couldn't see straight. "I'll pay for your tickets."

"You're paying for the whole goddamn thing, including a massage every single day and as much tequila as this body can hold. I've more than earned it."

Considering how much Moore had been through in the last few years, I figured the least I could do was foot the bill and told him as much.

Another round of glancing blows and Nate finally caught Tennessee on the edge of the forehead, and it was lights-out. Moore grumbled to himself as the big man went down and didn't get up.

"You going to go scrape your husband off the floor?" I asked.

"Nope. He got too cocky, and your little fuckboy put him on his knees. I figure he could use the embarrassment to knock him down a peg."

Snickering, I moved on to business while Nate flagged down some help. "Anything I need to know?"

Moore hummed, eyes narrowed as he watched Cameron and Grey pull Tennessee out of the ring. Their eyes flitted to us and back down to their cargo, gentling their hands immediately. My eyes narrowed just as fast when Dominic wrapped his hands to replace the big man.

Can't I get one fucking day?

The last thing I needed was him starting a pissing match with Nate like he did with Greyson. For once, I wanted some fucking unity in my household.

"Heavy is the head that wears the crown," Moore said with a grin that told me he was loving this. "Joaquin's been busy. I've caught him sneaking back into the house in the mornings, but when I ask, he says that he's got a new girl."

My uncle had so many mistresses stacked throughout the city that I wasn't shocked at him collecting a new one. It was his only hobby besides bothering me and ignoring my aunt. Thankfully for her, her friends were *more* than willing to satisfy the needs he didn't care about. "You don't believe him?"

"Hell no. He seems even more tense when he gets back, not like he just got laid. Also, he's always dirty, but he never smells like sex. I've run into him after one of his escapades, and he smells like he bathed in his girl of the month. But not lately. I mentioned it last time, and he told me I wouldn't know what pussy smelled like if someone waved it in my face and to fuck off. I may like dick, but I lived in the barracks long enough to know he's not diving headfirst into snatch every night."

Gross but true. I made a mental note to have the building cleaned more frequently. "What're you thinking?"

"He's doing something, and it isn't a woman."

From the corner of my eye, I could see my uncle holding court on the other side of the gym. His usual cronies and the capos were next to him, except Gabriele, who was working on a heavy bag with one of the new recruits nearby. It wasn't uncommon for them to help with the newbies, but this was one who had no affiliation with Joaquin. What did it say that Gabriele wasn't close to my uncle? Unsure what to make of the unusual distance between them, I filed it away in my brain to ask Greyson about later.

"Do you think he's making moves?"

"He's always making moves," Moore reminded me. "That man has been gunning for the throne since he took his first breath. The fact that it's passed him over time after time is bound to chafe. If he wasn't plotting, I'd be shocked."

Yeah, I thought the same. Dominic and Nate tapped gloves, and the match was on. They danced around each other, gauging the other's reach and strength.

"Who do we have on Joaquin?" I asked quietly.

"Warner. Though, Cameron's been out just as much as he has."

I wasn't surprised. If Joaquin had defected, his son would take that personally, especially after Rey's death. I knew I wouldn't even try to convince him not to follow. It was his prerogative, and if he needed to see proof that his father was a danger to us, that was none of my business.

The fight in front of us heated up as both Nate and Dominic seemed to decide playtime was over. They traded punches, Dominic getting one to the ribs that made my own creak in sympathetic agony. Nate got hit just right so his eyebrow split open. Blood covered half of his face, and I had to hand it to Dominic. It was a smart move. Head wounds bled like crazy, and it would essentially blind Nate in one eye if he wasn't careful.

"Are we taking bets?" Greyson said as he slid next to me, his fingers brushing mine before he slipped his hands into his pockets. He'd been doing it more since I got back, small touches that weren't noticeable to everyone else, and each one meant the world to me.

"My bet is on Nate," Tennessee said as he limped his way to

stand next to Moore. He leaned down to give Moore a kiss, only for his husband to turn away at the last second. Undeterred, Tennessee grinned. "You mad, baby?"

"Not mad, just ashamed. You baited him and lost."

Tennessee shrugged. "The kid's got more skill than I gave him credit for."

Moore snorted at his husband. "You gave him credit for nothing. It's your own fault."

Tennessee tipped his head in agreement. "Does that mean you're not going to kiss me better?"

"Go kiss your own ass." Moore rolled his eyes, and Grey and I both struggled to hold our laughs. "I'm voting for the kid, too."

"I'm voting for Dominic," Grey said. Shocked, I turned toward him, but he shrugged. "I don't have to like him to know that this is way more than just a single fucking match."

There were so many ways to take that comment, so I said nothing. I also didn't make a bet. The truth was, I didn't know who to bet on. Nate had the skill, but Dominic was angry. I could see it in every move, every swing of his arm, every step that he took. He had rage to release, and whether he had earned it or not, Nate was his target.

I also knew firsthand rage made you sloppy, so I wasn't surprised when Dominic swung a haymaker, only for Nate to duck under and drop him with an uppercut to the chin. Dominic's eyes were closed before he hit the mat, and my panties were soaked.

Why was that so attractive?

Greyson leaned in so his lips traced my ear. "That got you hot, didn't it?"

When I didn't answer, he laughed and gave me some space. Truth was, I'd been wet since Nate had climbed into the ring, but seeing him and Dominic fight had me drenched. I didn't know what it said about me that I was such a bloodthirsty bitch, and I honestly wasn't sure I cared.

I moved toward the ring to congratulate the winner—and yes, to check on Dominic—but before I could go far, Tennessee called me back.

"Forgot to tell you, we got a phone call earlier. The audit's done."

Finally. We needed to dive into our financials to see just how far Cash's claws had dug in before I could even attempt to scrape him out. "Set up a meeting."

"Already did. Ten a.m. tomorrow."

I nodded and went down to climb into the ring, where Nate knelt beside Dominic, lightly tapping his cheek.

"Wakey, wakey."

"If you touch me again, pretty boy, I'm going to beat your ass."

"I'm pretty sure we already played this game, and I won," Nate said, shoving himself to his feet with a laugh when Dominic swung at him. "Right. Up you go."

They clasped hands, and Nate yanked Dominic to his feet. When Dominic was steady, they shook and did that half hug, half backslap that men often did, and I felt the tension in the room die down a little. Dominic's obvious support of Nate was important for his success in the family, if he was truly interested in staying.

The fights were a show of strength we needed to prove he was capable by himself. My soldiers needed to see that Nate wasn't some little bartender I had decided to play house with—he could hold his own. I'd had enough faith in him for that, at least, but from now on, Nate would have to pass or fail the Marcosa tests on his own.

"Congrats," I said, leaning against the ropes. "Guess you're the winner."

Nate leaned down so that we were breathing the same air, and it was thick with tension that screamed *rip my clothes off*. "Do I get a prize?"

I hummed, not giving much of an answer. Having him close was addictive, and even though we weren't in the place for public displays of affection, I was still hot from watching him fight. His little smirk said he knew exactly what he'd done to me. The question was, would he help fix the problem he started?

His grin softened just a touch. Less cocky, more sincere. "Later, angel."

"Promises, promises." Nate laughed under his breath, turning away to gather his things. It gave me my first up-close view of Dominic, and I wasn't impressed. Minor cuts here and there, some blood matting his hair. At least everything was superficial. "You look like shit."

He barked a laugh, grimacing as he tried to push his hair back, only to get his fingers tangled in the blood. "The kid's got a solid punch."

"Considering what he was trained to do, he should. Go get cleaned up." I turned back to Nate. "You too. We have things to discuss."

The easy grin fell off his face, and he nodded solemnly. "Your office?"

My family's true identity was a secret I protected fiercely. Though I trusted my men and my family, recent events had me going for the only place I knew for certain was bug-proof. "My bedroom."

There was heat there, but also more than a little concern. It made me anxious to find out just what Nate Black had been hiding. "I'll be there in five."

Thinking of how I desperately needed a change of panties and five minutes to myself, I countered. "Fifteen."

Greyson wasn't the only one who smirked at me on my way out the door.

Chapter 10
Mari

I stripped on my way to the shower, not wanting to waste a moment. If I only had fifteen minutes, I wanted a good orgasm out of it.

The water warmed in seconds, and I was under the spray, rinsing off the sweat that had come from my workout earlier. I'd had to let it dry on my body to watch Nate fight, but it was worth every uncomfortable moment.

The reminder of him sweating, working hard as he tussled with Tennessee, sent my blood boiling, and the reminder that I didn't have long before he came for me got me moving. The feel of my arousal on my fingertips, warm and wet as I circled my clit, was everything that I didn't have time to appreciate. Trying to speed things up, I leaned against the tile wall and closed my eyes.

Imagining those wrapped hands on my body, us grappling on the mats, the firmness of Nate on top of me, had me panting. By the time I imagined him ripping off my pants and fucking me into the floor—with or without a few select guests watching nearby—my ears were ringing.

Maybe that was why I didn't hear my bedroom door open or the footsteps that came after. I heard nothing until—

"Mari, are you still—oh *fuck*."

My eyes snapped open, and there he was, wet hair and blazing blue eyes. He'd found another pair of athletic shorts, and I could see just how much my unexpected peep show affected him. *Fuck.*

I had to lick my lips before I could speak. "You're early."

"Only by a minute." His eyes darted between my face and my pussy. "I can leave if you want."

Looking at him, I wasn't sure an orgasm from my own hands would be enough. Now that something more was in front of me, I wanted it. The question was, would Nate give it to me? "And if I don't?"

"Then I'll stay," he rasped. "You're perfect."

Considering I was still bruised everywhere, I doubted that very seriously, but I wasn't letting my issues get between me and what promised to be an incredible time.

I ran my eyes down the length of him, stopping at the thing I wanted most. "Take it out."

Nate licked his lips but kept his gaze locked on mine as he pulled out his cock and gave it a rough stroke. Where Greyson was long and curved, Nate was thick enough that I knew the girth of him would stretch me, and I wanted it.

Moving forward, I reached for him. I wanted to feel him thicken in my hand, to see him break apart under my touch. After that, he could fuck me until I couldn't walk. Conversation be damned.

Nate had other plans. "No."

I stopped, throwing an arm out to make sure I didn't stumble on the slick tile. Not just because it was unexpected, but because "no" was a complete sentence for me. If he didn't want it, I wouldn't pressure him.

That didn't mean I wasn't going to clarify, though.

"No?"

"I'm not going to fuck you."

"Why the hell not?"

He threw back his head and laughed at my genuinely pouty tone. It felt too much like being a spoiled princess, but I didn't care. I'd been expecting a dick appointment, not whatever this was.

"Later, angel. Right now, I want you to show me how you touch yourself."

For a moment, I froze. He wanted to watch me masturbate when we'd never even kissed. For some reason, that felt so much more intimate than fucking. Maybe that was why every part of me clenched in anticipation. He wanted to see who I was when no one else was around to watch. He wanted to know what I needed.

Yeah, I liked that. "Only if you do it too."

His hand was already stroking, his thumb circling the tip when he reached it. "Try to stop me."

Moving back to my spot against the wall, I slid my hand all the way down my body and between my legs. Rubbing my already stimulated clit, I moaned at how close I still was. How much I wanted this.

I wanted Nate to see me because it felt like he already did.

"Does it feel good, angel?"

"Yes."

"You look incredible. Don't stop."

I wasn't going to. I touched and teased, fucked myself with my fingers and bit my lip hard enough to draw blood. Whatever it took to sate the need I was feeling. I was so focused on chasing the orgasm warming my skin that I startled when Nate caught me behind my knee and lifted my leg over his shoulder.

"What are you doing?"

"I need to be closer. I have to see you better."

"You're going to get your clothes wet." His shorts were already sticking to his legs, but he didn't seem to mind since he never took his eyes off me or my fingers.

"They'll dry." I was uncharacteristically self-conscious at having him face-to-face with my pussy, until he took a breath and shuddered. "Fuck. Do you taste as good as you smell?"

"Why don't you find out?"

He turned his face into my thigh, groaning. "Next time. Now, make yourself come."

I wanted to argue, but I could see how tight his grip was and how fast he was jerking his cock. It looked like he was in pain, but the kind that came from mind-bending pleasure. Like he was punishing and ruining himself all in one. I fucking loved it.

"Give me your hand," I demanded.

"I'm not fucking you."

"I know. I need you to hold me up so I can fuck myself."

Before I could slip my other hand into my pussy, he caught my wrist, dragging it to his mouth. I was wet enough that I didn't need the extra help, but watching him suck my fingers, the feel of his warm mouth around them, had me rubbing circles around my clit faster.

He pulled my fingers free of his mouth and slid them into my pussy, making sure the only part of me he touched was my hand. "I want to hear how wet you are when you come."

Fuck, fuck, fuck.

Cool blue eyes scorched me like nothing else could, and I shivered. Nate slid his hand around my other hip, pressing me against the wall just enough to keep me stable while we touched ourselves.

I writhed against him, hips chasing everything I had to give, but I was careful not to touch Nate any more than we were. It would've been so easy to press my pussy to his lips, to make him give me what I wanted. He would have done it happily; I knew that for a fact, but he wanted to play the game, and I wanted that too. I wanted to tease him with something he couldn't have. Not yet.

Plus, I liked torturing myself.

I was hooked on the way Nate stroked his cock, the way he watched as my breathing quickened with every plunge of my fingers and how his followed soon after. Despite how little we touched, we were more connected than I'd ever been with someone else besides Greyson. Coming didn't feel like just a possibility; it was inevitable.

"You're so close," he murmured in an awe-soaked voice. "Show me how you come, angel."

A few more seconds and I was there, riding my own fingers through the high. I hissed Nate's name, and he stroked faster until he was coming with mine on his lips as well, but not even his come touched me. It made it that much hotter.

When we were both finished, breathing slowly again, Nate stood and turned off the shower, reaching for a towel to wrap me in. When I tried to take it from him, he growled under his breath and snatched it back, carefully drying off every inch of my skin. For someone who hadn't fucked me, he was more comfortable with my body than I expected. Then he shucked his shorts and wrapped a towel around his waist. I didn't know if I could handle a conversation with him naked in my bedroom, but I vowed to try.

Neither of us spoke as he wrapped my hand in his, led me into my closet, and disappeared back out the door. Thinking he'd left made my chest ache, and I hated it instantly, even knowing he'd have to come back. Hated that, already, I could feel myself getting more attached to him.

It was only when I was dressed again and saw him lounging in my chair in nothing but a towel that I relaxed.

"What're you doing?"

"We need to talk." It was obvious he wasn't looking forward to our conversation, but he'd resigned himself to it.

"We do."

I let him prepare himself. Whatever he had to say wasn't something he was proud of—anyone could tell as much—I wasn't going to make things worse by pestering him. I needed him to tell me the truth.

"What do you want to know?" he finally asked.

"Tell me about the Osorios." He hesitated, and I knew the time for pussyfooting around the truth was gone. "If you have ties with the cartel, you can't be here, Nate. Family or not, I don't trust them, and that means I can't trust you."

For a moment, he just stared off into space, and I wondered if this was it. If I'd have to kick him out for good. Truthfully, I didn't know if I could do it. Finally, he blew out a long breath. "I do have ties with them, but not like you're thinking. I worked for them."

"The Osorios."

"In a roundabout way, yes." Frustration swamped me, and I tried not to swear. This conversation would take forever if he kept trickle-truthing me. I didn't want this to be painful for either of us, but my people were counting on me keeping shit together. That meant knowing who we'd let into our house.

"I wasn't actually in the Army my whole tenure." He said it so pointedly that it made my stomach sink. He was owning up to a lie already. What else would he admit by the time we were done?

I tried to stay calm and think through it. I'd read his military file and been impressed. They gave him incredible commendations, some of the best I'd ever seen, and we'd verified each and every one. Had he earned them, or had the government done it to hide his real job?

As soon as I thought about it, I knew. Then I really did swear. "Holy fuck. You went *merc?*"

If he was a former mercenary, it explained a lot. His skills were better than expected. Grey had taken him to the shooting range before they'd hit the gym and was blown away. Nate had nailed every shot asked of him without fail.

Nate laughed under his breath. "I can't believe I'm surprised you know about us. You know everything."

I didn't, but I wished I did, especially now.

Mercenaries were people even Mario wouldn't mess with. If they came through your city, you let them pass without issue. If they had to hunt on your territory, typically, they gave you a warning. But even if they wouldn't, who gave a shit? You didn't fuck with the people who could climb in your window and slit your throat.

Even mafia bosses had boogeymen, and the mercenaries were ours.

Looking at Nate, I couldn't see it. There was something about the way he was with me that made it feel impossible, even though my gut was screaming that it was true. That was emotion, though. When I considered things logically, it made sense, and as that sank in, the paranoia came roaring in with it.

I'd brought a government black ops agent into my house. *Holy fuck, Greyson's going to shit a brick.*

"Are you still active?"

"No. I was part of a certain sect of people who were taken from the recruitment pool. The government trained us, armed us, and housed us, but we didn't work for them. We weren't their weapons. We were ghosts."

And ghosts could go anywhere, including onto Osorio soil.

"You worked with the cartel."

"Surveilled some. Did contract work with them too, but it was mostly intel and recon."

There was more he wasn't saying, likely what his actual position was, but I wasn't going to press. Mercenaries were notoriously tough to crack, and if Nate had things he'd done because he had to, that was his business.

"Why did you join?"

"I needed out of Seattle, and the military was the only way. At first, I was just happy to be free. Then I got chosen for the mercs, and it was all high-energy. We were keeping the peace. It felt right. Plus, if we survived, we got the same benefits as a veteran. If not, our families would've been supported, and they would have wiped our memory from the earth. It wasn't a bad gig."

Maybe not, but for someone who had people waiting at home, it sounded like torture. "Last time we talked, you sounded close to your mom. Why go into the Army if you had a family like that?"

"She's got Alzheimer's," he admitted. "Late-stage now, but it started early. It came on when I was a preteen and got worse after we lost my brother."

Thinking back to the file, I frowned. "I wasn't aware you had a brother."

"I don't talk about him." It was a huge oversight on our part, but the way Nate said it made it clear that the conversation was over. His brother was off-limits. As somebody who had lost her brother, I could respect that.

"As close as Mom and I were, the city only ever held bad memories, bad decisions, bad choices. I wanted a chance to do something good with my life, so I left. She understood, but we both knew I was always going to come home."

"Even if it meant losing that part of yourself?" If people thought adjusting to civilian life after the military was hard, they couldn't imagine coming back after being a contract killer. *Everything* was different.

There was no hesitation in Nate's voice. Just surety. "Even if coming back meant giving up everything I'd earned."

"Did you get out clean?" Leaving meant becoming the mark. Because of that, very few mercs "retired" from the company and survived. It was *till death do you part* always.

He shrugged. "Ish. My last contract was fulfilled, and considering my mom's diagnosis, my superiors were good about letting me go. But I was told to keep my head down and go straight."

Then he'd found me. A stop to help a car on the side of the road uprooted his plans to stay under the radar.

Guilt swarmed me, my new favorite companion, and I started thinking up ways I could fix things for him. "We can get you out of here if you need—"

"I won't leave the city, angel."

"Because of your mom."

"Because this is my home," he corrected.

Not ready to wallow—that was a problem for when I was alone —I pushed on. "Do you see her often?"

"No." Guilt was thick in his voice. I could understand why. "She doesn't remember me. She was doing okay when I left, but when I returned, she was gone. I knew I couldn't take care of her on my own, but the thought of leaving her again was too much. Finally, she asked to be put into a home. I only sent her because it was what she wanted. That's where she's been ever since."

"Will the company use your mom against you?"

Something dark passed over his face, and then it was gone. "They could. That's also why I don't visit often."

"Is she safe? We can get security on her." I had more than enough favors to get some guards who weren't connected to me. Nate's mom would be safe.

"I appreciate the offer, but I've got it covered. I talk to her care-taker daily to make sure they're good. If something comes up, I'm sure I'll find out."

"That's who's been texting you." He'd been getting a lot of messages. Considering he was a loner and we'd gotten him a new phone number, it hadn't made sense to me. Nate keeping tabs on his mom was right up his alley, though.

"Yeah." His voice was thick, eyes shifty like he was embarrassed. "I know I should be doing more, but I just can't and not only because I don't want her caught in my mess. She's my mom, but she's not my mom anymore. You know?"

I didn't, but he didn't actually want an answer. Looking at him when he was so obviously hurting made my chest ache. I wasn't good at comfort, but something about Nate made it all too natural to climb into his lap, so I did. His body tensed, but he wrapped himself around me soon enough, taking what little solace I could offer just by being there. Letting my instincts lead, I pulled him into a hug and rested his head against my shoulder.

"You're not a bad person for not being there all the time. You're putting her well-being above your own. From what I've seen of you so far, it seems to be a character flaw."

He laughed, his breath warm against my collarbone, and I tried very hard not to squirm. Now that I knew what was underneath those shorts and how hot this thing between us could burn, it was going to be very difficult to hold myself back. But this wasn't a moment when he needed sex; he just needed me to be there.

Eventually, he leaned back and let me rest on him. We didn't speak as he ran his fingers through my hair, taking comfort in another person. At some point, he tipped my head up, and after a long look in my eyes, his lips were on mine.

Our first kiss was everything I expected from Nate. It was soft, sweet. All-consuming. It made me feel vulnerable and powerful at the same time. Then it was gone, and my lips tingled with the feel of him.

"What was that for?" I asked. He shrugged, tucking me back into his chest. I liked feeling the rumble of his words against my cheek.

"Because I wanted to. Because you're here when you don't have to be. Because you're giving me a chance. Take your pick."

Smiling softly, I shifted so I could run a hand through his hair too. His eyes closed happily with the feel of my fingernails on his scalp. "It's not exactly a hardship to be here for you, Nate. You're a good man."

"I'm not," he said, silencing me with a blind kiss when I moved to argue. "One day, you'll see that I'm right, but for now—for you—I'll try to be."

The way he said it made the hairs on my arms rise. "What else don't I know, Nate?"

"Admittedly, a lot. But there are some things I just can't tell you—either because I legally can't because the price is too high, they would put you in danger, or because I'm just not ready to talk about it."

It was a bad idea. I knew that, but I also knew history that hurt. Besides, Nate was Nate. New or not, I couldn't see him doing anything to hurt me if he could avoid it. "Are any of these secrets going to come back and bite us in the ass?"

I liked that he took his time to think about his answer. "I don't know, but I promise to be at your side if they do."

I wanted more, but I wasn't sure he had anything else to give. For as connected as we seemed to be, Nate was just as self-contained as Moore. He held himself and his secrets close. I either had to be ready for a fight for answers or be okay with knowing he was holding back.

The part of me that had too many lives to protect balked, but I'd already made my decision on Nate when he'd taken lives to save mine. "I'll accept it for now, but if your shit comes back to haunt us..." I left the warning unfinished. He knew what I meant even if I couldn't say it.

"I know, Mari." Mari, not angel. That earned him points too. He knew when to be soft and when to be a soldier.

We were quiet again for a while, him running his hand through my hair and me just listening to his heartbeat under my ear. Eventually, I knew the world would come for us, but I just needed one more minute.

"Was it worth it?" I asked when I couldn't help myself any longer.

"Was what worth it?"

"Leaving, joining the mercs, coming home?" *Joining us?* I didn't say it, but he heard it. I had a feeling Nate could read me just as well as the others, but that street went both ways. When I looked at him, I saw the broken pieces that longed for a home that was long since gone, the part that was as desperate to belong and be safe as I was. I saw myself, and I wanted to tell him that I could make it all happen, that this family could be his too. But I didn't. Nate wasn't ready for it.

That was fine. We had nothing but time.

His fingers tightened in my hair before they relaxed again. "Yeah, I think so."

Chapter 11
Mari

W e've got a problem, boss."

Veronica LaRue, known affectionately as Ronnie to her friends, sat across from me at Harris and Co.'s massive conference room table. I was fairly certain it was barely smaller than my dining room table at the mansion, but it was nearly empty today, with only Dominic and Greyson joining us.

Tennessee was by the door, but I'd left Nate with Moore to get up to speed with our security protocols. After our chat, Grey had done another, more in-depth background check—mostly using our little friends in the government—to back up Nate's claims. Everything checked out as far as we could see, and that meant we were all taking a leap and trusting him. The same could be said for him, considering he had given me no fewer than three knives on my way out the door. He was taking his bodyguard duties very seriously, and honestly, I was here for it.

But Harris and Co. wasn't the place to test out new trust. The auditors were longtime employees of the Marcosas, and they knew too much about us to let just anyone sit in on a meeting. Hell, even Mario had used them to make sure everything was running smoothly in our family.

If you lose track of your money, you lose track of your power. Another lesson I'd taken to heart.

I sat back in my seat, rubbing my temples and waiting for Ronnie to explain. The meeting had barely started and I was already getting a headache, but I knew her. If she said there was a fire, it was a fucking inferno.

With a few clicks of a button, the conference room windows darkened to black, highlighting the image Ronnie projected onto the wall. I could appreciate the privacy, especially considering the sensitive data she was sharing, but it made me nervous that she was going to that much effort to keep things hush-hush. Everyone in her office knew the truth about my businesses, so the secrecy meant some real potential for instability lurked in those slides. A peek at Greyson and Dominic told me they felt the same.

"Obviously, there were inconsistencies with the accounting." Ronnie clicked through slides until she found the ones that she wanted. "We expected that, based on what you found at the docks. The problem is that same inconsistency happened throughout all of the businesses."

Fuck me.

"So there's a rat everywhere," Dominic said, sitting back and crossing his arms. "Are we talking about a single rat doing all of this at once, or multiples in key places in the organization?"

"I don't know."

"Give us your best guess."

Ronnie frowned and placed her hands in front of her on the table. "That's just it. I can't. We couldn't tell."

"How can you not tell?" I asked.

"All of the deposits were made from or into different accounts at different times. That's not a big deal—your staff list has overlap, but not *that* much overlap. There's nobody who has access to every single place and can be accounted for at the same time. The schedules never match up. So, at the very least, you have one person who is playing rat. But we can't positively identify anyone or promise there's not more than that. Not without solid proof, which we don't have."

"What about the cameras?"

"She asked and we checked, but there's nothing on the recordings," Tennessee said. "She even gave us time stamps for each location, and everything was exactly as expected. No breaches, no tampering, no loops. Just nothing."

"Maybe they did it remotely," Grey said.

"It's possible, but improbable, that they managed it without alerting anyone."

Meaning it was likely that we had more than one traitor, she just didn't want to guarantee it. Smart of her.

Veronica fidgeted in her seat, fixing her skirt over and over, and I just knew I was not going to like what she said. "We originally asked you for six months of data, and you provided it. The overages were present in each weekly deposit for those six months. I decided to do a little bit of extra digging and go back as far as I could in the data that we had over the last few years to see if I could pinpoint when the overages started."

"And did you?" I asked, narrowing my eyes. I didn't like that she was being coy any more than I liked that she'd dug into our finances without telling me. I trusted Veronica, but blind trust was a fool's game that I didn't play.

"I did."

"And?" Dominic snapped. I realized that his playboy persona had fallen by the wayside since I'd gotten home from the hospital, and I wondered why. Had he been that scared for me after Cash took me? Had our breakup broken him in return? I wasn't sure if I wanted the answers to be yes or no.

"The overages have been happening for at least the last four years."

Four years. The words echoed in my ears, and I felt like I had tunnel vision.

"You're telling me this motherfucker has been in my organization for *years* unnoticed? How is that possible?" I couldn't even fathom the amount of damage he could have done under our noses. It was astronomical. He could have pulled the strings of my family until it fell apart without my ever understanding why.

No wonder he was so smug. If this was true, he had every right to be, and I had every reason to be very, very worried.

"That's just it. It's not just organization money that he has a hand in. I believe he's had access to the nonprofit."

No.

I was going to throw up. My ears were ringing. Were anyone else's ears ringing?

Toni's Table was a nonprofit that I'd started in honor of Antoni. It provided meals to the unhoused population. It gave scholarships to kids for schooling, including clothes, backpacks, and college tuition. It offered rent and housing assistance to people in need. Toni's Table existed to help, and Cash had been messing with it.

"In the case of the nonprofit, there were shortages." I'd heard the term seeing red, but this was more than that. It was a rage blackout being held back by a paper clip and a prayer. He'd stolen money from a *nonprofit*. I knew we were criminals, but Christ. We had to have some fucking boundaries. That was mine.

Under the table, Greyson grabbed my thigh on one side and Dominic grabbed from the other, the two men pining me down when I hadn't even realized I'd gotten out of my seat. Ronnie looked terrified, and that cleared the fog a little.

"I'm not going to hurt you," I told her. She relaxed a little, but neither of the guys did. I thought about brushing Dominic off, but I needed the anchor or I was going to blow.

"How much are we talking?" Grey asked.

Veronica grimaced but held eye contact. Props to her. "We've identified $2.5 million so far."

Rage warmed my skin until I thought I would set something on fire.

That piece of shit. I was going to kill him.

"I want him out," I snarled. "Find whoever the hell his puppet is and *burn him out.* The organization is one thing, but my nonprofit is not a fucking playground."

"Do we have any idea who it is?" Dominic asked. He ran his thumb across my thigh, but I could barely feel it. I couldn't focus on anything beyond the need to destroy Cash.

Fucking with me was annoying, but tolerable. Fucking with my organization was idiotic, but par for the course. Fucking with my brother's memory. My *family.* *Innocents.* That was a death sentence I'd gladly carry out.

Tennessee stepped forward. "Ronnie called last week, and with Grey's permission, we did some digging into payroll. We think we have a potential list of accomplices. These are people making way too much, considering what they do, and those who had a major pay increase for no reason. We also checked anyone who saved more than they should have."

"It's not perfect, and it's definitely not a guarantee, but here's the list." Ronnie changed the screen, and I got my first look at the potential traitors in our midst.

The list held almost a dozen names, and that was the low side of things. The likelihood was that there were twice as many, and the others were just much better at hiding their tracks. The only positive was none of my officers seemed to be on it, and I knew Tennessee and Ronnie. Both would have insisted we look all the way up the hierarchy.

I also wasn't surprised Joaquin wasn't on the list. He wasn't out to take my seat for money. He wanted the prestige and the power that went with it.

Checking the list, I found Ronnie, our ever-organized auditor, had made sure to separate everyone based on where they worked, so it was easy to find the dockmaster's men. Out of everyone, Micah was the only one who had two employees on the list.

I pointed to their names. "Tell me about those two."

"They're Micah's men, both lifers. Their families have been with us since before your father was even around. Very old-school, the whole lot of them."

Which meant the likelihood that they didn't appreciate a female Marcosa running things was high. At the very least, they'd be easily manipulated because of their biases. "Why are they on the list?"

"They made double what they should have made last year with no additional jobs, no Social Security, no inheritances, no lottery earnings. They just made double. It didn't make any sense."

"We didn't pay them extra?" I asked, reaching for the payroll logs.

Tennessee answered without looking at the notes. "No, and they didn't get the money as commissions. They're strictly freight guys."

"We had to dig into offshore bank accounts to find the money," Ronnie said.

The fact that our employees had offshore accounts wasn't uncommon, considering the line of work we were in. Offshore bank accounts made it less likely for their accounts to be frozen if they happened to get caught up in any charges, especially if they were secret or under a fake name. At least that way, their money would be safe, and they could take care of their family should the worst happen. Greyson and I each had ten total and recommended our people have at least three each. But they were required to give us the information for exactly this reason. Auditing was easier if you didn't have to do much digging.

"Both of them have at least two additional offshore accounts they didn't let us know about."

"Easier places to funnel and hide money," Grey mused. "What do you want to do, *reina*?"

I looked over the list again and hated every second of it. At least one person in every one of my clubs. Two board members of my nonprofit. Cash was everywhere, and we needed to hit back at him.

I pulled out my phone and made a call to the dockmaster. Thankfully, Micah picked up immediately.

"Mari." He was wary. Good, he should've been.

"The audit's back, and I have two of your men's names on the naughty list. I need to know which one of them is more likely to crack under pressure." I listed the names, and he cursed loud and long.

"I didn't know."

I had no doubt about that. Micah would've brought me their bodies if he had. "I know you're loyal, but you'll still need to replace them and re-vet every other one of your men. Tennessee has already started, but I expect you to have a more *hands-on* approach. If you need help, send them to me."

Obviously, my people thought I was getting soft in times of peace. That had to change.

"That's a gracious offer." Micah didn't take it, though I knew he would if he had to. He preferred to police his own team. "If you're looking for which one I think will crack, Derek is probably your best bet. He's a good kid, great at his job, but he doesn't quite have the strong disposition Jacob has. He's also younger, which will help here."

Not as much practice learning to keep his mouth shut. *Perfect.*

"We'll let you know if we need anything else. In the meantime, I suggest you clean house." I hung up the phone and looked back at Tennessee. "I want Jacob picked up immediately. Call Warner to do it. Make it loud, public, and in front of Derek."

"You got it." He turned away, already reaching for his phone.

I wanted out of the fucking building before I exploded, but I had more to do. We couldn't leave it like this, without any real answers.

Jesus Christ. "From now on, you'll work on my account solo. If you need extra help, Greyson, Tennessee, and I will vet them individually. I need to know how long he's been doing this. I don't care how far you need to go. We'll give you access to all of the rosters that we have in exchange for having a guard of my choosing present at all times. We'll also be leaving a guard on you twenty-four seven. I don't think I need to stress this, but I'm going to. This is urgent and very dangerous. You fuck up and leak this, you're dead—and so are we. Get it done, and keep it locked down. Understood?"

Ronnie nodded immediately. No hesitation. "Understood. I'll get to the bottom of it."

I had no doubt she would. It was dangerous giving anyone that much information, but I trusted Ronnie as much as I could. With the orders given, I brushed the men's hands off me and stood. It felt like I was seconds away from melting my skin off, I was so pissed. Grey stood with me, but Dominic didn't.

"What about the clients?" Dominic said. I turned back, confused. "The reason we caught this is because your client had an overage, right? Well, what about the rest of them?"

"We audited them too," Ronnie said. "You have a couple that we think are working with Cash, but they're all relatively new. They're small overages, ones that I can easily see us overlooking, but the biggest one is still René Porter."

Of fucking course it was. "Looks like we need to have a chat with him, then. If there's anything else, give us a call. In the meantime, get to work. I want to know when he got into our systems and how."

I didn't wait for an answer, storming out of the office and then the building itself.

No one spoke until we got home. I was too angry, and Greyson and Dominic knew better than to poke me. Even Geneva and Tennessee were silent. By the time we got out of the car, I thought I was going to explode. Tennessee split off from our group, heading toward the other end of the garage for his truck.

"Where the hell are you going?"

"Going to meet Warner and pick up your boy. Am I bringing him here or somewhere else?"

I considered taking Jacob to Gilded, but I didn't want to draw attention there right now if I didn't have to. Plus, I was avoiding the building in hopes Cash would forget about it. Unlikely, but I was still going to try.

"Here," I said. "I want him to be easily accessible when I'm ready to talk."

"We giving him the silent treatment?" Grey asked.

"Yeah, two days at least. I want to see what his little buddy does before we even attempt to do anything else."

"You got it. I'll be back in a jiff." Tennessee gave a little salute, and then he was gone.

The moment I stomped inside, Joaquin took one look at me from across the room and disappeared down the hall, his little sycophants following suit. I was in a mood, and everyone knew it was best to avoid me. At least until I wasn't ready to lop off heads for sport.

You're not Mario. Get changed, go to the gym, work this shit out of your system, then be the leader they need.

I could do that.

After a quick change, I headed down to my private gym where I could be alone with my thoughts. The only people with access were Dominic, Greyson, and me. Well, Nate now too, but he and Moore were out on the property for the rest of the day.

Good thing, too.

I was so angry, I was practically steaming, and that meant I was fucking useless as a leader. Leading on emotional responses was how people got killed and empires toppled. That would not do.

I went through my stretches and warm-ups with gritted teeth, hating every second I had to live with the energy roiling inside me, but I couldn't afford to exacerbate any of my physical issues that were finally healing from the warehouse. When I was done, I taped my hands up and immediately went for the heavy bag.

Punch, kick. Punch, kick. Every time, I pictured Cash's smug face as he stabbed me in the stomach. As he walked away from me while he took that fucking phone call. As he told me he killed my brother.

And every time I hit the bag, I did it with the intent to maim. Kill. Defeat.

By the time I felt the air shift in the room announcing someone's arrival, I had sweated through my clothes and my chest ached from breathing hard.

"You're going to hurt yourself."

Dominic. Of course it was him. The little nurturer couldn't bear to see one of his flock hurt.

"Go away, Dominic," I snarled, setting myself up for another kick. "I'm not in the mood."

He ignored me, stepping closer. "I understand that, but if you don't stop, you're going to hurt yourself."

"Did you ever think that maybe I want to hurt? Maybe this is preferable to the fact that someone else is destroying my life's work. My brother's memory. Did you ever think that maybe this is the only way that I can function?"

He stepped into my line of sight, and my first instinct was to punch. *Get ahold of yourself.*

"If you want to hurt, I know more productive ways that you can do it."

I laughed, rotating so I couldn't see him again. "I'm not fucking you, Dominic."

"I didn't suggest it. We're not there yet, but if you want someone to run you through your paces and wear you down, I can help."

The anger inside me was nowhere near sated. It wanted a target, and Dominic was offering himself up on a pretty little platter. Any conversation we had was going to get toxic quick. "It's a nice offer, but it isn't what I need. Go away." *Just listen to me, please.*

Regardless of how much he'd hurt me, I didn't want to hurt him back. Not like this. Because I was more like Mario than I'd ever cared to admit, and I'd go for a kill shot every time.

"Maybe you don't think so, but I do." He stepped behind the heavy bag, holding it still for me. "You think I don't understand you, but I do. You and I are far more alike than you think. That's why we fight so much, and it's why we're so good together."

"There is no we, Dominic. There is no us. You and I are not together anymore."

"I understand that, just like I understand that's my fault, but I'm telling you, I can help if you let me."

"I think I'll pass, but thanks." I couldn't decline again or I'd go postal. I just needed him to leave before I said something we couldn't get past. "See yourself out."

"That's fine. That's your choice. I just want to let you know that I'm here and I'm not going anywhere. I know I've made mistakes and I have a lot to make up for, but I'm going to do it. I'm not going to let you go again."

The pressure inside me was near to bursting, and I knew there was no stopping it now. I'd given him an out—more than one, really—and he'd chosen to stay. That was his fault. "Maybe not, but which Mari are you clinging to?"

"That's fair." He looked so serene, and it pissed me off.

I pulled off my gloves and tossed them to the floor. "Of course it's fair! You can't see me, Dominic. You only see her. *Your precious little mariposa.*"

"That's not true anymore."

"Are you fucking kidding me? What changed in such a short period of time?"

"You did. You almost died, Mari."

The rage was melting into sadness—for me, for Antoni's legacy, for all the bullshit I'd had to endure. For the way Dominic had hurt me. I hated it, and I hated him for pushing the conversation when I didn't want to have it. "Why did it have to take me dying for you to get there?"

"I don't know, but it did. Almost losing you was the worst moment of my life." I scoffed, and he circled the heavy bag, keeping his distance but making sure I could see him. "I know you don't believe that. I know you think that because you broke up with me that I don't have feelings for you, that watching you lie in the hospital bed didn't do anything to me, but it did. I've loved you since the first time you kissed me."

Oh, fuck no. The anger disappeared in a wave of disbelief as Dominic dropped to his knees at my feet. I knew he'd told me he loved me at the warehouse, but we'd been dancing around it. I didn't have the mental bandwidth to do more than that. Yet here he was, bleeding his heart onto the floor.

"I've loved you since the first time I held you in my arms, Marianna Marcosa. That hasn't changed. Both of us may have changed, but that hasn't. I loved you then, I love you now, and I'll love you until the day that I die."

"I don't believe you," I whispered, raw and agonized.

"I know, but it's true. I just got lost because I couldn't recognize you at first. That's not your fault, it's mine. I came here expecting nothing to have changed, and I couldn't accept the fact that you had other people who had replaced me. So, I hurt you. I will always live with that regret."

I was frozen, staring at him. How did someone respond to a love declaration from their ex? "I can't say it back."

The disappointment I expected never manifested. "I know. I'm not asking you to. But you should know I'm going to earn it. I don't care if it takes a year, five years, ten years. I'm not leaving this city. I'm not leaving your side. I'm not walking away."

Pretty words that I didn't believe he could back up. "What happens when you see something you don't like? I can't go back to who I was, Dominic. Not only is it impossible, it would get us all killed."

"I don't want you to go back. I see the person you were trying to show me before, and she's incredible. Your strength is what really made it sink in. You're still my *mariposa*. You've just evolved."

"I'm not. I'm not her anymore."

"Okay." He was placating me, but in the aftermath of so much emotion, I didn't care. I just wanted to sleep for a year. "I'm going to prove myself to you, Mari."

Stepping around him, I headed for the door. I needed a stiff drink and a fucking nap. "Good luck."

I didn't want to believe him. Not when he'd let me down before. But part of me would always want Dominic. So maybe I couldn't give him my all, but I was willing to watch him try to earn it.

Chapter 12
Nate

If someone asked me what I thought a morning in a kingpin's house would look like, watching Dominic and Greyson bickering at the table while I cooked pancakes for the woman we all wanted wouldn't have been my answer.

It was all so *normal*, especially if I ignored the insane mansion and the armed guards strolling past the windows every few minutes. It felt like I'd always been there, like I always would be.

The feeling was even stronger when Mari walked into the kitchen, hair flattened on one side from sleeping on it. Clad in nothing but an old men's T-shirt and a pair of shorts that barely peeked out from under the hem, she looked edible.

"Good morning," she said, leaning down to kiss Greyson. Again, I couldn't stop thinking that it was all so easy, so casual. Though I could practically feel the ache from where Dominic sat across the table, eyes burning with jealousy.

"Morning." Her greeting to him was far more subdued, but he didn't seem to mind when he returned it.

She padded softly over to me, kissing my cheek before wrapping her arms around my waist. I liked how comfortable she was touching me, like we snuggled every morning over the stove. "What are we making?"

"*I* am making breakfast," I clarified, sliding a cup of coffee over to her. I directed her to sit, but I stopped her before she could get far. Greyson said she'd had a rough night and had taken a sleeping pill before dinner was even served. "Is there anything I need to know?"

"About yesterday?"

"About him." Her little frown was adorable, showing she definitely wasn't awake yet, so I gave a very quick glance at Dominic. She hummed into her coffee, smiling when she found it exactly the way she wanted. "We're...working on things?"

That was an understatement, and Mari's lack of belief he could fix the absolute shitshow he'd caused was beyond noticeable. I handed her the plate and kissed her forehead. "It'll work out."

Her smile was shaky at best as she took her seat beside Grey, and I hoped I was right. I didn't know Dominic very well, but he seemed like the type who wouldn't give up until he got what he wanted. My only hope was that what he wanted was actually Mari.

I shoved the rest of the pancakes onto a platter and set them in the middle of the table next to the fruit salad and bacon that Greyson had not so subtly suggested.

"No personal service for us?" Dominic joked.

"I think you can handle getting your own fucking pancakes. Besides, she's special."

Dominic grumbled something under his breath until Greyson kicked him in the kneecap.

"Thank you for making breakfast." He sounded like he was

swallowing porcupine quills, but I would take it. I figured I wouldn't like me right now either if I were him.

We made it through breakfast without interruption, talking about the weather, people's plans for the day, and even dinner. We ribbed one another comfortably, and when I laid my arm over the back of Mari's chair, she leaned into me like it was nothing. It felt like a dream I didn't deserve.

That all changed the moment Mari was done. As soon as her fork hit the plate, Greyson and Dominic sat at attention. It was like they could feel the shift in her before it was even complete. I wondered if she realized how in tune they were with one another and with her.

"I'm paying a visit to René Porter today."

I didn't know the name, but I did know the look on Mari's face. Someone was going to die. And because I knew her, I was also positive that they deserved it.

Greyson frowned, peering over his schedule on his phone. "With the wedding and everything, I don't know if I can go with you."

Mari waved him off. "I wasn't planning on bringing you anyway. I need you running interference with O'Bannon."

Dominic and I winced.

"Honestly, I'd rather take the torture," Dominic said.

Agreed. O'Bannon had come into Gilded a few times once it opened, and he'd been warned every time to keep his hands off the waitstaff. He was a pig and a shitty tipper to boot.

Grey glared at Mari from his seat at her side, but she smiled innocently. "The wedding planners will be here in an hour or so, and since problem-solving is your specialty, I need you to figure out how to make Ash's dream wedding happen in no time flat. Talking to Sean is part of it."

She was laying it on thick, and I tried not to laugh at how

obvious it was that she didn't want to be involved. Maybe opening night had scarred her. I'd heard it was a logistical nightmare.

For a second, Greyson looked like he'd refuse, but I should have known better. This was Mari's shadow. What she wanted, he gave her.

I may have been new to the family, but even I knew that much.

He leaned in close, speaking low, though we could all hear him. "You're an asshole, and you owe me for this."

Mari smiled, all sex and seduction. "Don't worry, baby. I'll let you fuck me later."

"Deal," Greyson growled, nipping her lips before getting up. "Better go tell the lovebirds before you go. If we don't warn them, Cameron will go off script, and we both know he won't be able to resist baiting his future father-in-law."

We all grimaced. Cameron's dislike of the Irishman had been heard far and wide inside the Marcosa walls. Aislynn's, too, for that matter.

Mari stood, fluffing her hair absently as she looked at Dominic and me. "You two have thirty minutes to get changed and meet me by the front door. Dress like a badass. The theme for today is intimidation."

When she was gone, we looked at each other. "I think we got the better end of the deal."

Dominic snorted. "You say that now, but it's time to show your guts, pretty boy."

Normally, I wouldn't play his game, but he'd been seething since Mari walked in, and he thought it was okay to take it out on me. I was the newest member of their little troupe, but I wasn't the weakest. He couldn't play me, and he'd learn that I had no problem stooping low if he came for the knees.

"Trust me, Mari knows exactly what I'm capable of. Can you say the same?" The words were heavy with innuendo, and Dominic's face twisted in irritation.

"Fuck you, Nate." Yeah, didn't think so.

Nate, 1. Dominic, 0.

I could feel the heat of his glare as he stalked out of the room, but I didn't care. I was dying to see Mari in her element again. She was hot as fuck when she was in her power. I *needed* to see it again, if only because I was wearing out the memory of the ambush we'd both been in. I had to get new material until I could have her the way I desperately wanted her.

Plus, I would get to prove myself to her. I could hang with the kingpin and be an asset. She just didn't know it yet.

* * *

When Mari said we were going for intimidation, I didn't think she meant kicking in the door to someone's office. Yet, there I was, trailing her and Dominic through the door to the sound of surprised screams.

"What the fuck?" That came from the man struggling to cover his dick since his pants were around his knees.

From the scant details Mari had given me on the way over, that was our mark.

René Porter. Forty-three, chronically single, no kids. According to the intel, he was a low-level importer, longtime Marcosa customer. He sold weird shit—never the same thing twice—and was scared of his own shadow. Up until recently, he'd been a model client.

Mari wanted to know when and why that changed.

Avoiding the sight of dick so early in the morning, I peered around. His office was deceptively high-end for a low-level importer, but money couldn't replace taste. Hand-tanned leather couches mixed with '70s mod rugs and existentialist paintings that made me want to gouge out my eyeballs. Every square inch of the room was filled with something that was supposed to show his prestige, but instead made him look like a hoarder.

Dominic stepped forward, covering Mari while the guy covered himself, but she barely glanced at either of them. Her focus was solely on the woman cowering beneath the desk with messy hair and swollen lips.

"Aren't you the assistant?" she asked.

The woman brushed her hair behind her ear, wiping her mouth. "Yes, I am."

When she dropped her eyes almost immediately, Mari's gaze narrowed and she turned to Porter. "Do you normally require your assistant to have such a *hands-on* role in your company?"

It was very obvious that little Porter was using his power to get his rocks off. If he wasn't dead before we walked in, he was now.

"Of course not," Porter said, glaring at the other woman. "Get out."

She didn't hesitate, shoving to her feet and stumbling halfway to the door. Dominic caught her with gentle hands and escorted her out, locking us in as best he could after she disappeared down the hall. We'd done a number on the door, so it hung slightly off-kilter. I kind of liked it, though. It added to the unstable feel of Porter's treasure trove.

"Why am I not surprised that you're an idiot and a predator?" Mari asked.

Porter sat back in his chair like it was an everyday occurrence for the queen of the city to break in to his office. But he was *too* calm and cool, and I saw beneath the mask. The barest shake of his fingers betrayed him. He was petrified of Mari.

And I was not ashamed to admit it made me hot.

"I have no idea what you're talking about. She was willing."

"You're wrong. In places where power is so imbalanced, consent is never black and white. Did you threaten her livelihood?" Mari asked with a sneer.

"No." *Liar.*

"Did you threaten her safety?"

"Of course not." *Lie.*

"Did you promise her something in return for her *cooperation?*"

"No." *Lie.*

Not one of us believed him.

Porter cleared his throat, straightening his position. "Did you come all this way to talk about Miss Antoinette?"

"No, I came all this way to talk about our mutual friend, Cash Beckstrom. She's just an added bonus."

The name hit me in the chest like it had every time I'd heard it, but I forced myself not to react. Cash was the one attacking the Marcosa empire. He'd taken Mari, nearly killed her. And one day, he would pay for his sins, but not today. Another man was on the chopping block this time.

If it was possible, René paled even further. "I don't know a Cash Beckstrom," he stammered. Christ, he wasn't even trying to be convincing.

"Of course not," Mari said, walking around the desk until she could perch along the edge of it. She set her hand down on the surface and froze, seeming to remember what had just happened in the area, before picking it up with a frown. "Do you have hand sanitizer?"

Porter glanced between her and the desktop. "It's not like we fucked on it."

"Forgive me if I don't take your word for it," she said. "The hand sanitizer. *Now.*"

Perplexed, he fished out a bottle and held it out to her. I didn't think Mari cared that much about the germs—though, gross—it was the power play of it all. The way she reminded Porter that he was a disgusting little urchin without saying a word. The way he sank a little in his chair as she rubbed the liquid into her hands, looked at him, and did another round? Brilliant.

I'd learned a lot about manipulation in the mercenaries, and Mari played him flawlessly.

When she'd finished her show, she set down the bottle and smiled at Porter, though it was about as warm as an iceberg.

"Cash Beckstrom, Seattle's most irritating resident," Mari droned. "He's been messing with my shipments. Yours, in particular."

"Can't say I've noticed anything missing from them. Besides, isn't that your job to fix?" Porter asked, trying and failing again to gain some of the power back.

"You wouldn't have," Mari told him. "Not when your shipments were over. He never shorted you. Isn't that fascinating?"

She stood, and as she talked, she trailed her fingers along the various belts and scarves he had tossed over a coat rack near the window. I didn't understand why he needed so many, but considering what we were planning to do to him in this dragon's nest of an office, I couldn't have been more grateful. Just because we'd brought our own supplies, didn't mean we necessarily *wanted* to use them.

Mari fingered a solid leather belt and then another for good measure. When she took them off the rack, Dominic and I rounded each corner of the desk, boxing Porter in. He panicked, standing so the chair rolled out from underneath him, but we shoved him back down. There would be no escaping Mari's wrath.

"Hold him down."

Dominic and I each held one wrist to the armrest while the other hand kept his shoulders back so he couldn't bite her if he got the balls. He didn't, though. He stopped fighting the second she held up the belt.

Once Porter was tied, Dominic dug through his pockets and fished out his phone, holding it up so that the facial recognition would open it. *Facial recognition.* On an *importer's* phone. Looking over his shoulder, I could see he had no additional security beyond that. What kind of idiot didn't secure the phone he did his business on?

Dominic muttered something similar under his breath as he dug through the apps, finding a hidden folder with a simple password of 0000.

"Christ, you can't even be creative for that," he mumbled.

"I have a bad memory." Porter's defense was weak.

"Then you're in the wrong business."

While Dominic dealt with that, I added the software Greyson had sent with us to the computer and watched Dominic while it loaded.

As he looked through Porter's secret folder, I could see a couple of messaging apps, some extra banking ones, but nothing crazy. It was what we found when we delved deeper into them that was interesting. We expected conversations with Cash, obviously, but we hadn't expected how much money Porter had gotten out of that gig.

"Your bank account shows you're ten million dollars heavier than you should be. Care to explain?" Mari asked. I turned back to the computer, diving into his files as the sound of flesh on flesh echoed in the room. Porter's groans were music to my ears.

"I sold a few extra pieces," Porter said, trying and failing to make us believe it.

Except, the invoices said otherwise. Dominic came up behind me, reading the page and whistling between his teeth. "Christ, you may be too stupid to live, Porter. Your invoices aren't even password-protected, let alone encrypted. At this point, you're going to die because you're a fucking liability."

I rotated the screen to show Mari, but she waved me off. "I don't even need to look. You want to know why, Porter? Because I pay attention."

She hopped from her perch at my side and threw a solid right hook. "I know exactly who you sell to, how much your pieces cost, and what you should be making."

Another punch and Porter spat a wad of blood onto the floor with a tooth included.

"You're way above your threshold here. You should've stayed in your happy little hobbit cave. Instead, you get to deal with me, and I want answers."

"I don't have anything to say. I earned that money."

"I'm sure you did, Porter. I want to know how. Why did you do it? How long you've been batting for the wrong team. Because make no mistake, any team that isn't mine is going to lose."

When he didn't answer, she punched him in the nose, and the crack of cartilage told me she'd done some damage.

"I don't know what you're talking about!" Porter screamed.

"You do, and you're going to tell me, even if I have to use more creative methods." She slipped a knife from her pocket, and I had to adjust myself. Who knew I had a knife kink?

Maybe it was just a Mari thing. That sounded more likely. I liked her for who she was, messy bits, weapons, and all.

I leaned into her, talking low. "Do you want me to do this for you?"

Dominic's eyes met mine, and I thought I saw a glimmer of respect in them before he turned back to trolling Porter's phone.

Mari pressed her cheek against mine. "No. I want you to watch."

Fuck yes.

I wasn't a sadist. I didn't enjoy hurting people once it was no longer my job, but I had a feeling watching Mari interrogate Porter was going to be a different experience for me.

Mari's knife cut away the front of his shirt, slipping through the fabric like butter. "I want to make this clear. For every lie you tell me, I cut you. Omit the truth, I cut you. Unless you give me perfect honesty, you're going to bleed. Do you understand?"

Porter nodded and Mari began. "When did you meet Cash?"

"I don't know what you're talking about."

Slash. "Try again. The truth this time."

Porter shook as she pressed the knife into his flesh. Not cutting, just holding it there. A promise and a warning that he didn't heed.

"I-I don't know what you're talking about."

Slash.

For the next thirty minutes, Mari interrogated him. Every time he refused an answer, he got cut. Every time he lied, he got cut. Every time he tried to disappear inside his little brain, he got cut.

My eyes went between Mari and Dominic as she sliced and diced her mark, because as beautiful as it was to watch her in her element, the real beauty was in the way Dominic watched her. Not like she was some new puzzle he needed to put together or some animal at a zoo, but like he really saw her. Like he finally understood who the Mari right in front of him was, not the girl he knew before.

Seeing that, I had actual hope for them. I didn't know why it mattered to me, but Mari deserved all the love she could get, and there was no doubt in my mind that Dominic loved her. He just had to get over himself and love her the way she needed to be loved.

Fiercely, recklessly, without fail.

It wasn't what people in the underground cared about, but it was what she needed. A foundation to hold her steady, a family to keep her grounded and give her something to fight for. People to fight for her, not because she ruled them, but because they wanted to. Because they loved her. We could be that for her.

None of us were good men, but I had no doubt we would be Mari's monsters if she let us. We would be good when she needed us to be, and when she needed us to be bad, we would be downright awful in her name.

Every queen needed knights; Mari's were just darker than normal.

By the time Porter gave up, he was soaked with blood and listing in his seat, but he still hadn't given us an answer. I was almost impressed with the little twerp.

"I don't know what you want from me," he whined when Mari cut him again. Her cuts were all smooth, all methodical. She never once cut too deep, even when he goaded her. She showed more patience than I would've had in the same situation.

It was interesting watching Mari's darkness come out. I'd known it was there; I'd even seen glimpses of it, but having a front-row seat to the control she had over it was beyond my wildest dreams. Mari kept herself on a leash so tight, there was no way it could escape. I wondered if Dominic saw it the same way I did, how she made it work for her and not the other way around. It showed a lot of restraint on her part that she didn't have to have.

She tsked at Porter. "You do. You're just worried that I'm going to kill you when I find out. News flash, that's already the plan. *Tell me what you know.*"

"Why should I if you're just going to kill me?"

"Because if you don't, I'll make your death very painful." Mari leaned in close, dragging the knife across his skin. "I can keep you alive for days. Weeks. Months. Barely enough to eat, barely enough water to wet your throat. I'll skin you, burn you, pull out every nail and hair on your body. I'll make you wish for death. Does that answer your question?"

I'd never seen a man turn that shade of green so fast. Only quick thinking kept Mari and me from getting covered in vomit as the nerves finally got to Porter.

Torture a man for thirty minutes, nothing. Promise to make him hairless, and he barfs.

Side-eyeing him, because vomit was something I did not suffer well, I dug back into the computer while Dominic threw one of Porter's coats over the pile. Gross.

"Why did you join with Cash?" Mari asked again. This time, he answered.

"Because he was offering me money, and I needed it. Things haven't been going well."

"I'm shocked," Dominic deadpanned with a look around the room.

"You got into bed with Cash because you couldn't afford your lifestyle. That's what you're going with?" Mari didn't seem to believe him. I couldn't say I did either. Not when he had ten million in the bank.

"It's true."

"No, it isn't. Not fully," I said, clicking deeper into his email. As expected, nothing was protected. No encryption, no passwords. *Moron.* "He did it because Cash promised him your throne."

There was a pregnant pause as Mari read the email thread once, twice, three times. Then she tipped her head back and laughed.

If I'd thought she was incredible before, nothing beat the sound of her laughter. She seemed like someone who hadn't had enough of it. Even Porter looked a little awestruck.

"You think you can wrest the city from me and keep it?" she asked when she finally calmed down. Her eyes were glittering with tears of mirth even as she sneered at him. "You want to be *king* that badly, Porter?"

"I-I just think I could do a good job," he stammered.

"*Anyone would be better than that Marcosa bitch,*" I quoted, anger making everything a little hazy. I'd always had an anger-management problem, but the mercs had burned it out of me. It'd been a long time since I'd felt that mad. I didn't hate it. "Bold words for someone who can't even protect his intel."

Mari leaned in close, making sure Porter understood every word was true. "You wouldn't last a day being me and not just because Cash would kill you the moment you became less than useful. The others would see you as a threat. They'd hunt you down like prey and rip you apart with their teeth. You should thank me for saving you from that fate."

"I'm sorry. I shouldn't have done it. I knew that, but I did it anyway. I got greedy. I'm so sorry."

Christ, she was good.

"You did, and now I have to clean up your mess. Apology not accepted."

Porter started crying, and I could almost feel for him. Looking headfirst into your own death was brutal. I'd been there more than once. But when you committed to a cause, you stayed with it. He'd committed to the Marcosas, to Mari, and he'd jumped ship the second a better offer came around, without remembering the number one rule of underground life: traitors didn't survive long.

"I'm starting to think I've been too lenient with you, Porter. All these years of you being a quiet pain in my ass, and I let it slide because money is money. Now it's time to rectify that." She pulled her gun from its holster, and I met Dominic's eyes across the room. Needless to say, we both liked seeing our woman with a weapon in her hand.

"You don't have to do that," Porter babbled. "I'll tell you whatever you want. You don't have to kill me. Please don't kill me."

"I think I do. See, I need a message for Cash, and getting rid of you is the perfect first move. Well, second move, but he doesn't know about that one yet. I'm going to leave your body as a reminder of who runs this city." She twisted to look at me. "Can you get all the information off the computer?"

"Sure. Grey could too."

"Good."

Pop. Pop.

That was it. Two shots and René Porter ceased to exist. "We need to get the assistant a severance package and some fucking therapy."

"I'll tell Grey," Dominic promised.

With Porter slumped in the chair and Mari's hands and wrists covered in blood, she turned to us. I was certain she'd never looked more beautiful.

"This is who I am. This is who I'm always going to be. If you don't like it, there's the door."

That was it, the summation of our trip. She wanted to know if we would stay when we saw her ruthlessness.

"I'm in." There was no choice for me. There hadn't been in so long. I wasn't a believer in fate, but something divine had pulled us together, and I'd be at her side until I had to leave.

"I already told you I'm not going anywhere," Dominic said.

I could see that Mari didn't take his words as truth the way she did mine, and that kind of trust was a weight I knew I'd have to carry.

The silence was tense and stilted until Mari obliterated it with a single nod. She'd laid down the challenge, and we'd promised to meet it. Now, she just had to see if we'd keep our word.

After a quick shower and a change of clothes, Mari and I headed downstairs. Dominic stayed behind to arrange for the cleanup, though we were delaying it a few days. Hopefully, long enough for Cash to come looking for his missing man and find nothing but bloated body parts. I helped Mari into the SUV, and my phone beeped loudly as I climbed in behind her.

"What's that?" she asked, twisting in her seat to see me.

"My mother's caretaker," I said, checking the text before deleting it as always. I didn't like it on my phone. "Just an update for the day."

The furrow in her brow smoothed, and she reached over the seat to rub my shoulder. "I'm sorry. You didn't have to tell me."

"It's fine. I wasn't hiding it."

"You know, if you ever want to go see her, but you don't want to go by yourself, I'll go with you." Guilt festered in my stomach, souring the moment.

"You want to visit my mentally incapacitated mother with me?"

Mari shrugged as Dominic climbed into the passenger seat beside Geneva. "I wouldn't say want, but she's important to you and you're important to me. Why wouldn't I go?"

She started to pull away, but I clasped her hand, forcing her to stay connected to me. To remind me that I wasn't alone in this shitty world. That I didn't have to shoulder the burdens of my family on my own. I didn't respond—couldn't, really—but I didn't need to. Not everything between us needed to be said with words, and the same was true for this.

I didn't deserve Mari, but I was going to keep her as long as I could.

Chapter 13
Mari

There's never been a more beautiful bride," I told Aislynn. She stood on the pedestal in her wedding dress with pins here and there, places that needed to be tucked and hemmed.

Hell, the whole skirt still needed to be lined, but it was incredible. Her team had worked day and night to make her dream a reality, even with the tight deadline.

Yet Ash didn't look happy.

"It is beautiful." Ash turned, scrutinizing the gown in the mirror. "It's not quite right, though. Maybe we need to shorten the train or remove some of the bustles. There's a lot of work that still needs to be done and no time to finish everything."

The guilt that had been weighing on me grew heavier.

"No," Gretchen snapped, throwing a glare in my way. "Come hell or high water, you'll have the dress you are meant to have. If the *queen* doesn't like the new overtime budget, she should have stuck with the original timeline."

"The queen has no problem footing the bill." There was no use arguing with her. No doubt we'd be at each other's throats until the end of time.

The two talked and planned, making small adjustments until things were as perfect as they could be, then Gretchen helped Ash change and left.

She joined me in the armchairs as one of her assistants dropped off a tray of drinks and small snacks before leaving. We each grabbed something small, nibbling here and there.

For once, we were alone. Dominic was busy checking on some things, Nate was with Moore and Tennessee, getting some more practice with our systems, and Grey was dealing with the fallout from O'Bannon's shitfit. Even Cameron was busy. I was grateful for the alone time. It'd been too long since we'd talked.

"Has your father contacted you again?" The moment I uttered the words, I was reminded that we'd grown up the same. Both daughters of the mafia, born and bred to hold secrets beyond the grave, and Ash had learned how to do it well. If I hadn't been looking directly at her, I wouldn't have seen the minute wince. As it was, she said nothing.

Guilt may have held me prisoner in my own head, but I couldn't just turn a blind eye to something so obvious.

"Are we lying to each other now, Aislynn? I didn't realize we had reached that point of our friendship." I kept my voice light, non-accusatory. The last thing I needed was to alienate her.

Another wince, this time noticeable. Finally, she sagged into the chair. "Yes, he has. Sorry, it's been a source of contention with Cameron lately, so I told myself to keep it quiet."

I thought about my cousin, who had all but cornered me this morning. *"If that O'Bannon prick speaks out of turn to my fiancée one more time, he's going to find himself six feet under and his son crowned king."*

"I can't imagine that's been easy for you," I told her sympathetically. As expected, she waved me off.

"He's angry that you took away his spotlight. He'll get over it or he won't, but that's not really my problem. Is it?"

She peeked at me, uncharacteristic fear in her eyes. It made me wonder how much different the O'Bannon household was from mine. Mario had been an asshole, but he was more negligent than abusive. He preferred to put us in our place by reminding us of the power he held. That type of manipulation took tact and patience, neither of which Sean O'Bannon possessed.

"I'll take care of it," I promised her.

Ash smiled with relief, reaching over to grip my hand lightly. "I know you will."

That faith buoyed me. Maybe I hadn't fucked up her life completely.

"How's everything with Cameron? Is he treating you well?"

She smiled a little, though she tried not to. "Cameron's great, maybe too great. It makes me nervous. Men in this life should have red flags, right?"

I thought about my own men, about how long it had taken Greyson and me to get to where we were now. About Dominic's inability to see me as I was because of who I used to be. About my position being too much for him and for Nate. We'd made it through, though. Well, mostly.

Then there was the possessiveness, the jealousy I saw them try to hide. The over-the-top protectiveness. The fear that it would be too much and one of us would walk.

Were those problems that came from our world or the fact that I was building a relationship with more than one man? Maybe things would be different for Ash because it was just Cameron. Though, thinking of my cousin's near-feral need to keep her safe, I wasn't so sure.

"Maybe too many green flags is a red flag, but you also haven't been around healthy relationships. Neither have I. As much as I want to hope that this is good for you, maybe it's best to go into it with no expectations."

"You're right." She took a long sip of her drink, looking away as if it hid her disappointment. "Already, I feel like I'm his roommate, not his wife. Maybe that's all I can hope for."

Neither of us said anything. While not ideal, it could've been far worse.

Finally, Aislynn cleared her throat. "He's gone a lot, which is nice. The transition between living on my own to living with him has been a little easier with him being out at all hours."

I didn't explain what Cameron was doing because I knew my cousin. If he wanted her to know about Joaquin, he would have told her.

"Maybe taking your own space is a good thing for now," I said. "Start slow, be friends. You don't have to fall in love right away, or at all. Even if you're strictly platonic, at least you'll be safe and protected. He will take care of you, even if that means you find love somewhere else when things are more settled."

Because an affair early on would not only make us look weak, but send her groom over the edge. Cameron's stress levels were already maxed; a secret boyfriend at the moment—even a consensual one—would have deadly consequences for everyone involved.

Ash laughed, settling back into her chair with the air of someone who'd just lost the weight of the world. "I hear your warning loud and clear. No relationships."

"Wait and see what happens with your husband before you go making plans." She nodded, taking another sip of her drink. Guilt and curiosity beat at me until I had to ask. "Look, I know things have been hectic, but are you sure you want to go through with this?"

"We just had a fitting for my wedding dress, and now you're asking me if I want to run? A little late, don't you think?" Ash laughed, and the sound was so happily carefree, I took it as her answer.

"It's not that I'm worried about you running. I just want to make sure that I'm not pushing you into something you don't want."

Guilt had made me restless. The understanding that I was burning Aislynn's bridges for her ate at me. Her being married off was what we'd tried to prevent, and yet here I was, shoving her toward my family, as if we were better than the O'Bannons. We weren't—we just had more power.

It was hypocritical at best and cruel at worst. I wanted—no, I *needed*—to make sure that I wasn't hurting my friend in the process. I didn't want to lose her over something like this.

Too little, too late, my mind screamed at me.

Aislynn set down her drink and stared right into my eyes like she knew I needed the connection. "I'm the one who said yes. We both know you would have let me walk if I had asked, and I didn't. You're right. Cameron is a good catch, and he'll be a good husband, even if it's just as a friend. I want to do this, and frankly, there's no way for me to go home now anyway. My father thinks of me as a deserter. If I try to go back, he'll either marry me off to some geriatric abuser or kill me in my sleep as a message to all the other daughters who dare bow to anyone other than their king. I can't go home again."

For a moment, she trembled, and that killed me a little more. Despite how awful O'Bannon was, I'd just taken Ash from the rest of her family too, and we were both realizing it. Granted, she'd been trying to leave anyway, so maybe that blame wasn't all mine to hold, but the crown was heavy, and mine felt a hundred times too big some days.

"Besides, who will mediate the arguments between Cameron

and my father, if not me? No one else would stop them before they come to blows," she joked.

I wanted to keep talking until she absolved me of my guilt, but she obviously didn't want to and we didn't have the time. Being queen meant living with the consequences of my actions, even when I hated them. I'd just have to suck it up and deal.

"I'd bet on your husband any day of the week. He's a real protective type, and O'Bannon's been on his shit list for years."

Aislynn laughed for real, and I let that sound worm its way into my heart and dampen the worst of the guilt. It wasn't a long-term fix, but I doubted anything would be. All I could do was hope that my plan turned out well for her and she found happiness. My phone buzzed on the table, and I found a text from Dominic.

Downstairs whenever you're ready.

"Our chauffeur has arrived," I joked, standing and brushing off the smart pinstripe suit Ash had made me years ago. After another touch-base with her team and another glare from Gretchen, we finally made it downstairs.

"Where's your driver?" I asked as the valet pulled an SUV I'd never seen to a stop in front of her and handed over the keys.

Ash passed the valet a tip and snatched the keys. "I gave him the day off, especially since I'm planning to go right home."

I wondered if my cousin had agreed to that. He wasn't the type to shirk on protection detail, especially not with Cash running around. The moment I thought about it, I decided it wasn't my problem. Their arguments bordered on foreplay, and frankly, my cousin's sex life was none of my fucking business. If they wanted to play boss and bad girl, that was on them.

"And the bodyguards?"

She shrugged, looking more insincere than ever. "Must've given them the wrong schedule. They could've found me, but I had this car delivered earlier today, so no tracker yet. Oops."

Christ. Before I could warn her of the upcoming freak-out, Ash climbed into the driver's seat with another wave and a smile toward the valet. Knowing she didn't have backup, I climbed into my own car to find Dominic shaking his head. "What?"

"Cameron's going to tan her ass when she gets home."

Remembering the blush on her cheeks when Shara and I asked, I had no doubt Ash would enjoy it. "I take it he doesn't know she's out for a joyride?"

Dominic threw back his head and laughed. "Oh, he knows. He was losing his shit earlier. By the way, he broke two candelabras and threw a table. Apparently, *he* thought they'd agreed that she'd take the driver and the guards wherever she went. According to the bodyguards she left tied up in their suite with pantyhose and boob tape, *she* thought they were optional."

Snorting at the absolute mayhem my friend had unleashed, I buckled in.

I loved my cousin desperately. He was an incredible man, one of the funniest people I'd ever met and one of my favorite people on the planet, but he was also a fucking hothead. Making matters worse, he'd never learned how to channel that anger into anything more than a temper tantrum. I felt sorry for Aislynn, but knowing that she could hold her own had me wishing for popcorn and a front-row seat to that fight.

It would be one for the ages.

Ash pulled away, and I directed Dominic to stay close. It would be just our luck for her to get rear-ended and have Cameron turn into a fucking warden.

The ride was silent but comfortable. After our meeting with Porter and the subsequent body dumping of our little traitor, Dominic and I had found ourselves in a sort of easy peace.

While I'd been leaving my message on Porter, I thought

Dominic would run—or maybe I was just expecting him to balk. Instead, he stood right by my side the whole time. It gave me hope for a future where we might actually have a chance with each other. I didn't know if it was foolish to want him anymore, but hope was a fickle thing. It burrowed deep at the slightest chance of redemption and clung until it had to be pried off.

I wanted Dominic to prove me wrong. I wanted him to earn me back. I just wasn't ready to admit it.

We were nearly home when his fingers creaked against the steering wheel and he cursed under his breath, a habit I noticed he'd taken up since moving in with us.

"What is it?" I said, instantly on alert.

"We're being followed."

With Ash's car in clear view, I pulled out my phone, tapping a message to Greyson to get everyone we had ready in case we brought a fight to the mansion.

He called me immediately. "We sounded the alarm. You think they're planning a shootout or something else?"

Something like a bomb in the car. It wasn't the type of warfare we generally allowed in the city, but Cash was unhinged. I had a feeling nothing was off-limits to him.

Dominic answered for me. "Looks like surveillance, so let's hope not."

All of a sudden, the growl of a shitty engine echoed through the car. As it swerved around Dominic to pull up to our side, I grabbed my gun and climbed into the back seat so I could shoot without risking my driver. Before I could even roll down the window, the car raced off. "What the fuck are they doing?"

"Maybe they realized they were caught and wanted to get out while they could."

It was possible, but it didn't feel right.

It wasn't.

One second, the shitty sedan was gunning it to get ahead of us.

The next, it was driving straight for Aislynn. Metal groaned and tires squealed as the sedan T-boned her, shoving her over the sidewalk and into a telephone pole.

"Holy shit." Dominic yanked the wheel to the side as I screamed into the phone. "Ash's been hit!"

We'd barely stopped before I threw myself out of the SUV and ran straight for her, only pausing to make sure the other driver wasn't about to shoot me. Blood dripped down the side of his unconscious head, though he was still breathing for now. He'd likely hit his head on the window or something. Frankly, I didn't give a shit.

Motioning for Dominic to take care of him, I moved on. The slam of a body on the ground was music to my ears.

I stood parallel to Aislynn's door, waiting for Dominic to finish. Logically, I knew it wasn't a good idea to wait to check on her, but I didn't want someone using the moment my back was turned into an ambush. Besides, fear rode me hard. I didn't want to see Ash dead, and I was very, very worried that was the case.

Please let her be alive.

Finally, Dominic rushed over to me, gun in hand and warily eyeing the area. "I tied him up and put him in the trunk. How is she?"

"Keep an eye out while I check."

He twisted immediately and shielded my body with his. My hackles rose, but I held down the urge to tell him to move. It was his job to keep me safe, and like he'd told me about Rey, he considered it an honor. My own issues were exactly that—mine. I had to get over them. Still hated it, though.

Aislynn's driver's side door was destroyed from impact and unopenable, so I opted for the passenger side instead, and there she was. Slumped over in her seat with the airbag deployed and blood trickling down her face from a cut at her hairline, she looked dead. For a moment, I panicked, but the sight of her chest moving with easy breaths hit me like a sucker punch.

"She's alive." My voice cracked, but I didn't care. She was alive. That was all that mattered.

"Thank fuck," Dominic murmured, his fingers squeezing my hand once like he knew how scared I'd been. He probably did.

I pulled a knife from my pocket and deflated the airbag before I cut off the seat belt. I knew it wasn't smart, but I couldn't leave her here. We were sitting ducks in the middle of the street. Another damned if you do, damned if you don't scenario I didn't want to be in, but I figured Ash would prefer to be alive with any complications that might come from my involvement over being dead.

Before I could pull her all the way out, more footsteps arrived with the sound of colorful curses and snapping voices breaking through the strange silence that had somehow befallen the area. One voice echoed above the others.

"What the fuck happened to my wife?"

Again, all that rage, all that passion. I didn't blame him. My cousin's protective instincts were firing on all cylinders. He crept up behind me, and I didn't have to see his face to know he went nuclear the second he saw the blood.

Twisting, I grabbed his arm before he could kill Aislynn's attacker. "Help me."

"I'll be right back," he growled. He tried to shake me off, and I had to plant my feet against the doorframe to keep him there. The fury on my jovial cousin's face was so abnormal, it looked like a mask.

Speaking carefully, I tried to get through to him. "We need to get her out in case his car was rigged to blow. I can't do it alone, and I don't want to hurt her worse."

I could see the war welling up in him, the need for retribution. Regardless of feelings they might or might not have—and I had a feeling they'd left plenty unsaid—Ash was his, and Cameron always protected what was his.

Then that feral energy banked, giving way to a slow, begrudging acceptance.

"Later."

It wasn't a question; it was a demand. He was going to get his blood debt whether I allowed it or not. Considering I'd do worse if my men were hurt, I accepted it.

Forced to focus on helping rather than hurting, Cameron called over a few of his most trusted men and laid out the plan. Between all of us, we painstakingly pulled Aislynn from the wreckage, trying to jostle her as little as possible. The private ambulance pulled up right after with EMTs ready to take her to the Marcosa ward at Seattle General.

Seeing her alone and fragile in the back, I wanted to go with her. I had the handhold gripped, about to leverage myself in, when Cameron threw himself in at her side and snapped at the driver to go. He hadn't even seen me; he was just taking his place as her husband. It was how it should've been.

So why did it feel so shitty to step back?

"We'll follow you." My cousin barely acknowledged my words with a nod before the door slammed shut and the ambulance peeled off.

"You okay?" Dominic slid up beside me, hovering again.

The answer was no. No, I wasn't okay.

I wanted to be there holding my best friend's hand, but someone else had taken my place. Someone who deserved it more.

He was her husband, and I was just the woman who'd almost gotten her killed.

Chapter 14
Mari

When Greyson told me he'd bought a wing at the hospital, I thought he was kidding. For years, we hadn't gotten hurt enough to need more than an on-call doctor. It bothered me that we were giving the hospital enough activity to justify keeping it open.

"Oh great, my favorite patient," Dr. Grant snarked at me as she steered her way into Aislynn's room.

Dominic and I were crowded against the window, staying as far away from Ash and her gargoyle of a fiancé as we could. Cameron had taken one look at the nursing staff and lost his shit. Apparently, they were good enough to work on me, but they seemed incompetent when working on his future wife. It was almost laughable how quickly he had fallen into the protector role for Ash.

As expected, Dr. Grant refused to be steamrolled by my cousin's mood and poked and prodded Ash without giving him a glance. "Outside of the cut on your face and maybe some bruising from the

146

seat belt, you seem pretty good. Must not have been too bad of an accident."

"It could have been much worse," Aislynn said clearly, glaring between my cousin and me from her place on the bed. Apparently, she was sick of our hovering. "I'm assuming Cash saw me as an easy target or as a way to piss off my father enough to get him to defect. I'm not, and my father won't. He's nothing if not a decent business-man, and the second you signed the contract, he was your ally. I'm fine. End of story."

Cameron scoffed. "Maybe you're *fine* now, but you definitely won't be after I've taken a piece out of you for your stunt today."

"Oh, great. We're back to threats." Ash rolled her eyes and jabbed a finger at him. "Stop trying to control me, and I won't have to pull anything."

"I'm trying to keep you safe!"

"You're suffocating me."

"At least you're alive!" Cameron's breathing was heavy and the air thick with unspoken words and grief. I could practically taste it on my tongue, familiar and unwanted. Rey's ghost haunted us in different ways. Ash softened and reached out, brushing her fingers down his arm until he gripped her fingers. It was the touch of someone who understood. Someone who cared.

Whatever he said was too low for me to hear, and I intended to keep it that way. Dominic, in obvious agreement with me, cleared his throat to softly call the doc over to us. "Is there anything we need to know while she heals?"

Dr. Grant frowned but seemed to realize she was going to tell us or no one. My cousin and Ash were busy. "Only what I'm sure you already do. Keep the bandage dry, watch for signs of a concussion or infection."

Aislynn's voice trickled between us. "Does that mean I can go? I want out of this awful gown."

She'd refused to remove her other clothes until Cameron had

made it very clear that if she didn't change of her own volition, he would make sure she had no other choice. Every time she rubbed the fabric of the gown between her fingers, I could see her disgust growing. I made a mental note not to tell Greyson or he'd end up buying the most expensive hospital gowns he could manage for the ward, and that was the last thing we needed.

Dr. Grant smiled warmly at her. "You can, but I suggest bed rest for a day or so and no driving for a week."

"That won't be a problem," Cameron said with a dirty glare her way. "My wife is taking the week off."

"Like fuck I am."

"Here we go again," Dominic murmured.

"Aislynn," Cameron warned.

"I don't have time to take off! I have a whole wedding to plan."

"Delegate."

"I have! There are no more bodies to delegate to, and this has to be perfect. The family needs this, especially now." Ash turned to me, a little desperate and a lot fierce. "I want to throw it in Cash's face that he failed. He came after me, and I'm still alive. We can't stop now."

It didn't feel right disagreeing with her, considering that was the whole point of moving up the wedding, but I didn't want to put her in any more danger.

While my cousin and I had been pulling Ash from the wreckage, Dominic had checked over our newest friend and found a phone. None of the others had one. We hoped it was sloppy work, and it was. He'd used GPS to get to Aislynn's dress shop and followed us from there. There was no doubt Cash had come for her directly.

We finally had a starting point because none of the little birdies in the city had any clue where he was hiding, but at what cost? How much more would the war cost us? I was hesitant to find out.

"We won't," I said. "We've got an idea of where to go first, but you have to rest."

Tears shimmered in Aislynn's eyes, more frustration than sadness. "I can't take a full week off, even with the wedding planners. It won't work."

"Three days, then." I shot a look at Cameron, who looked ready to unleash hell on me, and he shut his trap. "*And* I'll hire an additional execution team for the wedding planners to make sure things get done. Will that help?"

The happy couple glared at each other for long enough that I thought they were trying to learn pyrokinesis. Finally, Ash nodded, and the beastly edge of my cousin's temper dulled. Until he leveled a finger her way. "As long as Ash is safe, I'm happy. But you leave the house without a guard again, and I'll spank your ass so hard you won't sit for a month."

Ash looked like she was ready to bite the appendage clean off. "When do I get to punish *you* for breaking the rules?"

"I'm already being punished," he muttered as Dr. Grant left my side to go back to theirs. After running through all the signs of a possible concussion with the pair, just in case, she dropped off a set of scrubs and shooed us out the door.

Cameron leaned against the wall, folding his arms defiantly. "Get dressed, princess."

In practiced moves, Dominic and I made for the door, trying to get out before the coming storm. Aislynn was generally even-keeled, but she was hurting, and Cameron was stomping over boundaries he didn't understand.

If I thought she'd looked mad before, she was about to go nuclear. When Ash spoke, it was with the cool, crisp edge of frosted glass. Cold enough to burn and sharp enough to kill. "I am entitled to my privacy, Cameron. *Get. Out.*"

With all the grace of a boar, Cameron dug his heels in, and his voice echoed through the doorway. "Like fuck am I leaving you—"

"If you don't get the fuck out, I'm going to burn all of your clothes in the middle of our living room. I'll take a bat to every car you own and shred everything else. I may be quiet, but I'm not passive or meek. Don't test me. Now, *out.*"

I looked back in time to see Ash point a single angry finger toward the hallway. Frustrated grumbling and pissed-off stomps came soon after.

The door was barely closed before my cousin turned to me, seething. "He's dead for this."

Of course he was. We all knew that, so I didn't even bother answering.

Dominic, of course, couldn't leave it at that. "Not that I disagree, but what part of this has you so worked up?"

With his heel kicked against the wall and his eyes sweeping my cousin's frame, Dominic poked the bear like a fucking idiot. Still, it was nice to see the antagonistic side of him back again. He'd been too morose.

Cameron turned blazing eyes on Dominic. "He attacked my wife, and an attack on her is an attack on the family. We can't let this stand." He turned to me, and his eyes were dark with vengeance. "I want the little shit who hit her."

Again, I knew this. "Of course. *Tomorrow.* Tonight, you have other duties."

"Like what?"

Christ, men were thick sometimes. "You said it yourself. Your wife got attacked. Despite how strong she is, she needs to know that she's safe and protected. That's your job."

"Why bother? She doesn't listen to me anyway." The sulky, grumbling man resembled nothing of my happy-go-lucky cousin, and I relished the realness. Maybe the marriage wouldn't be the worst thing I'd ever done.

Still, the image of Aislynn in the hospital bed burned too

brightly in my mind to forget. "Because you're trying to command her like she's a soldier," Dominic pointed out.

"She's your wife, man. You've got to learn to compromise."

Cameron crossed his arms over his chest, though he seemed less angry, more thoughtful. "Safety isn't something I'll compromise on."

Dominic shrugged. "Then find something you will. Relationships are about give-and-take."

I didn't know where he'd gotten the relationship advice, considering how badly we'd burned out, but I was grateful he was giving it anyway. My cousin and Ash needed to find some kind of peace, or their marriage was going to be nothing but fighting. I wanted more for them.

"I don't know what I'm doing with her. I can't seem to keep my temper." Cameron sagged a little, and even if I felt obsolete, it was eye-opening to watch their conversation.

"I've never seen you this uptight before, man. The old Cameron would've wooed her to his side by now with sweet words and thoughtful gifts. Instead of spanking her raw, why don't you try that?"

"Because she's my wife." Why did he say *wife* like it was the answer to the question?

"Exactly. Arranged or not, she's yours for life. Why not make the most of it?"

Cameron said nothing, so Dominic carried on. "Ash is fierce, but she's still a woman who wants to be needed and loved. It's plain to see, just like it's easy to see that you need that. Someone to love and protect. You two can be happy together if you put down the weapons and just *try*."

Dominic looked at me, eyes brimming with honesty and self-loathing, before jerking back to my cousin. "Don't push her away because you've got shit dragging you down, man. Pull yourself up so you're on her level, or you'll regret it every second for the rest of your life. You either try now, or prepare yourself for watching her find what she needs with someone else later."

I didn't know what to say, and thankfully, I didn't have to figure it out because an irritated Aislynn stomped out in scrubs that were three sizes too big and rolled up too many times just to get them to stay around her waist.

A smirk twitched on Cameron's face, but before he could tease her, she cut him off. "Don't. Start. I've had a bad night, and I am not in the mood."

"Okay, princess," he said, reeling her into his side and pressing a kiss against her temple. Ash looked frozen, stunned, as he dragged her down the hall to the elevator. "I'll save it for tomorrow."

"You're going to bodyguard me, aren't you?"

"Every step of the way," he agreed. She grumbled a little but melted into his embrace like she was meant to be there.

Dominic and I grinned at each other, and my heart clenched in my chest at how easy we were again. How well they fit together. I tasted a bitterness at the back of my tongue that said I wanted that too. Maybe I already had it; I just had to decide whether I could forgive the past and move on.

"What's the fallout from this car accident?" Ash asked when we were back in the SUV, batting Cameron's hands away from the seat belt he was trying to tug over her. "I can do it!"

With his arms up in surrender, he sat in his own seat, though I noticed he put Ash in the middle while he took the window. *The better to protect you with, my dear.*

"We are not going to allow you to get hurt," Cameron answered pleasantly once Dominic pulled out of the parking lot. We were boxed in like a convoy, with extra guards sticking close in their own vehicles. There wouldn't be a second accident with Aislynn. "Not only because it looks bad on us because you're family. That means you will take the guard with a smile on your face. No sneaking out without one again. No driving alone, and until Cash is dead, you're borrowing one of Mari's armored cars."

He looked at me in question, but I was already nodding. A car was the least I could do.

For once, Ash didn't complain. "What about the guy who attacked me? Do you know who he is?"

"Oh, we've got plans for him," my cousin said darkly.

For a moment, they watched each other. Finally, she sat back with an equally dark smile on her lips. "I accept your deal, *if* you let me watch."

"Watch what?" Cameron frowned.

"Watch you interrogate him."

Shocked, he looked over at her face, trying to find the deception, but there was none. Aislynn was an O'Bannon, a mafia queen in every way that mattered, including her own thirst for blood. If my cousin thought she was an innocent little flower, he was sorely mistaken. Only the strong survived in our world, and Ash was one of the strongest people I knew.

Apparently, her husband was about to figure that out.

"Do you really want to see that?"

"I asked, didn't I?"

"Fine," he said reluctantly. "You can watch, but you promise to leave if it's too much."

Ash laughed, patting his leg with a condescending slap. "Don't worry your pretty little head about me. I'll be just fine."

We shared a small grin that convinced me she was fine more than any test could have.

"Should I be worried here?" Cameron asked in the silence after.

"Yes," the rest of us answered with laughter that almost covered my cousin's whispered *fuck me*.

He had no idea what was coming.

Chapter 15
Dominic

I waited until we were home to corner Mari. "It wasn't your fault."

She didn't flinch, didn't move from her spot against the wall where she watched Cameron carry a sleeping Aislynn to their suite. There was no use asking how my girl was doing. Anyone could see the guilt weighing her down.

"Yeah, it was." Her voice was rough, ragged. Like she had razor blades carving up her insides. I knew firsthand it probably felt like it too. "Cash went after her because of me."

"That's on him, not you."

She scoffed, staring at the door even after Cameron closed it behind them. "I goaded him into it."

It killed me seeing her so devastated, and she was. She was heartbroken and angry at herself, doubting if she'd made the right choice. I could relate since that was how I felt every day now.

"From what I've seen, Cash Beckstrom is a grown-ass man with a fucked-up mind. He would've gone after Aislynn eventually because she's a weak spot for you, and that's how he plays. He doesn't hit you from the front like a man. He snipes at you from the back like a little bitch. That's not on you, Mari."

My girl had always been stubborn, so it was no shock that none of my words penetrated, but I couldn't let her hold on to this. It would eat her alive.

"I should've made her get in the car with us when I saw she was alone."

"Then we all would've gotten hit." Mari narrowed her eyes. "Aislynn knew what she was getting into, baby."

Irony stabbed my gut with every word. I was the least qualified person to have this conversation with her, considering she'd *just* had to spell it out to me, but Greyson and Nate were busy. I was all Mari had, and I was determined to rise to the challenge. To prove that I had the guts to support her when shit got bad. She needed me, and she'd have me, even if she didn't like it.

"No, she didn't," Mari argued. "*I* put her in danger when I should've gotten her out, and it nearly got her killed. *I* did that."

"No, you didn't. She chose to stay."

Mari laughed, loud and forced. "Because I asked her to."

The Mari in front of me was so like the girl she'd been before that it was painful to look at her. I'd meant it when I said that I was all in with her as she was. I didn't want the young Mari I'd had before; I wanted this one. Every strong, beautiful, infuriating inch of her.

The urge to keep fighting swelled in me, but I shut it down. Arguing wasn't getting through to Mari, so I had to change to a new tactic.

"That's very conceited of you." I leaned nearby, casual as could be. Pulling on the friendly asshole mask was easier this time since I was doing it for her. I had to rile her up, force her head back into reality instead of letting her get caught up in it. I needed to get her feet back under her before things went south.

If the queen got lost, we were all doomed.

Mari twisted, eyes fierce. "Excuse me?"

She looked like she wanted to hit me. *Good.*

"Oh, don't take offense. I just mean that you, of all people, should know better than to believe you were the be-all and end-all of Ash's decisions. She's a big girl who can make her own choices." I waved her off, negligent as ever.

It felt wrong to do it, but the poison she was shooting at me was exactly why she needed to find her balance again.

"I'm aware of that," she gritted.

"Are you? Aislynn was always going to be a target. You said it yourself—this was always going to be her life as a mafia daughter. She knew that, and she still chose to stay. Don't take that from her because you feel like shit that she got caught in the crossfire. Honor her choice, learn a lesson from this, and move on."

I picked at my fingernails, watching her tense out of the corner of my eye. Mari had never liked being ignored and she'd never liked games, but what else was I supposed to do? Reason wasn't working, so frustration was the next best thing.

"Who made you the fucking expert?" She planted her hands on her hips, and I tried not to grin. There was rage in her, sure, but fear had her mixed up inside. She needed an outlet for it before it poisoned her. I didn't mind being her punching bag until she got herself under control again. In other circumstances, I would've considered it foreplay.

Now there's an idea.

"You did." Her lips parted, and I had to force myself to look away. They'd been the star of many a fantasy since we split, and I was almost desperate to taste them again.

Christ, I was a grown man with a near hard-on for a fucking kiss.

I wasn't sure if it was pathetic or not, but since it was Mari, I didn't care.

"You walked away from me because I couldn't accept that this was always going to be your life," I reminded her. "I haven't been idle since then. I've been thinking. Learning. Growing as much as I can in such a short period. The truth is, you were right. I used my guilt to ignore the facts. You were always going to be in danger. You were also going to be in power. Nothing I did could've changed that. Aislynn is the same.

"She's the O'Bannon princess, baby. She was always going to be a tool. Even if you'd gotten her out, there was no guarantee that her father wouldn't have yanked her back in when he found her again. No guarantee that she'd be safe even if he didn't. Ash took the information she had and made the best decision for herself with it. Don't take that away from her."

For a moment, I thought I'd gone too far. Bringing our breakup into the conversation was a risk on a good day, and I didn't want to hurt her any more than she already was. When she deflated, relief and success washed over me like a tidal wave.

"You were listening," she whispered.

"I was, but it's always easier to see things when love isn't clouding the view. You love Aislynn like you love Shara. They're family to you. It's important for both of us to keep the people we love safe, but we have to remember that we can't smother them. They're free to make their own decisions. We've just got to love them through the rough patches."

"I feel so awful."

I crept closer, letting our shoulders brush. When she leaned into me, I threw an arm around her shoulder and pulled her in tight against my side. God, it felt good to hold her again, even if the circumstances were shitty. "Then listen to your friend. She told you to your face that she was fine. Trust that if she wasn't or if she wanted a way out, she'd ask."

She looked up at me with desperation so heavy in her eyes, it struck me like an arrow. "Will the guilt ever go away?"

The ache of it in my chest said no, but I couldn't tell her that. I'd do anything to take it from her, but I wouldn't lie. Not any more than I had to. "I'll let you know when I find out."

The house was silent around us, but I was content to stand in it with Mari. Finally, she yawned, her body listing into mine just a little, and I knew it was time for the night to end. "Come on. I'll walk you to bed."

Immediately, she jerked away, hands up like she was warding me off. "I can't."

"You need sleep."

"I know. I just...can't. Not yet." She shook her head, and I didn't like how wild her eyes got.

Looking at her harder, I realized it wasn't just guilt making her struggle. It was adrenaline. Her body shook because she was exhausted, but she was also too wired to sleep and too stressed for her brain to shut down. She was one more bit of bad news away from a mental breakdown that none of us could afford.

As much as I wanted to, I didn't think I could fix it. Not alone. "Come with me."

She stared at my outstretched hand like it was a cobra ready to bite. I didn't take it personally, though I wanted to. "Dominic—"

"I'll take you to get Nate or Grey, and they can help with the crash." I wanted to be the one to do it, but I wasn't pushing her for the world. We needed time to rebuild the trust I'd broken, and sex was a bandage, not a cure.

Mari shook her head. "They're busy."

"They'll make time." There was no doubt in my mind. We'd all make time for whatever she needed. Mari came first.

"No. I need them focused." Her hands shook, and she tucked them into her pockets when she saw.

"You *need* help, Mari."

She lifted her chin, haughty and proud. Every bit the queen she was. "So do it."

I froze. "What?"

"Help me with the crash. I assume you have something in mind, or you wouldn't have mentioned it."

I did, but... "It's not a good idea."

"Why?"

"Because my idea involves so many orgasms you can't think anymore. It would be best if one of your boyfriends did it."

Her lips parted again, and I had the desperate urge to run my tongue across them. Just a lick, a little taste of the forbidden fruit. Fuck, the mere thought made me hard. She had no idea how difficult it was to say no.

"So do it."

Just kidding, *that* made me hard.

I wanted her so badly I could taste her on my tongue, but it didn't feel right to say yes yet. I needed to know she wasn't having reservations. "Are you sure about this?"

"No, but you're right. I need it."

The hesitation was enough for me, sinking deeper than any of my former guilt could. I'd done that. I'd made her unsure of me, and it sucked. "I'll get one of the others."

"I just said I needed you, and you're walking away? Is that your MO now?"

She was snarking at me because she felt rejected. I knew that. But it was too much. Frustration and the ache of not having her pushed me forward until she was caged between my arms, back flat against the wall.

"I'm not a second choice, Mari. If you want me, *really* want me, I'll make you come until you cry, but I won't touch you if there's a sliver of doubt in your mind. That's not fair to either of us."

"You'll give me to one of the others, even though it's obvious that you want me?" She pressed her hips forward, rubbing herself against my cock. I barely held back my groan. "Why? Why walk away when I'm right here for the taking?"

"First, I can't *give* you to anyone. You aren't a toy, a prize, or my property. Second, I already fucked this up, and I don't want to do more damage that can't be undone. I want to keep you more than I want to fuck you," I admitted, stroking her hair.

Believe me.

For a long, heavy moment, she just stared at me. I wondered what she saw. Was it the boy who took her firsts or the man who'd broken her heart? Could she see the future that I could, or was she still too blinded by everything I'd done wrong?

Could she see the one thing I was still trying to hide?

Finally, she melted, her hands at my hips pulling me as close as I could get. Having her against me felt like a heaven I never wanted to leave. "I want you, Dominic. I'm just not ready for more."

She was scared to trust me with her heart, but the way she clung to me told me she was being sincere. She wanted me, and tonight, it would be enough.

"I know, baby." I gripped her under the thighs and hauled her into my arms. She gasped, nails digging into my shoulders as I started up the stairs at a jog.

"What the fuck are you doing? My men—"

"Are occupied." I'd sent most of them out of the house myself before we got back from the hospital. "It's just us here."

Greyson and Nate were probably watching us on the cameras, but it didn't bother me. I'd been known to put on a show before.

The idea of having her in front of them, making her mewl and cry while they watched but couldn't touch, pushed me to move faster. It was a dream more than a hope, but I wanted it.

I wanted to share Mari with them. I wanted a place in her bed and her heart. I wanted to make up for all the things I'd done wrong.

When I did, I'd have everything I ever wanted. Mari and the family she was building. I could see the bones starting to form, stronger than anything else. That was something I could be patient for.

A quick readjustment got us into my room. Mari didn't even have time to breathe before I tossed her on the bed. Hearing Mari's laugh echoing off my walls made everything better.

Reaching for my shirt, I stripped it off, loving the way Mari's eyes snapped to me the second I showed skin. Her gaze roved over all the newly exposed ink, and her tongue peeked out to wet her lip. "Stop looking at me like that, or I'm going to eat you, baby."

A smirk tipped those dangerous lips. "Is that supposed to be a threat?"

Smirking back, I didn't answer. I knelt on the bed and hauled her underneath me with a hand around her ankle. She fit perfectly. "Here's how tonight's going to go. I'm going to get you out of your head, wear you down enough so that you can sleep. That means as many orgasms as you can handle and maybe one or two more. No strings, no stress. That work for you?"

"Please." Even as she gnawed on her lip, I saw the relief in Mari's eyes. The hope that I could fix her problems, even just for a night. The need to not be anything but a woman who wanted to feel.

I couldn't do a lot for her, but I could do this.

I wanted to touch her, but I needed both of us fully coherent for a bit longer. Still, I slipped my hand under her shirt until I could feel the warmth of her skin against my palm. It was steadying to have her close again. "Pick a safe word, Mari."

"Blade." She arched into my touch with a breathy little sigh, like even that small bit of contact made everything better. If that was true, she had no idea what was coming.

"I'll be checking in a lot, but if you ever need me to stop immediately—no matter what we're doing—you say 'blade.' Got it?"

"Yes."

"Good girl." I wanted to kiss her, but I was too terrified she'd turn away. I could handle a lot, but that would be too much.

Instead, I skimmed her shirt up until I could see the edge of her bra. The urge to kiss along the band, nipping and sucking here and there, won out, and I ran a trail of kisses across her ribs. I shouldn't have, we had things to discuss, but I couldn't force myself to stop when she tasted so sweet. "What are your hard limits, baby?"

Mari's breaths were coming quicker, and she moved easier under me, like she'd given herself the okay to enjoy this. To enjoy me. I wasn't going to let her regret it. "Basics only, no breath or waterplay. I don't like restraints, but I like being held down. Hair-pulling is fine. Biting to bruise, not bleed, though I'd prefer those be in easily covered areas. No bodily fluids other than come, no spitting, light impact play on the ass and thighs only, toys are okay, but no tools. I prefer pleasure as a punishment."

Which meant orgasm denial and forced orgasms were okay. Since that was my plan, I was relieved. Spanking was out since she was still healing. I'd take her to the brink of pain, but I wouldn't do more than she could handle. The image of Mari writhing on the sheets, overstimulated and desperate for a break, was one I planned to keep with me until I died. With any luck, I'd get to see it in action someday.

Needing a moment to gather my thoughts, I pulled back and stripped her out of her pants, and *fuck me.* She had on the tiniest lace panties I'd ever seen, and I wanted them on my floor immediately. Dipping my thumbs under the band, I smoothed my fingers over her skin. A little calming, a lot teasing. A prequel of a touch that made her squirm even more. The unsatisfied grunt she gave when I left the panties on made me laugh. "Penetration?"

A pause and I wondered if she'd say no. I wouldn't mind, but fuck, her clit was going to hurt tomorrow if not. "Vaginal and oral, only. I don't care if you're rough with either, though we need condoms."

I was clean, hadn't touched anyone else since I'd come home, but that didn't matter when our trust was cracked nearly beyond repair. Doubt seeped in, and I wondered if it was really a good idea to do this. We needed more time. Then I looked into her eyes, and I couldn't say no. "What's your goal for the night, baby?"

"I just want a minute to breathe."

For the woman who carried the weight of the world on her shoulders, I imagined those were hard to find.

"Everything I have is already yours. You just have to trust me to give you what you want *and* what you need."

Brushing her hair back, I pulled her a little lower, so her hips were tight against me. When I rocked against her, careful to press hard enough for her to feel me through the panties, she groaned, and I knew I was never going to forget this moment. "Can you do that?"

She squirmed, desperate for more pressure. "Dominic, please. I need you."

Fuck, that was a trip. Marianna Marcosa, the woman who didn't need anyone, needed me. Grey and Nate could've helped, but we both knew I was the one who would push her as far as she needed to go tonight. It was a heady feeling to hold that kind of power in my hands. "Can you do what I asked? Can you trust me, baby?"

"I trust you with my body." I hated that she had to clarify, and even though I tried not to, it got to me. Mari's trust was fractured. She wasn't sure that I was in it for real, that I'd stay. I knew better. We were forever. I just had to earn back what I'd lost first, one day at a time, until she was back in my arms where she belonged.

Still, it was at that moment that I realized I couldn't do it. I couldn't fuck her. Not until she was ready to trust me all the way. Which meant I had to think of a new plan for the night.

I'd give her anything she wanted *except* my cock.

Chapter 16
Dominic

I had seconds to rethink my plan, and when I did, I liked it almost better than the original. "Do you want to know what I'm going to do to you?"

"Yes," Mari breathed, arching desperately for more contact, more touch. More, more, more.

I ran my hand along her thigh, teasing while I could. "I'm going to slip my fingers into that sweet cunt until you're dripping, then I'm going to lick you clean. You're going to come so much, you'll be too tired to hold yourself up."

She bit her lip. "Keep going."

"When I'm through with you, you'll be too blissed out to care that you're covered in come." Carefully stripping off her shirt, I groaned at the matching bra that was all straps and lace. I couldn't stop myself from giving one nipple a long lick, and Mari shuddered at the contact. She muttered under her breath, and I had to lean close to hear.

Please, please, please.

Mari needed release more than she needed to play, so teasing was out. Slipping my hand between her thighs, I palmed her pussy, grinding the heel of it against her clit. Her cry was fucking perfection. "First, you're going to come on my hand like this."

Her body jerked as I worked her over. My hand covered her whole pussy while I rested my fingers at her slick entrance as a reminder for us both. Mari was mine. Now and always.

"You're so wet already," I whispered into her shoulder, crazed at the taste of her skin on my lips. My hips rolled against hers each time my palm rubbed her clit.

It was a tease, a taunt, a mimicry of what fucking her would be like, but I was desperate to come already. To paint her with my come and claim her as mine. It wouldn't take much, a shift here, a condom there, and I could come inside the woman I loved. It wasn't just the urge to fuck her, but the need for connection that had me panting against her. I wanted it so bad my bones hurt.

Keep it together, asshole. This isn't about you.

Pulling back, I adjusted so I could finally slide my fingers inside her. Perfect pink lips dropped open on a sigh, and I bit back a curse. She was so wet, so warm. I couldn't look away from the sight of my hand between her slick thighs, her body twisting and rolling to meet me as I fucked her with thick fingers. Her throaty cries as she flushed so perfectly under my touch. It was almost too much.

Focus. I watched the light sheen of sweat appear on her skin, dipping to lick it off. I kept her bra on, working her nipples through the lace with a warm tongue and cool breaths. When I nipped the points, rolling my tongue across them while I kept a firm grip with my teeth, she jolted so hard she shoved my hand deeper, and we both swore.

All I could see, smell, hear, taste was Mari, and I never wanted it to end.

Her every move told me she was wound too tight, and the way she clenched around my fingers said she was close. Another bite across her breast and a long suck of her nipple, and she was gone.

"God, *yes*." Mari gripped my wrist, holding on for dear life as she rode out the pleasure. Only when she was pliant and panting below me did I lift myself away. I was hard enough for a light breeze to hurt, and it was a Herculean feat to leave my cock in my pants when all I wanted was to slide home inside her. After a painful adjustment of my dick, I shifted her farther up the bed so I could lie down.

With a palm on either thigh, I spread her out and groaned at the sight of her pussy. Wet and sweet and ripe enough to eat, and I was starving. "Look at you, spread out and dripping on my sheets. You're aching for it, aren't you, my sweet little *mariposa?*"

"Don't call me that," she snapped. One wrong word and all the looseness from her first orgasm was gone.

Arching an eyebrow, I massaged my fingers into her suddenly tense thighs. "Why not?"

"I'm not soft and sweet anymore, Dominic."

"Not always," I agreed. "That doesn't mean it's the wrong name."

"What does that mean?"

How could I explain this to her? How could I put into words what I'd only just realized?

Needing to be closer, I lay down between her legs and rested my head against her thigh, close enough to let my words drift over her pussy without actually touching it. Just the smell of her was enough to make me high, and just like I thought, the barest hint of *something* was enough to start her writhing again.

"Butterflies are beautiful and noble. They make the world

brighter with their presence. Butterfly knives are sharp and deadly. It takes practice to wield them correctly without hurting yourself. You're all of those things. Cunning to your enemies and sweet to the people you love. It's an apt description."

"That's not why you gave me the nickname, and you know it."

I shrugged, dragging my tongue through the heat of her when the urge to have her got to be too much. Mari's taste exploded on my tongue, and I groaned against her clit, making her moan. "God, you taste good."

When I'd lived in Chicago, I'd dreamed of Mari every night. At first, they were memories, reminders of who I'd left behind. As the years passed, it was living out my fantasies like she was with me. Sex on the balcony of my penthouse, sneaking off at parties, fucking her in a room full of strangers. No matter who I went to bed with, Mari was always there when I closed my eyes, but in all those years, I never once remembered how she tasted. It was as if the memory was snatched from my brain the second I walked away.

Now I knew I'd been missing out.

Mari tasted like sin and sweetness. Promise and poison. She tasted like home and heaven and a death I'd welcome with a smile. Reacclimating myself to every curve of her pussy, every single centimeter, was a wish I'd never thought would come true. She tasted like my future, and I wanted to drink her down until I was too full to move and she was too sated to remember why we weren't together.

"Reasons change, *mariposa*. Just like people do."

"Do you expect me to believe that you've changed?" she panted, fingers clawing at the sheets. She was trying so hard not to show I affected her, and I relished the struggle. We both knew she wanted this, wanted me.

"Not yet, but I'll prove it. Now, hush. I'm hungry."

I ate her out with all the grace of a man on death row, desperate for one last taste of life. True to form, Mari wasn't a passive partner. She rode my face, shoved her hands in my hair, and directed me exactly where to go, praising and cursing me with every lick, suck, and gentle nibble I gave.

And every time she came, it was with my name on her lips.

By the time she'd had two more orgasms, my jaw ached, and I could feel the wet spot my precome made on my boxers. Mari had tangled waves, glassy eyes, and lips that she'd chewed almost to bleeding. Not to mention that she was covered in sweat and panting like she'd just run a marathon. She looked wrecked, but there was still something unsettled about her.

"Almost done," I promised, smoothing my hands over her hips and gently sliding them up her sides. Reminding her I was there and she was safe.

"Are you going to fuck me?" She gripped my cock, squeezing tight enough that I jerked against her. I was too close, too sensitive for more. If she stroked me even for a second, I was going to come.

"Do you want me to?" I gritted.

"Please." Gently extricating myself from her grip, I pressed a kiss to her palm and climbed off the bed. Mari's confusion was palpable, but I didn't stop and explain, dipping into the closet to find what I was looking for.

I'd intended to wear the strap-on for some one-man DP action, but it would work fine as a substitute for now.

I made a show of opening the brand-new box and cleaning the dildo. Mari needed to know that it was unused and intended for her only. She watched warily as I slid into the harness, groaning under my breath as I adjusted it over my rock-hard cock.

Only after I stroked the soft texture of the toy with a lubed hand did she ask, "What the fuck is that?"

"A strap-on." I crawled over her, running the tip of the toy through her swollen lips and bumping her overstimulated clit as I went.

She exhaled, trying to hold herself still. "What are you doing with it?"

"Fucking you."

"Why?" The confusion on her face was cute, especially when she scrunched up her nose like that.

I leaned down, ghosting my lips over hers so she could taste my words on her tongue. "I already told you I wasn't fucking you until I've earned you. That's doubly true now. I'll make you come, but I won't get to feel that pussy around my cock until you've forgiven me."

I never stopped rubbing the toy against her, and she panted every time I got close enough to shove inside her but didn't. "What if it never happens?"

The thought kept me up at night, but I couldn't tell her that. "Then it doesn't, but I'm not going to fuck up my chances to have you the way I want. We're not friends with benefits, baby. We're forever."

"Dominic—"

She was overthinking it again, and I was so close to getting her down from the edge. "Do you want to stop?"

While she considered, I stilled, stroking her thighs. After an unholy amount of time, she answered. "No."

I kissed her cheek. "My perfect, beautiful girl. You're going to look so good on my cock." Before she could say anything else, I flipped her onto her belly. A hand between her and the mattress leveraged her up long enough to squeeze a pillow under her hips. By the time she settled, I had her thighs tight between mine and her pussy on full display.

"God*damn*, you're beautiful."

Unable to help myself, I ran my tongue through her soaked lips again, catching her clit with the tip of my tongue. She jolted, groaning under me. Leaning back, I ran the tip of the toy through her wetness to tease her once more before I sank into her. It was a slow, steady thrust, and Mari cursed, her head falling to the bed even as her hips jumped to meet mine, burying me to the hilt.

Seeing her stretched out by my cock, real or not, was a sight I'd never get over.

"This one's going to be hard and fast, baby." She was almost where I wanted her. So fucking close. She just needed to be fucked within an inch of her life first.

Mari mumbled into the sheets again, and I gripped her hair, yanking her head back so I could hear. "Yes, yes, yes."

Well, okay then. Dropping her head back down, I planted one foot on the bed, and I pulled out, just to slam back into her. Her breathy sighs turned to loud moans as I did it again and again and again. Her cries echoed off the walls, and I had no doubt the others could hear.

Good.

"I made this cock for you, baby," I panted, going as deep and as hard as I could. "Wanted to fill you up with my cock in every hole, so I had them replicate me."

She froze, and even exhausted, I heard the anger, the jealousy. "You let another woman touch you for that?"

I laughed under my breath. My possessive little queen. "I did it myself just for you, baby."

She settled, and I took the relief to heart. She still wanted me. I still had a chance. "What do you think, *mariposa?* You want me to stuff you full of cock one day?"

Her body answered for her. The orgasms before had been tough on her, but not like this. Her fingers clawed the sheets, and I could see her pussy drawing the toy in, clenching around it. My pants were getting soaked by her come, and I didn't care.

Let it seep into my skin so I can smell like her forever.

I didn't let up. "You're taking it so good, baby."

She tried her best to meet me with each thrust, but my grip on her shoulder yanked her hips to mine without any help. Even as her legs twitched with aftershocks, her muscles pulsing with the force of it, she begged for more and I gave it. Each thrust rubbed the base of the toy against my cock and it was painful torture forcing myself not to come, but I didn't slow down. I'd go however long she needed.

Her next orgasm came fast, taking us both by surprise, and by the time it was over, she was practically wheezing.

Almost there.

"Last one, *mariposa*. One more and you're done."

"I can't," she sobbed. When she turned her head, tears wet her cheeks, but I saw no pain or sadness in her face. Just relief. Pure, utter relief.

"You can," I soothed, rubbing her hips and peppering her back with kisses as I slowed my thrusts again. "Just one more."

Honestly, she barely had enough for one more, but I knew if I didn't wear her out to the point of exhaustion, she'd never rest.

"Can you come for me again?"

"Yes."

"Good girl." I adjusted my position so every thrust hit her G-spot just right.

We were going with more than a bang. I wanted a splash.

Wedging my hand under her, I strummed her clit as she wiggled and whined under me. It was too much stimulation, but I could feel the little bead pulsing under my fingertips, desperate for a break, desperate to come.

So close.

"Almost there, baby." Her cries got sharper, louder, and I knew I'd done it. "Come for me, *mariposa*. Soak my fucking sheets."

As expected, she came with a gush that drenched us both. I played with her fast and hard, keeping my hips moving and forcing the orgasm to continue until her whole body twitched with aftershocks. Only when she pushed my hand off did I lean back so I could look at my handiwork, still giving her slow comedown strokes with my cock.

Just like I'd promised, she was covered in sweat and dripping in come. It was just her own. Little spots dotted her body where my fingers had left bruises, but I wished I'd marked her more. Still, Mari completely undone under me, both of us sticky and messy and thoroughly fucked, was enough to make me come too.

"Fuck, Mari." I leaned over her, moaning with my teeth in her shoulder as I rode out my orgasm. Mari's breath caught, and she moved in shaky thrusts to rub me against the toy. It was the best orgasm I'd had in ages, and I didn't even care that I'd come in my pants.

I ran my hands lightly over her body, helping her come back to the real world a little more with each touch and kiss and soft murmur against her skin. After she drank some water, her eyes cleared of the glassiness that came from too many endorphins.

"What do you need?" I asked.

"Clean, please." Christ, that sex-rough voice hit me straight in the dick.

We both groaned when I finally pulled the toy from her. For me, it was the sight of her pussy clinging to it that had me biting my lip. "God, you're so pretty."

"Fuck off," she slurred. That was it, no other comeback. She was too exhausted.

Laughing to myself, I ran to the en suite for a warm washcloth, stripping while I had a chance. The toy and strap went into the sink to clean later, and my clothes were swapped for clean sweats. I'd shower once she was asleep and work out the ache in my balls that a single orgasm hadn't cured.

Washcloth in hand, I found Mari unmoved. A shower would've been better, but she didn't have the energy to stand long enough, and I didn't want to force her into a second wind. She needed rest. I washed her carefully, making sure to get every drop of come off her as gently as I could. When she was clean, I put her in one of my shirts, loving the way it dwarfed her frame.

She yawned, her jaw cracking and her eyes drifting shut. Pride surged through me. I did that. I took her stress away. "You ready for bed, baby?"

A soft nod was my only answer. Careful not to fully wake her, I pulled Mari into my arms, kissing her temple as I walked her across the hall to her room.

"Thank you, Dominic," she said as we stopped so I could open her door.

"Anytime, baby."

Using my hip to open the door, I let us in, unsurprised to find Greyson reading in their bed. He looked up with a raised eyebrow. "She okay?"

"Just needed a break." I laid her down gently, tucking her into the sheets and brushing hair off her face. "Hopefully she'll sleep through the night."

"Your lips to God's ears."

I snorted, pressing one last kiss to her forehead. "Goodnight, *mariposa*. I love you."

She said nothing back, of course, too far into sleep to do more than sigh at my touch, but I kept the sound close as I stood. Maybe one day she'd actually say it back. For now, it was time for me to go.

Before I could even climb off the bed, a hand clamped down on my wrist, and Mari's sleep-drenched voice uttered a single word. "Stay."

I wanted to more than anything, but she was tired and worn out. I didn't want her to wake up and regret asking. "I don't—"

"You heard her," Greyson said. "Climb in."

It was obviously a command, but as much as I tried, I couldn't get upset about it when this was where I wanted to be. Still, I worried that staying would do more damage than good.

"Are you sure about this?"

"She is. That's what matters."

Fair enough. Careful not to jostle her too much, I climbed in next to Mari, boxing her between our bodies. I expected her to go to Greyson, but she wrapped herself around me with a contented sigh that relaxed every muscle in her body. Her cheek pressed to my bare chest, and her fingers dug into my hip like she belonged there. Because she did.

She was in my arms again. My *mariposa. Finally.*

I wrapped an arm behind her back and pulled her flush against me, dropping kisses anywhere I could reach.

Grey watched her settle, his eyes coasting over Mari with the barest hint of a smile on his lips. "You worked her over well."

"She needed it."

"She needs you."

I didn't miss the word choice. The idea that Grey was rooting for me, for Mari and me together, made it seem possible again. But whatever the future held was up to her. I'd made my peace with that, even as I hated the possibility of losing her for good. "Thanks, man."

"Don't thank me yet. Fuck her over again, and it'll be the last time."

"I won't." I'd walk away before willingly hurting her again. A tiny kernel of guilt dug at me, but I buried it. We weren't in the place to share secrets yet, but one day, we would, and Mari would know everything. Then we could really begin.

"Get some sleep," Grey finally said, clicking off the bedside lamp and settling at Mari's back with a hand on her hip. We lay in comfortable silence while he fell asleep.

I never did.

Hours passed, and my eyes refused to close, worried that the next time they opened, I'd realize this was all a dream. I didn't want this moment of peace to end, so I memorized the weight of Mari against me, the seconds between those deep, sleepy breaths that skittered across my chest. The softness of her skin. The feel of her heartbeat matching mine.

I memorized it all. If she woke up and put me at a distance again, I'd always have this night to look back on.

If this was all I ever got, it would be enough.

Chapter 17
Mari

L ike Gilded, the Marcosa mansion had a basement suite packed with everything we could ever want for an interrogation. We even had a deprivation chamber in the back of the house specifically for the people who were tough to break.

So far, it looked like that wouldn't be needed. The man who hit Ash was strapped to a chair, arms and legs immobile and mouth gagged shut. Cameron paced like a feral lion next to him, eyes blazing with rage.

He wanted blood. He demanded penance, but he had to wait, and it clawed at his skin.

Just a little longer.

Nate was at my back, and Dominic took up a position in a nearby corner. Tennessee and Greyson were busy, but Moore was close too, though he kept his eye on Nate. He'd done well defending himself, but that was different from outright torture. We were all wondering how he'd do or if he could handle being in this world.

If not, I'd let him go, but I was honest enough to admit I didn't want to. Nate had snuck under my defenses the first day we met, and I didn't want to pull him out. Not when it felt like he'd been made to stand at my side.

So far, all he'd done was study the driver with a healthy dose of concern and skepticism, and I found myself watching him more and more, waiting for his reaction.

Moore cleared his throat, and I looked away, ignoring his teasing grin. After our talk, he looked lighter. Not perfect by any means, but he seemed to be healing or making progress to. I understood, though. Nothing would ever cure the loss of Rey or my brother before, but if the only thing we could do was heal, I'd be glad for that too.

Aislynn sat at my side, poised and regal as ever, despite wearing the comfiest pair of clothes I'd ever seen her in. No doubt the hoodie and sweats were courtesy of Cameron, considering I was certain they were his. The glare on Ash's face when he'd helped her sit had me keeping that thought to myself, though. On her other side, Shara munched on a bag of popcorn like we were readying to watch a heavyweight title match.

Is that sanitary?

She threw another handful into her mouth and grinned at me when I frowned. "What? I used to love when Antoni had interrogations. It's like watching a movie in real life."

It was a reminder that as kind and cute as she was, there was a reason Shara had almost been queen. She was just as ruthless and bloodthirsty as the rest of us, and she had no qualms about either.

Ash straightened in her chair, Cameron's head whipping around when she adjusted slightly, like he was prepared to rescue her from any hint of discomfort.

Of course, she glared at him.

"Things seem to be going well with the two of you," I drawled. Nate and Moore snickered.

"Oh, shut it," she snapped, then winced when Cameron shook his head slightly. "Sorry, forgot where I was."

Thankfully, the only people in the room were men I mostly trusted, so I didn't have to correct her. I wasn't sure my cousin would've handled that well so soon after her accident.

Aislynn slouched until she leaned a lot of her weight on me, but I didn't mind. Especially when she let out the most contented sigh I'd ever heard. "We've been home for less than twelve hours, and he has been a mother hen the whole time. If I thought I was losing my shit before, I'm definitely losing it now."

Shara smothered her laughter with another mouthful of popcorn. "At least you know he'll never let things slide. I mean, look at him. This is not a man who is ambivalent toward his wife."

"Future wife," Ash corrected absently. "And this isn't about me. I may be his wife, but it's the *his* part that he is focused on."

That was partially true, but the dismay she was trying to hide urged me to clarify. "It's not a property thing. It's more of a protective instinct. I'm not sure if he was like this before Rey died, but my cousin just can't handle someone hurting his people."

"I know. I know, and I'm grateful. The last thing I want to do is be left to fend for myself, but it's still a lot. Especially when he goes overboard for a paper cut."

"What, not a fan of getting your boo-boos kissed?" Shara teased.

"No one's ever done it for me before," Aislynn said quietly.

The reminder that Ash's life as an O'Bannon was borderline negligent unless she was needed as an asset or tool for the empire hit hard. The Marcosas weren't perfect, but we were a family that went to bat for the people we loved. Every. Damn. Time. Ash needed to know that someone out there would kill and die for her. It was the least she deserved.

Cameron stalked over, agitation bleeding into every step. "How much longer?"

"We're just waiting on Greyson."

As if we conjured him, Grey strolled in. I tried not to ogle him, but he looked so damn good. As usual, we matched—this time, his shirt was coordinated with mine—and I realized he probably did it on purpose.

Little freak.

With everything going on, we hadn't been able to connect as much, and I missed him. I was also grateful that he was around, helping out wherever he could so I didn't have to be involved in the everyday parts of the business. He slid into the seat next to me, pressing a kiss to my temple before nodding at my cousin.

"Is it done?" I asked.

"We have twenty-four-hour surveillance on the starting location from the GPS. No one in or out without our knowledge."

Aislynn let out a happy, satisfied sound, and that eased some of my worry that the crash would have long-term effects on her mental health.

"Can I start?" My sigh was enough to make Cameron grin as he walked back to his victim.

"What about Jacob?" The dockmaster's man had been on my mind since I'd woken up. Not a shock since he was the next resident of the room, but he just wasn't a priority. Money was important, but not more important than my people's lives. So, he got to live a little longer.

Pity.

"Still comfortably waiting for you." Greyson laughed under his breath as my cousin got close to the driver, whispering something that had the man paling. "He looks like he's losing it, though, so I'd suggest we get to him sooner rather than later."

I didn't really have the time to be interrogating someone else, but if Grey suggested it, it meant poor Jacob was much worse than I expected. *Maybe Dominic would do it for me.* That would go a long way to show me he'd changed.

The first punch rang out with the reward of a pained gasp right after. Shara laughed, and I peeked at Aislynn to find her face flushed. Shara and I glanced at each other and leaned closer.

"Those are some rosy cheeks." I tried to keep it casual, but Shara didn't get the memo.

"Are you telling me that the Irish princess gets hot watching her fiancé beat someone up? Because I can respect that."

Ash was less than impressed. "It's not the fact that he's beating someone up—it's the fact that he's doing it for me. I've never had anybody defend me like that before. To be honest, I could get used to it."

Dominic's version of therapy helped a lot, but hearing Ash happy at the turn of events was exactly what I needed. Though, the reminder of his body on mine sent a rush of heat through me, and I had to consciously remind myself not to fidget in my seat. Not that it mattered when Grey's low chuckle hit my ear.

Fuck. He totally knew I was turned on.

"Shut it," I whispered.

"I didn't say a thing. Though I am curious what about this turns you on."

"Nothing, I was thinking about Dominic."

The man in question looked over at me, and I hated the greedy smirk that crossed his face, so I flipped him off. His laugh was so light, cutting through the sounds of Cameron's interrogation with ease. "I'm glad he helped." With a brief squeeze of my thigh, Greyson leaned back and watched my cousin work.

The questions he asked were simple and easy, things that anyone in Cash's organization should've been able to answer.

Where is he hiding? What does he want? What are his goals? Why did he go after Ash? Who else is a target?

I could barely hear the words over the grating sound of a small drill. It wasn't smart to use your fists for too long, especially early in an interrogation. The last thing you wanted to do was cut it short because you'd hurt yourself.

Intentionally, yes. Accidentally, no.

I couldn't see what my cousin was using the drill on, but I wasn't sure I wanted to anyway. Cameron was creative on a good day, but Ash's accident had brought something out of him that I wasn't sure we'd ever be able to put back on a leash.

"Fuck, man. I already said I don't know anything. She was a job. That was it."

"A job." Cameron was obviously unconvinced.

"Yeah, a job. They gave me a cell, told me where to go and what to do, and I got paid."

"How much?"

"Twenty grand."

Aislynn scoffed next to me. "I'm worth at least fifty."

"Amen," Shara agreed.

"No job is worth attacking a Marcosa, especially when that Marcosa is also an O'Bannon. Not for ten thousand, not for a hundred thousand, because everyone knows crossing the Marcosas is a death sentence. According to your ID, you've lived in Seattle your whole life. You grew up knowing this. So, why do it?"

"I needed the money."

"Not that badly, Paul. No one needs money that badly."

Yet the look on Paul's face said he did.

"Come on, man. I don't want to kill you. I just want to know how to protect my girl. You can understand that, right?" Cameron's good-ol'-boy voice worked, and Paul nodded solemnly. It made me wonder who he'd thought the money would protect. "Help me out here. What is Cash's end goal?"

"I'm a glorified paper boy," Paul said woodenly. "They don't give the peons anything more than breadcrumbs. Even if I wanted to tell you, I can't, man. I really can't."

Watching him, I tried to figure out how a man like Cash, who had such little care for his people, inspired such fierce loyalty. Only to realize it wasn't loyalty.

"He's terrified of Cash," I said more to myself than anyone else.

Grey hummed. "I think that will be the problem with all of them."

"But how? He uses them as cannon fodder, and they thank him. How does he do it? Do you think he's blackmailing the army?"

"It would be stupid of him if he did," Dominic said, coming to stand beside Nate. It felt good having all three of my men so close. "Who's to say they don't all rise up against him?"

"They won't rise up against him if he's got decent enough leverage," Nate pointed out.

Dominic snorted. "Nobody cares about somebody's coke problem in the grand scheme of things."

"Maybe not, but they would care if he was threatening their families, their friends, the people that they love. They may not be good guys, but they still have people they care about, too." Merc or not, Nate had been eyeing the man in the chair warily the whole time, and I could practically feel his discomfort under my skin. I patted his hand where it hung near my shoulders. "You don't need to be here."

He twisted his grip so he could hold my hand where no one else would see. "I do and I am."

His tone made it clear: end of discussion.

Over and over, Cameron asked the questions, changing the wording and the torture he inflicted beforehand. He threatened fingers and toes and teeth. There was burning, cutting, even waterboarding.

Every time, Paul gave the same answer, *I don't know.*

How do you contact Cash? *I don't know.*

How do you get paid? *I don't know.*

Where is he? *I don't know.*

The situation felt similar to someone pleading the Fifth, and I didn't understand. Why wouldn't he give us what he knew? He'd already clarified that he wasn't a higher-up, so why not toss some fire at his former employer while he had the chance?

The longer it went on, the more I began to think that Nate might be right. Maybe it wasn't about the blackmail itself, but the threat of what would happen if they crossed Cash. Even the worst of the worst had people they wanted to protect most of the time.

Two hours in, Shara wandered away, stating she needed to get to Gilded, but we all knew she was just bored. The rest of the men in the room filtered out soon after, leaving just my men and Ash. Cameron never wavered. He never even looked up as the door shut. He was focused, determined to figure this out for his bride.

It wasn't until he got a look at Aislynn's jaw-cracking yawns that he finally stopped.

Paul's head dropped to his chest as he heaved in breaths of relief.

"Come on. We need to get you back," Cameron said.

"You aren't finished. I can walk myself back." Ash stood, groaning as she stretched her spine with a gentle stretch.

"Absolutely not."

They both tensed, gearing up for an argument that none of us wanted.

"I'll take care of it," Nate said, nodding at our captive.

At the sound of his voice, Paul—who looked like a horror movie extra—pried open his eyes. For the first time since he'd been brought in, he looked excited, and that made me angry. Suddenly, I understood why my cousin was so obsessed with keeping Aislynn safe.

The idea that this man knew who Nate was and that Cash would go after him because of me set all of my instincts flaring.

I marched over and threw a punch that rocked the chair.

"Eyes to yourself," I snapped. Grey's soft chuckle filled the air, but I couldn't step away. Something primal drove me to protect. To defend. To claim.

Get ahold of yourself, Mari.

I couldn't. They were my men, and I wouldn't let anyone take them from me.

"Don't worry, boy toy. I've got this." Dominic swept past me, laughing at the pained exhale his own hit made.

Blow after blow after blow, Dominic punched until Paul finally, blessedly, passed out.

"What was that for?"

Dominic shrugged. "I'm all in, even if it means defending one of those assholes."

My heart clenched, and something in me started to shift. Dominic hadn't walked; he hadn't balked. He'd stayed with me. He'd helped Cameron.

Could we really do this?

"Thanks, man. I appreciate it." Nate stared at Paul with relief, though it was a painful sort of relief after I gave my orders.

"Drop him by the docks when you're done."

"Wait, you're going to kill him?" Nate said.

My hackles rose, and I tried to tell myself he wasn't asking to make a problem; he was genuinely curious. Still, I had the worst urge to defend myself. It was part of the damage Dominic caused, and it would take time to accept and move past.

"If we let him live, Cash will kill him, and he'll do it worse than we ever could. We'll make it quick."

"I don't doubt it. I was just surprised, is all," he said, still looking incredibly uneasy.

Despite Nate's being a merc, he still maintained something so innocent in his character. Maybe it was just how he saw the world as it was and accepted it. I didn't want to ruin that, but if he didn't get a handle on it, it would get him killed. I wanted to help Nate, but I didn't know how. I couldn't stop what had to be done, and sending a message to Cash was necessary.

Cameron bundled Ash up, tucking her under his arm, and she glared at me. "With that settled, I expect you at my bachelorette party this weekend. Shara knew you were busy, so she planned it, which means dicks and chicks everywhere. Don't be late."

And the worst maid of honor award goes to me.

"I'll be there. With bells and whistles on," I promised.

"Good. I want a night of no drama. Just the three of us. Dancing, drinks—"

"And no strippers," my cousin snarled.

Neither of us agreed. There wasn't a snowflake's chance in hell that Shara hadn't hired strippers. Double—no, triple—the number, if he'd commanded her not to.

Poor Cameron had no clue how to handle women like us, despite growing up with me.

He'll learn, though, I thought with a grin. Ash wouldn't have it any other way.

With them gone, Dominic and Grey helped Tennessee remove Paul from the room. Normally, we wouldn't move him, but we could all see something was up with Nate. He just kept staring at Paul like he was a puzzle Nate wanted to solve.

When they were gone, I pulled him into Ash's chair and slid into his lap. Things were still so new with us that it felt a little awkward at first, especially when he made no attempt to move closer or hold me there. I was about to get up when he grabbed me around the waist and settled me firmly against his hips.

We hadn't done much more than the shower and I was dying to get him inside me, but things kept popping up. I couldn't walk away from my responsibilities to get laid. Especially when I wasn't sure that Nate was ready for this. For me.

"Are you okay? I know this was a lot." I ran a hand through his hair, trying to mimic what I liked when I was upset.

Nate snorted. "I did worse than that for the mercs."

"Then what is it?"

"I don't know. I think I'm annoyed at Dominic."

"Because he knocked the guy out?"

"Yes? I'm not sure." He took a breath and ran his hands up my thighs as he thought about it. "I guess I hate that he took away my opportunity to show you what I'm made of."

"You don't need to do that."

"I know." He cut me off with a kind smile and pulled me so close, nothing but our breaths were keeping us apart. "I just want you to know that I'm here and I'm in this and I can be a useful part of this team, too. I'm not just your little fuckboy. I want to help protect you."

My first instinct was to say no. When people protected me, they died, and if I lost Nate—if I lost any of my men—I didn't think I could handle it. But his eyes told me he needed it. He needed purpose. Moving in with me, Nate had lost his identity. He wasn't a bartender, he wasn't a mercenary, he was just my live-in man. And even though he'd been introduced to the systems that kept my empire running, we hadn't done anything to make it official yet.

He was in stasis, and if I wanted him to be fulfilled and happy in his role in my life, that needed to change.

"It's a good thing we have another little birdie just for you, then," I said, patting him on the chest. Shoving aside the part of myself that didn't want to sully Nate, I continued. "How about you help me with the dockworker?"

"Yeah?"

"Yeah."

As nervous as I was, the smile he gave me made it all worth it. "You're not going to regret this."

I knew I wouldn't. It was Nate. I hadn't regretted anything that had happened since we'd met, and I hoped that never changed.

Chapter 18
Nate

According to Mari, one of her men, a dockworker, had been taking payouts to mess with shipments. She gave me a list of questions to go on, and that was it. I didn't mind, though. I'd worked with less.

Settling into the routine of interrogation was like putting on an old coat I hadn't worn in a while. It felt a little stiff, but it was still the right size, the right shape. I'd once hoped I'd never put it on again, but I knew better now.

I was never going to escape being death's hand. It was my lot in life.

Brushing off the melancholy, I set down the recording device on a tool bench near the man's head and clicked it on. Mari hadn't been comfortable with the idea of it at first—*why would I want evidence recorded for the Feds to find, Nate?* —but she'd accepted it after I explained my routine. I had to be able to go back through the information later and see if I'd missed anything. If everything checked out, the man would die quickly. I wasn't one to drag things out unnecessarily, so as long as the information was confirmed, he'd be killed promptly. If there was something else I needed, we'd do it all over again, as many times as it took, like a fucked-up merry-go-round.

I didn't look at the tools as I stood behind the man's head, intentionally shuffling my feet to seem nervous. Uncomfortable. As always, he fell for it.

They always did.

"You've got to help me. I didn't do anything. They've got the wrong guy." He craned his neck, desperate to catch my eyes, to convince me of his innocence. "I swear, I didn't help anybody, and I didn't steal anything."

Gotcha. "How did you know what we wanted to talk to you about, then?"

I saw the moment he realized his mistake. He gulped, eyes darting around the room before he came back to me. "The guys who took me mentioned it."

Except they didn't. "Of course."

"I'm serious. You've got to help me. She's going to kill me."

"No, she isn't. I am."

The man looked at me like I'd just shot his beloved. All betrayal, confusion, and anger. He was pale and exhausted, likely from his stint in Mari's cold room. One of his eyes sported a fading bruise that Tennessee explained he'd gotten for fighting back when they'd originally picked him up from the docks. Jacob wasn't the target they expected information from, but I was told to try my best to get it anyway.

Who approached you? How did you contact them? Who else is Cash working with? How long has this been going on? What else do you know?

"Jacob Collins, where do you work?"

"Seattle docks, under Micah Fitzgerald. Been there since I was twelve, working alongside my father, brothers, and uncles until they all retired. I'm the last Collins left."

"What a shitty way to end a family legacy," Mari snapped from her seat on the other side of the room, with Greyson and Dominic at her back. Jacob said nothing. He didn't even look at her. It was as if she didn't exist.

I didn't like that at all.

"Here's what's going to happen, Jacob. I'm going to ask you questions, and you're going to answer them. No lies, no half-truths, no omissions. If you do what I ask, I'll go easy on you. If not, I will do whatever it takes to get the information I need, even if it means pulling out every single tooth and fingernail and knuckle in your body."

To his credit, Jacob tried to stay tough, but I saw the whiteness of his knuckles against the chair and the hard swallow that bobbed his Adam's apple. He was petrified, but too proud to admit it.

The darkest parts of me cheered with glee. The tough ones were always fun. That was the part of myself I didn't like, the one born from a boy who'd had to steal and hurt just to make sure he ate. The one who'd done terrible things to make sure he survived.

But he was part of me, just like the man who cared for Mari was. They were all Nate, even when I wished they weren't.

"Let's get started." I grabbed the first instrument I could reach and cracked it down on his hand as a warning. Then the interrogation began in earnest, and I let muscle memory and the familiar sounds and smells of torture take me away. Before I could understand what was happening, I was back in a time when there was no Mari, no Greyson, no Dominic. No empire in need of my help.

Just me and my team trying to survive.

"What are you gonna do when you get out of here, Nate?" Jorey asked, flipping a knife between his hands. It was an annoying habit. One of his many.

"Nothing," I said. "I just want a chance to do nothing."

I'd never had that before. I didn't want warm sand and cool water, just a few days in a place of my own to decompress.

Franklin grunted as he bandaged a bite mark on Stowe's upper arm, smacking him when he wouldn't quit wiggling. "Knock it off."

"Can't believe that fucker bit me," Stowe grumbled. I peered at the wound again, but it looked far better than the stab wound on his left leg. He'd been first in the door, and apparently, our mark had impressive aim.

"How about you keep your fucking distance next time?" Franklin muttered.

"What can I say? I'm a team player." Stowe's annoying grin turned to a pained hiss when Franklin poured antiseptic on him. "Damn, dude. That hurts."

"Do you want whatever that asshole had in his mouth? I didn't think so. Shut up."

That asshole was now a body we'd buried in a shallow grave five miles away in the middle of bumfuck nowhere. I didn't even remember what country we were in, to be honest. I rarely ever did. While we were working, there was nothing but the chase. The hunt. The kill.

Gather information, take down our enemies, survive. I didn't have room for anything else.

Franklin and Stowe continued to bicker as usual, so I tuned them out. We were brothers. Just the four of us against the world, fighting bad guys most people didn't even know existed.

We were the ones who snuck into homes and slit throats while our targets slept, ending regimes under the light of the moon. There were no songs singing our praise, no medals waiting for us at the end of the road as we crept through the shadows. Just another mission to complete.

This one was no different. A trafficker was setting up to take his business through the US, carting people across the pond and using the airports as hubs to send them all over the world. If we didn't stop them, millions of women and children would be at risk.

We'd been trying to crack into the network for almost a month, with no luck. The biter had given us the intel we needed to finally end it all, and tomorrow, we made our move.

Franklin and Stowe glared at each other until their lips tipped into smiles while I oiled my knives with Tsubaki oil, trying to brush off the horrors I'd committed for honor and country. Meanwhile, Jorey tossed that goddamned knife in time with my heartbeat.

Catch, throw, catch, throw.

The first bullet hit him while the knife was in the air.

He was dead before it hit the floor.

"Ambush!" I dove to the floor, fighting the urge to pull Jorey to safety. He was gone, though.

When faced with death, there was a moment when the inevitability of it hit you. You realized that everything you thought you cared about didn't matter. It was the immaterial things, the intangible, that you wanted to keep with you in the afterlife.

My mother, who had given up everything for us, my brother—or who he was before we lost him—those were the things I wanted to remember. I hoped she knew how much we'd loved her. I promised myself right then and there that if I got out of this, I'd figure out a way to give her the care she needed and change the fate awaiting me back home.

I just had to survive this shit first.

The first wave of men came out of nowhere and, without hesitation, took out Franklin.

Fuck.

The way they killed my team said a lot. Jorey was a loose cannon, more likely to set us all on fire than to make up a plan. Franklin was next because he was our medic. If we got hurt, we were as good as dead, and Stowe was already injured.

This wasn't an ambush. It was an assassination.

Grabbing Stowe, I pulled him out of the room we'd been holed up in, knowing there was almost nowhere we could go. The old school building was practically rotting around us. We hadn't cared before because it was meant to be a rest stop before we took out our target and got the hell out of dodge.

"Not going to make it, man," Stowe huffed. The wound in his leg obviously hurt, and when I looked down, I cursed at the blood trail it left.

"You don't have a fucking choice. I'm not going back alone." I was practically pleading, even as I could see the writing on the wall. Stowe was already dead, even though he was still breathing. We both were.

"If you don't leave me here, none of us are coming home. Jorey and Franklin, they deserve better than this. Bring us home, brother. Give us the burial we deserve."

Life was unfair, I already knew that, but nothing would ever beat this. The moment I watched another brother disappear forever.

"Whatever it takes." It was the promise we'd made to each other years ago, when our team was first formed. I'd just never imagined I'd be the last one to say it.

Footsteps pounded through the room beyond, and I knew my time was up. Quickly, I helped Stowe to the floor, kneeling to hand him his weapon. "You gotta tell my girl I'm sorry. I didn't mean to break my promise."

"I'll tell her." I'd fly to Wisconsin, where I knew his girlfriend of four years was waiting for him to be done with this tour so she could finally get the engagement ring he'd been hiding for years. Stowe had promised her this was his last tour. He'd been right in the worst way.

"I know you will, man." He clapped me on the shoulder, and I did the same before yanking him into a hug. It wasn't something I had consciously thought of before, but everyone deserved a hug before they died. Stowe should know that someone in the world cared that he'd existed. He held me tight, pounding my back once, twice, three times before he shoved me away.

"Don't die because of this. I'm telling you to go so you can live for all of us." Survivor's guilt already weighed heavily on my heart, so I didn't say anything, but Stowe knew. "Whatever it takes to survive, Nate. Now, go."

I went.

I was barely out the door before the gunshots started, each one ringing in my ears. Stowe never yelled, never cried out. He just kept saying it over and over again.

Whatever it takes.

They found me just as I was exiting the last hallway, ten steps from the door. Guilt-ridden or not, I fought. I cut. I sliced, I hit, I kicked, I bit. I did everything I could to make sure I survived so someone could be sure Stowe and Franklin and Jorey made it home. I didn't fight for me. I did it for them.

They deserved better than to die in this shithole.

My arms were tired, my legs heavy, my soul weary and dark. I thought it would go on forever. That I'd never be free.

Then I heard her voice.

"Come back to me, Nate."

My angel. It confused me. There were no angels where I'd been. Only the blood on my hands and the echo of long-lost gunshots.

"Open your eyes, Nate."

It was a command, and I followed it. The first thing I saw were imploring brown eyes. The second, my bloody hands.

"Fuck," I gasped, shoving myself away from the body.

Jacob. His name was Jacob. I couldn't think of him as a body. He was someone's son. If I forgot that, I worried I'd lose my humanity for good.

"Are you back?" Mari asked cautiously.

"Stay back, *mariposa*," someone commanded.

"Fuck off, Dominic," she snapped.

Behind her, Grey held him in a choke hold, while he was nearly foaming at the mouth with Mari so close to me. I didn't blame him.

"I'm good," I rasped. "I'm good."

"I know you are." Mari's smile settled me a little more, and I pulled her close with shaking hands, bowing my body over hers. All I could do was breathe in the smell of her hair, feel the soft puffs of her breath against my neck.

I just needed a minute to wipe away the memories. Just a minute.

When I felt more stable, I cleared my throat and pulled away, my heart warming when Mari stayed close. It was obvious in the way she watched me—head on with no ulterior motives—that she wasn't waiting for me to break down again. She just wanted to be near. I liked that. Maybe too much.

I turned toward Jacob, grimacing at the sight of his unrecognizable face. Christ, I'd fucked up. There was nothing like abject failure to humble a man.

I was supposed to do a job for Mari, and instead, I let myself get caught up in a past that no longer mattered. I knew better than that. "Did we get anything from him?"

"Yes. You were surprisingly coherent throughout," Greyson said, shoving Dominic behind him and stepping forward. It said a lot that he didn't put himself between Mari and me. He trusted that I wouldn't hurt her. I didn't know if it was blind faith, but I appreciated it, nonetheless. Grey paced his way around Jacob's body. "Do the flashbacks happen often?"

"Not now," Mari admonished.

I didn't want to be coddled, but I felt like I owed them. "No. I haven't had a flashback in months."

"Until you came here as my guest." Guilt was thick in Mari's voice, and I tried to get myself to say something, to fix it, but someone else beat me to it.

"It was bound to happen anyway, *mariposa*," Dominic said, stepping close. He glared at the space between Mari and me but kept his distance, likely because he knew she wouldn't appreciate his interference. "Some things scar you so badly, the only way to escape them is death."

He spoke like he had firsthand experience, and I wondered if we'd ever be close enough for him to tell me. It shocked me that I hoped so. The longer I stayed with Mari and the others, the more I felt like I'd finally found the one thing I'd always craved.

A family of my own, as strange as it looked from the outside. "Do you need help with this?" I motioned to Jacob.

"No. Go clean up," Greyson replied.

"I'll check in on you later," she said, coming up to give me a kiss. Blood spatter covered my hands and wrists, and it felt like it was seeping into my skin. The urge to scour myself until I was down to the final layer of epidermis rode me hard, and I couldn't handle touching her. Letting it stain her too. I stepped away, and she sighed, the sound hitting me straight in the chest.

"You did good, Nate. We got everything we needed and more. Go shower."

She didn't have to tell me twice.

The second I was in my bathroom I turned the water to boiling hot and scrambled to rip off my clothes. I'd burn them the first chance I could. The second I was naked, I was in the shower, hissing as the hot water rained down on my skin, but I didn't make a move beyond letting it burn me.

When I felt like I could move again—and the water ran clear-ish —I grabbed the washcloth and got to scrubbing. Only when I was as raw on the outside as I felt on the inside, did I get out and slip into my comfiest pair of sweats.

I knew someone had been in my room the second I opened the door. I expected Dominic, ready to beat my ass for being a threat to Mari.

Instead, I smelled popcorn.

There on my bed in nothing but a T-shirt and a pair of boxers, both mine, was Mari. Her face was clean, hair pulled back like she was ready for bed.

"What're you doing here, angel?"

"Thought we'd watch a movie," she said, pointing to the TV, where she was scrolling through choices.

"That's sweet, but—"

"Don't even think about finishing that sentence."

"Mari," I sighed.

"We don't have to talk, and you don't have to touch me. Hell, I won't even look at you. You don't have to tell me anything that happened. Not today, not tomorrow, not next year. Your story is yours, Nate. I just can't in good conscience let you be alone. If you want to get rid of me, you'll have to go to a different room. And I'll be honest, I'll probably follow you there too. It'll be much easier if you just accept that I'm not leaving."

She didn't even look at me when she said it, didn't mention the recording or the interrogation at all, and I couldn't help the feeling that bubbled up in my chest.

This woman. This amazing, powerful, kind woman who fought for her people with everything she had was mine. *How did I get so lucky?*

True to her word, Mari kept her eyes averted when I unfroze myself and climbed in next to her. She stayed in place as I settled, only moving when I snatched her waist and dragged her over to me. "Hey! I'm trying to give you space."

"Well, don't. If you're in my bed, you'll be wrapped around me. Understand?"

Her grin seared my chest where her head rested. "Yes."

"Good, because I don't plan on going anywhere." My voice was grumpier than usual, and she laughed under her breath but didn't say anything else. Just held me tighter as she started whatever movie she'd picked out.

As I watched every expression on her face, as the press of her body against mine grounded me, I knew without a shadow of a doubt what I thought I'd always known.

I was in love with her. Wholly, completely, unchangingly.

Hell, I think I loved her the very first time I saw her, and that was a problem. As much as I rejoiced at the idea of having her, it was unlikely I'd survive the coming months.

When this war with Cash was over, I'd be another name on the list of men who'd gutted Mari. Even as I hated it, I knew it was true.

I spent most of the movie trying—and failing—to figure a way out of it, but there was none. I knew better than most that even silent battles had casualties.

Mari's eyes crinkled with laughter at something on-screen, and the lightness in them shifted something in my chest. I knew what I had to do.

Whatever it takes.

I might not survive, but Mari would. This time, I was going down with the ship.

Whatever it takes for her to survive.

Chapter 19
Mari

I was putting the final touches on my outfit when Greyson came into the room. He took in the royal-blue slip dress and comfortable heels, raising an eyebrow when I hiked up the hem just enough to adjust the knife strapped to my leg. Party or not, I wasn't going anywhere unarmed until Cash was taken care of.

"You look beautiful, *reina*," he said from his place against the wall.

"Good enough for wherever we're going?"

Shara had given me explicit instructions to dress nice, but that was it. No other clues about what we were doing for Aislynn's bachelorette party. She'd also been clear that the only men at the party would be the strippers she'd *absolutely* hired and whoever was on bodyguard duty. My men were not invited, and neither was the groom.

But I knew Greyson. There wasn't a chance in hell he hadn't gotten the details from her by now.

"The outfit is almost perfect," he promised, pushing off the wall.

"Almost?" I turned back to the mirror, trying to figure out what I was missing. "What does it need?"

He came up behind me and pressed a kiss to my neck. "I'll show you."

That low voice sent shivers down my spine, and heat pooled between my legs at the filthy way he watched me like I was his own personal fantasy.

"Greyson." I tried to twist around, wanting a kiss, a touch, anything, but his hand between my shoulders pushed me forward and kept me still. Only when he was sure I wouldn't move, did he plaster himself to my back, caging me between his hips and the dressing table.

"Don't move," he whispered, nipping my neck and kicking the insides of my ankles to spread my legs wider.

We were still dressed, but I felt naked under the weight of his stare in the mirror.

My heart was pounding, and I had to swallow more than once to respond. "What are you doing?"

"Giving you a goodbye present since you'll be gone all night."

Oh fuck. I could feel myself getting wetter. I wasn't sure what it was about my men, but I needed them more than I'd ever needed anyone else. The moment they were close, I *wanted.*

Grey slid his hands under my dress, large palms skating across my skin and into my panties. I was already panting, but he didn't touch my pussy, just pulled the lace down to my knees and left it there.

"I'll be late." *Do I care?* Honestly, no.

"Not if you hurry." All I got was a sultry smirk in the reflection before he dropped to the floor behind me. I had a moment to think, *yes*, before he shoved his head under my dress. The first caress of his tongue made my knees shake.

"Christ, I needed this." He'd barely touched me, and I was already leaning heavily on the dressing table.

"I'll always give you what you need," Greyson promised as he wrapped his lips around my clit and sucked.

Fuck me, that's good.

"You taste so good, *reina*," Grey rasped between licks, alternating from long and slow to quick swipes that made my hips jerk against his hold. He tightened his fingers on my thighs, pulling me back into his face. If his hands weren't holding me down, they were rubbing expert circles around my clit while he fucked me with his tongue. His grip was firm and sure. He knew he had every right to touch me, so he did.

Even though he was on his knees for me, we both understood that he owned me.

In that moment, I was wholly Greyson's.

All while I got a front-row view of my own pleasure.

The mirror showed me a panting mess, hips writhing as I desperately tried to ride my way to an orgasm, but Grey's grip wouldn't allow it.

"Greyson," I whined. The edge of an orgasm was just out of reach, and I wanted it bad.

"You want to ride my face, baby? Slide that slick cunt over my mouth until I make you scream?"

"Yes."

"No."

"No?"

"You'll take what I give you and nothing more. Are you watching what I do to you?"

Of course I was. The mirror was an unpaid actor in this scene, and I couldn't take my eyes off it. Off us. I couldn't see more than the tip of Grey's chin, slick and shiny between my spread thighs, his body still completely covered up behind me.

Fully dressed men fucking me was absolutely a kink, especially when it was Greyson. It felt far dirtier than it should have, like we were stealing pleasure while the world waited on us. Like he couldn't resist putting his hands on me. I loved it.

"You're such a good girl, *reina*. Taste so sweet on my tongue."

"Please make me come." I wasn't too proud to beg. Not for him.

He made a noncommittal sound and went back to eating me out. On and on, Grey toyed with me until I thought I would scream, not quite edging me but skirting the lines of pleasure. My fingers cramped against the table, and my voice was getting hoarse from pleading, but I didn't dare move.

Whatever he was doing, I wanted.

Finally, he gave me more, and the wave of my orgasm rose to meet me.

"I'm close. I'm so close," I panted, desperately reaching for the peak I knew was coming. It felt powerful, and I had no doubt it was going to be the best orgasm I'd ever had. Another long pull from his lips around my clit, and I clenched my fingers against the tabletop and—*there it is.* "Oh, fuck yes. I'm coming."

There was nothing but sweet relief on my tongue. *So. Fucking. Close.*

"That's too bad. It's time for you to go." He pulled back, shattering the orgasm before it could even begin.

No. *No, no, no.* I could feel the warmth of him and the orgasm floating away. He hadn't just denied me; he'd ruined it. The best orgasm of my life, gone with nothing to show for it.

I blamed the fog of endorphins for how long it took to come up with a coherent response. "What?"

"You have to go. You're going to be late." Like he'd conjured them, I heard footsteps and the sound of an irate Shara.

"Mari," she growled. "If you don't get out here right now, I'm going to break this door down and drag you out."

"I'll be right out," I promised, my voice cracking. Slumping against the table, I glared at Grey. "You're seriously going to make me go out like this?"

"You mean wet, dripping, highly unsatisfied?" he asked as he slowly slid my panties up my thighs until I was put back together again. "Yes, I am. I think it'll be good for you."

I wanted to rip his face off then cry in a corner because *what the fuck?!* "The only thing that would be good for me is if you finished what you started."

"Tempting." He gripped my hair and pulled me close, sliding his tongue into my mouth so I tasted myself, but he wouldn't let me touch him back. "But I'm going to have to pass."

He had just gotten me all hot and bothered right before I was set to leave, and he was going to *pass?*

Are you fucking kidding me?

Had it been anyone else, I'd have finished myself off. Or found someone else to do it for me. I had no doubt that Nate would enjoy the challenge, but it didn't seem right. "You know I'm going to get you back for this, right?"

Tying him up so I could make him feel my pain sounded wonderful.

Greyson grinned. "I have no doubt. But for now, just trust me. You know I wouldn't do this without a reason."

"Of course you would." I grabbed my purse, making sure to slide my body against his erection on my way out. I hoped he got blue balls. "Have fun with your hand, asshole."

I absolutely slammed the door on him and his laughter.

Shara took one look at me and shepherded me into the SUV that was acting as our limo. Bulletproof, of course. "I should have known he was going to do something when he offered to come get you."

Ash took one look at what I assumed was my unhappy face and

hid her smile behind the champagne flute. "What's wrong? Someone not get laid?"

"No," I snapped, instantly regretting it. It was her bachelorette party, and I was yelling at her. I blamed Greyson for that too. "Fuck, sorry."

Because I was feeling generous, I explained the situation. As expected, my so-called best friends laughed their asses off.

"I'd be cranky too if someone started something they wouldn't finish." Ash smiled gently at me. "Though I would settle for being touched again. It's been a while."

Considering I knew that she and my cousin weren't fucking—or at least, I was pretty sure—I could only imagine. I wasn't willing to ask, though. Close as we were or not, my cousin's sex life was none of my business.

But Greyson's was, and since my thighs were sticking together under my dress, I was considering becoming celibate. Just from him, though. What was the point of having three boyfriends if I was going to be celibate from all three?

My brain caught on the word *boyfriend,* but I ignored it. This was not the time to consider appropriate word choices for my men.

"Where are we going?" I asked, turning back to Shara. Moore and Tennessee were in the front, laughing together since Geneva had the night off.

"Where else would we go? Wicked, of course. Although I will admit that none of your men were all that pleased."

Since two of the three knew the club had once been my hunting grounds for companions, I could imagine.

"Screw them." I downed the rest of the champagne Shara had wisely prepared for our drive. "We deserve some fun tonight, even if it involves getting hit on by men who don't have an iota of a chance with us."

"Hear, here!" Shara downed her glass.

"Serves them right," Aislynn said with a pissed-off frown.

"Cameron walked in when I was getting dressed earlier, and he told me I looked *easy*."

Christ. *What a fucking moron.* "He really has no idea what he's doing, does he?"

Ash snorted. "Does any man?"

"Idiots, the lot of them." Shara raised her glass. "They should thank god we like dick."

We all drank to that.

* * *

Wicked looked the same as it always did, except for one noticeable difference.

It was empty.

"What the hell?" I turned in a circle, trying and failing to come up with an excuse. "Where is everyone?"

"I closed the club for us," Shara said with a grin. "That way, we can have all the fun we want, and the menfolk aren't losing their shit about their precious ladies being in danger."

"Or getting hit on every five seconds," Tennessee muttered.

"Last thing we need is a pile of bodies at a party," Moore agreed.

Knowing my men absolutely would have made it happen, I could applaud Shara's problem-solving skills, but as the owner, my mind was focused on dollar signs.

"Relax, the boys chipped in to pay the private-party fee."

Oh. That made more sense, though I wondered how Nate had handled it. It was tens of thousands to shut down our club for a single night. Grimacing, I decided against asking him. It was none of my business, though I did need to get him working again, for his own sake. The man obviously needed a project to keep him busy.

Thinking of him in his bed earlier in the week, body curled around me like he couldn't stand to let me go, warmth flowed through me. We hadn't talked, though I was dying to. I wanted to know everything there was to know about Nate Black.

Who he'd been, what he'd done, the future he wanted.

He'll tell you when he's ready, I told myself. I just had to have faith. For now, I'd work with him to find a position in the family—but *not* in the family—that would pay him well without relying on his former career. I had enough interrogators; I wasn't interested in re-traumatizing another one.

"Let's get some drinks before the show begins," Shara suggested.

Aislynn and I glanced at each other as Shara ordered a round of drinks from the bartender and shepherded us to a table with a perfect view of the go-go cages. They were on the floor for once, and a lick of something close to anticipation coiled in my stomach. "Show?"

"I thought we deserved some fun, so I may have hired a bit of extra entertainment." Her grin turned positively feral when the lights flickered, and three masked dancers I knew we didn't employ slipped into the cages.

It was muscles for miles, and I wasn't complaining a bit.

"Are those strippers?" Aislynn asked, laughing when all three started to undress to the beat.

"Oh god. I knew it. Cameron's going to lose his shit."

"Good," Shara said with a sharp grin. "Had he *asked* me not to hire them, I would've respected his wishes, as long as they were yours too. Instead, he commanded me like I was his dog. I am not his property, and neither are you. It's time he was reminded of that."

"You're a holy terror." Ash's smile was just as deadly, and I realized these two were exactly the type of women I'd have asked for if I could've handpicked my sisters. Beautiful and deadly, like Rafael had said.

The reminder that my uncle was playing opossum in my city ran over my skin, as did my nerves about meeting the Wolf, but I ignored it. Ash's party wasn't the time to borrow worries from the future. Besides, they hadn't reached out to me yet, so no news was good news.

Though I really needed that information on Cash.

I sat back, nursing my drink, knowing I wouldn't get sloppy. Just because we were having a fun night out didn't mean that Cash wasn't planning something, and I was not willing to give him an easy target. Even as I laughed and joked along with the others, my eyes drifted to every entrance and exit, diving into the shadows like I could ferret out danger if I looked hard enough.

Maybe that was why it took me so long to realize one of the cage dancers looked familiar.

Too familiar.

Is that...?

No. It couldn't be.

And yet, it was.

Nate danced in the cage in nothing but a pair of tight black briefs.

What the actual fuck?

I must've said it out loud because Aislynn and Shara peered in the same direction. I knew the moment they recognized him, too, because Ash choked, while Shara started cackling loud enough to be heard clearly over the music. All three men's eyes landed on us, but Shara didn't care. "Oh, he's in so much trouble."

"Yes, he is. Now put your eyes back in your head," I growled.

I'd never been a territorial woman before, but the idea of anyone seeing him nearly naked... No. Not okay. The need to yank him out of that cage and teach him a lesson struck me in the chest, and I welcomed it. It wasn't anger but passion, and I wrapped it around myself like a favorite sweater.

That fire had been missing for me since Rey died; it felt good to sense it again.

I tapped my fingers against my leg as I debated what to do. If I pulled him out of the cage, I'd ruin Aislynn's party. If I didn't, I'd end up killing someone. Thankfully, Ash made the decision for me.

"Go get him before someone else tries."

A glance at the bar told me she was right. The servers were all making eyes at Nate.

My Nate.

Absolutely fucking not.

"Oh fuck," Moore groaned. "Just what we need."

"Come on, baby. This'll be fun. We may get bodies tonight after all," Tennessee joked.

I stood carefully, making sure every step was measured. Calculated. I hadn't been this on edge in months. I didn't want to kill anyone tonight, just teach them a lesson they'd never forget.

Instead of going to the cage, I headed for the bar first. Suitors first, then I'd deal with my errant boyfriend.

Benji saw me coming and got to work on a new drink, sliding it down the bar, though I obviously didn't need one. The other workers weren't so astute.

"He's so hot," one of the servers whispered from where she leaned against the bar. "Seriously, I'm going to need a shower to cool off soon. Think he'd join?"

"I don't know, but do you see the outline of that dick? It would break me to pieces," another said.

"It really would," I said calmly, sipping from the glass Benji had slid across the bar. "Too bad he's not available."

"He got a girlfriend or something? Because I can be discreet." She winked like it was funny that she'd just suggested being Nate's side chick *to my face.*

"Oh fuck." Benji backed up, eyes wide and nervous.

"What?" she asked, looking between the bartender and me. "Oh shit. You're his girlfriend."

The first server, all blonde hair and blue eyes, looked like she wanted to puke. "We didn't know, Ms. Marcosa."

"Ms. Marcosa?" the second one squeaked. "Oh god. I'm so sorry. He's just so hot and—"

I cleared my throat as her friend elbowed her in the side *hard*.

"Sorry, sorry. I didn't know, I swear."

"Now you do. Unless you'd like me to teach you a very painful lesson about hitting on one of my men, I'd suggest you keep your eyes, hands, and opinions to yourselves."

"Of course," they said, and suddenly, every eye he'd garnered looked away.

Magic.

Moore chuckled nearby. "I expected a bloodbath."

"Trying to keep the body count low, but I make no promises if they look at him again."

"That's my girl."

"Benji?"

"I'll take care of it," he promised.

I had no doubt that if they even looked at Nate again, they'd be handed pink slips and a ticket out of the city.

I wasn't interested in ruling solely by fear, but sometimes it came in handy.

Knowing Benji would keep the servers in check, I made my way over to the cages. Nate was slick with sweat. I'd seen him mostly naked in the shower, but the flashing lights showcased the scars on his body. He didn't have a single tattoo, unlike Greyson, Dominic, and me.

I wanted to see all that blank skin spread out under me.

Would he let me tattoo him?

A question for another day.

"Is this a fucking joke?" I asked, crossing my arms under the cage.

"Not sure I know what you mean. Care to elaborate?"

Cheeky fucker.

"Whatever the hell this is, it's over."

Nate's grin was something I expected Dominic to give. Flirty and joking and absolutely the wrong fucking move. "Sorry, I don't give lap dances. My girlfriend wouldn't approve."

"Agreed. Now, get out," I snarled.

"What's wrong, baby? You wanted strippers, you got strippers." When I said nothing, his eyes darkened. "What, you don't want me flaunting the goods to your friends?"

No. No, I did not.

Keeping my voice level was so much harder than I expected. "Let me make this clear, Nate. If this is some sort of game where you try to make me jealous, I can assure you it's not going to go the way you want it to. You've had your fun, but whatever this is, it's over. Now."

Whatever look I gave him must've been bad, because his grin dropped. "Angel—"

"I swear to god, I am on the cusp of a murder spree, Nate. *Get. The Fuck. Out.*"

"Okay. Okay, I'm coming."

Maybe it was the frustration of being left unsatisfied, or maybe it was truly just the fact that I didn't want anyone else to see him, but the longer it took him, the more irritated I got. To his credit, it wasn't his fault, but I hated it.

Hated that those women had looked at him.

Hated that they'd fantasized about him. That they'd probably keep fantasizing about him even though they had no right to.

Nate was *mine*.

And I was going to remind him of that.

Chapter 20
Nate

Somewhere between dancing in the cage and Mari demanding I get down, I made a mistake.

Anger, I'd expected. Possessiveness, I'd hoped for.

Ice-cold rage was not part of the plan. Especially when it was paired with the world's smallest sliver of hurt.

Fuck.

I wasn't sure what set her off, but I had to fix it. If I didn't, my sexy surprise was going to end up a deadly one.

"Let's go, Nate."

I reached for her, grabbing her just above the elbow. "Mari—"

"Don't." She tore her arm away. "I'm so pissed off, I can't right now."

I could see that, and it made my stomach ache. "This isn't how this was supposed to happen."

"What *was* supposed to happen, Nate?"

"I didn't come here for anyone but you."

She stared at me, eyes narrowed like she was trying to spot a lie. She wouldn't find one. When she realized that, she prowled forward, pinning me against the cage. My dick, already hard from the possessiveness of her shooting down the servers, pressed between us. "Do you think it was smart of you to take your clothes off in front of other women?"

Focusing was a chore with her body against me, but I tried. "I wasn't doing it for them."

"You didn't want them to look?"

"I wanted you to look. Only you." Because even after the shower, things were slow with us, and I wanted more. I needed more. I needed *her*.

Besides, the dancing thing was Dominic's idea. Greyson helped too. Hell, even Cameron was part of this charade.

And I'd throw them all under the bus if I had to.

"How did you even get in the group?"

"Not exactly a real group, angel."

She peered at the other men again, and when the one closest to me winked, I knew the jig was up. Like a switch, Mari's anger dimmed. "Oh my *god*, I did not need to see my cousin like this."

"Then don't look," Cameron said behind his mask.

A lighthearted laugh lit up her face, and the sight made my breath catch. Not only because she was beautiful, but because I knew we were okay. Or, we would be. "Ash's going to be *so* pissed at you."

"Good. We'll match."

Considering the lap-dance portion was right around the corner, I couldn't wait to see what happened.

"Who's the other guy?"

"Someone your uncle recommended."

Her brows screwed up. "Joaquin?"

"No, Rafael."

"Huh. Didn't know he had fun."

She had no idea the type of fun Rafael had, and I wasn't going to tell her. Not now when things were unstable between us again.

"Can we start over?"

"No."

Fuck. I scoured my brain, trying to come up with some way to salvage the evening.

The plan was clear: dance in the cage and seduce Mari. That was it.

We hadn't made contingencies for her reaction. A massive mistake if ever there was one.

The music changed, and the remaining two dancers exited the cages, prowling toward their victims. "Unless you want to see your cousin give Ash a lap dance, we should get out of here."

Mari narrowed her eyes at me, then winced when Aislynn's irate voice echoed over the music.

"*Are you fucking kidding me?!* You couldn't give me one night, you controlling prick?"

We were moving toward them before she was done talking. Her face was twisted with rage, and while Cameron looked more relaxed, I knew he was seething.

"You wanted strippers, you got them!" Cameron yelled back. "What's the problem?"

"The problem is *you*, Cameron. It's always you."

"Better get used to it, then. I'm not going anywhere."

Mari glanced at her friends, glaring at the dancer who was grinding all over Shara. Though, it looked like she was more than enjoying it. Apparently drama wasn't enough to distract Shara from what she wanted, and with the way she was undressing him with her eyes, Rafael's man was just the flavor she was looking for.

"What do you want to do, Ash?" Mari's fingers twitched at her sides, though she tried to hide it. She was pissed too.

"Go take care of your man." Ash waved us off, voice deepening with irritation as she turned back to Cameron. "I'll take care of mine."

"Is that a threat, princess?"

"It's a promise, baby."

"You heard the lady. Let's go." Mari grabbed my wrist, barely touching me as she towed me through the club and toward a side hallway. Everyone was watching us out of the corner of their eyes, but only Aislynn and Shara were brave enough to do it outright.

Why did that turn me on so much? The way Mari wielded her power in every situation was just *hot*. Would she use it on me if I asked? I wasn't someone who enjoyed being commanded, but thinking of Mari naked, telling me exactly what to do to make her scream? I was pretty sure I'd be okay with that.

We didn't say anything as we wound down the hallway to the last door on the right. She unlocked it with her fingerprint and shoved me inside. Yeah, I definitely didn't mind the manhandling.

The office was fancy but nothing special.

It was all moody florals, dark and dangerous. I was pretty sure all the flowers in the prints were poisonous, though I doubted many others would know that. Rich, luxurious fabrics and high-quality furniture. A velvet couch and matching armchairs that looked pristine, expensive booze on the bar cart. It was all very Mari, and I loved that she'd brought me here instead of somewhere else in the club.

The second the door closed, she turned on me.

It was in Mari's nature to hunt the prey in the room, but this was something else.

Every step forward was measured. Every sway of her hips was intentional. Even the way she stared at me, eyes burning with residual anger and lust, was controlled.

All of it added up to one unavoidable fact.

I was harder than I'd ever been, and it was because of her. For her. *Only* her.

"I think we've had a miscommunication, so let's clear it up." She stopped in front of me, head tipped up to see my face as she ran her hand down my chest. "You're mine, Nate. That means this body is mine. My arms, my legs, my cock." She gripped me through my briefs, squeezing until I groaned, hips flexing against her touch. She pulled me down with her other hand, so her deadly whisper went straight into my mouth. "You ever think of showing it to someone else again, I'll cut it off."

Christ, this woman. If I wasn't hard before, that did it.

Before I could do anything other than lick my lips, she shoved me onto the couch, straddling my lap while I was still bouncing.

"Do you understand me, or will you need a visual reminder?"

"I understand, and it'll never happen again," I promised, wrapping my hands around her hips. "It's yours. I'm yours."

Mari's chest brushed mine as I flexed my fingers, using the barest touch to grind her on my cock. "I've dealt with more than my share of jealousy with the other two, Nate. I don't want to deal with it with you."

"I'm sorry. I made a mistake. I just thought—"

"You thought what?" she asked quietly.

"*We* thought it was the push you needed."

The whole charade was a risk, but all four of us—even Cameron— agreed Mari needed a push with me. She was so scared to corrupt me that she was taking too long to realize I was already corrupted. There was nothing left in me to save.

I wasn't afraid of the darkness if it got me her.

"You were trying to push me?"

"Yes. You see me differently than the others, even though I'm not. I may not have grown up in the life like you three, but I'm not fragile. I chose to be here. I choose you. Don't keep me at arm's length, hoping I'll change my mind."

"So you decided to manipulate the situation in your favor? Get me angry enough to fuck you, if only to prove a point to everyone else."

"No. Yes. It wasn't meant to be like that."

I hadn't intended to, but she was right. I could've talked to her.

"I'm sorry. I should've told you how I felt instead of sneaking around trying to trick you. That's not fair to either of us."

"It isn't, but you're not wrong." She sighed, collapsing against me just a little. "I haven't been comfortable letting you in. You seem too good for this life."

"I've killed hundreds of men for my country and plenty more before that. I'm not some pristine pretty boy, Mari. I'm a grown man with more secrets than you can fathom."

"Your trauma doesn't negate your worth, Nate."

"I know that, but I don't like how it affects me. But that's a problem for another time. Right now, I need to know how to get you to *see me*."

She flinched, and I wondered if I'd said the wrong thing and how to fix it.

"I'm sorry," she eventually whispered. "I'm doing exactly what Dominic did without even realizing it."

Was that true? Thinking it through, I agreed. She hadn't meant to, but she'd been following his logic the whole time. I hoped feeling that same thing he did would help them come together again. Anyone could see that we worked best as a foursome.

Oh fuck. I wanted to see what that would look like. Three mouths, three cocks making our girl come.

My hips flexed again, rubbing my cock between her legs. Greyson told me all she had on under the dress was a tiny pair of lace panties, and I desperately wanted inside them. "If I promise to forgive you, and you promise to stop treating me like I'm too good for you, can we move on to what I had planned for the rest of the night?"

"Maybe. Why try to trick me? I want the real truth, Nate."

"Because you think I'm worth saving."

Something shuttered in her eyes. "You are."

"I'm not." Her eyes flickered and I knew she'd argue, so I continued. "I've seen and done terrible things. I've been part of this world long before I wanted to, but you refuse to see that."

"So you tricked me to, what, get in my pants?"

"No. To give you a push to take what you wanted. You won't break me, baby. I was shattered before I met you."

"What, no sweet words about me putting you back together?"

"I did that myself, or I'm trying to. But you give me a reason to keep trying. Is that close enough?"

"Yeah, I guess so."

"Don't push me away, Mari. I've made my choice. I'm where I want to be."

"Okay."

"That's it? *Okay?*" Admittedly, I was skeptical. Mari was incredible, but she was also fucking stubborn. Giving in wasn't part of her vocabulary.

"I'm trying to take people at their word from now on."

No doubt that had everything to do with Dominic, but I wouldn't look a gift horse in the mouth. She was trying, and so was I. That was all that mattered.

"Don't manipulate me again, Nate. It won't end well."

Her warning was clear—*do it, and I walk.*

"I won't. I promise." I leaned forward and nipped her ear. "Let me make it up to you."

"Okay."

Fuck. Yes.

I ground her against my cock, rocking her hips so that the lace rubbed her just right. Two strokes in and there was a serious damp spot on my briefs, making me groan. "You're so wet, angel."

"You can thank Greyson for that."

"I know."

She glanced at me, and her eyes narrowed in fury. "That fucking asshole. *That's* why he wouldn't let me come?"

"He did it for me. He knew you'd be mad, but he hoped that you'd lean more to claiming than killing."

"I don't know if I like you three ganging up on me."

"I can think of a few applications that would make it worth your while."

"Hmm, maybe." She rocked over me again before she slid off my lap, spreading my legs so she could kneel between them.

Oh god. Just seeing her waiting for me, mouth so close to my cock, made it hard not to come. "You don't have to."

"I want to. Consider it payback for your little stunt back there."

Oh, she was going to torture me with a blow job. As she pulled out my dick and stroked it, I wasn't sure that would be a bad thing.

Then she slipped me into her mouth and went to town.

I'd had blow jobs before—I wasn't a monk—but *fuck.* I never wanted to leave Mari's mouth. She was warm and wet, and she had no problem taking me. Her hand was rough as she stroked me between sucks, dipping to pull my balls into her mouth one at a time.

Every time I felt myself tensing up, she backed away.

Over and over, she licked and sucked, teased and nipped until I thought my balls would fall off. When I was covered in sweat and nearly desperate to get inside her, I shoved my hand through her hair and pulled her off my cock. It was that or shove her down on it, and we hadn't established if that was okay yet. "Mari. Angel. *Please.*"

"Do you want to come, Nate?"

"*Yes.*"

"Tell me who you belong to."

Fuck me. "You."

"Whose cock is this?"

"Yours." All day, every day.

"Mine," she agreed, sliding her hand down my shaft again. "Only mine. So, give me what I want."

"Anything."

"Come down my throat. Then you can fuck me until I can't even crawl out of here."

Oh fuck. Fuck, fuck, fuck.

The moment she put her mouth on me again, I came. I couldn't help it. Her possessiveness turned me on. I wanted her to claim me, and I wanted to claim her back.

When I was done, she sat back on her knees and licked her lips.

"You even taste like mine," she whispered.

If I thought it would take me long to get hard again, I was wrong. Five words had me raring to go. "Get up here," I rasped.

"Excuse me?" Her eyes glittered as she leaned down, letting her warm breath caress my sensitive dick. It hurt so good. "You're not in charge here, Nate."

"I know. I'm sorry. *Please* sit on my cock."

"You're such a good boy."

I was. I really was. And I wanted my reward. "I'll beg if you want me to."

"Maybe next time. Do you have a condom?"

I dug into the briefs, happy that Dominic had told me to grab one. She rolled the condom on and stood, lifting her dress just enough to bare those panties to me before she slid them—and the dress—down her thighs. She straddled me again, and I reached for the hem, desperate to see her, but she smacked my hand away. "Nope. No pussy for you."

Record scratch. "Wait, what?"

"Oh, you can fuck me, but you can't look. No tasting either."

"Are you serious?" She wasn't going to let me touch her? I couldn't even watch as I fucked her for the first time?

"Deadly. Consider this payback for helping Greyson edge me."

I stared at the apex of her thighs, even as it was hidden behind the fabric. "Will we be even after this?"

"Yes."

"And I'll be able to watch next time?"

"You can take a fucking picture if it'll make you feel better." Her voice was tight as she ran herself over my cock, coating me in her.

"Fuck, fine." I'd make it up to her next time. I'd eat her out for hours as long as she let me fuck her.

"Good boy."

She lifted onto her knees, gripped my cock where she wanted it and slowly, *so fucking slowly*, slid me inside her.

"Mother*fuck*, angel. You feel so good. I knew you would. This pussy was made for me." I was babbling, but I couldn't stop.

"Maybe you were made for me," she panted, gripping my shoulders as she rolled those luscious hips over me.

I could believe it.

Mari kept the pace she wanted, but it was still too teasing. I needed more. I needed her to come.

"Touch yourself."

"Excuse me?"

"I can't touch you, so I want you to put your hand under that dress and rub your clit until you come on my cock. Will you do that for me because I've been a good boy and I want it?"

She narrowed her eyes, but I saw how much she liked hearing me say it. How much she wanted it to.

I was proven right when she was clamping around my dick in no time. "There you go. Fuck, you're so pretty when you come."

"Nate." Now she was begging, and I didn't mind at all. We could trade off. I'd be more than happy to play games with Mari every day of the week.

I gripped her hips over the dress, holding her still as I fucked into her from below with long, deep strokes. I wanted to ruin her.

"Oh fuck. Yes, yes, yes."

"Kiss me," I demanded, grinning when she immediately complied.

We slid together, grinding and gasping and touching as much as we could. The only sounds in the room were labored breaths, whispered words, the sound of skin on skin, and the faintest beat of the bass from the club.

It wasn't long before Mari was poised to come again. "That's right, angel. Soak my cock. Be my good girl this time."

"Yes." She clenched around me, and while she was still riding that orgasm, I pulled her against my chest and sped up, making sure every stroke hit her where I wanted.

I wanted her to ruin me too.

"You ever squirt before, baby?"

"Yes."

"Good. You're going to do it again. Soak me in your come so everyone out there knows who I belong to."

"Mine."

"Yours."

Mari screamed into my shoulder, her hips jerking as she came with a gush, and just as her last orgasm hit its crescendo, she fixed her teeth in the crook of my neck and bit. *Hard.*

I wasn't typically one for pain with my sex, but the feel of Mari's teeth in my skin and her pussy clamping hard on my cock was enough to make me blow.

"Mother*fuck*." I slammed into her, letting her body milk me with every stroke. It felt like the orgasm that wouldn't end, and I didn't mind at all.

I'd happily die buried in Mari's pussy.

We stayed connected as we came down, neither of us wanting to get up. I rubbed her back, pressed kisses and I'm sorrys into her skin. Finally, she leaned back with flushed cheeks and eyes bright with pleasure.

I'd never thought I'd seen a woman look radiant before, but Mari was that and more. She was everything.

"I really am sorry."

"I know, Nate. Let's stick to being honest from now on, though."

"Agreed, though I like the punishments."

"Of course you do," she laughed. Then her eyes caught on my neck, and her whole body winced. "I'm sorry, I—"

"Don't. I like it." And I did. It said that I was hers and anyone who saw me was going to know it because I was. I was hers, mind, body, and soul.

And I didn't give a single fuck who knew it.

Chapter 21
Mari

The week after the bachelorette party was quiet. Almost too quiet. With Aislynn and Cameron distracted by final wedding prep, family flying in from the Emerald Isle, and my entire household moving to a mansion on the waterfront, I expected Cash to blow up the plane or set one of my businesses on fire. Hell, I half expected him to mow someone over with a tank.

Instead, there wasn't a single whisper of him the entire time. It made me twitchy.

The only thing that kept me stable was knowing that we had eyes on at least one part of his operation and Derek was under constant surveillance. Thanks to Tennessee and Moore, we could watch him slowly disintegrate into paranoia in real time, and he'd been doing it beautifully. Especially once Jacob's body turned up.

Now, Derek couldn't take two steps without looking over his

shoulder. Exactly the way I wanted him. Broken men were far more willing to give me the information I needed, either with their mouths or their actions.

From what we could tell, the business Paul used as the GPS starting point wasn't Cash's, but since we'd put eyes on the entire neighborhood, we'd definitely seen an uptick in Aces. Even if it wasn't the right building, we were in the right place. On top of that, I'd sent a message to my uncle requesting the information on Cash he'd promised us. Apparently, he was having trouble with the Wolf, but he'd get it as soon as he could. Once we knew his history, we could guess his future.

Everything was coming together. I just had to be patient.

"You look beautiful, *mariposa*," Dominic said as he entered my room.

Since our evening together, he'd been around but not available, and I wasn't sure if he was trying to tease me or if the goal was to give me space. We'd crossed a line, but the more time went on, the more I thought it was good that we'd done it.

"You look handsome yourself." Dominic in jeans and a T-shirt was hot, but put him in a fully tailored suit with a pocket square to match my dress, and he was droolworthy. He'd even swept his hair back, though it still had that just-fucked look I liked so much. The man was a walking wet dream, and I had to clench my thighs together at the sight.

"If you're good, I'll show you what's underneath the suit." He said it with a flirty smile that fell soon after, and I hated it. Despite everything going on, the longer our estrangement continued, the less I wanted it to. Dominic had proven over and over again that he was there for me how I needed him to be. At some point, I either needed to trust him or let him go, and the idea of him finding happiness with someone else made my chest hurt.

Had he earned me, though? I thought so.

Still, it was a new kind of hell to take steps to bring him back into the fold and into my heart when he'd already decimated it once.

"I may take you up on that offer."

The way his smile brightened washed away the discomfort of taking that first step. I had made my decision. We would either live with it or we would die by it, but either way, we owed it to ourselves to try. *One more chance.*

Dominic crept closer, taking my hand in his. "I'm not going to let you down again, Mari."

"I know you won't." And I did. We'd have our issues, but he'd never hurt me like that again. He'd never question who I was. I had no doubt about that.

He'd walked into the fire with me, and we'd be reborn together.

"Where are the others?"

"Here." Greyson stepped in, with Nate close behind him.

If I thought that one of my men looked incredible in a suit, all three of them lined up together was a whole new experience. Each one had something on that matched my dress. For Dominic, it was the pocket square, for Nate, his button-up, and Greyson matched with the faint pinstripes of his suit. They were subtle but more than obvious to anyone with eyes and a brain.

I loved it.

"No one told me we were having matching costumes," I joked.

Greyson grinned. "All the better to claim your property with, my dear."

My eye roll was automatic. "You're not my property."

"We are," they argued. No question, no hesitation.

"Maybe not property, but we are yours, and it's best to walk into a situation like this showing that to everyone." Nate grinned, and I realized his shirt was unbuttoned, so my bite mark was visible. Another form of claiming for him that sent a bolt of heat through my body.

"We should go." Grey opened the door, leaning down for a kiss as I passed, and I couldn't help but grin.

Despite everything, these incredible men were not only mine—they *wanted* to make it obvious that they were. How had I gotten so lucky?

I wiped the smile off my face as we made our way through the house. The chatter of voices echoed down the hall, growing louder until we came upon the cluster of people standing at the bottom of the stairs. I spotted the usual suspects, including O'Bannon meandering through the throng, but no couple of the hour. Aislynn and Cameron would arrive after my entrance. O'Bannon glared, and I knew he was pissed that I'd snubbed his entrance. Well, too bad.

Everything he did in my city, he did because I allowed it. It was time he was reminded of that.

I walked down the stairs alone, allowing everyone to see me, though the soft footsteps of my men behind me said I had backup if anything went wrong. I refused to let it, though. Ash deserved two peaceful days to get married, and I was going to give them to her.

Before I could formulate a plan for mingling, one of the servers from Gilded stood before me, tray wobbling as she bowed slightly. I scrutinized her face as I took the offered glass. She looked so familiar. My suspicions mounted the longer she stayed in place, until finally Nate confirmed them.

"Ivy, what are you doing here?"

Right, Ivy. The girl who'd panicked when Nate killed the Ace.

"It's my last job working for Gilded," she said. "I'm leaving the city."

"That's a good idea," I told her, not unkindly. Things were going to get messy, and the last thing that we needed was someone unprepared for the chaos that was coming.

"Good luck. I hope things work out for you wherever you end up," Nate told her.

Ivy's eyes flicked to me, then the men behind me, with a look of barely banked terror. "I could say the same."

I almost laughed at what she probably viewed as a final act of bravery, but I didn't. Not everyone could handle what I was and how I lived, and that was okay. Besides, I refused to make her last moments with Nate be anything but pleasant.

"Where to first?" Grey murmured, taking his own glass before Ivy disappeared.

I opened my mouth to suggest charming Mama O'Bannon when Joaquin stomped his way through the crowd.

"Apparently our first stop is a showdown."

All three men tensed, and I could feel their combined protective energy coiled at my back, waiting to strike. For the first time, it felt like I had an army at my back. Like I wasn't alone. *That's so damn nice.*

Nate stepped up next to me, eyeing my uncle's movements as they got jerkier with every step in our direction. "I'm assuming there are rules for tonight. How far are we going to let him go?"

It was a good question. "Just far enough."

Nate's face screwed up. "I'm going to need more than that. Something more concrete, if possible. What should I be looking for?"

Trying to explain something that I'd learned as a child was harder than I expected, so I turned to the others for help.

"If he crosses the line to disrespect, we'll need to make an example of him," Dominic offered.

"Anything else?"

"If he tries to harm Mari or undermine this alliance, he dies here and now. There are too many eyes here to let it slide," Greyson added. Dominic quickly agreed.

Nate looked at me for confirmation, and I nodded, albeit reluctantly. "I prefer punishing my people in private, but we can't afford to look weak. If he makes a play, he dies."

Killing my uncle would have consequences I wasn't ready for, but if it came down to me or him, I'd deal with those later.

"Done." Nate's eyes narrowed in concentration. "He won't get through me."

"He won't get through any of us," Dominic corrected. "We're a team. It's going to take all of us to protect her."

For the first time, I really believed it. We were a team, and nothing was going to change that.

Before I could get too sappy, Joaquin was there, and so was the reek of whiskey.

"Are you halfway through the barrel, Uncle?" I asked, my lip curled.

"This is my only living son's wedding. Am I not allowed to enjoy myself?"

The hit landed but didn't penetrate. Rey was dead and I missed him desperately, but I couldn't let myself fall into depression over his loss again. None of us could afford it.

"Of course you are, but need I remind you that while we are family, we are *new* family. It would be best to keep your head in situations like this."

"Don't trust your new patriarch?" he sneered.

"Watch yourself," Dominic said, angling himself so that he was between us. It was instinctual, because sober Joaquin was annoying, but drunk Joaquin was a wild card. Still, I couldn't let Dominic defend me.

"Dominic." That was it. One word. I could feel the urge to deny me, to argue that he was doing his job as underboss. For a second, I worried we were right back where we started, with him thinking he knew best.

Then, he moved. Every step was clearly angry, but he did it, and that was more than I expected. It gave me more hope than anything else he'd done had.

He was trusting me to take care of myself, and once again, I felt hope bloom in my chest.

Could I really have it all?

Maybe. I just had to get through the clusterfuck that was the incoming war, then we'd see.

"What seems to be your problem today, Joaquin?" If I let him lead the conversation, we'd be finished on the Fourth of Never.

"My problem is we're shot gunning a wedding that should be the celebration of a lifetime. For Christ's sake, when your father ran the family, weddings took months—sometimes *years*—to prepare for."

"And yet, my father's dead," I said bluntly. "I'm running things now, and this is how we're doing it."

"But *why*?"

People were beginning to stare, and I didn't have the energy to watch him wrap the noose around his neck and pull. "Are you questioning my authority, Joaquin?"

"No, I'm asking for clarification."

"Then you should've done that two weeks ago," Greyson admonished. "*In private.*"

"How could I when she's been holed up with you three for months? Do you expect me to watch you fuck her?"

Nate stepped up, clenching his fists with anger. "Watch yourself."

Joaquin huffed with disbelief. "You've got the new guy fighting your battles now, Mari? This isn't how we trained you."

No, he and my father had trained me to fight my battles on my back, legs spread. Surprise. I'd found my own way to win.

If my uncle's words bothered Nate, he didn't show it. "I may be new, but I'm not stupid enough to poke the bear in front of a crowd. Keep going, and I'll grab popcorn while she rips your face off."

Joaquin opened his mouth, and I'd had enough.

"We're here because we need allies," I said clearly. "O'Bannon has the second-biggest territory in the city. If we don't maintain his alliance, we'll be dead."

Another drunken scoff, this one colored with anger. "So this is about *him*."

It didn't take a genius to know he was talking about Cash. "This is about staying alive, Joaquin. Fortifying our defenses in a time when war is imminent. It's about making smart decisions to prolong the survival of our family."

"What happens when that family decides that the way you're doing things no longer works?"

It had been years since any of my uncles had flat-out threatened me. Oh, they were big on sharp words and pointed tones, but threatening the current leader of the family was a big no-no, even if they all wanted to.

A mistake that Joaquin had just made in front of friends and foes alike. *Idiot.*

Dominic stepped into Joaquin's space so far, the latter was shoved off-balance. He stumbled a step before he caught himself. "I don't know what the hell you think you're doing, but you're not going to do it here."

Dominic's voice was low and dangerous, and it slid over my skin like velvet. I wanted him to talk to me like that while he fucked me senseless. *Would he do it?*

I bet he would.

Joaquin sneered, eyes roving over all four of us. "Of course you'd say that. You and your little friends are clearly pussy-blind."

"No, we're just not idiots. We follow the ruler of the city, the woman who's earned our loyalty," Greyson replied.

"For now. What happens when another leader comes in and snatches that crown off her head?"

All three men growled low and menacingly in their throats. I wasn't sure what it said about me that I liked it, but I did. I really, really did.

Because Joaquin was quickly veering into dangerous territory. Treasonous waters.

It was looking more and more like we'd be celebrating my cousin's wedding with a funeral.

Dominic leaned closer, keeping his voice low enough so he wasn't overhead by anyone but us. "I don't know what your problem is with Mari, but it needs to end. She's the only reason this fucking family has survived, and instead of being grateful, you're dead set on making yourself her enemy. Let me remind you what she does to her enemies, Joaquin. She doesn't let them go. She doesn't give them a pass. She *annihilates* them. It may take weeks or months, but she dismantles them until they're nothing but ashes on the wind. Don't put yourself on the opposing side when we all know you won't survive it."

Joaquin's face reddened with rage, and Greyson stepped forward. "Don't be an idiot, Joaquin. Sort your shit out before your prejudices get you killed in front of everyone."

"Until then, you can take your temper tantrum somewhere else." I flicked a negligent hand.

"This is my son's rehearsal dinner," he seethed.

"Then act like it. If you want to be here out of respect for Cameron, then you will do so with the utmost politeness you can muster. If you can't keep your mouth shut, I will have you escorted out. The last thing we need is your drama. Understood?"

"Understood," Joaquin said through his teeth after a long, tense silence.

The only reason he walked away was because I knew my cousin was having him followed. Day by day, my uncles were becoming more of an obstacle. Despite not wanting to lose more family, I was starting to see the situation as them versus us, and I intended to be the survivor of that Marcosa massacre.

Greyson cleared his throat, pulling me out of thoughts of duty, and I looked up to find Cameron staring down at his father's retreating form with something like malice.

"Keep them away from each other tonight."

"On it," the boys agreed.

With a few words and a smile, I introduced the happy couple.

Cameron and Aislynn were picture-perfect, her in a custom champagne dress and him in one of her suits, shirt a shade darker than her dress. He walked carefully, measuring his steps and making sure his bride didn't trip. He didn't have anything to worry about.

Like me, Aislynn had trained for this.

When they reached the bottom of the stairs, we led everyone to the dining room to eat. The space was filled with candles, flowers, and low lighting, so that even though it could easily seat thirty people, it was still intimate and comfortable. O'Bannon held court at the opposing head, a seat of honor. Not that he seemed to think so, as he spent more than one course complaining about everything from the speed of the wedding to the fact that it wasn't Catholic. The worst part was, I couldn't call him on any of it. Most territory leaders learned how to insult someone to their face without ever crossing the line of disrespect, and O'Bannon was no different. His words were honey-sweet, even if the point of them was closer to a wasp sting.

Still, we had to grin and bear it.

Each time his braying laugh filtered across the table, Dominic and Cameron both clenched their fists. If the Irishman wasn't careful, he was going to get much more than he bargained for during the wedding festivities.

As dessert was served, Cameron helped his bride stand.

"We don't want to keep anyone from the lovely dessert that Amara and her crew made, but we just wanted to thank you all for being here today." Ash's eyes gleamed, her mask perfect. "Especially Mari, for hosting not just the rehearsal dinner tonight, but the wedding. We wouldn't be here without you, and we both appreciate you so much."

This time, I knew the joy was manufactured. It was pure mischief, and I loved it. Especially when I realized Cameron shared it.

"To the O'Bannons, especially Aislynn's father. Thank you for giving us the best gift we ever could have asked for. Ash is everything we wanted for this family. Kind, smart, and beautiful. An asset we'll never take for granted."

Sean was seething mad, red rising up his face until I thought his head would explode at the table. His chair screeched across the floor, and heads turned toward the angry father of the bride.

"For now, we'll have dessert in the living room. Cigars will be available for anyone who wants them as well." Greyson stood, smoothly intercepting everyone's attention before O'Bannon could even open his mouth. All the guests looked between us, the tension crackling in the air at our unspoken conversation.

You won't get away with this, O'Bannon said.

Submit or die, I replied.

Because that was the truth. O'Bannon would either fall in line, or I would not only take his territory, I'd take his life too. He wanted an alliance with the queen; he got one.

His hand twitched, reaching for his side, and the tension ratcheted higher. Under the table, I slid my hand into the slit of my dress, palming my knife. If he moved, I'd hurl it through his throat and end the problem for good. Dominic, Greyson, and Nate were stiff next to me. Hell, even Joaquin was ready to throw down.

In the end, Ash was the one to defuse the tension. "I'd prefer if this marriage weren't sealed in blood, Father."

O'Bannon didn't back down for a heartbeat, two, three. Then he dropped his hand and stormed out of the room.

"What a fucking child," Ash muttered. Cameron and Nate grunted, making me laugh.

I threaded my arm through hers, leading our group to the other room. "Let him have his tantrum. We'll win in the end."

For the next hour, O'Bannon kept his distance. Oh, he seethed, snarled, and snapped at everyone who came within ten feet, but he stayed the fuck away from us. Considering my men were ready to skin him alive, it was the right choice. My cousin stayed close to Ash the entire time.

Until he didn't.

Cameron left the room after whispering in his bride's ear, and the second she was alone, O'Bannon took advantage. He moved toward his daughter with a head of steam. Nate and Grey tensed at my side, while Dominic's sharp eye watched from the other side of the room. Greyson stepped forward to intercept, only for Sean to stop short. He yanked his phone out of his pocket with frustrated motions, but whatever stopped him also seemed to help. The relaxation of his shoulders made mine tense.

Something wasn't right.

Sean threw a scathing glare at his daughter, nodded to his sons, and then all the men of the O'Bannon empire left without saying a word to their bride. It was beyond rude—it was unheard of.

What the fuck was going on?

"Because that wasn't suspicious at all," I said under my breath. Nate's laugh eased some of the paranoia. Though, it ratcheted back up when I found Joaquin similarly glued to his phone.

"What are the chances they got separate text messages?" I asked as Joaquin left in the same direction as O'Bannon.

"Slim to none," Cameron said as he threw an arm over my shoulder. I hadn't realized he'd come back in. "He's been sneakier than usual. Don't worry, though. I've got someone else tailing him tonight."

It seemed to be the theme of my empire lately. Nate's phone chirped once, twice, then three times. He frowned, pulling it out and frowning even harder. I peered over his shoulder to see MOM'S

NURSE flashing on the screen with a text that read, *Call me when you can. I have news.*

"Call them back," I said. Nate leaned down, ghosting his lips over my cheek with a grateful smile before heading out the door with his phone to his ear.

"His mom's sick, so he's in constant contact with her caregiver." I answered my cousin's obvious confusion.

Cameron hummed, eyes brushing over Nate before resting back on Ash. "I like him. He seems like a good guy. The others too."

"They are."

Cameron's smile was contagious, and I found my own echoing it. "Good for you. The last thing you need is mediocre dick for the rest of your life. You've earned better than that."

I laughed, because even though it felt crude to say it, I agreed. I'd been through enough. Maybe I really did deserve something easy, something long-lasting. Something stable.

Maybe those men were exactly the future I'd earned.

Chapter 22
Greyson

The morning of the wedding, Tennessee, Moore, and I led three separate teams to scour the grounds. We checked every garbage can, flowerpot, gate, and trash more than once. Slid a metal detector under every bush and hedge and ran scanners for bugs of every kind. Searched for everything that could've held a bomb or a weapon in it.

We checked from top to bottom once, twice, three times before anyone else was even awake, and when we were done, we looked through security footage.

We'd just finished by the time the wedding planners and their entourages arrived, and yes, we checked them out too.

Only after I was sure that absolutely nothing was going on in the house did I get ready for the wedding, and even then, I kept my phone on the security feeds the entire time.

I was pretty sure that Cash wasn't going to attack a situation so obviously perfect for him, but Mari didn't agree. She needed things to go well today for her own guilt and for her empire. The family.

That was why, when I found Sean O'Bannon with a bottle of whiskey in his hand at ten in the morning, I moved on autopilot.

Snatching the bottle, I body checked him into the corner of the room. Florists were everywhere, setting up vases overflowing with bouquets, but not one of them looked at us. They knew better than that.

"What the fuck do you think you're doing?" Sean growled, as if he had the means to intimidate me.

I wasn't sure he could intimidate an ant even when he wasn't trashed.

"I'm making something clear before the day begins. As a family, we prioritize one another. Our happiness, our joy, our lives. That means that on days like today, we like to put down the pitchforks and celebrate." I leaned close, dropping my voice in case any intrepid ears decided to listen in. "If you ruin this for anyone, you are not only going to end up on your daughter's shit list, you are going to be starting your alliance with the Marcosa family on shaky ground. Do you understand what I'm saying to you?"

O'Bannon was smart. He knew how to read between the lines. If he didn't tread carefully today, he would fuck up the entire purpose of the alliance, and the next time he called, Mari wouldn't come to help. Like he hadn't helped us in the ambush that had nearly stolen Mari's life. If he thought she'd forgotten that, he was an even bigger idiot than I imagined.

Family was family, and he wasn't one of us. Yet.

With angry eyes and a tight jaw, Sean nodded before snatching the bottle out of my hand again and stomping off. I rubbed my face with a sigh, knowing it likely wasn't the only temper tantrum I'd have to quell. Sometimes made men were no better than toddlers fighting over a toy.

Exhaustion weighed heavily on me, but I couldn't stop. Not

until the newlyweds were safely on their way out of the city and Mari was back in my arms. It was my job, both as her partner and as one of her seconds.

With O'Bannon taken care of, I checked my watch, only to grimace. If I wanted to see Mari before she left for Aislynn's suite, I needed to move. Sprinting up the stairs, I took the corners at a clip. I made it to her room, only to find that instead of the woman I wanted, two other men waited.

"Seems like we all had the same idea," I said, moving to sit in one of the armchairs. Dominic's surly self was leaning against the wall as always, while Nate was laid out on the bed like he was seconds away from a nap. Considering he'd been with Moore's team all morning surveying the estate, I could relate.

"She left early," Dominic grumped.

"So, what do we do now?" Nate asked. "Do I have time to sleep?"

"Now we go find the groom."

No one but Cameron and Aislynn would stand at the altar, but the three of us had somehow become Cameron's pseudo-grooms-men. Which made it our responsibility to make sure that he made it to the altar in perfect condition. Thankfully, he wasn't terrible to babysit on a normal day. As long as Joaquin stayed away, I didn't think there'd be a problem.

"Think he'll act like he's not excited to marry Ash?" Nate popped off the bed and went to the closet, pulling out all three garment bags. "We all know he's interested."

"Maybe, but Cameron's version of interest isn't everyone else's. He'll be interested on the principle that she's his and his alone."

"For now," Dominic corrected.

No one knew what their marriage would look like in the future, but for now, monogamy was the game.

With nothing left to say, Dominic and I grabbed our bags from Nate, and we all headed toward Cameron's suite. I kept my eyes peeled, desperate for even a glimpse of Mari, a moment to reassure her. Sadly, I got none, so I pulled out my phone.

> Checked everything. We're good. Don't stress. Wish I could've seen you already.

> I needed to hear that. Thank you. You'll see me soon.

> Maybe I'll steal you away later. I love you.

> I wouldn't complain. Love you too.

Smiling, I tucked my phone away and thought of where in the day Mari and I could disappear without raising suspicions.

Is this what our wedding will be like? Missed glances and stolen moments?

The thought shook me, causing me to trip over my own feet. Was I really thinking about marrying Mari?

Yes. Yes, I was.

I'd wanted her our whole lives and only stayed away for Antoni. Even though we hadn't been together long, I couldn't remember why we were waiting. Most people needed time to get to know someone before marriage, but we'd been best friends since birth. She knew everything about me and vice versa. Would it really be rushing if we got married soon?

I didn't think so, but I wasn't the only person in the equation. Mari had to agree. I knew she would, though. I had no doubt that one day, Marianna Marcosa would be my wife.

The idea of Mari with my ring—the one I'd bought years ago and kept hidden outside the city—on her finger made me smile. I just needed her to know for sure that I was fine with the others too. Practice and theory were two different things, and as much as I didn't mind having the idiots around, I hadn't had a need to challenge my perception of the situation either. Kissing was one thing, but could I handle more? Could I handle knowing that they were fucking her when I wasn't?

I'd handled Dominic just fine. I'd helped Nate win her over.

Hell, I'd had the image of both those situations in my head more than once while I was alone.

It wasn't that I was interested in the others; it was the idea of Mari's pleasure that got me hot. I wanted to see her fall apart in front of me, and I couldn't always focus on her when I was part of the action, but more than one of us with her gave me the perfect opportunity.

Now that Dominic was back in the game, my wildest fantasies could come true. I just had to get the others on board too. I doubted they'd mind, though. We all wanted Mari to be happy. What better way than to give her all the pleasure she could want?

As the picture formed in my head, I knew that it was perfect. We were all going to have a memorable night.

My smirk was the first thing Cameron saw when he flung open the door. Jerking back, he narrowed his eyes at me. "Who's dying today?"

"No one, if we can help it."

"Then what's with the creepy-ass smile?"

My grin got wider as I stepped past him and hung my garment bag in the closet. "Just came up with a good plan, that's all. Happy wedding day, by the way."

"Thanks," he said skeptically. "Do I want to know about this plan?"

"Considering it's about us fucking your cousin—"

He held his hands up. "Nope, nope. We're not doing that."

"Hence why I didn't tell you."

"Right. I'm going to take a shower while you three do whatever it is you're doing." He was already in the bathroom, shower running, by the time Dominic and Nate stepped in and closed the door to the suite behind them.

"So, what's this plan?" Nate inquired.

"I think we've been going easy on Mari."

Dominic snorted, dropping onto the couch in that lazy sprawl he preferred. "I think she's got enough going on without us making problems."

"Not problems. Solutions."

"Are you planning on killing Cash while she sleeps? 'Cause I'd be down for that," Nate said.

"I'm not talking about Cash. I'm talking about this relationship she's got with all of us."

Dominic's eyes narrowed. "She's not worried about the three of us."

"Not now that you've sorted things out—kudos for that, by the way—but we also haven't shown her just how good it can be between us. No date nights out, no play, no romance."

"There's been no time."

"It's been all about survival," I agreed. "That's why I think we should make time."

Nate, who had taken his seat in one of the chairs across the room, leaned forward, elbows on his knees. "What exactly are we thinking?"

"How do you feel about a special after party?"

When they grinned too, I knew I had the right idea.

Tonight was the start of something new for all of us.

* * *

The wedding went off without a hitch. Aislynn's dress was perfect, not just for her, but for the mansion venue Mari secured as a last-minute gift to the couple. Even Cameron had trouble taking his eyes off Ash as she walked up the aisle to their future.

I wasn't sure if it was just me, but it looked like he watched her like she was his everything. Did he love her? I hoped so. Or at least, I hoped for his sake that they found even an inkling of the kind of love Mari and I had. One that would transcend lifetimes, even if it was built in friendship.

As the two said their vows pledging themselves to the other forever, I kept one eye on Mari and not only because we were surrounded by allies and potential enemies. Despite how quickly we'd pushed the wedding, everyone important had shown up. Public figures, police chiefs, judges, and lawyers all sat in awe of the couple of the day. Clients and the other leaders of the city stayed silent as they watched history being made. All watched, not just the alliance between the two families, but the Marcosa queen herself.

She had to be perfect, and she was. She didn't show an ounce of uncertainty, not a single tear—though she dabbed her eye like there was.

But I knew her better than almost anyone.

Longing filled her eyes as she watched Aislynn and Cameron slip rings on each other's fingers. She wanted something like that. Not an arranged marriage, but the commitment between two people. The echo of her needs so soon after I'd come to terms with my own made my heart race.

One day, I'll give you the world, reina.

When the wedding was over and sealed with a kiss, Mari stood to congratulate them both at the altar, and I took that moment to lean over toward Dominic and Nate, whispering the truest thing I'd ever said. "I'm going to marry that woman."

Nate laughed under his breath, while Dominic narrowed his eyes in irritation. Though, I wasn't sure if he was irritated at me or himself. We both knew he could have had her as his wife if he'd made different choices.

For now, there was no world in which Mari accepted a proposal from him anytime soon. I had a bet with Cameron that it would be at least a year before she even considered discussing it with him. The other one, however... I was pretty sure Mari would throw the rule book out for Nate.

He was her Achilles' heel.

"You don't have a problem with that?" I turned to Nate, finding his eyes glued to Mari's ass. To be fair, she was in a jumpsuit that molded to it perfectly, so I couldn't fault him for looking, but we were in public. I slipped my hand behind him, casually smacking him upside the head. He started but turned to me with an unrepentant grin.

"We aren't there yet," he said simply, though he didn't sound sure. "I'm fine as boyfriend for now."

"Boy *toy*," Dominic corrected.

"Nah, we're past that. I'm aiming higher." We didn't say anything else, not only because Mari came back, guiding us out of the room just after the happy couple.

As she shook hands in the receiving line, I stayed right behind her. I watched everyone who passed, eyeing them as if I could see beneath their clothes to any weapons they could be holding. All the while waiting for a lull to lean in and whisper in her ear.

Finally, I got it.

"We're going to have this one day," I told her. "The party, the celebration, the love. Maybe it'll just be us. Maybe it'll be the other two idiots too. But we're going to have this. I promise you."

Mari said nothing, but the corner of her mouth tipped up in something close to a smile, though it was gone before it could really manifest. I wasn't worried, however.

I had no clue what our future held, but I did know that I'd be at Mari's side, no matter what. Where I belonged. Where I'd always belonged.

Chapter 23
Mari

"You can't glare at him all night," I warned, sitting down beside the irritated groom. The reception had been going for two hours, and he'd been glaring at his father the entire time.

"He's a shady fuck," Cameron spat, downing his glass of whiskey and slamming it down next to three others. Discreetly, I glanced at Greyson, who counted the glasses with a wince.

We both knew a drunk Cameron was a combative one.

Knowing Aislynn was already worried about her father starting a fight at the reception, I decided to poke at my cousin's protective instincts. Subtlety worked well with Cameron, but in certain situations, the best option was to beat him with the right choice.

"Lots of shady fucks here tonight," I said innocently. "Who will protect your bride if you get too drunk?"

Cameron twisted, glaring at me, and I fought my smile. "I'm not drunk. I'm numbing myself. Unless you want me to kill him tonight."

Though my life would've been easier without Joaquin, I declined. We'd managed to make it through the wedding and dinner without a fight. I was hoping to continue the streak. "That would be one hell of a way to celebrate, but I'd prefer to end the day without bloody clothes."

"Hence the drink."

"What if it's not what Aislynn needs, though?" My cousin's face lightened at the mention of his wife, and I pushed forward, hoping to get him to listen. And if I embellished a little, I knew Ash would forgive me. "She needs you now more than ever. She needs you to guard her and protect her from her family, and she needs you to make sure she's taken care of. That's your only goal for tonight. Take care of the bride."

"But he—"

"Is tomorrow's problem," I interrupted. "Focus on your bride, Cameron. She's all that matters."

He didn't like it, but he didn't have to. Everything I said was the truth. This was his wedding too. The last thing he needed to worry about was Marcosa drama.

He lifted his hand, motioning for another drink, and I slammed it down. The server took one look at me and bolted into the crowd.

"What the hell?"

Oh, goodie. He was glaring at me now. "I think you've had enough."

Another glare and a slight snarl. I carefully slid over my untouched glass of water with a single finger. "Take this and go to Aislynn. Try to enjoy the rest of your night. This time tomorrow, you'll be alone in paradise."

It was very obviously a command, one he took. Thankfully.

Cameron didn't look back as he snatched the glass and found his way to his bride. Ash looked relieved that he'd come for her, blushing under her makeup when he wrapped a hand around her waist.

They look perfect. I just hoped they were happy.

I wasn't alone for long before someone else took my cousin's place.

Two-Bit had cleaned up for the occasion. Face shaved, hair slicked back; he'd even put on a nice suit. Everything about him spoke of someone's first taste of having money, all flash and pomp, but it didn't quite fit him right. I didn't have an adequate way to describe it, but I got the feeling he was used to *more*. Like maybe he was comfortable with the finer things in life already.

But how did that happen to a kid who supposedly grew up in the worst parts of the city? The nagging sensation that Two-Bit wasn't what he seemed poked at me.

"Congratulations on the union," he said, shaking me out of my thoughts.

"Thanks for coming." I sipped from the glass Greyson had quietly slipped me before heading back into the crowd, grateful when I discovered it was water. I had no problem letting loose, but an event with every potential enemy besides Cash in the room wasn't the place for it.

Two-Bit snorted. "Like I'd miss history in the making. Never thought I'd see the day O'Bannon and Marcosa would unite."

"You're new. Besides, times change," I said, wondering what he wanted.

He let the silence stretch, glancing at me before looking across the room. "Yes, they do."

When his eyes fixed on a certain point, I had to force myself not to react.

Rafael stood next to Cameron and Aislynn, obviously congratulating the couple. He was all smiles, all kindness. It made me very leery. Family or not, I didn't know my uncle well enough to predict whether he was here as friend or foe.

Nate and Dominic watched him with something like alarm in their eyes, but I didn't know what the best course of action was.

I hadn't invited the Osorios. I certainly hadn't invited Rafael, who had been slinking through Seattle for the last few weeks. He touched base here and there, but in general, he kept his own space, and that was irritating enough.

He had information to give us, and he hadn't delivered. The longer he dragged it out, the more I wondered if he was playing me. And if he was, what the fuck was he doing in my city?

"Seems like you have more than enough allies now. I hope it doesn't bite you in the ass."

That prickling sensation at the back of my neck intensified, and I remembered just how much Two-Bit knew.

My mother. The Osorios.

Was he a plant? How did he have information that nobody should have known?

My paranoia was getting worse every day, but it didn't feel out of place. Two-Bit was a master at hiding things. Peering at him from the corner of my eye, I leaned back, playing casual. "You're a very smart man. Too smart to let random information slip when you shouldn't. Is there something I need to know?"

"Not necessarily," he said, copying my posture with a lazy sip of his drink. I could smell the whiskey. Top-shelf, but a brand I hadn't included in the bar. Which meant he'd brought it himself.

Who the fuck was this guy?

"And yet your *not necessarily* comes from knowing information that has been practically burned from the history books. Who's your resource for that?"

His smile reminded me of secrets whispered in the dark and never repeated. "Do you really think I'm going to give you that?"

Of course he wouldn't. Nobody would give up their intel source without a fight, especially one who obviously had access to more than they should.

The fact was, there were only a few ways he could know about the hidden parts of my life, and none of them were good. Lucky for him, I didn't want to wage another war when I had at least one on the horizon, but I no longer believed that Two-Bit could be ignored. Greyson had to look into him again. Soon.

Knowing that, I glanced back into the crowd. "Keep your source close. I don't like people knowing too much about me."

The threat was clear, but Two-Bit didn't seem concerned. He dipped his head, though I saw the little smile that spoke heavily of *I know something you don't know.* "Whatever you say, Mari. You're the queen."

"I hope you remember that. I'd hate for our future conversations to get messy."

"I assure you, I'll never forget." He knocked his knuckles against the table once before leaving me, only for Shara to take his place.

The chair was turning into a fucking merry-go-round.

"Isn't she gorgeous?" Shara gushed; eyes glazed from too much booze.

I peered over to find Ash smiling and laughing on my cousin's arm, and she really did look incredible. Like every other bride. Happy, hopeful, in love. "She's beautiful. Her team did a great job. Even Gretchen."

The old dragon glared at me from the other side of the room like she'd heard every word, and I gave her a cheeky finger wave. Movement had my eyes snapping over to find Rafael moving toward me.

Well, fuck.

Hastily, I turned to Shara, who hadn't seen him yet. "Do you remember when I told you about my uncle? The new one."

"The one who looks like Antoni." She bobbed her head to the music, looking as carefree as Ash. I hated to ruin it for her.

"He's here, and he's coming over. If you'd like to leave now, no one will fault you for it."

Hesitation crossed her features along with a longing so intense it made my own chest ache. Then she straightened her shoulders, her eyes clearer than before. "No, I'll stay."

I'd never been prouder of a person in my life. If given the chance to meet my dead beloved's doppelgänger, I wasn't sure I'd do it, but Shara wasn't me. She was born to confront pain, to heal wounds.

Under the table, I gripped her hand, hoping it gave her strength.

"I'll be here the whole time," I promised as Rafael stopped on the other side of the table with a slight inclination of his head. The only indication that Shara saw him was the tight grip she had on my fingers.

"Mariana, you look beautiful."

"Thank you, Uncle. This is Shara, Antoni's fiancée."

Rafael held out his hand, but Shara was frozen. I turned to look at her, and her face gutted me. All I saw was heartbreak, pain, and grief so acute it swam in her eyes. My chest squeezed just looking at her. "Shara?"

"Antoni," she choked, tears falling down her cheeks.

Everything about Rafael softened. He leaned forward and gripped her other hand gently, bringing it to his mouth for the faintest kiss. "I'm so sorry for your loss. My nephew was a good man."

Shara stared, taking in everything from the laugh lines around his mouth to the streak of white in his hair. Then he smiled, and all at once, she seemed to shake from her stupor. She flung my hand away and nearly toppled the chair in her haste to gain some distance. "I have to go."

Before we could say anything, she disappeared into the crowd. Greyson caught my eye, motioning that he'd make sure she got home. Knowing Shara, she'd hole herself up inside her apartment until she was ready to come up for air.

I made a mental note to send a delivery of her favorite foods and movies to keep her company. "I didn't mean to upset her," Rafael said, staring after her with self-loathing.

I waved him off with a sad smile. "Antoni was the love of her life. Her soulmate. I don't think she'll ever be over the loss of him."

"I doubt it," Rafael agreed. "It's funny, though. She's exactly my son's type. Must run in the family."

For some reason, I'd never considered that Rafael had children. I wanted to know more about them, but we were still on unstable footing. I couldn't give him something to hold over my head. The family tree would have to wait.

I pointed a sharp-tipped nail at him. My fingertips had healed enough for nail extensions until my own nails grew back. It wasn't perfect, but I couldn't wear the gloves forever. "You better not have ideas for Shara. She's not for sale. Especially if your son looks anything like you."

"I never said I did. I merely mentioned that she was exactly his type. As for his looks..." Shadows passed over Rafael's face. "He takes after his mother."

Grief was something I knew well, but I hadn't recognized it on his face before. Maybe because he was older, more settled into his own pain, if that was a thing. Still, I saw it then. "I'm sorry for your loss, Uncle."

His smile was more of a grimace, but he did his best. "It's in the past. As much as I wish it was possible, nothing brings back the ones who've left."

I could see his desperate need for a break, so I gave him one. "How is Grandfather?"

Had I not been watching, I wouldn't have seen the slight wince. It made me nervous. Getting into a war with Cash was one thing. Pissing off the Wolf was another entirely.

"Angry," Rafael finally admitted. "I knew he would be, but he's making things difficult."

"Hence why we haven't gotten our information." I'd known that was the case, but it still sucked. We were depending on Rafael's intel. If he couldn't get it... "Do we need to rethink our plan?"

"No. I'll get what you need. It's just taking me more time than I thought it would."

As O'Bannon glared at me from one side of the room and Joaquin from another, I sighed, though I tried not to let the weariness show on my face. "Time is the one thing we don't have."

"I'll fix it," Rafael promised, but how much did his promises count for? The truth was, I didn't know him. He could've been lying through his teeth, and I'd be none the wiser.

When I didn't answer, Rafael turned as if he'd walk away, and I couldn't help myself. "Will you be all right with...things?" I didn't want anyone knowing who Rafael was, and I definitely didn't want to let people know how close the Wolf was to our doorstep.

If the other territory leaders got wind of the danger, they'd kill me the second they could.

"I'll handle my father. You don't have to worry about me, *tesorita*."

But I would. I always worried about my people. That was my job. Regardless of how uncertain I was about him, Rafael was family.

"I hope you're right."

He was almost out of earshot when he muttered, "So do I."

After Joaquin and O'Bannon took their separate entourages and left, the reception felt almost normal. The bride and groom cut the cake. They smiled. They drank. They had too much fun. Then we cheered them off as they left for their honeymoon, as far away from the city as they could safely get.

No bloodshed. No death. No threats and no Cash.

It was as perfect as it could've been.

With the guests of honor gone, the crowd disbanded, and people congratulated me on everything from the party to the alliance before heading out. I was watching the last of them climb into their cars—thank god for chauffeurs—when arms banded around my waist. I felt a moment of tension before I realized who it was and relaxed in his grip.

"I have a surprise for you," Greyson said. It wasn't the words that clued me in, but the timbre of his voice. Slow and teasing, like he wanted to say every word against my skin. "Are you too tired?"

"I'm never too tired for you."

"Perfect."

"Where are the others?" I asked as he pulled me along behind him. I'd been too busy networking and threatening Joaquin with bodily harm if he drank another drop of booze to keep track of my men.

A travesty when they looked good enough to eat.

"You'll see."

Moore and Tennessee shared a grin as Grey all but dragged me past them. "We'll get the stragglers out and lock down the house. Have a great night."

We were almost upstairs when I whispered, "Do they know something I don't?"

"Possibly."

"Why doesn't that make me as nervous as it should?"

His dark chuckle sent a delicious tingle down my spine. Oh yeah, I was in for it.

Back at my suite, anxiety crept through me as Grey gripped the door handle but didn't open it.

"Should I be nervous?" I asked.

"You know I won't do anything to hurt you."

I don't know what I was expecting, but it certainly wasn't Nate and Dominic sitting on the bed together.

"Are we having a family meeting?"

Joy lit up in each one of their faces at the term, and I realized that all of us had the same desire in life.

We wanted a family of our own. *This* family.

The realization caught my breath, and something like gratitude warmed me from the inside out.

"We realized earlier that we haven't had time to show you the good part about having so many partners." Greyson closed the door, locking it behind him, the sound echoing in my ears like a gunshot.

My pulse tripped because all three watched me like I was their last meal and they couldn't wait to eat.

"Someone's always available when I'm in the mood." I joked.

"Something like that," Dominic said, thumbing his bottom lip.

Nate stood, eyes roving my body as he circled me. "This jumpsuit is incredible," he whispered, stepping so close I could feel his breath on my neck. "I've been staring at your ass all day."

My laugh was strangled by the playful nip he gave my earlobe.

"I can't wait to take it off." His fingers brushed my back, and then the fabric loosened as he slowly, so slowly, unzipped me.

"What are you doing?" I asked, glancing between Dominic and Grey.

"We're showing you how good it can be," Nate said. "All three of us."

All three of them.

Oh fuck. Desire swamped me.

I couldn't say I hadn't dreamed about having them together, but I'd never thought it was possible. Things still felt fragile, and I didn't want to ruin them by asking. I figured I'd wait it out and use the fantasy as spank-bank material until they were ready.

But all three of my men touching me, teasing me, pleasing me? I wanted it *bad*.

Nate helped me out of the jumpsuit, though he clicked his tongue in disagreement when I went for my shoes. "Leave them on."

"They're sharp."

"I like the marks."

"I know." He'd kept my bite in clear view until it faded, then asked me to do it again. He liked the idea of being marked by me, and it turned me on to see it.

Nate laid the fabric carefully over the edge of a chair before taking his place next to Dominic again. "Unbelievable."

"Goddamn," Dominic cursed he when got a good look at what I wore underneath. "You look amazing."

Two down, one to go.

"Well, how do I look, Grey?"

"Absolutely irresistible." My first love circled me, hands sliding around to cover my rib cage as he pressed himself against me. I could feel the hardness of him against my ass as he slid one hand into my panties.

He glided his fingers through my folds, dipping inside me just far enough to wet them before coming back to my clit. "But you know that already, don't you? Is that why you're wet? You know what you do to us, don't you? It gets you hot knowing that we're aching for you every time you're in the room. That we want you more and more with every breath. I think it makes you feel in control."

It did. As Grey slipped my panties to the side with his hand, letting the others watch as he worked my clit like a pro, my men looked at me like I was their salvation. Wearing nothing but hand-sewn lingerie and deadly high heels, I'd never felt more powerful. I never wanted it to end.

"Greyson," I breathed, pressing myself against him. I needed more. Wanted him.

"Relax, *reina*. I'll give you what you need."

"We all will," Nate corrected. His eyes were locked on my pussy as Grey slipped his fingers inside me, stroking as he ground his palm against my clit.

"Oh fuck." I couldn't help myself as my hips rode his hand. Just having the guys watch had me close to coming already. "Grey."

"Patience, baby." Nate came to my side, running his hand along my collarbone and down my chest until he had it wedged in the cup of my bra.

The thought of destroyed lace made me tense. "Don't you dare rip it."

It seemed like a silly thing to get mad at when I could afford more, but I loved this set.

"Never. I want to see it more than once." Carefully, he pulled off the bra, the slightly chilled air hitting my already sensitive nipples. "You're so pretty."

Nate wrapped his lips around one, biting hard before giving it a long suck. He did it again and again, using his teeth to pull my nipple taut, making it ache before he soothed it with his tongue. Grey found his pace, fucking me ruthlessly in time with Nate's attentions until I was panting and whimpering against them.

All the while, they made sure Dominic could see everything.

The first orgasm stole my words, and the second stole my breath.

I was soaked and panting and wobbling in my fucking shoes. "What now?"

Greyson grinned, eyes dark as he sucked me off his fingers. "We fuck until you can't go anymore."

Chapter 24
Mari

O h, fuck *yes*.

"Who's going first?" I asked as I crawled onto the bed, panties gone. Their deep groans as I swung my hips were music to my ears.

"Do you have a preference?" Greyson asked.

"Just curious."

"All you need to know is we've got you." Nate climbed onto the bed, wrapped his hand around my neck, and lifted until I was kneeling with my back to his chest. His other hand teased its way down my spine to squeeze my ass, and he groaned when my thighs clenched, pressing the tips of my heels into his legs. "How comfortable are you with anal?"

I'd been too busy the last few weeks to have it recently, but Greyson and I included it in our activities often. "I'll need some prep, but I'm not a newbie."

"I am."

I tried to twist, but Nate's grip held me immobile. Knowing I couldn't move unless he let me made me dizzy with want. I loved when they took control. "You've never done it before?"

"You're my first."

The traitorous, jealous part of myself preened with happiness. *I'm your only.*

I didn't say it, but it felt obvious to me.

Nate was mine. They were all mine. I'd tattoo it on them if they needed the reminder.

Grey pulled a bottle of lube out of the drawer, and while Nate pressed kisses and nips along his favorite path up my neck, he worked his wet finger into my ass a little at a time. I could hear the slick of the lube as he worked himself too.

When my pussy clenched on nothing, Nate felt it too. His soft laugh ruffled my hair. "Fuck, this is going to be fun. I'm so glad I waited."

I'm so glad I waited for you, went unspoken, but I knew that's what he meant.

Greyson stood next to us, watching Nate warm me up, but Dominic settled in against the pillows.

"You don't want to watch the show? Oh god," I exclaimed, panting as Grey slipped his fingers inside me again so my pussy was full too. I was so full. "Fuck me, that feels so good. More. I want both of you."

I hadn't meant to say it, but I was still surprisingly disappointed when Grey answered. "Not tonight. You need more practice before we decide to double-team you."

Twisting, I opened my mouth for a scathing response of *Fuck practice,* but Grey rotated his hand just right, stealing my breath. "I'm not going to let you get hurt because we want to fuck you all night. We take this slow, and soon enough, you can have all of us at once."

It was reasonable, but I was so far past reason, I wanted to argue anyway. As if he knew I would, Nate added another finger and squeezed my neck. It wasn't hard, just enough to get my attention, and damn, he had it.

"Next time, angel," he promised. "We'll take turns fucking you into the mattress tonight, but next time, we'll all take a hole."

Holy. Fuck. "Please."

Hadn't meant to say that out loud either. Whoops.

"As for your question, you are the show, baby." I couldn't respond when I was *this* close to coming. Especially not when Dominic's filthy grin melted my brain cells. Temporary insanity, I hoped. "I'm not interested in either of them. I'm interested in you. How you feel. What you like. What you want. Fuckboy's just another toy in my arsenal."

"Fuck you, asshole," Nate laughed.

Dominic just grinned, but I knew he meant every word. "You want to come again, baby?"

"Yes."

"Is she ready?" Dominic asked.

Nate and Greyson both did something at the same time, and the slow simmer of an orgasm they'd been stoking raged red-hot. "Fuck, fuck, *fuck*."

"I'll take that as a yes." Dominic leaned forward, hovering over my mouth so I could feel his command on my lips. "Show us how pretty you are when you come, *mariposa*. I want the whole house to hear it."

Looking away wasn't an option as the orgasm swept through me, tightening every muscle in delicious agony until I was crying out just like Dominic wanted. Greyson and Nate fucked me through it before they both slowly pulled out.

I'd never felt so empty, and Dominic's smirk said he knew it.

At the edges of my vision, Grey sat back, mirroring Dominic on the opposite side of the bed. Too far to touch, but close enough to see every reaction. "Delicious as always, *reina*."

Christ. These men.

Dominic looked me over with that irritatingly smug smile. "You looked like you enjoyed that. Ready to be a good girl and get another?"

No. "Yes."

Four orgasms in a night felt greedy, but I didn't care. I wanted it, even if I was sure it would kill me.

"Face against the mattress, baby. Give Nate a good view while he fucks you."

"No." Before I could catch my breath, Nate flipped me onto my back, yanking me down until our hips were flush. Once again, he wrapped a hand around my throat, gently tipping my face so all I could see was him and his lubed-up cock.

"If I'm going to take your ass, I want to see your face when I do it. Wrap those legs around me, baby. Give me a good visual for later."

Dominic choked on a laugh as I did what he wanted. "Christ. Fuckboy's got a mouth on him."

"You have no idea," I joked, trying not to wiggle as Nate tried to find the right position.

"Put this under her hips." Grey tossed us a pillow, and Nate slipped it under me, elevating my hips to a position I knew would make it easier to take me and more pleasurable for the both of us.

"You ready, angel?"

"I can take anything you give me," I promised, pulling Nate down for a kiss. "Do it."

He pressed in slowly, his brows furrowed with pleasure so good it was painful. The kind that made you worry you couldn't hold out long enough. "Oh fuck."

"Yeah?"

"Yeah. I still love your pussy, but this is unreal." He pulled out, slowly pushing back inside me with a low groan. "I want to feel you stuffed with cock next time."

"I can go get a toy," Dominic offered, but Nate shook his head.

"No toys tonight. Just us. Just this."

I had no air to answer when Nate's thrusts changed. He picked up his speed a little now that I was warmed up to take him, but each one drove him as deep as he could go.

It felt good, but I wanted more, so I slipped my hand between my legs. Greyson shuffled over, slapping my fingers out of the way. "We're taking care of you tonight. If you want something, ask for it."

"I want to come."

"Of course you do," he agreed. "Do you want me to rub that pretty little clit until you do?"

Was that a serious question? "Obviously."

Grey glared down at me but still went back to my clit, though he made sure he was *barely* touching it.

Nate noticed and laughed, the sound so low and dark, it sent goose bumps rippling over my arms. "Better be careful, or Greyson may decide not to let you come at all."

"That seems more like Dominic's speed," I panted. Another thing I hadn't meant to say. I blamed Nate's magic dick because, newbie or not, what he was doing was working for me.

Three orgasms deep and a fourth coming on fast. Maybe I don't need Grey's help after all.

Dominic laughed, shifting so I could see him. "It is, and I can't wait to play with you, baby."

It was then that I realized he was still dressed. Fucker even had his shoes on.

My stomach dropped at the idea that he was just spectating. I didn't know how they'd planned things or what we were going to do, but I wanted all three of them. It felt important.

"Are you joining us?" I asked.

"Do you want me to?"

I didn't even have to think about my answer. Dominic had always been mine, and he belonged with us.

"Come here, Dominic." In a flash, he was naked and at my side, dipping to press his mouth against mine in a hot kiss.

Just like every other time we kissed, Dominic consumed me. He breathed me in like I was the only air he needed and held me like I was the most precious thing in his world. For the first time in so long, I believed he actually meant it.

Dominic pulled back enough to whisper in my ear. "I won't fuck you tonight."

Oh, come on. "Are you fucking kidding me?"

"No, I'm not."

Whoops, said that out loud too.

No part of me was willing to push past a hard no, but— "Why?"

"I'm not letting our first time after so long be in front of these two assholes. I'll make you come and I'll join the party, but when I fuck you again, it's just for the two of us."

I couldn't exactly argue with that, so I didn't. "You owe me a rain check."

"Don't worry, baby. I'll be collecting sooner than you think." With a devious grin, he lifted his head and commanded the others. "Flip her over."

They looked at one another for a moment, and then hands were on me. Pulling me back onto my knees.

Dominic slid underneath me, planting my pussy firmly on his face while Nate slid back into my ass. I was so close to having all of them. I leaned over to take Grey in my mouth, but he redirected me to Dominic.

"Come back to me later," he said with a grin. "I want to enjoy this before you make me come."

Dominic, who had attacked my clit with fierce nips and bone-shaking licks, must not have heard, because he jumped when my mouth closed around him, shoving himself farther inside. I felt his growl against my skin, and it just made me want more, so I took him deeper, harder.

All the while, Nate's slow, deep thrusts were sending me closer and closer to the edge. The harder I sucked Dominic, the harder he worked me. The more I squirmed, the deeper Nate went. We were an endless circle of pleasure, with Greyson stroking his cock as our only spectator.

We are absolutely doing this again.

My orgasm crested in no time, and I pulled myself off Dominic, begging and pleading with every breath I had for something, anything.

Release. Relief. Control.

"Please, please, please, please, please."

Nate cursed as I clenched around him.

"I'm not going to last long, so neither are you." One hand tightened on my hip while the other fisted in my hair and guided me back to Dominic's cock. "If we're going to come, he should too. Suck him off, angel. Show him how good that mouth is."

He released my hair in favor of a grip on my shoulder, pulling me back onto his cock so that every thrust was deeper than before. Harder than before. Just *more*.

It was exactly what I needed.

Dominic clamped his lips around my clit and sucked, and I moaned around him, digging my nails into his thighs as his cock thickened in my mouth. Then my orgasm was there.

My gasps and groans were muffled as Dominic pumped his hips, fucking my mouth from below. The vibration of his sounds against my pussy turned me on, and I took him as deep as I could, swallowing him down when his orgasm hit too.

One down, two to go.

"Fuck me." Dominic's voice was wrecked, and the deep rumble of it against my pussy made me squirm harder. He slid out from under me and hauled my lips to his, stealing my gasps as Nate fucked me. Dominic's fingers dug into my shoulder, marking my skin. The only thing he was capable of saying was my name. Or maybe he was cursing it.

All I knew was I loved to hear it in that sex-drenched voice of his.

Mari. Mari. Mari.

Dominic lay back, adjusting so he braced me against Nate's thrusts as he chased his orgasm. He pressed kisses into my damp hair and whispered praise like it was going out of style. "You're taking him so well, *mariposa*. You're doing so good. Look at that perfect ass of yours. I can't wait until I'm inside you again. I'm going to fuck you on top of him next time. We'll show Fuckboy how it's done."

I laughed at that, and Nate swore when my body tightened around him. Driving into me one last time, he tensed and came. Even when he was done, he didn't pull out, instead continuing with more slow thrusts until he was soft. It was like he never wanted to leave.

I could relate.

When he did pull out, the two of us collapsed as one, landing on Dominic with a three-way "Oomph."

We were panting, sweaty, and sated. It was damn near perfect.

Nate kissed the back of my neck sweetly. "Thank you for that."

"My pleasure," I whispered, unsure if I could talk any louder.

"Still alive under there, baby?" I tried to lift my head to look for Greyson, but I was too tired. Instead, I flapped my hand in what I hoped counted as a response.

Suddenly, the weight on my back was gone, and Nate disappeared into the bathroom. In minutes, he came back with a warm washcloth, cleaning the both of us off before Grey pulled me off Dominic's chest, spreading me out next to him. When Nate returned, he boxed me in between them, so all I saw were miles of bare skin.

"You look worn out, *reina*," Grey mocked, though I could see the pleased glint in his eye at how spent I was. And I had no doubt I looked like I'd been fucked within an inch of my life. Felt like it too.

"I am." Christ, my voice croaked like I'd spent my life smoking two packs a day. I needed to hydrate.

All Greyson did was laugh. "Don't worry. You're almost done."

"There's more?"

"There's more. You rest. I'll do all the work this time."

I didn't think I could take another, but as Greyson slid inside me, I couldn't stop myself from reaching for him. I wanted to make him happy, to give him what he wanted. If that was another orgasm, I'd pull one out of thin air if I had to.

I thought he'd fuck me hard and fast, maybe try to prove how quickly he could get me to come, but despite the near-painful hardness of his cock, he set the pace slow and deep. He ran his hands over my skin, tweaking my nipples and rubbing my clit and dipping to suck and nip and leave marks here and there. Every time he did, I felt over sensitized.

His skin burned me, his lips hurt and healed. I wanted him in me, around me, always.

"Do you have any idea how good you looked with them?" he whispered. "Like a goddess taking your pleasure from mortals. Will you do the same for me?"

I didn't know how, but... "If you want me to."

"I always want you to." Grey leaned down, whispering in my ear. "Are you happy, love?"

"Yes," I sighed, settling into the rhythm with him. What we did wasn't just sex; it was connection on the rarest level. Emotional, spiritual, physical. The type of sex I'd always imagined soulmates having.

"You going to come for me too?"

"Yes." And as easy as breathing, I did.

Keeping Grey close with a hand around his neck, I leaned up to nip him back. "Are you going to come for me?"

Like he'd been waiting for my words, he groaned and panted, praising my name under his breath as he spilled inside me.

I couldn't move as Grey pulled out, eyes laser-focused between my legs as his and Nate's combined releases leaked out of me.

"Almost perfect," he said absently.

"Next time," Dominic promised. Slipping his hand between my legs, he slid his fingers inside me, keeping the rest of Grey's come from dripping out. "Next time, we'll show her she's really ours."

Chapter 25
Dominic

The morning after the wedding, I woke up to Grey and Nate creeping out of bed.

"What's wrong?" I whispered, trying not to wake Mari. She'd fallen asleep on top of Greyson almost as soon as he'd cleaned her up. It was fucking adorable.

"Nothing. We're going for breakfast." Nate slid into his jeans and stepped to the door. "I'll get the car ready."

"Do you need us to come with you?"

"No, we're not going far." Grey's gaze was steady but pointed as he looked between Mari and me.

Anticipation thrummed through me, along with a heavy dose of gratitude. They were leaving so we could be alone. Giving us the time to reconnect.

Fuck, I think I like those assholes.

"Thanks, man."

Greyson watched Mari, whose breathing was getting lighter. They must've woken her up when they climbed out of bed. "Don't thank me. Just be good to her and make the most of your time."

I absolutely would.

Mari sighed, shifting to lay her head on my chest. "I don't know what's going on, but be safe."

"We will. Love you, *reina*." Grey blew her a kiss and left.

She groaned as the door snicked closed, grumbling under her breath. "What *are* they doing?"

"Getting you breakfast." She had to be starving, but she didn't move an inch. Just hummed under her breath and tossed a leg over mine.

Mari first thing in the morning was something I'd never get over. She was unguarded. Unmasked. Relaxed and calm. Still naked and sated after last night, but there was heat in her eyes when she blinked them open to look at me. Love too, though she wouldn't admit it.

That was okay. I could be patient. When she finally did, those three words would be the best reward I'd ever won.

"I love you," I told her, because I couldn't look at her and not say it.

"I know. Wake me up when they get back." She nuzzled into me, desperate for a little more sleep. It was cute, but we had plans.

"I want my rain check."

For a moment, I thought she'd fallen back asleep. Then her hand slid down my body. It took all my willpower to stop it, especially when she pouted. "I thought—"

I rolled her, pulling her back to my naked chest and nestling my hard-on against her ass. I wanted her hand on my cock, yes, but I craved something else on it more.

"I want you like this. Slow and lazy like we're spending Sunday in bed. Like I woke up and had to slip my cock in that warm pussy before I could even open my eyes." I kissed up her neck with greedy inhales of that scent that was so perfectly Mari. "Do you like that?"

I didn't have to ask, though. She was squirming before I'd finished talking. "Yes."

Fuck, that husky *I want you so bad* voice. It did things to me.

"Good girl." I slid my hand down her body until it cupped her, pleased to find that she was swollen, but more than wet enough. "Are you sore?"

"No. Just fuck me, Dominic. I'm dying."

Adjusting my grip so I had a handful of luscious thigh, I pulled her leg back and over my hip, adjusting so I could do exactly what I'd said. "Don't worry, baby. We've got all the time in the world."

The slow slide in was torture, and it took serious effort not to come the second her pussy wrapped around me. Being inside Mari for the first time in years was like finding where I was supposed to be after being lost for too long.

"I've been dying to have you," I groaned, forcing myself to take it slow. To feel every inch of her so she could feel every inch of me. "I missed this. I missed you."

"I missed you too. So much. I'm almost worried this won't be as good as I hope it will."

"It'll be better," I promised. I wasn't an inexperienced teenager losing his virginity. I knew what I was doing now. "Nothing but the best for you, *mariposa*."

She had no idea. I wanted the world for her, as long as I was part of it.

I wanted to surround her, fill her, be inside her all the time. I wanted there to be no place on her body I hadn't touched or a space in her life that didn't remind her of me.

Briefly, I wondered if that urge was jealousy from watching the others claim her, but no. I just wanted to reclaim her as mine whenever and however I could. She could be ours and mine at the same time.

But does she think so?

"Are you mine?" I asked, needing to hear it.

"Yes," she moaned, her fingers diving for her clit.

Grabbing her arms, I pinned them to her chest with the arm holding her leg, making her lie there and take me exactly how I wanted. Giving up some of the slowness, I started moving faster, harder. "Does that mean this is my pussy?"

"Oh god. Yes."

"It's the only one I want." The only one I'd ever have again. "No touching unless I say so."

"It's my pussy."

"Not right now, it isn't." I wrapped a hand around the back of her neck and jerked her closer, plastering her against me so not an inch of space was between us. Exactly how I liked it.

Tilting Mari's head back, I watched every fleeting emotion rush over her face. Pleasure, devotion, love. "I'm obsessed with watching you unravel. It's my new favorite thing."

Was it obsession? The need to keep her close at all time, the urge to devour her, if only to have a part of her with me everywhere I went. I wasn't sure I cared if it was. There were worse ways to spend my life than devoting myself to the woman I loved.

"Dominic." Her legs twisted against me as she panted, clawing at my arm desperately. I could already feel her clenching around me.

I pulled her head up, whispering against those lips I adored. "You like this, don't you? You like being at my mercy, forced to take whatever I give you."

She didn't answer, just attacked my mouth, nipping my bottom lip hard. I squeezed her throat, more out of reflex than anything else, and every part of her tightened. She had no idea how much she turned me on. Again, I had to force myself to focus, to put off the near-painful need to come.

"I like it too. I want this forever." It was too much, too soon, but I didn't care. Feeling her against me, wrapped around me, it was everything. She was everything, and I was so sick of not telling her.

Dark eyes clouded with all the things she couldn't say fixed on mine. "I want to come."

"So do it." Shifting my legs for leverage, I gave her more. Still a lazy morning fuck, but hard enough to send her careening over the edge. I muffled her cries with a kiss, almost desperate to keep them between the two of us.

Greedy. I was greedy for her.

"You're so pretty when you come." I dropped her arms, cupping her pussy with the same possessive grip as before so I could feel myself thrusting inside her. "I want to die in this pussy."

Pretty sure I was going to if I didn't come soon.

Mari's hand crept toward her clit, but this time, I didn't push it away. If she wanted another orgasm, she could have one. Instead, those lithe fingers settled over my hand, the sensation of them touching me as I pulled out, just to push back in again, driving me crazy.

The gasp she gave was even better.

"You feel so big like this," she whispered.

Well, fuck. Apparently, that was all it took.

I bit her shoulder, moaning her name as I pumped my come into her. Refusing to stop until she was stuffed with every drop, absolutely full of me.

We didn't move, even after I was soft. We just stayed there, with my body curled around hers and come leaking onto our legs. I almost didn't want to move. I could practically feel her thinking, and I was worried that even though she'd invited me to bed last night, it hadn't been more than sex.

If she regretted this, I didn't think I'd ever recover.

"Was it worth the wait?" she finally asked.

That was what had her mind racing?

I pulled her head back, diving down for a filthy kiss. "You were always worth the wait, baby. You always will be."

"You are too, Dominic."

I hoped she always felt that way.

* * *

It took more effort than I'd ever admit to get out of bed, but by the time Greyson and Nate returned loaded down with food, Mari and I were showered and dressed. Though, admittedly, we'd gotten more dirty than clean.

"You went to Little Sal's? How is everyone?" Mari asked. She had an uncharacteristic squeal in her voice that made me grin. Looking around, I saw I wasn't the only one who heard it. Mari's joy was quiet by design, so having a front-row seat to it was an honor I'd never get over.

"They're great." Nate directed her to the table with a hand at the small of her back. "They sent well-wishes and far too much food. Seriously, we only ordered half of this."

Greyson laughed. "I already told you, it's normal. They're in love with Mari."

"I know the feeling," I whispered, pressing a kiss behind her ear as I sat at her side. She flushed just a touch, while Grey handed her a coffee.

It was almost unreal how docile she was, how easily she let us care for her. I wanted to know what I had to do to keep her like that, so soft and sweet and relaxed. So easy to please and happy to accept what we were offering.

Don't get any ideas, I told myself firmly. *It's only safe for her to be like this with us.*

Mari was the protector. *She* was the power, and even though I hated it, I couldn't forget it. Even when every part of my brain was screaming *my girl to protect,* that wasn't my role. I had to accept it or risk losing the love of my life again.

The four of us sat squished around one end of the long dining table as Grey and Nate started unpacking food. Despite not being in our own home, it felt normal. Routine.

Would we do this more often now that things with Mari and I were settled? Start our day off as a family?

Was that what we were?

"Seems like you have enough there to feed an army."

The voice interrupted my thoughts, and I had a knife poised and ready to fly in less than a second. Mari's hand on my thigh was the only thing stopping me from throwing it at Rafael's face.

Fucking Osorio.

"Uncle," she said with marked wariness. "I thought you were gone to wherever the hell you've been."

He smiled, though he didn't offer up any more information than that. "Thought I'd stick around until you got out of here. The morning after a huge party seems like the perfect time to take you out."

Though Mari would never get trashed in the middle of a war—she wasn't a moron—Cash could've assumed she would and made plans to get her when she was too hungover to protect herself. When my phone buzzed in my pocket, I knew Greyson was thinking the same thing.

I planned for this, but let's add an extra car to the detail.

With somebody other than Geneva driving Mari.

Mari cleared her throat, and I tipped the phone toward her so she could read. We weren't making plans behind her back. I just didn't trust Rafael to keep the information to himself, family or not. Apparently, Grey agreed.

"Thank you for your consideration, Uncle, but we've got it covered." Mari squeezed my thigh gently, her unspoken acceptance of the change of plans. "Would you like to eat with us?"

"I'd love to."

As Rafael took his seat across from me, Mari sent me a *please don't be an asshole* look, so I swallowed the urge to tell him to fuck off. As if it was any other normal family meal, we talked about nothing important. The weather, traffic, baseball. All boring, surface stuff. The one thing we didn't talk about was work. It was almost as if there was an unspoken rule hanging above our heads. It made me antsy and nervous, especially with Rafael being so secretive.

I didn't trust him. I didn't trust any of the Osorios, with good reason, but Mari didn't know what I did. Or why. I could tell her, but I wasn't ready yet.

I just had to hope that when I did, she'd understand why I'd kept it from her.

"How have you been liking my city, Uncle?" Mari asked after she finished, leaning back in her chair with her hands resting on her belly.

"It's beautiful. I've been enjoying the sights and the people very much."

It was the perfect answer. Vague and uninteresting, absolutely no detail. When Nate's and Greyson's eyes narrowed, I knew they thought the same.

"What have you been doing with your time?" I asked casually.

Don't mind me. Just your niece's boyfriend trying to get to know you.

As if the heir to the Osorio Cartel would ever believe that.

"A little of this, a little of that." Another evasive answer that sent tingles down my spine while my mind was chanting, *Danger.*

"What about your father? Is the Wolf hearing all about your adventures in the city?"

Greyson leaned back in his chair, deceptively relaxed, but I saw

Nate's hand slip under the table. Meanwhile, Mari pinched me on the inside of the thigh, and I could almost hear her hissing *What the fuck is wrong with you?*

But she didn't say it. Because as much as we didn't want to talk about work, work would always be there, and as of now, the Osorios and the Marcosas were not friends. Which meant she couldn't undermine her own leadership team in front of a potential enemy. Though I was going to get an earful later.

Rafael flashed a predator's smile, all sharp teeth and sharper intent. "Even if he was, I think you're aware there are some things I can't tell you, Dominic."

"Of course not, but you can see how things look from our perspective. You blow into town in the nick of time, then disappear into the ether when it's done, offering information you haven't been able to produce. It seems shady, don't you think?"

He wasn't expecting me to be honest, nor for Mari to back me up silently. He thought I'd let his non-answers go for the sake of politeness. He was wrong.

Rafael cleared his throat and set down his fork. When he looked at Mari, his face was open but serious. I wondered if it was real or just a ploy to play on her emotions.

"To be honest, I've been digging into things here. The entire city is in chaos. Allies betraying allies, friends betraying friends, and a new party ready and willing to take over it all. It's the perfect time for a revolution." Mari's eyebrow ticked, and he lifted his hands in surrender. "I'm not judging, nor am I here to take over. Just offering my observations."

"Why did you feel the need to observe at all? Seattle isn't your city." I didn't need to remind him of that, but it didn't make sense.

"But it is my niece's. I have my reasons for looking into things."

"Sounds like someone bringing in more secrets when we can't afford them," I drawled.

"Maybe I just don't want to ruin such a lovely weekend. I do love weddings. Don't you, Dominic?"

Rafael's eyes twinkled as he popped the last bite of almond French toast into his mouth. There was a heaviness in his words. A weight that shouldn't be there.

He knows.

The thought hit me like a ton of bricks. I didn't know how or why, but like Greyson, Rafael knew what he shouldn't. What he couldn't.

What should have gone to the grave with Mario.

With Greyson, I didn't have to worry. He would spare me to spare Mari. Rafael didn't give a fuck either way. He was the new guy in Mari's life, the outsider, and I had no doubt he'd throw me under the bus if it kept him in her good graces.

Shit, shit, shit.

Grey glared at me, and his expression screamed, *Get your shit together.*

Easy for him to say; he was on the fast track to forever, while I'd just gotten permission to get in the fucking car again.

Thankfully, Mari didn't poke at the statement. "Secrets or not, you promised information and have yet to deliver. Why?"

There it was, a wince. A chink in the armor. It wasn't a lot—minuscule, really—but it was something I'd dig into if I wanted to keep what he knew out of Mari's ears. I'd just gotten her back. I couldn't let her shut me out again because I wasn't a fool. This time, it would be for good.

"I'll get you your information by the end of the week," he promised. "I've finally found something that I believe my father will accept as payment for it."

"Payment?" Mari's confusion was almost laughable, until I realized how much Mario had fucked us by not giving her more information on the Osorios. Maybe he hadn't been expecting her to lead, but the fact was, she didn't know how to deal with them, and it put us at a disadvantage. "I wasn't aware there was payment beyond my presence at a meeting, which I've already agreed to."

Rafael shrugged, though it was uncomfortable. "Giving out intel isn't exactly normal in the family, especially when it won't directly benefit us. I had to promise him something on top of your meeting to get the permission I needed."

And that rankled. Anyone could see how much he hated having to bow to his father's whims.

"What is it that the Wolf wants that badly?" Greyson asked.

Like me, he didn't get much consideration. All of Rafael's attention was on Mari. "I can't tell you what he's after, only that it won't harm you or put anyone you love in danger."

"Just information, then."

"Just information," he agreed.

"That you found in my city," Mari said skeptically.

"I did. But again, it won't do anything to harm you or yours."

"Will it put innocents in danger?"

Rafael's face softened as he looked at his niece, and it was obvious that he loved her, even though their relationship was new. She was important to him, and seeing that she cared, it mattered to him. "There will be no innocent lives lost."

Mari stared at him for a long time, breathing deep and even until, finally, she sighed and rubbed the bridge of her nose. "Why don't I believe you?"

Rafael smiled a little wider. "Because you are wise beyond your years, *tesorita*."

"Hmm," was all she said.

Rafael cleared his throat as he stacked his plate and stood. "I have to go, but I'll have the information for you soon."

"I know you will. Because we both know you don't want me digging for it on my own."

Grey grinned, obviously thrilled at the very pointed threat to hack the cartel's systems.

"Understood."

"I'm sure it is." Mari's smile was predator-sharp, and I had to admit, it made me hard. "Be safe, Uncle."

When he was gone, she turned to Nate with a thoughtful expression. "What's Rafael's specialty?"

He looked down at his plate as if he was recalling the information. "Sharpshooter, I think. From what we gathered, your grandfather used him for local assassinations. Stuff he didn't want to use his team abroad for."

She tapped her fingers against the table as she thought. "Is there any way he's the reason we haven't seen any activity from Cash lately?"

It felt like too much of a coincidence to say no, even if I didn't want to give Rafael that much credit.

"There's always a chance," Nate said diplomatically.

"My uncle's chasing around my biggest enemy and refusing to let me help. Why is that not the weirdest part of my life right now?" Mari said with a sigh.

She was so tense, all the softness of our time together gone.

I hated it.

Maybe I can get it back for her.

I reached for my shirt, stripping it off before the others caught on. Mari was so busy thinking, she didn't even notice until she heard the clink of Nate's belt hitting the floor.

"Oh shit."

Yeah, we were definitely getting home late.

Chapter 26
Mari

Three weeks after the wedding, my phone rang as I was getting ready for the day. The desire to let it go to voice mail swelled until I glanced at the screen.

O'Bannon.

"Christ, I was hoping to get more time without him." Three weeks definitely wasn't enough.

Things had been stable since the alliance was solidified, and though Aces were still out there taking swipes at us, they were small nuisances. A broken window in a protected shop, an attempted robbery at a bank we used, three separate bar fights in my territory, but no real change with Cash. Just irritating, petty shit.

I wasn't sure if that was intentional to lull us into a false sense of peace, or if Rafael had been extra busy.

With the wedding over, O'Bannon was back to the polite

distance we'd previously employed, and I definitely preferred it to interacting with him daily.

"Do you want me to take that, *mariposa?*" Dominic asked as he curled himself around me. He'd been sitting on the bed watching me get ready for twenty minutes, and I liked the weight of his eyes on me. Since the wedding, none of us had slept apart. I liked that too.

I almost said no, but then realized it was his job as much as it was mine. "Please."

With a few taps, he had us on speakerphone. "What do you need, O'Bannon?"

"Where's Mari?"

"Occupied," Dominic said with a grin, slipping his finger underneath the strap of my bra like he'd pull it down. I flicked it off, glaring at him in the mirror. While I didn't have a problem with voyeurism, I didn't want to do it with O'Bannon on the phone.

Gross.

Dominic rolled his eyes but kept his hands to himself.

"If I wanted to talk to you, I would have called your phone."

"Yet I'm all you've got. What can I do for you?"

The Irishman growled. "You can come pick up this body."

Everything in me froze and I reached for the phone without thinking, but Dominic pushed my hand away. All the teasing bled from his face, and I was left with the sight of an underboss. *My* underboss.

When the hell had that happened?

"What body?"

"An Ace," O'Bannon spat. "Left on my doorstep like a present from our deranged friend."

"He's not a friend," Dominic corrected.

"I don't give a shit either way. The whole reason for this alliance was to make sure we had help if we needed it. A dead body on my doorstep says we need help, so I want her over here *now.*"

I stood, gathering my things, as Dominic glared down at the

phone. "Before we go anywhere, I'd urge you to correct your tone. Mari isn't yours to command."

I could practically hear O'Bannon grit his teeth, but only because Dominic was right and he knew it. "I would appreciate some assistance in the matter, if the Marcosa queen has time."

Dominic looked at me for permission, and I nodded. "We'll be there in thirty minutes."

He hung up before O'Bannon could respond.

"Let Greyson know what's happening." I immediately headed to the closet. The suit I had on was fine for checking in at the clubs, our original plan for the evening, but you couldn't get dead body stink out, and I didn't want to ruin the fabric. Instead, I changed into an older suit. Still clean, still sleek, just one I didn't care about incinerating since I had a whole closet of them.

I pulled off the jacket and let my mind wander. I wondered why Cash had waited so long. Why now? Why hit O'Bannon instead of us directly? Was it a warning, a sign that things were ramping up again? Had he ended his self-imposed exile to toy with us some more?

"Why now?"

"What do you mean?" Dominic propped himself against the doorway, watching as I stripped.

"Cameron and Aislynn's wedding was weeks ago. Why wait until after the distraction of the wedding is over? Why not attack in the middle of the chaos?"

I was just spit balling, talking over my shoulder to get rid of the thoughts in my head, but it made sense. Wedding planning was atrocious even when there wasn't a deadline. Why had Cash walked away from an opportunity to get us then? It didn't make sense.

I'd learned to hone my instincts a long time ago, and I didn't like that they were screaming at me.

"Maybe he worried you'd be too overwhelmed with everything that you would snap back and blow him sky-high."

"If he's been watching like I think he has, he'd know that's not my MO."

I was collected. Strategic. I tried to take out enemies without killing unnecessarily. It was a fine line to straddle, and Cash was beginning to feel like one of those situations where, to kill a monster, I had to let go of my principles. I didn't like it.

Shrugging into the suit jacket and a pair of heeled booties I could run in if I had to, I declared myself ready to go. "Guess we won't know until we get there."

Dominic straightened from his slouch. "I'll go with you."

"No. I need you and Greyson to check on the clubs for me. With all the wedding shit, we've been neglecting them, and they're a perfect target for Cash. Take Tennessee and Moore with you and make a show of it."

"Grey and I will be fine. You take the wonder twins."

"They'll go with you." Dominic opened his mouth to argue, but I held up a silencing hand. "I'm taking Nate, and Joaquin has to go with me anyway."

With Cameron still out of the city on his honeymoon, I'd given Joaquin more responsibility as a way to keep an eye on him, and so far, my uncle had done everything perfectly. Maybe too perfectly. Bringing him with me would keep him close, because family or not, there was no trust there. Not on my end.

"This doesn't feel right. We should be with you," Dominic insisted.

"Then split the clubs with Grey so you can meet up with us faster." *He won't listen to you.* I hated that my mind was screaming at me, hated that we weren't in sync. I especially hated how deep his questioning hit those wounds we still hadn't healed. "I need you to trust that I know what I'm doing. You promised you understood my position."

"I did, and I stand by that promise. I also know Nate will protect you, no matter what."

"Then what is?" Because I didn't want to leave it like this. Unfinished and uncomfortable.

Dominic sighed, pulling me into a tight hug. "It's the situation I don't trust. O'Bannon and the Irish. Joaquin and his sycophants. Cash. There're too many variables, and it makes me nervous, but that's because I love you."

Every time he said it, it made my heart pound. I never wanted him to stop.

But I couldn't make myself say it back.

"It's okay," he whispered, knowing I was struggling. "I don't mind waiting until you're ready."

"What if I never am?"

He shrugged like it didn't matter, but we both knew it did. It would hurt Dominic if I kept the words from him. I didn't want to; I just *couldn't* say them. Not yet. "Come on. The sooner you leave, the sooner you get home."

"Are we okay?"

He kissed me sweetly, pecking my nose once with a smile. "We're good, baby."

Okay. I took a deep breath, smoothing out my jacket and redirecting my attention to my duties now that I knew my relationship was good. "Have Nate and Joaquin meet me in the car in five. Send Warner's team to O'Bannon's to run the scene before we arrive."

"I will." Dominic gripped the back of my head and gave me another kiss, this one much harder. "Be safe."

"I'll see you later," I promised.

When I got in the car, I was surprised to find only Nate waiting.

"We couldn't find Joaquin," he said with a grimace.

"Of course not," I grumbled. "Has he even been home tonight?"

Geneva shifted into drive and shook her head. "Haven't seen him all day."

Foreboding slithered through me, but I refused to give it purchase. I'd been paranoid since the warehouse, and it only got worse as days progressed. I wasn't made for Cold War tactics, but steel and blood and chaos.

Mental games weren't my fortitude unless I was the one orchestrating them.

Settling in, I gave Nate the rundown of my expectations. "When we get there, I need you to listen to everything that's said but don't react. O'Bannon is likely going to make an issue with me because that's what he does. Don't engage. Stay quiet and photograph the scene."

"Mouth shut, eyes and ears open, guard your back. Got it." Nate's lips tipped when I turned to him with a raised eyebrow. "I was expecting this, Mari. Cameron briefed me before he left. Speaking of, I didn't know he was the Marcosa bomb dog."

The term made me roll my eyes. "He's not a bomb dog. He's just very good at figuring out where they are."

"So, he's a bomb dog."

"Yeah, I guess so." I laughed.

While we talked, I pulled out my phone, sending a text to the security team about Joaquin in hopes one of them knew where he was, but no dice. He hadn't been seen all day, and he'd left his Marcosa cell phone at the house, probably since that was the device we tracked.

More and more, I wondered if I had a rat in my house and what I'd have to do to exterminate it.

* * *

The O'Bannon estate was located in an area designed with new money in mind. There was no history, no depth. Everything was sterile walls and boring ceilings. Just standing on the street felt like living in an animal's cage.

I hated it.

When we neared the gate, a single guard waved us through, and none were on the fence line. *What the hell?*

Every other time I'd visited, they'd walked the walled fence around his compound, rifles on display. It was overkill, but that was how O'Bannon worked. All brute force. All intimidation.

Then we drove up the driveway and into pandemonium.

Guards covered every square inch of the drive, most of them in a thick knot around the front door, where I assumed O'Bannon was waiting for me.

"I guess that explains where everyone is," I murmured.

Nate grunted, his bodyguard mask firmly in place. "I don't want you too far from me."

Considering we only had a few men on-site, I agreed. O'Bannon often acted like a cornered cat, and I didn't want him swiping at me because he thought I'd brought an army into his territory.

"I'll head back down to the gate," Geneva said as we stopped, knowing we needed the space.

"Thanks, G."

Stepping out of the car, Nate walked carefully before opening my door and blocking everyone from sight as I got out. It was his job, but the lack of breathing room spoke more of nerves than duty.

"You can't guard me from everything," I said softly.

"Watch me."

It was so like something Greyson or Dominic would do that I almost laughed. The only thing stopping me was a furious O'Bannon and the very dead Ace on his doorstep.

"Apologies for being out of touch earlier. What happened?" I peered at the body. The man looked like he'd only been dead for a day or so, but something about him looked...off.

Warner, Cameron's second, knelt and pressed a single fingertip against the dead man's skin. "They froze him."

"They *what*?"

"Froze him." Warner poked somewhere else then shrugged. I

didn't work much with Warner since he was close to my cousin, but I had every faith in his abilities, especially when it came to bodies. He'd been a coroner once upon a time. If he said that was what happened, it was probably accurate.

"Probably killed him and shoved him straight into the freezer." Nate's suggestion made sense, but what the actual fuck?

"Dead guy popsicle," one of the newbies whispered. Warner glared, and the guy shut his trap with an audible click.

O'Bannon's scowl deepened. "Why the fuck did he drop this on my porch?"

Sometimes I wondered if O'Bannon was genuinely obtuse or if he was playing me. After years of not having an answer, I was going to ask Ash when she got home.

"You just signed a treaty with us. That makes you his enemy too." When he continued staring at me like I was speaking in Klingon, I rolled my eyes. "It's just a warning, O'Bannon. It's not that big of a deal."

"There is a dead man on my porch, and I had cops here when he was *delivered*. It's a very big deal to me."

That got my attention. "Why were the police here?"

Any semblance of helpfulness he had was instantly gone. "That's none of your concern. The treaty allows me to continue my business as I see fit unless you need me, or did I read the contract wrong?"

He hadn't, but I didn't like that he was keeping secrets. O'Bannon was a boaster. Him hiding things made me wary.

Since I couldn't show it, I gave him my most condescending smile. "You do whatever feels right."

Unwilling to dig further when he was obviously on edge, I continued. "Warner will finish the investigation and remove the body for disposal. We'll need the security footage to see exactly how it got past all of your guards."

O'Bannon's scowl deepened to the point that I wondered if his face would freeze like that. Finally, he nodded at his son and underboss, Kieran. "He'll send over the necessary videos immediately."

That was very clearly a *doctor the videos so she can't see our security system* answer, but whatever. His loss if he didn't want my team to help.

As I waved Warner over, my phone rang in my pocket. Given O'Bannon's mood, I didn't want to take my eyes off him, so I handed it back to Nate.

"Yeah?" I tuned Nate out. The call could wait.

"Have you done a bomb check yet?" I asked Warner quietly. After our first run-in with bombs years ago, Cameron had built a protocol to check the area. With him gone, it should have fallen to Joaquin to run through, but that obviously didn't happen. I was pretty sure Warner knew the protocol, but I had to be certain.

"Did it before you came. It's clear," he promised.

Good. "Search it."

I watched as Warner began systematically searching the frozen body as best he could, prying fabric up when he had to. They hadn't bothered cleaning him up, so blood covered him to the point of being a hindrance.

All in all, it was a good body to drop. Messy and inconvenient. Point to Cash.

At some point, Nate returned to his position at my back, slipping the phone into my hand. "Greyson is on his way."

Good. I didn't like how outnumbered we were, and Grey easily counted for three men on his own. Warner, who had finished his search, laid out his findings on the steps, but there was nothing out of the ordinary. Phone, wallet, and a pair of keys. Nate flipped the older than dirt wallet open to find it empty.

Shocker.

The phone was also blank, though redial worked. I texted the number to Grey to investigate later. Warner did his best to check the body over again, but with the way he'd been frozen, it just didn't work.

Finally, he stood. "What do you want to do about this, boss? We have room in the freezer if you don't want to thaw him out, but I don't see the point."

I stared at the body, wondering what purpose the man's death served and coming up blank. It felt like a warning no one could read. "Just get rid of him."

"That's all you're going to do? Take the body away and clean my stairs? What the hell did I call you for?" O'Bannon sneered.

And I was done. "What else would you like me to do, O'Bannon? Do you need me to put a protective detail on your home? If your forty-plus-man security team isn't enough, I will absolutely procure you some new ones. Hell, I have plenty of men I could *personally* lend you. Would that suffice?"

We both knew he couldn't say yes. The second he took that much help from anyone, he'd be deader than Popsicle Man. It didn't mean he liked my insinuation that he needed it, though.

"I don't need your help protecting my people."

"Then what *do* you need my help for? You called me here, and I'm taking the body off your hands. What else do you want from me?"

Silence was my answer. Despite our supposed alliance, it felt like tensions would always be high with O'Bannon because he wanted territory and power, and I had it. That kind of desire wasn't going to disappear just because I put a Marcosa jersey on him and claimed we were family.

Not for the first time, I wondered if it had even been a smart idea to take him up on the alliance in the first place. Then I realized it didn't matter. I'd done it, and I had to suffer the consequences or kill him and hope his sons were better.

"Whatever you think is best," he said finally.

I nodded to Warner, who called the rest of his team over. "Since we already wrapped the back of the van in plastic, all we need to do is put the body in and head out. Unless you want us to send a message, boss?"

I was already shaking my head. "If he was willing to kill the Ace, he's not important enough to send a message. Get rid of the body and make sure he's in pieces. The last thing we need are the Feds finding out our body count is rising."

"Got it, boss."

"Call me if anything changes," I told O'Bannon as Warner's team prepared to lift the body. "Whether you like it or not, we are allies. I intend to honor that commitment."

I turned, heading for the car with Nate close behind.

For a moment, there was only grunting as the men slid their hands under the heavy body and lifted, the sound of Nate's footsteps behind me and the grumbling of O'Bannon as he stomped his way toward the front door.

It was normal. Easy.

Too easy.

I wasn't even surprised when the blast came, when heat raced over my skin, burning my arms.

It was the scream that got me.

Nate's voice, echoing in pain.

I twisted, reaching for him even as I lost my footing. Then he was on top of me, shielding me with his body as the front of the house fell.

After that, there was nothing but echoing silence.

Chapter 27
Greyson

A moment of stillness hung in the air before chaos erupted. A moment where all the hair on your body stood up. It was almost like being in the eye of a storm, the only safe place.

Then the moment was over, and pandemonium reigned.

We'd just pulled past the gate when the bomb went off, and I watched from the edge of the driveway as the house fell. As Mari was buried.

"Call Dominic," I barked at Tennessee, bolting out of the car before he'd even stopped. I didn't wait to consider whether there were people waiting to pick me off as I ran into the open. All I cared about was what was under the rubble.

Who was under it.

Mari. Alone and terrified. Hurt.

Not alone, I told myself. Nate was there. He would protect her. He had to because she couldn't die.

None of us would survive it.

As I hit the edge of the debris, I realized I didn't see where the blast had thrown her. Panic stole my breath as I looked around. The house was half gone, and people were screaming. Smoke and the heavy tang of blood floated on the air, and I didn't know where Mari was.

If she was hurt, the delay in treatment could kill her. If she wasn't, the lack of oxygen could.

The whole situation felt doomed.

Shoving the panic away, I decided to start somewhere. Anywhere. I picked up chunks of stone, throwing them in a pile near one of the destroyed cars. Not caring as they scratched my palms and my fingers. All I cared about was the love of my life buried under it all.

Every heartbeat that pounded in my ears had the sound of her name. *Mari. Mari. Mari.*

I didn't know how long I worked. Tennessee was with me, but we still weren't moving fast enough. I could feel the clock ticking away on us. On her.

We needed more men, but I couldn't call them. The explosion was obviously an attack, one Mari wouldn't want me to advertise. *We can't afford weakness.*

I didn't give a shit, so long as she lived.

Eventually, the sound of a motorcycle hit my ears, and a single sigh of relief rolled through me. Dominic would help. We'd find Mari and Nate. They would be safe. They had to be safe.

I must have been saying it out loud because Dominic clapped his hand against my shoulder. "We'll find her."

His voice, usually full of laughter, was grave, and fear wrapped itself around my heart and squeezed.

What if we didn't?

Together, the three of us dug in silence. Each stone we upended was one step closer, but every time the space below was empty, I felt a little more desperate.

An eternity later, we heard it.

The faintest whisper of a voice. "They're coming for us."

Mari.

She kept speaking softly as Dominic and I moved as one, carefully pulling rocks from the direction of the voice until finally we saw something dust and debris covered. A shirt? A jacket?

Lifting more rocks than I'd ever lifted in my life, I caught sight of what it was.

Not a something. A some*one.*

Nate.

He'd covered her body with his. Taken the brunt of heat and stone so Mari didn't. He'd saved her.

Dominic cursed under his breath, and he and Tennessee gently began to pull Nate out, only to stop when a startled gasp hit our ears.

"The rocks aren't stable." Her voice, so clear in my ears despite the persistent ringing, sent a frantic burst of energy through me.

"We have to get her out first," I said.

"We've got him." Dominic adjusted his grip on Nate's limp body. "You get our girl."

I did. I dug and threw stones, carving a circle around Nate's body, so we could pull him out without burying Mari again. If we did, she'd have no protection this time.

Finally, a hand slithered between Nate and the ground. One I'd recognize anywhere.

Dominic and Tennessee lifted Nate as Mari's other hand slipped out to grasp both of mine like a lifeline.

"Almost there." I pulled gently, trying not to hurt her. The second she was free, I hoisted her into my arms and practically jumped out of the rubble and away from the others. They had Nate, and I had Mari.

She's alive. The relief nearly took me to my knees.

"Are you okay?" I ran my hands all over her, brushing her hair back, checking her scalp, finding nothing more than scratches and a few burns. Thank god.

"I'm fine," she rasped, coughing hard. "Nate?"

"Dominic's got him."

Or, he had. As we looked over, the others hauled Nate to the private ambulance that had shown up at some point, though I hadn't heard it. The EMTs put him on a backboard, and Mari gasped at her first glance at him. Nate looked rough, and it dawned on me that I didn't even know if he was breathing.

We both stared as they checked his vitals, jumping when Dominic came over and hauled us both to our feet. Well, he hauled Mari, and when I wasn't willing to let go of her, he got me too.

"Christ, I'm glad you're okay." He pulled her into his arms, and we wrapped ourselves around her, insulating her from everything else. The second she was hidden, she started crying these soft, barely there sobs. Ones she could hide. I didn't care if we stood there forever. I'd hide her for as long as she asked me to. As long as she was alive to ask.

Finally, Mari lifted her head, showing dirty, tear-streaked cheeks. "Is he dead?"

"No." We all looked over at the EMT who had apparently been coming to brief us. "He's alive, but we need to get him out of here."

"We're coming," I said. No hesitation.

The three of us climbed into the private ambulance, despite the EMT's annoyed sneer.

"Send an ambulance for the O'Bannons, then follow us to the hospital," I told Tennessee.

"Already on the way."

I looked back at the carnage that a single bomb had caused, and every part of me raged. "Find out where the hell Joaquin is too."

Because while Warner was one of Cameron's men, Joaquin was the one who should have been there and wasn't.

Joaquin, who had disappeared over and over for months.

Who had failed Mari.

I refused to let him do it again.

It was time he answered for his actions.

The trip into Seattle General was short and discreet, thanks to the private entrance in the basement. It was the only way we could get inside without alerting anyone to Mari's presence. We didn't need people thinking she was dead again.

As soon as we stepped inside, nurses and doctors whisked Nate to the Marcosa wing, and I'd never been happier we'd bought the damn thing. Since Mari's attack, I'd hired a full-time staff to run it. When they weren't busy, they did checkups on our people and their families.

I'd even convinced Dr. Grant to work for us, though she demanded we pay a higher salary that included a hefty donation to a charity of her choice every month. Considering she'd saved Mari's life, she could have whatever she wanted. Fuck the expenses.

Mari refused to leave Nate's side, and Dominic and I refused to leave hers, which led to more arguments and teeth-gnashing from the medical team than my patience could handle.

Finally, Mari snapped. "Your opinions don't matter here. Your knowledge does. Do your job, and make sure he's okay. Everything else can wait."

They all looked at her, and despite the dirt and blood shrouding her, they saw the queen that they expected. When I looked at her, I saw something different. Her hands shook, her voice wavered, and she kept dashing tears off her face before they fell.

My beloved, who had seen more death in her early years than most people saw in their entire lives, was breaking. The idea of losing Nate fractured her right in front of our eyes, and I didn't know what to do about it.

Probably because there was nothing I could do.

He would live or he would die. Either way, we would face the consequences together.

* * *

For the two hours that it took to do tests on Nate, Mari didn't speak or look at us. She just paced the length of his room on repeat.

Finally, the door opened, and his bed was wheeled in. Nate was clean and asleep. I thought he looked better, but I couldn't be sure I wasn't projecting my desires on to the situation. Either way, I let out a sigh of relief that he'd survived.

The little bartender who threw our world into chaos. The Good Samaritan who saved Mari's life the first day he met her. In the midst of everything, I had grown to trust him with my whole world, and for the first time outside of the Marcosa family, I had somebody I considered a friend. Family. Someone I could see becoming my brother. When had that happened?

I didn't know. I also hadn't realized how much it meant to me until I'd almost lost it.

Dominic sank into the seat next to me as Dr. Grant explained the test results to Mari, squeezing my shoulder reassuringly. "Those two have nine fucking lives," he muttered.

"Let's hope so." We didn't need any more bad luck.

Dr. Grant gave Mari's hand a pat before heading out the door, and our girl immediately came over, dropping her ass into my lap like it was her normal seat. Not that I was complaining. Any chance to have her touching me was one I took.

She pulled Dominic's hand into her lap, playing with his fingers idly as she repeated what the doc had said. "He's got a possible concussion and some burns. They had to get some debris out, but we were far enough away that it's nothing serious. As long as we keep everything clean, he'll be fine."

"That's a fucking miracle," I said under my breath.

Dr. Grant came back in, wheeling a tray behind her, and Mari gave Dominic and me a kiss before joining her. As the good doctor talked her through redressing certain wounds, my phone buzzed in my pocket.

The call was a welcome reprieve from the throat-closing relief and the rage I'd ignored festering in my gut, coiling and slithering like a snake lying in wait. "You find him?"

"Yeah. Won't say where he's been, though," Tennessee said.

Of course he wouldn't. Shady fuck.

"Does he know about Mari?"

Tennessee grunted. "Don't think so."

"Keep it that way. Joaquin is no longer in the inner circle. Treat him as we'd treat a rat, and keep your mouth shut until further notice."

Tennessee's sigh echoed down the line. "Do we call Cameron?"

I watched Mari's face, her brows furrowed in concentration as she wrapped Nate's arm under the careful watch of Dr. Grant. She would want her cousin in the loop, but I knew more than anything, what she really wanted for him was a fucking break.

"No," I finally answered. "We'll tell him when he gets back."

It was only another week before he and Ash returned from their honeymoon. We'd give them that long. When they arrived home, war would be on the horizon.

As I hung up, the sound of arguing hit my ears. I found Dr. Grant and Mari squaring off. The good doctor had cornered my girl and was trying and failing to clean a cut on her temple.

"Would you just sit still?" she snapped.

"If you let me get my phone, I will," Mari snapped back. A smile tipped my lips. If she was fighting, she was feeling good.

"Your phone's trashed," I said, walking over to hand her mine. "Who do you need to call?"

"Rafael," she growled, snatching it out of my hand. "People died today. Good people. My people. *Nate—*" She looked at the bed, and her face crumpled before she built it back up. "I'm done playing nice, and he's done hiding. The Osorios promised us information, and I intend to get it."

Chapter 28
Mari

As I sat beside the hospital bed with one of Nate's hands clasped in mine, I knew the way the world worked around me wasn't normal. Some things were too fast and others too slow. I knew I was in shock, but I didn't care. All I could focus on was the gradual hiss of Nate's breath, the beep of his heart monitor, and the *tick, tick, tick* of the clock.

"He's here."

I slowly lifted my gaze to see Greyson on the other side of the room. He was dirtier than I thought he'd ever been, even as children. His hair was mussed, his suit trashed, fingers wrapped in bandages. My eyes caught on them and couldn't move.

Why were they wrapped in bandages? What had happened to his fingers?

"I dug you out," he said, voice hoarse. "Scraped them on the stone."

Had I ever seen him so raw before? The terror that blanketed his features felt too much like it had after the warehouse and I wanted to make it all better, but I couldn't. I could barely keep pushing forward myself.

Get your head in the game, Mari.

Unwinding myself from my chair, I stood, then hesitated. I still had Nate's hand gripped in both of mine, and I didn't want to let go. I felt like if I left him alone for even a single second, he would leave me too, just like everyone else.

"I'll stay," Dominic whispered, replacing my hand with his. "I won't leave him."

It should have looked funny, the two of them sitting there holding hands when I would barely consider them friends, but it looked like family. *My* family. What would I be like if I lost Nate? With that part of my heart dead, would I still be able to love Dominic and Greyson the same way? Would I be able to be whole with them if that part of me that Nate brought out was missing?

I didn't think so.

If one of them died in this godforsaken war, I would never be the same, and we would all suffer for it.

"Let's go," I croaked, letting Greyson escort me to the door. It was a fight not to look back every other step, but his hard grip on my hand kept me grounded.

The second we walked out the door, I buried everything Nate-related in my head. I couldn't be his girlfriend right now. *She* hadn't called her uncle.

The queen had.

We met Rafael at the same entrance we'd come in, and before he had a chance to breathe my air, I threw a punch that rocked him into the wall.

"What the fuck was that for?"

"That was for taking your fucking time," I snapped. "Do you have it?"

Rafael arranged his face like he was going to try to placate me, manipulate me, and I lost it. I lunged for him, shoving him against the wall until we were nose to nose.

"Do you understand what happened today? I nearly died *again*. One of the men I love is in a hospital bed because of Cash. Because of *you*."

"I didn't set the bomb," he argued.

But the fact that he knew about it when I knew no one had called him told me everything. Uncle Rafael hadn't been hunting Cash like we suspected; he'd been following us. *Me.*

He could've had Cash followed too, but I doubted the psycho was his priority. I was. Had Grey not been there, would Rafael have dug us out or stayed hidden to save his own skin? I didn't know, and I no longer trusted his answers.

"You may not have known about the bomb, but your information could have ended things before they ever got this far. You should've given it to us months ago, but you didn't, and now here we are."

"I didn't have any control over that," Rafael ground out.

"Fuck your excuses!" I roared. "I lost people today. My boyfriend nearly died. What do you think would have happened if he had? Do you think I would have allowed you to live? No. I would have welcomed the Wolf into this city just so that he could burn the place down around my ears. Do you understand?

"I don't care about power, I care about my people. My family. And you, who was supposed to be part of that, couldn't give me the one thing I needed to protect them because you were scared of hurting Daddy's feelings."

"I understand that you're upset, but it isn't like that."

"Isn't it? You told me I wasn't what I could've been if I'd grown up with you. I wasn't a black widow. You were wrong. If Nate dies because you've been jerking us around, I'll kill you too. Wolf be damned."

"He'll gut you."

My laugh was hollow and empty. "I'll already be dead."

Because I couldn't lose Nate. I couldn't lose Dominic or Grey either. They were the pieces of me that clung to humanity, to love. If I lost them, I lost me too, and the Mari who would rise after wouldn't give a fuck about anything but revenge.

Warning issued, I eased back, giving him enough room to breathe. "Where is the information?"

Rafael stared at me for a long time, looking at me as if he was finally seeing me for the first time. Maybe he was. Osorio-raised or not, I was a Marcosa. I was a queen.

And I was really fucking pissed.

Finally, he pulled a file from the bag at his feet and held it out. I reached for it, only for him to grab my wrist before I could pull away.

Faster than I could blink, Greyson had a gun trained on my uncle's forehead. "Let her go, or you die right here, right now."

There was a pregnant pause before Rafael dropped my wrist and stepped back. He looked chagrined, but I no longer believed his face. He used it too often, offering up pretty lies for my grief-stricken mind, and I'd let him. I'd been too focused on seeing my brother that I'd let Rafael manipulate me. Another mistake.

No more. Antoni was dead. End of story.

Rafael took a step back, then another. "I wasn't going to hurt you, *tesorita*."

"What were you doing?"

Rafael sighed, then stood to his full height, taking up more space than I'd ever seen him do. "I was told to give you a message. Prepare yourself. The Wolf is coming to Seattle."

Had it been any other day, I probably would've been scared. Emmanuel "The Wolf" Osorio had a reputation for a reason. But nothing could penetrate the numbness in my chest. "When?"

"Three days." Rafael looked like he wanted to say something else, but I didn't care to wait.

"Noted." I jerked my head toward the elevator, and Greyson followed, covering my back in case Rafael wanted to take a shot. He didn't.

He was gone before the doors closed.

Back upstairs, we found Dominic in the exact same position next to a still-sleeping Nate. "Did you get it?"

"We got more than just the file." As Grey shut the door and locked it, I took my place at Nate's side again but didn't touch him. I was too wound up, and he needed calm. Peace. Healing.

I settled for watching him.

We'd settled into a routine of checking the room and everything brought into it for bugs, so I knew we were okay to speak freely. "The Wolf is coming in three days."

Dominic's eyes jerked to mine, and something flitted through them. Fear? Anxiety? I wasn't sure, and I didn't trust my mind. "What do you want to do?"

I didn't know. I was too focused on the *now* to care about tomorrow.

"We'll deal with the cartel later," Greyson suggested. "What's the file say?"

"Let's find out."

The three of us huddled together at the side of Nate's bed as I read the first page out loud.

"Cassius Ace Beckstrom, age forty-six. Seattle native. According to the file, he's the sole living son of a Katherine Beckstrom—waitress at some diner down south—no father in the picture. Younger brother died by drowning at age five. Supposedly an accident, but the investigator wrote in his private notes that all signs pointed to Cash doing it, though they never found enough evidence to arrest him."

Something prickled in the back of my mind, something I needed to remember. I almost had it when Dominic's voice shattered my focus. "Christ. What a fucking psycho."

Shaking off the sense I was missing something, I flipped through more pages. There was some background on Katherine, who was as blue-collar as it came. Grew up poor, was still poor. No ties to the underworld at all and, by all accounts, a good mother.

There was a vague timeline of Cash's life up until he joined my father's empire. High school, where he'd run track and played football until he injured his shoulder and was forced to drop out. There was speculation from his teachers—how the fuck had Rafael gotten *those* notes? —that he'd become addicted to pain pills. Those rumors grew when he dropped out to get his GED and joined the Marcosas a month later.

That was the end, though. No information on what he did for the family or where he went when he left. The last twenty-five years were just...blank. How had he been off the grid for so long?

Moving on, we found a list of known Aces and accomplices, including a few he'd kept long-term. One of them, a man who had been around since Cash was in school, was listed as a weapons specialist. The bomb maker, no doubt.

There was a special place in hell I was dying to send him.

The more I read, the more holes I found, and the more certain I was that Cash had been home for far longer than I'd thought. If he'd left at all.

Pointing to the list of known addresses, I frowned. "Look at these places. Seymour's Deli, Wayward School, Sevenroe Hospital, The Mine. Do those sound familiar to you?"

Dominic and Greyson shared matching frowns, but Grey was the one who figured it out first. "Weren't those hideouts that Mario used?"

"Yeah." I kept reading, confirming the theory with the pictures Rafael had included. Cash was using Mario's hideouts as his own.

"He stole Marcosa safe houses?" Dominic asked.

"More like hidey-holes," I corrected absently. I wanted to explain more, but my mind was racing.

Thankfully, Greyson took over. "Mario was beyond paranoid, always thinking someone was out to get him. Because of that, he didn't give up his safe houses to anyone, but the crew still needed somewhere to hide in emergencies, so he created protected pockets all over the city. Places to bunk if there was trouble. They weren't widely known, though. Only the very top of the Marcosa food chain would've known that many locations."

"So, Cash wasn't lying. He really was close to Mario."

Or he stole more than product. There was only one other way he could've known about the safe houses.

"I don't remember any mention of him in my father's files." The handwritten journals were hidden in the library of the mansion. Some were Antoni's and mine, but most were my father's. I tried to remember if I'd ever seen anything Cash- or Beckstrom-related, but I recalled nothing. Though, I'd only read the last ten years, certain that nothing else would be relevant.

What a foolish mistake.

What if the answer to our problems is in those fucking journals?

"You mentioned that he was around when you were a kid, right? How far back did you read?" Dominic asked, reading my mind.

"Not far enough."

The idea that somewhere in my house was a potential land mine of knowledge I'd missed seared my stomach. The numbness I'd been swaddled in since the blast disappeared, and I was left with nothing but agonizing rage at Cash, at the bomb, at myself.

"It's okay, Mari. We'll read them when we get home." Greyson's attempt to soothe me didn't work because it wasn't okay. It would never be okay.

I'd made a mistake that could've cost Nate his life. Could've cost Greyson and Dominic theirs too.

I thought about Nate's mom, who had no idea that her only son could've died today. The realization that I would've had to look that woman in the eyes and tell her I was the reason he was gone was too much.

Everything was *too fucking much.*

Rationally, I knew the shock was wearing off and I was headed straight into an epic breakdown, but I didn't care.

For once, I wanted to be the emotional waif all the big men of the city thought I was. I wanted to rage and burn until I knew for certain that no one was coming after my family again.

I reached out, hoping the warmth of Nate's hand would ground me, but even that only did so much. He was in that bed because of all this shit. The rage wanted revenge. It wanted retribution. It wanted an eye for an eye.

If the whole world went blind, then so be it.

Chapter 29
Mari

I was giving Tennessee patrol instructions when it happened. "Split up the teams between the east and the west side. Try to keep them as far out of the other leaders' territories as possible. I don't want anyone to think—"

"Angel."

It was nothing more than a whisper, but I whirled around, phone call forgotten.

Holy shit. Nate was awake. Three hours after we'd arrived at the hospital, he'd finally woken up.

Suddenly, I was at his side, fingers gently running over his face. "Are you okay? Are you in any pain? I can call Dr.—"

"I'm fine, Mari." He grabbed my wrists, pulling them down to rest on his chest. "I'm fine."

"You are not fine," I snapped.

I could feel the terror of being trapped under the rubble welling in my stomach again, ready to swallow me whole. Nate must have seen it too, because he yanked me off-balance, pulling me onto the bed with a soft grunt.

"You idiot, you're going to hurt yourself."

"Then I'll hurt myself," he said. "I'd rather be hurt than watch you be in pain."

Sweet, irritating man. "I'm only in pain because you almost died."

"That feels like an exaggeration," he said, though he twisted to look at Dominic standing guard by the door. "Isn't it?"

Dominic's head rocked back and forth. "Yes and no." His eyes fell to the phone still clutched in my hand. "You want me to finish that?"

"Shit." I pulled the phone back up to Tennessee yelling down the line, and I winced. "Sorry, sorry. Nate woke up."

There was a brief pause and then, "Is the kid okay?"

I smiled softly at the very obvious concern in Tennessee's voice. "Yeah, I think so."

"Good. Should we bring Cameron's team in to do the south side?"

The reminder that my cousin had just lost some of his men sat heavy. "Give them the night off."

Tonight, they could be blissfully unaware of what they'd lost. Tomorrow would come soon enough.

"Three teams means leaving a potential opening for Cash to get through."

"Then he gets an opening," I sighed. "We'll deal with the south side tomorrow."

"No, we won't. We'll take care of the south side tonight." Nate, who'd obviously been listening, snatched the phone from my hand. I tried to grab it back, but he gave quick assurances to Tennessee and ended the call. "How soon can I get out of this joint?"

"You have a concussion. You're not going anywhere."

"Possible concussion and it's a small one," Dr. Grant corrected as she stepped into the room. "Glad to see you awake, Mr. Black."

Nate winced, probably at the volume of our voices. *Because he had a concussion.* "Thanks. Now, when can I leave?"

I glowered, but Dr. Grant just laughed. "If your tests come back fine, you can go home within the hour."

"Perfect." Nate turned to me with a serious expression. "We have a stop to make on the way."

Before I could climb farther onto the bed to strangle my irritating boyfriend, Dominic grabbed me around the waist. I was still debating whether I should attempt to get free when he sat and arranged me on his lap. "Don't worry, baby. We'll make it quick."

"We won't be making anything at all. We're going home."

I was surly as I watched every second of Dr. Grant's assessment. She checked Nate's reflexes, his eyes, and even got a portable ultrasound to make sure he had no internal bleeding anywhere. Nothing.

That fucker passed every test.

Goddammit.

"Other than the possible concussion, which does seem very mild, if anything, I see nothing wrong. Pay attention to yourself, keep those burns clean, and take it easy for a few days." Dr. Grant's smile was just as wide as Nate's. "You're a very lucky man, Mr. Black."

Nate's eyes found mine from across the room. "Trust me, Doc. I know it."

Dr. Grant dipped her head, trying to hide the small smile, but I saw it. She liked Nate, and I had a suspicious feeling we were growing on her too. "Stay away from screens for a few days, if possible."

"Don't worry. He's going home and straight to bed."

Dr. Grant patted my hand on the way out the door. "I'm sure you'll take great care of him."

The second she was gone, Nate started unhooking himself from the monitors.

"What the fuck are you doing?!" I shoved off Dominic, but he wouldn't let me go.

"I'm getting out of here," Nate said, ignoring my growl. "The doc said I'm good, so we're going."

"You need to rest."

"And I will. After we check the south side."

"You have *got* to be kidding me." I tipped my head back, glaring at the ceiling. "You're not going."

"Yes, I am."

The door opened as I slammed my mouth shut, only to find Greyson walking in. We were all silent as he passed out the bottled water he'd gone to buy, tossing the last one to Nate. "Nice to see you awake."

"Thanks." Nate took the water with a grateful sigh. "Maybe you can get through to her."

Grey settled in a chair near the bed and kicked his feet up. "What are we arguing about now?"

"Nate wants to go patrolling," I said with more than a little snark. But what did it matter? Greyson was the one person I could count on to side with me.

He raised an eyebrow, and after Nate's quick explanation of the phone call, he seemed to shut down. No, he hid himself from me.

What. The. Fuck.

"If he wants to go, then we should take him."

Et tu, Greyson? "No."

Grey sighed. "Mari."

"I said no, Greyson." Why didn't they get that this was for his own good? He was hurt, for fuck's sake!

"You don't command me," Nate snapped, chest heaving as he ripped off the last of his monitor wires. "I'm not your servant. I'm not a Marcosa. I'm not a dog. I'm your fucking boyfriend."

"I know that!"

"No, you don't. You're scared for me, and instead of thinking with your head, you're thinking with that fear."

I wanted to deny it, but hadn't I just thought the same thing? Hadn't I *wanted* to think with my heart for one fucking second?

Was it so bad that I was scared for him? "I don't want you to get hurt because of me."

"I know, baby." Nate's voice softened, and he held out a hand for me to hold because Dominic still hadn't let me up. "I'm sorry I scared you, but it can't stop us from getting things done. We have to push through when shit gets tough. We can't afford to give Cash an out."

We really couldn't, but every part of me was screaming *no*.

"I promise I'll be careful the entire time. We'll get in, check it out and leave so you can mother me to death in our own home. Does that sound like a deal?"

It wasn't what I wanted, but if this relationship was to be built on equity like I wanted, I couldn't pull the queen card. I had to respect Nate's choices. "Fine, but you go to bed as soon as we get home."

Was I pouting? Yes. I didn't even care that I was a grown woman doing it either. If my men had issues with it, they could suck it up, because agreeing felt like it stole all my energy. Nate smiled, reeling me out of Dominic's grip and into his chest for a hug. "I'll let you hover all over me for the next two days if it means we can do this."

"I was going to do that anyway."

"Of course you were." He laughed into my hair, pulling me in for another kiss. "I'm proud of you, baby."

"Don't be. I'm going to bitch the whole time."

"I wouldn't have it any other way." Then he pressed the button for the nurses station. "We need discharge papers, please."

* * *

An hour later, the south side was quiet. Too quiet.

Or maybe that was just my paranoia.

I had to wonder if it was smart to be out with a walking target on my back and an injured man, but I'd lost the argument. We were patrolling, even as I reeled with the fear of almost losing Nate. The fear that next time, we might not be so lucky.

Focus. Break down later.

We were at the last stop, carefully checking alleys, streets, and buildings for any sign of Cash or his fucking Aces, but we found nothing but silence.

"Everything seems fine," Dominic whispered.

It was his first time on patrol with us—Nate's, too—and seeing him so straight-faced and serious felt different. Like he was really in it and we were actually a team. I didn't hate it.

My phone buzzed in my pocket, and habit had me stepping closer to Greyson before I pulled it out. I liked to tell myself that blocking the light hid our vantage point, but I knew better. He was guarding my body, and I hated every second of it.

The phone buzzed twice more before I opened the text thread. All the other teams were done.

"Looks like the rest of the city is clear. No Aces, but plenty of graffiti for them," I said under my breath, slipping the phone back into my pocket. "Let's just get this done so we can go."

I slid a glance toward Nate, who was grinning, even as he limped behind us. *Fucking idiot.* I wanted him in bed where he could rest, and instead, he chose to roam the fucking streets. Because that had to be good for his burns.

"Quit glaring at him before you make this a real problem," Dominic said, exasperated. "He's a grown man, Mari. He can make his own choices."

He was right and I knew it, but the day had been long and emotionally taxing. I whipped my head toward him, ready to rip him to shreds, only to see a faint flash across the street. My body reacted before my brain caught up to what it was.

Metal glinting in moonlight.

On a lunge, I shoved Dominic out of the way.

"What the fuck—"

"Gun!" I hissed, pulling him behind a parked car. The thing was small and new, more plastic than metal, so it wasn't going to do shit to give us actual cover, but it was the best I had at the moment.

Thankfully, Greyson heard and hauled Nate behind a car with him too. I pointed to give him a general place to look as Dominic's heavy hand landed on my shoulder. I shook him off. There was no time for distractions as I searched out that glint again.

Someone was close. I could feel it.

Less than a second later, Dominic had me twisted, back pinned against the car. "What the fuck do you think you're doing?"

Was he serious? I looked over at the others. Nate was focused solely on the shadows, while Greyson's eyes bounced between them and us. "There was a gun."

"So you step in front of it?"

The answer was obvious, so I didn't respond.

Wrong move.

Dominic crept closer, eyes burning with rage even in the low light. His voice was a dark whisper that slid along my skin like a razor blade. "*You* don't do that."

Was that a joke? Hadn't he *just* told me that Nate was allowed to do whatever he wanted with his body? Did I not have the same rules for mine?

Apparently not. How fucking typical.

"Next time someone saves your ass, how about a thank you?"

"I'm not going to thank you for putting yourself in danger," he snarled.

"And I'm not going to argue right now. If you have a problem, save it for later."

"No. We're going to finish this now."

"Dominic."

"I'm not saying this as your boyfriend, but as your partner in crime—literally. You don't have the luxury of putting yourself in the line of fire for me. You have hundreds who depend on you." He wrapped his hand around my throat, a warning to pay attention. Even angry, even horrified, he stroked his thumb softly against my pulse. Gentle. "You'd survive my loss, but the city wouldn't survive yours."

I didn't agree, but we seriously didn't have the time. Anticipation and adrenaline were racing through my veins, and I could feel the tension getting higher in the air. "I need you to let me go."

We were sitting ducks the longer he decided to make a point. "Tell me that you agree."

Yeah, not going to happen.

I tried to push forward, but he shoved me back. "This isn't a conversation, Mari. As your underboss, I am telling you, *you do not get between me and a bullet again.* You asked me to respect your job, I'm asking for the same courtesy. Let me do mine. Let me protect you."

Well, fuck.

Dominic managed to trap me between a rock and hypocrisy. Asshole.

"Fine," I growled. "You win."

"It's not about winning, *mariposa*. It's about keeping you safe for all the good you do for the city. We're on the same side."

The frustration was still there, but the defensiveness the conversation created eased out of me. "Okay. But Dom—"

He immediately let go of me. "I know. Never correct you like that in public. I'm sorry, I wasn't thinking."

It felt wrong that he understood so fast, like part of me was still expecting him to argue. But he hadn't argued because he didn't want me to be me; he argued because he had to. Because whether I hated it or not, he was right. His job was to stand between me and danger, and mine was to let him.

Greyson caught my eye and motioned across the street.

"They've got him," I whispered, refocusing on the task at hand. "Let's go around and see if we can jump him without a shootout."

Dominic and I circled the car on quiet feet, knowing Grey would understand the plan immediately. The street was a dead end, but with trash cans and bushes around, we had enough cover to get us almost on top of the guy. I couldn't see more than a lanky shadow and the glint of that fucking gun.

Dominic held up his fingers, counting down.

Three.

Two.

One.

Go.

We lunged at the same time that Greyson and Nate stood from their positions. The distraction startled the Ace, who lifted his gun to shoot them. Except we were there first.

Dominic wrapped his arms around the Ace's leg, taking him to the ground. I jumped for his arms, trying to pry the gun out of his hand. He let himself fall flat, groaning as his head hit the pavement, but the move kept his arms free. He swung wildly, hitting me in the cheek when one of them slipped from my grip.

It'd been a while since I'd been hit in the face, and it was always a bit of a shock. Still, I didn't let up, sitting on his other arm so I could grab the one that was flailing the gun around. "Will you hold still, you fucking idiot?"

"Bite me, bitch."

That's it. I reared back and gave him a swift punch to the head, knocking him out.

"Feel better, *mariposa*?"

I really did. By the time the guy was trussed up like a holiday turkey, I was sweating buckets, but it was done. We had an Ace.

Now we just had to see if he'd talk.

* * *

The boys hung him in the cold room, a giant meat locker in the basement of the mansion. Nate was unanimously voted out of interrogation duty and relegated to grumbling in the corner about overprotective families.

"How long do you want to make him wait?" Greyson asked as we stared at our swinging captive, who hadn't woken yet. I was starting to worry I'd hit him too hard.

"We don't have time to wait. I'll take him now."

It had been a long time since I'd felt blood on my skin, and after the day we'd had, I needed it. I needed the control, needed to know I was the only thing protecting him from death. It probably made me some kind of psychopath, but I didn't care.

Beating the shit out of an Ace was the perfect way to get my head on straight, which I desperately needed because as the man swung, phantom aches echoed through my fingertips, my ribs. I knew it was in my head, but it was so hard to ignore.

Was that what I'd looked like when Cash had me hanging? Had I really been that vulnerable? I didn't know, but I made a promise to myself that I would never be that way again. He would never get another chance to hurt me like that.

"You don't have to do this, Mari," Nate said seriously. Dominic stood close to him, giving me distance after our disagreement, so Greyson was the one to wrap my hands, finishing with brass knuckles custom made to fit over them. I could've worn them alone, but the extra padding meant I wouldn't break a finger by accident.

Probably.

He kissed my palms before stepping back to stand with the others. "She'll be fine, Nate."

Dominic nodded. "Besides, she's got something to prove tonight."

"You don't need to prove anything to us," Nate told me.

"I didn't say we were the ones she was doing it for," Dominic corrected.

Fucker was right again. I had to prove to myself that even though I'd failed more than I'd succeeded lately, I was still Marianna Marcosa, Queen of Seattle.

And no one fucked with me.

I stared at the Ace on my hook, frowning. The longer I looked, the more certain I was I'd seen him before.

I tried to remember, but with everything else, my mind was still fuzzy. "Do we have Cash's file?"

Greyson pulled out the small tablet he had in his suit jacket, tapping away on the screen. "I uploaded it to the cloud while Nate was getting discharged."

"You mean while Mari was arguing with the nurses," Nate corrected.

"They weren't giving me the right instructions."

"Like you didn't already know them."

Grey laughed under his breath, handing me the device with the file open. It was just pictures of the pages for now, so I flipped through until...*there.*

Known accomplices. Cash didn't have many, so the long-timers had caught my attention as people he seemed closer to.

People like Enzo Morelli, the man on my hook.

The photo was definitely old since he looked like a model. In person, he looked very different. Flatter hair, face wrinkled, and a complexion shades lighter—almost sickly. Only the tattoos and the scar across the side of his neck told me the two men were one and the same.

They need to update their photos.

Reading the file, I realized why I remembered him. Good ol'

Enzo was the weapons specialist. The one who had been connected to Cash since they were teens. The one I suspected set the bomb.

I wasn't naïve enough to think Cash would come for his lifelong bestie, but I had hope Enzo knew more than the others had.

My captive woke as I handed the tablet back to Grey. "Enzo Morelli, I wasn't expecting you tonight."

He lifted his head wearily, eyes widening when he saw me. It was just a second before he schooled his face into a frown, but I recognized the look in his eyes.

Fear.

He knew why he was in my cold room, and he knew he wasn't leaving it alive.

"I want to talk about your little friend Cash Beckstrom."

"Don't have any friends," Enzo said.

"That's right," I said with a snap. "He's not your friend. He's your boss."

"Don't have one of those either." Enzo's eyes narrowed, and I tried not to grin. Men were so easy. Made men, even more so. Hit their libido or their pride, and they'd fold like a house of cards.

"We both know that's not true, but fine. Let's call him an acquaintance. What do you know about Cash?"

"That he's a psychopath who's going to chew you up and spit you out."

"He already tried that and failed."

"He'll just keep coming until he gets it right."

"I'm looking forward to it."

For a moment, he just watched me, like a tiger pacing in its cage. Then he scoffed. "You two are more alike than you know."

What a terrifying thought.

Enzo sighed. "Look, he's a vault. Even if I wanted to help you—which I don't—I couldn't. There's nothing for me to give. No information. No plans. Nothing. Your best bet is to kill me now and move on with your life."

"That's certainly one option."

The punch hit him out of nowhere, rocking him back on the hook. I fell into muscle memory, treating his body as a heavy bag to exorcise my demons. Occasionally, I stopped to let him catch his breath. When he did, I asked him questions.

Where is Cash hiding? I don't know.

Why did he come back? To get the power he thinks he deserves.

What does he really want? To take your place.

They were answers, but unhelpful ones. I asked about the docks, Porter, Jacob, and Derek too. I asked about every little thing I could think of. Enzo gave me nothing, and the longer it went, the angrier I got.

I was seething when I stopped, letting Enzo swing. Seeing him, bleeding and broken, did nothing for me. There was no satisfaction in killing a dead man. Especially one who kept his secrets well.

"Why is Cash taking Marcosa properties?" I tried again, hoping for a different answer.

"What can I say? He's got a thing for hospitals...and bothering you," Enzo panted, face lined with pain.

"Is that why you tried to blow Nate and me up? Because it would bother me." I flicked my hand toward my boyfriend.

"Of course not. The kid wasn't supposed to be there." Enzo scoffed, though his eyes followed my hand. When he looked at Nate, it was almost...remorseful.

Is that a conscience?

So, he *was* keeping tabs on Nate. I'd already known there was no way Cash wouldn't see a new inductee to our world as an easy target, but it pissed me off, nonetheless. "Did you see him as a way in? You kill him, you wound me."

"It's not that deep, man. We get our orders, we follow them. End of story." Enzo said it like he didn't believe it, but I could tell I'd hit closer to the truth.

Cash wanted to hurt me, and he knew Nate was an easy way to do it.

I leaned in, letting Enzo feel my breath on his face. "I'll tell you a secret. You're not wrong. The idea of you hurting him enrages me. The fact that you already have... Well, I'm *very* unhappy right now."

Enzo looked between Nate and me, as if he realized he'd finally made a mistake. It wasn't his fault. My patience for Cash and his need for attention was spent.

He'd taken Antoni from me.

He'd taken Rey from me.

He'd nearly taken my men.

I wasn't going to give him another opportunity to hurt the people I loved. It was time to hit back, and I'd just found a two-for-one special.

Quick as lightning, I pulled my gun and shot. Men like Enzo didn't get last words or a chance to repent for their sins. They got a bullet between the eyes before I forgot them entirely.

I considered it a mercy.

"I take it you're done, then?" Greyson drawled.

"Not even close. It's time we hit back. We're going to fight fire with fire."

And thanks to Enzo, I knew exactly where to go.

Chapter 30
Mari

Sevenroe Hospital had been abandoned in the seventies after a gas leak nearly blew up one of the wings. The patients were immediately moved to another hospital, and Sevenroe closed.

At the time, the city was focused on budget cuts, and after getting an insane quote for a new system, they shut off gas access and did the least amount of fixes they could get away with before locking the doors.

Fifty years later, the place was wrecked. The exterior was worn and faded in what few places the weeds and vines didn't cover. Doors fell off their hinges, windows were broken or black, though I couldn't tell if that was from paint or grime. The whole thing had the air of desperation that came from abandonment.

Since the city had evacuated the entire area in case the place ever blew, my father had considered it a good hiding spot for his men and the perfect training ground for Antoni and me. I doubted

Cash knew, but by the time I was ten, I could navigate every square inch of that hospital blindfolded.

And I knew exactly how to burn it down.

"Are you sure about this?" Nate asked as he limped beside me. His breathing was rough but steady, and when he caught me watching, he smiled. "I'm fine, angel. More worried about you, anyway."

"I'm fine," I parroted back.

I wasn't fine. I was fucking fed up. I was so tired of Cash and O'Bannon and the other men in the city thinking they could take and take and take.

Seattle was my fucking city.

I had been too lenient on them, too smothered with grief to do anything when the hints of unrest started to appear. Too overwhelmed to put Cash in his place before things got too bad.

This was the outcome. A man who had walked into my city and thought he could take it from me.

Yeah, fucking right.

I was done playing nice. Trying to beat Cash from the high ground was going to get us killed. It was time to sink to his level, or as close to it as I could get. I could never condone collateral damage the way that he did, but eradicating the Aces one man at a time? I could do that.

"Don't worry, boy toy," Dominic said, clapping a hand on Nate's shoulder. "*Mariposa* is very accustomed to setting shit on fire."

He would know.

Before we'd ever gotten together, he'd said something cruel to Antoni. His whole life had been uprooted and he was hurting, but I couldn't let it stand.

No one mistreated my brother.

That night, we got Dominic too drunk to speak, wheeled his favorite car into the center of the driveway, and set it on fire. It was the only time I wondered if my father would actually snap and hit one of us, but he didn't. He'd spent the rest of the night screaming about consequences, but the second we stepped out of his office, it was as if it had never happened. He bought Dominic a new car, and we never spoke of it again.

It was a memory I cherished.

I blew Dominic a kiss, and he laughed.

"How do you want to do this?" Greyson asked.

It had been years since I'd been inside Sevenroe, but I still knew every part of it.

In all the years we'd come, my father had never explained the issues with the hospital to me, but I was curious. I wanted to know why they'd shut the place down. So, I did my own research. I pulled the blueprints from city hall and looked over every report I could find. If I knew every inch of the place by feel and smell and sight, I knew the guts of the hospital by memory. Which was how I knew the malfunctioning pipes ran through the entire hospital. A veritable treasure trove of gas, if one knew how to get it working.

"First, we need to check and make sure they're actually in here." Though the guards we'd knocked out, tied up, and dragged into the bushes were a good indication Cash was hiding something inside, we didn't know what.

I desperately wanted it to be himself.

The west wall had a first-floor window. It was barred shut—another sign Cash had something valuable inside—and black, but I wanted to look anyway.

Together, we spread out across the wall, Nate and Dominic keeping watch on either side, and Greyson next to me, keeping an eye above in case any guards were roaming the roof. When they were in position, I inched forward, staying as low as I could. Crouching under the window, I thought it looked the same as all the others. Black and inaccessible.

Except it wasn't.

In one of the corners was the barest hint of light. A place where whatever he'd placed on the glass had peeled up. Carefully, I peeked up until I could look inside the tiny space, and when I did, I swore.

Behind that window, Cash had turned the first floor into a fully functioning garage. He didn't just have usable cars either. There were beaters the Aces could drive to hide in plain sight, but expensive cars too. Classic cars. Cars that could cover mortgages for families around the country.

Cars that spoke of wealth Cash shouldn't have. *My* wealth.

He'd stolen from me, then spent *my money* on fucking trophies?

That shit boiled my blood.

"Take a look," I told Greyson.

My finger shook where I held my gun, and I had the desperate urge to break a door down and go in shooting, but I wanted more carnage than that. If Cash wasn't home, then destroying an entire parking lot of cars would have to do.

"Holy shit," Grey whispered.

"Let's get to the electrical room," I said.

As expected, the room had been unlocked, and since it wasn't important to them, the morons hadn't bothered to replace it, further cementing my theory that Cash hadn't done his research.

Lucky me.

Silently, I snuck inside. It was almost pitch black, barely enough moonlight to see in front of my face, but I couldn't use a flashlight and risk exposing our location. Carefully, I slid my backpack onto the floor, rooting around until I found the night vision goggles. I almost never used them because the risk was too great most of the time. If you got caught with a flash of light, it killed your eyesight. Since the guys would cover my back, I didn't worry.

A few minutes later, I yanked off the night vision goggles with a grin, shoving them back into the pack, and cleared my throat softly as a warning.

"Done?" Nate whispered.

"Almost." I stepped out of the room, letting my eyes adjust to the night again.

"What else do we need to do?"

I couldn't help the smirk that tipped my lips. "Play ball."

All three of them looked at me for a beat before Nate sighed. "Why does that make me nervous?"

Dominic grinned. "Because it should."

We crept through the shadows, making sure to stay covered in case somebody happened to look out a window. This was a covert mission. No shootouts.

I found a decent spot for us to wait. It wasn't an ideal position, but the coverage was excellent, and that mattered more than a good view.

Checking my watch, I hunkered down on the balls of my feet. "We should give it a minute."

"And then what?"

I zipped my lips, not wanting to spoil the fun yet. Ninety seconds later, I couldn't wait any longer. Carefully setting the bag on the ground again, I started unloading things.

Dominic swore under his breath. "You've been carrying grenades this whole time?"

"Yeah." I shrugged. What else did he want me to do, start a campfire on the ground floor?

Holding the first grenade out to Nate, I gave it a gentle wiggle. "You want to do the honors?"

I figured he was the one whose whole life had been uprooted by this shit. He'd lost his carefree existence, his job, his future, all because Cash had put him in my line of sight. The least I could do was give Nate the first swing back.

He crept forward, wrapping his whole hand around the grenade in mine. "I don't regret it."

I could hear what he wasn't saying. *I don't regret you.*

"I know." I even believed it most days.

Nate stared, making sure I knew he was serious before he took the grenade. Hands free, I gave the others theirs and palmed my own. We didn't need more than four for this. The gas would do most of the work.

"Where do you want them?" Nate asked.

"Ideally, through one of the windows, but as close as you can get works."

"Are we far enough back?"

"Absolutely." Probably.

"This is a terrible idea," Nate said under his breath.

"No, it isn't. He thinks that he's cowed us, that he's the big bad in this city. It's time he remembers that it's always been me." When Nate still didn't throw it, I rested a hand on his arm. "Do it for your mom. If he keeps going, she's not going to be safe either."

We hadn't spoken about it, but the reality was, this war would bleed over into everything. The mundane lives of those outside our world would be affected. Nate's mom's care would be compromised if we didn't end things soon. I hated that the responsibility lay heavily on his shoulders, but he couldn't avoid it anymore. The longer this continued, the more likely it was that we'd lose more than we could accept.

With another look at me, Nate cranked his arm back and tossed the grenade, sending it through the only other window on the first story. For a moment, all was silent beyond the tinkling of broken glass.

Then, *boom.*

The second the yelling started, Dominic, Grey, and I sent our grenades flying through the windows too. I waited as the heat from the burning structure crept closer, wondering if it was going to be the hit I wanted. Then the front doors crashed open, and the roar of an engine echoed through the night.

"He's here." Something in me knew it like I knew my own name.

The car raced down the front stairs just as the final explosion hit. Whatever wasn't on fire from the grenades caught with the gas, and the whole place shook. From my protected crouch, I watched the car be lifted into the air with a whoosh of heat, and I heard the crunch of metal as it was thrown roof-first into a nearby tree. I had no way to know for sure that Cash was in the car, but I hoped he was.

"We should check the car," Nate said, eyes trapped on the crunched-up metal. "See if he's there."

I wanted to. God, I wanted to, but the roar of more engines was a battle cry we couldn't ignore. "We have to go."

Nate didn't move, and I wondered if he'd run off and finish the job himself. I would've done it, but we really couldn't risk getting cornered without backup. Stealth was the key for now.

I held out my hand, watching the flames flicker over Nate's face. "Let's go home."

He grabbed it immediately, letting me drag him down the road and back to our car.

By the time we got home, his limp was more pronounced, his brow furrowed in pain.

Checking my watch again, I cursed. He was well past due for some painkillers and a nap. I slipped his arm over my shoulder and wrapped mine around his waist to support him. "Let's get you to bed."

We were halfway up the stairs when his phone went off. He reached into his pocket, and I took most of his weight as he pulled out the device.

I saw the name, and my heart sank like it knew something I didn't.

Mom's Caregiver.

"Is everything okay?"

"No."

He tipped the phone to show me four words.

Time to come home.

When he looked down at me, his eyes were watery, his whole body slumped in defeat, and I knew. I knew everything was about to change for him.

Nate was going to lose the only person he had left. His mom.

"Are you okay?" I whispered, brokenhearted for him already.

Immediately, I winced. Of course he wasn't. Who would be?

He didn't respond, though. He just clung to me, bringing me close so he could bury his face in my hair.

Nate gave me the softest kiss just over my pulse, leaving his lips there as he spoke. "I'm going to have to be."

Chapter 31
Nate

I understood from an early age that my life would be nothing like the movies. Chaos, torment, blood on my hands. That was my future. I'd long since come to terms with the idea that the ghosts that plagued me when I closed my eyes would be my only companions if I lived to old age.

Happily ever after was for people who could pay for it, and I'd always been poor.

Cash poor. House poor. Life poor. Love poor.

Then came Mari.

From the moment I saw her, I knew who she was. I *saw* her. All those sharp edges hiding softness she couldn't show. All that pain she was drowning in. The grief that felt so similar to mine, I wondered if they were twins. Pushing her away was supposed to be easy. She was exactly what I needed to avoid. She was a king-pin, for fuck's sake. But Mari had a way of digging under walls if you let her, and if she let you tear hers down in return? It was everything.

But there were no fairy tales for people like us. Not in life. All we could hope for was more kindness in death than we'd been granted on earth.

"What can I do?" she asked quietly.

We hadn't moved from the stairs, not since I'd gotten the text. I just stood there, staring at the four words that would change it all.

Time to come home.

My chest was tight, and every breath was a struggle. *Is it hot in here?*

I didn't know. It all sucked. Everything sucked. Life sucked.

No, my past life sucked. This life, the one where I got Mari and Greyson and Dominic? Where I had a family that would kill for me? Die for me?

This one was good. So good.

I should've known it would never last.

> When?

> Tomorrow.

It's not tomorrow yet.

Even as I looked at the crest of dawn in the sky, I knew the answer. Tomorrow, decisions would be made, but I had time. With a hard click, I turned off the screen and returned the phone to my pocket. Everything was changing. By the time the sun set on the day, everything would be different. *I* would be different.

If I only had one night with Mari before my whole world shifted, then I wanted it.

No distractions. No sharing. Just her.

Greyson cleared his throat, looking at me with a kindness I didn't deserve. "We're going to crash."

"We are?" Dominic asked.

Grey gave him a pointed look that said *Pay attention, fuckface.* "We are."

Dominic glanced at Mari and me, softening when he saw my face.

"Ah shit. Night, *mariposa.*" Dominic kissed Mari, running his hand up her back gently before disappearing up the stairs.

"Don't worry about tonight. I'll let everyone know to keep an eye on things in case Cash retaliates."

"Thanks, Grey. You going to be okay?" Mari's voice was fragile, like she knew there were too many people who needed her and not enough parts of her to go around.

She and I had been buried, but Greyson was the one who'd seen it happen. Who'd dug us out of the rubble alone when he wasn't sure there was anything to save. He was hurting too.

The urge to be selfless came, but Grey spoke before I could.

"I'll be fine, *reina.* Take care of Nate." Grey caught my eyes, and I knew he wasn't just doing it for Mari. He was doing it for me because I needed her. I gave him a grateful nod, a little over-whelmed at the thoughtfulness, and he returned it before leaning in for Mari's kiss. "Goodnight, baby."

When we were alone, she tipped her head to look at me. "What now?"

"I need a shower." All I wanted was to sleep in her arms and forget the texts on my phone, but I wasn't wasting my chance with Mari.

We have tonight.

"I'll take you to your room."

She'd do more than that.

I kept most of my weight off her as we took the rest of the steps. When we entered my room, I pulled her into the bathroom with me. She propped me against the counter and turned to the shower, fingers wiggling under the spray until the temperature was to her liking.

"I can help you cover the dressings and give you some privacy, if you want." Her brow was furrowed, and she chewed on her lip, a nervous gesture I'd never seen before.

Mari's losses had always come out of nowhere, a blow when her face was turned. This was head on with warning, and for her, I imagined it was like watching a train crash and being unable to look away. She wanted to help, but she didn't have the experience to know what I needed.

She had no idea that having her close was all I could ask for.

I said nothing as she stripped me out of my clothes and helped me with the dressings. I kept silent as she led me toward the shower. It was only when she turned to walk away that I grabbed her by the wrist. "Stay."

One word was all it took.

"Always."

It beat around my head, *always*. She said it like we had forever, like this thing between us was something that would never change. But I knew better.

Everything was changing.

I watched carefully as she stripped out of her clothes and climbed in, wetting a washcloth before covering it in soap. "May I?"

I liked that she asked me, even though I hoped she knew she could touch me anytime she wanted. Anywhere. I was hers. I would always be hers. "Please."

Just like that night she'd crawled into my bed to watch movies, I let Mari take care of me. I closed my eyes to the feel of her fingers in my hair, bent slightly backward as she washed the strands, then kissed the top of my head when she was done.

I watched as she lifted my arm, rubbing each and every finger to make sure it was clean. As she knelt between my legs to get the backs of my knees, my calves, my ankles. When she washed my cock, it wasn't sexual. She was methodical, damn near clinical.

And so fucking pretty.

With her hands on my thighs, she angled me into the water, and I tilted my head back, letting the soap wash my sins away.

When it was over, Mari brushed the washcloth over her skin before I took it from her. "I'll do this."

"You don't have to."

"I want to." I clung to her hips, trying to bring her closer, but she resisted.

"Nate," she sighed. "Not tonight."

With a rough tug, I pulled her back to my chest, wrapping an arm around her to hold her still as I ran the washcloth from her shoulder to her fingertips.

"I need this," I whispered. "I need to take care of you. I need *you*."

More than I could ever say. More than she would ever know, I needed her.

My angel.

My light in the dark.

I needed her touch and her voice and her love. I needed to know what she felt like against me because I worried if I didn't have one more memory, I would forget what it felt like *before*.

Because this was the *before*, and tomorrow would be the *after*. Nothing could change that.

Time didn't wait for us; it crept by in moments too fickle to hold in our memories. I wouldn't let this be one of those cases. I would cling to her scent and the feel of her skin like it was a life raft.

Even if I lost every other memory, I refused to lose this.

Mari said nothing, but she stopped moving away, letting me touch every single part of her. Dipping her head so I could rinse the shampoo out of her hair, holding still while I brushed it with conditioner still heavy in the strands, coiling the ropes into curls with my fingers. Whatever it took to stay a little while longer.

Then it was done, and I watched as she tipped her head back and let the water rush over her too. In that moment, more than the pain, sorrow, or fear, I hungered.

I needed her on my tongue. My lips. My fingers and my cock. I needed her everywhere. I needed her to fill in the hole in my chest that was growing with every second.

When Mari opened her eyes, she dipped them to where my fist was wrapped around my cock.

"I need you," I whispered hoarsely.

"Is this a good idea?"

No, but I need it all the same.

I reached out to palm the back of her head, tangling my fingers in the hair I'd just painstakingly combed and yanking her to my front. "You said you wanted to help. This will help."

But even as I wanted her, I wanted to make sure I wouldn't hurt her. I couldn't hurt her. "If this is too much, if you feel like I'm using you—"

"No," she said firmly. "It's not too much. I need this too."

I saw it then, the fear she'd been pushing down. Fear for me. For us. The future. She was worried. Scared.

I was too.

She rose onto her toes and kissed me, and it was as if she'd opened an escape hatch. The breaths that were so hard for me to take on my own were suddenly easier. I groaned into her mouth, palming her ass to lift her into my arms.

She yanked back with an indignant huff. "You're hurt."

I really was, but there was nothing on earth that would have stopped me from taking her. "Ask me if I care."

She rolled her eyes. "At least take me to bed. I'll do all the work, and you can lie back and think of the queen." The joke fell flat, but I loved her all the more for it.

Christ, I loved her.

Urgency quickened my steps out of the bathroom, where I completely ignored the idea of a towel as I threw her soaking wet onto the bed.

Words weren't my strong suit, especially not when change was so close, but I needed her to know where we stood. I needed her to know that I loved her before everything went to hell.

I told her every thought in my head as I kissed her, licked her, slid my fingers inside her.

You're beautiful. You're perfect. You're everything to me.

When I notched myself inside her for real, I gave her the most honest thing I could. "You're the best thing that's ever happened to me, angel. You feel like home."

Because she was.

From the very first moment she'd smiled at me, she'd been my home.

At first, she said nothing, letting the pleasure roll over her. Then I saw the look in her eyes—the love—and I silently begged her not to say it.

Don't. Please God, don't.

"I love you." She whispered it like she couldn't hold back, and I shoved my head into her neck so she couldn't see my face.

I didn't want the words. I didn't deserve them.

They ached. They killed. They burrowed inside me like poison.

I didn't deserve them, but Mari did.

She deserved to know everything, but she'd have to settle for what I could give her.

"I love you." Three words that changed my life this time. Three words pulled from the very depths of my soul.

I didn't know a lot about life or love, but I knew Mari was so deep inside me, there was no getting her out.

I knew soulmates were real because she was mine.

My Mari. My angel. My heaven.

"I love you," I said again. "I'll never stop loving you."

Now that the words were out, it was like I couldn't stop saying them. I whispered them against her skin, breathing them into her mouth, her hair, her fucking fingertips as we writhed together.

I didn't have a real plan for the future, just a promise I couldn't help but make. Every inch of her would know how much I cared. How real we were. How deep this love ran.

If I could change nothing about tomorrow, at least I could do that much.

Because after tomorrow, I could never go home again.

Chapter 32
Mari

The invitation came sometime after Nate fell into a fitful sleep. We'd stayed locked together long after morning arrived. He'd only crashed because I'd fed him a pain pill by hand, lavishing him with praise and kisses until he passed out in my arms.

We had a few hours of blissful sleep before Amara knocked on the door, envelope in hand. I knew what it was before I'd even opened it.

Cash Beckstrom, leader of the Aces, requests your presence this evening for a meet-and-greet. Cocktails and cigars will be served, as well as dessert. One guard for each invited guest is allowed.

Under the address—one of my office buildings, no less—was a handwritten note.

Loved the fireworks, Little Queen. I didn't think you had it in you.
See you at the meeting. Don't forget to bring your men.
--C

"It's a trap," Nate said when he found me reading it again over an early dinner because there was no way I was eating anything Cash had made.

Nate had woken up reserved, distant. I reminded myself that he was grieving and to give him space if he wanted it, even when my instincts were screaming to keep him close.

"Obviously," Dominic said, slathering his pancakes with butter. Anxiety fueled me with the urge to cook, but pancakes were all I could make without burning them, and even they had to come from a box.

I set another plate of pancakes in front of Nate, trying to pretend I couldn't see him stiffening in his seat as I got nearby.

Greyson and Dominic looked at each other and back to me with twin looks of sadness that I turned away from. I didn't need their pity. Nate was struggling, but we'd work through it eventually.

I just had to be there for him, and I would.

Clearing my throat, I went back to the stove to work on my meal, though I wasn't hungry. My stomach was tight with nerves. "If he were going to get retribution for the hospital, he'd blow the house up, not invite us to a meeting. Besides, he didn't just invite us."

He'd included the head of every other major family in Seattle to *my* office building. I had to admit, it took balls.

Whatever Cash had planned, he wanted to do it publicly.

"Moore, Tennessee, and I checked the security footage at the office, and there's been nothing out of the ordinary in the last week. They sent a team down to make sure there weren't any bombs either. They'll stay until after the meeting's over."

Even if there were, they'd probably be the last ones we had to worry about for a while. Cash's bomb maker was chilling in the freezer downstairs until I decided what to do with his body.

We finished our meal in silence, the weight of the day heavy on our shoulders. Only when I'd scraped the last bite off my plate did I lay out the plan. "We go in armed and ready for anything. The safe room is prepared in case there's an emergency, but I doubt Cash is going to invite us all to a bloodbath. There'd be too many people out to get him after to enjoy the spoils of war."

"Most of the families have rules about avenging their fallen leaders," Greyson agreed. "Even the ones who want them dead."

Wasn't that the truth. I had no doubt that if Cash succeeded in killing me, my uncles would kill him first, then fight to see who would take my throne as their own.

"So, we're agreed?" Three heads nodded. "Good. Grey and Dominic, get ready. Meet down here in an hour."

I finished my coffee as they left the room, putting the cup in the sink before turning toward my own shower. It would take every second I had to get ready.

Before I could leave, Nate caught me by the elbow, spinning me around to face him. It was the first time he'd willingly touched or spoken to me since we'd woken up. "I'm coming, too."

My chest ached when he let me go, that distance between us gaping like a canyon, but I understood protecting yourself from pain. "No, you aren't."

"I am." His eyes glittered with stubbornness, and I didn't know how to do this. How did I gently tell my boyfriend that his priorities were out of whack? That he was needed somewhere else?

How did I tell him he was wrong?

"Nate, your mom…" was dying. He had to go to see her. He had to spend those precious last moments with her.

I would've given anything to meet my mother just once. I wasn't going to let him destroy his last chance to say goodbye for anyone. Certainly not Cash fucking Beckstrom.

"I talked to her caregiver, and she'll be all right for a few hours."

"They can't know that." I'd been around death enough to know that things could take a turn in seconds. I didn't want him to regret this. To regret choosing me.

"I promise, I've got it handled and I'll go right to her after. But I don't feel comfortable letting you go without me." He sighed when he saw me gearing up for another fight and wrapped me in his arms, pressing my cheek to his chest. "Mari, I need to do this."

The urge to say no rose and fell. Hadn't I learned this already? Nate was his own person. I couldn't command him. All I could do was hope he made the right choice.

Besides, I didn't want to say anything to bring back that distance again. So, I didn't.

Selfish. Coward.

"You'd better go get ready, then."

* * *

We walked into the building that evening looking like a team. Dominic and Nate took Greyson's typical approach and wore something to match the delicate lace bralette I wore under my black suit. The pops of deep blood-red suited them in their matching suits. My own suit—an Aislynn Marcosa special—was tighter than I usually wore. The shoes were higher too. Hell, I'd even left my hair in waves down my back.

Everything about me was feminine and dangerous. Beautiful and deadly. Rafael was wrong about me; I'd always been a black widow. It seemed people needed a reminder I was all too glad to give.

The conference room was the same as always, except for the seating arrangement. Kosas, Ajilon, O'Bannon, Two-Bit, and Haru crowded around one end of the table and the single empty chair at the head. A half dozen chairs separated them and the other end, where one man sat alone.

Cash.

Ignoring the elephant in the room, I allowed Nate to help me into my seat. When I was settled, he didn't retreat. After a long conversation, we'd decided that he would take the typical bodyguard position just behind my shoulder. It was obvious Cash thought of him as a weak link, and if I wanted the attacks to stop, I had to show my faith in his abilities.

So, he got a temporary promotion. Or maybe not so temporary.

Folding my hands on the table, I finally looked up and feigned a frown at the sight of gauze on the side of Cash's face, even as it filled me with a visceral kind of joy. "Oof, that looks bad. Did you get a new tattoo or something?"

Cash's stupid smile wilted just a touch, and I couldn't help my smirk.

Payback, motherfucker.

"Apologies for the delay, gentlemen. We had a late night." I made sure my laugh was low and heavy with innuendo. The other leaders would assume we'd spent the night fucking, but Cash knew better. As expected, the men chuckled under their breath, though none were stupid enough to look at me while they did it. To his credit, Cash didn't take the bait. Not that I expected him to. He was too smart for that.

Smoothing his suit, he waved an arrogant hand. "A few minutes won't matter in the long run. I'm just glad you could make it."

The dig was subtle, the reminder that *he* had called the meeting.

It gave him the upper hand, but not by much. Especially when he'd forgotten the most obvious fact.

He could call all the meetings he wanted. They didn't start until I arrived.

Cash knew it, I knew it, and so did everyone else at that fucking table.

"Still, I appreciate your waiting for me." I smiled benevolently at him. "Shall we start?"

"Let's. Why are we here, Beckstrom?" Kosas asked, leaning back in his chair. "We're all too busy for this cat-and-mouse shit. So if you're here to play games—"

"On the contrary, I think it's time we let bygones be bygones. I'm here to propose a truce."

After losing all the capital he had stashed in Sevenroe, I wasn't surprised. But admittedly, I was a little disappointed. I wanted to beat Cash at his own game. Still, a truce without bloodshed would be a win for the entire city.

Surprisingly, O'Bannon was the one to laugh. It was loud and angry. A warning if I'd ever heard one. "You've been dicking around the city for months, fucking with supply lines and making things harder for all of us. Why should we agree to a truce when we could kill you and be done with your shit for good?"

"Because I've got an army that won't stop if I die."

"Why is that?" Ajilon asked.

"Let's just say they're very radicalized."

Of course they were. If our suspicions were right, half his army wanted to be there, and the other half was being blackmailed. I didn't fault them for it, though. I understood doing anything for your family.

"What would a truce look like to you, Cash? I think we're all dying to know what we're signing up for if we agree." I lifted a hand to encompass everyone at the table, and they all nodded.

Cash sat back, calm and in control. "Our gangs integrated under one banner. One ruler."

The men at the table stilled, predators ready to strike, and I swallowed down the instinctive spike of panic. He'd just thrown gasoline on a raging fire. Most of the other leaders had gotten their positions through blood, sweat, and death, and they'd do no less to keep them. Especially when Cash was suggesting one throne to rule them all.

I chose my words carefully, knowing that if I spoke wrong, I'd end up as dead as my father. As Antoni.

"Let me guess, you think you should lead? Because I'm not interested in a coup that kills everyone at this table." I let a condescending smile tip my lips and saw Kosas and Ajilon relax into their chairs.

"On the contrary. I'm willing to let you take the helm, provided I get to maintain a certain power level."

"And how would we do that? Give you your own territory to run under her banner?" Haru asked quietly. The quietest of the bunch, he listened more than he spoke, and I got the feeling he knew more than the others because of it.

"Marriage."

The men at my back growled as one while I fought to keep my posture loose and comfortable instead of tensing up with them. Marriage had not been on my bingo card for the day.

As expected, the table exploded in a flurry of angry words. My marital status had been a heavy debate for years, with everyone wanting to make an alliance and unite their families with mine. O'Bannon was the first to succeed, and the only reason he had was because I'd refused to lose Greyson.

Cash walking in and asking for my hand right out of the gate was an insult they couldn't allow.

Surprisingly, Haru laughed. "She's not going to marry some

upstart whose only claim to strength is that he's good at hide-and-seek."

Taking the out, I teased Cash. "Sorry, Beckstrom, but he's right. Besides, you're not my type."

Uncowed, he laughed. "Don't worry, I have someone else in mind. Someone I bet you'll really enjoy." He tipped his head, intense eyes meeting mine. "My little brother."

Alarm bells rang in my head, especially when his smirk turned into a full-blown smile that sent eyes darting between us.

I'd read the file so many times in the last day that I could recite it from memory. Cash didn't have a younger brother. He'd drowned decades ago. I'd even had Greyson check his Social Security number and his mother's history to verify it.

So, what the hell was Cash playing at?

Two-Bit caught my eye, and the look on his face... He knew something. He knew something, and it had everything to do with this.

Fuck me running.

I sat back in my chair, feigning relaxation despite the way my body thrummed with anxiety, and my mind raced. I had to play my part perfectly, or the sharks would swarm and my men and I were dead. "I'd rather chew my arm off than be related to you."

"I wouldn't say that quite yet. You haven't even been properly introduced."

But hadn't I? My mind went back to the warehouse and the call that had made Cash leave. The reason I was still alive, other than Rafael.

Fuck, Rafael. Did he know that Cash's brother had survived too? I hoped not, or I'd have to kill him and deal with those consequences as well.

Nate's hand rested on my shoulder, a silent reminder to get out of my head.

Throwing off the potential homicide of yet another uncle, I clapped like Cash had promised me a unicorn. "Okay, Cash. Introduce us. Show us this mythical, reincarnated brother of yours. I insist."

"You heard her. Come here."

At first, there was nothing but silence. Unease blanketed my skin as Cash's grin got wider and wider. "Come on, little brother. Cat's out of the bag now. Show the queen what she's buying."

There was a moment of stillness, reminding me of the moment before the bomb strike, one that promised carnage and pain and blood on the other side.

Then Nate's hand dropped from my shoulder.

I twisted, wanting to be sure he was okay. I wouldn't have put it past Cash to have hurt him right in front of us, but there was no blood that I could see.

His face, though. That caught my attention.

Brows furrowed with pain and a thousand emotions flitting across his face.

Longing. Heartbreak. Regret. Acceptance. Fear. Remorse.
Guilt.

I saw it all in a heartbeat before he shut me out. The warmth I was used to, the humor and mischief, the joy—all of it gone. Nate opened his mouth like he was going to say something but stopped. Instead, he straightened his shoulders, tipped his chin, and crossed the room without even a glance back.

No.

My fingers shook, and I slid them under the table where I clenched them so hard my nails carved grooves into my palms. I didn't care. Not then or when the skin went sticky with blood.

All I could do was watch and fight to keep my mask on so no one could see the horror I felt. Dominic and Greyson practically vibrated with rage behind me, the emotion so heavy I could feel the blister of anger against my skin.

This couldn't be real. I wouldn't survive it.

It has to be a mistake. Please let this be a mistake.

Deep down, I knew it wasn't.

Every step Nate took was a knife to the heart as the man I loved dropped in pieces to the floor. It was like he transformed the farther away he got, his posture more arrogant, his steps more assured.

When he took his place at Cash's shoulder—a mirror to where he'd stood behind me—I actually looked down, sure the useless fucking organ would be flailing on the table. I looked anywhere but at him because I couldn't correlate the man who'd whispered *I love you*s last night with the one who stood at my enemy's side.

Nate—*my* Nate—was a traitor.

A liar.

An Ace.

White noise was so loud in my ears, I could barely hear the words direct from Cash's filthy, smirking mouth, but I did.

"Esteemed leaders of the city, I'd like you to meet Nathaniel Beckstrom. My little brother and heir to the Aces."

•••

The GILDED EMPIRE series continues in **FIERCE MONARCH**

About the Author (Janie Crouch)

"Passion that leaps right off the page." - Romantic Times Book Reviews

MJ Crouch is the alter ego of USA Today and Publishers Weekly bestselling author Janie Crouch. Her books have won multiple awards, including the Romance Writers of America's coveted Vivian® Award, the National Readers Choice Award, and the Booksellers' Best.

After a lifetime on the East Coast, and a six-year stint in Germany due to her husband's job as support for the U.S. Military, Janie has settled into her dream home in Front Range of the Colorado Rockies.

When she's not listening to the voices in her head—and even when she is—she enjoys engaging in all sorts of crazy adventures (200-mile relay races; Ironman Triathlons, treks to Mt. Everest Base Camp...), traveling, and hanging out with her four kids.

Her favorite quote: "Life is a daring adventure or nothing." ~ Helen Keller.

facebook.com/janiecrouch

amazon.com/author/janiecrouch

instagram.com/janiecrouch

bookbub.com/authors/janie-crouch

Also by Janie Crouch

All books: https://www.janiecrouch.com/books

HEROES OF OAK CREEK

Hero Unbound

Hero's Flight

ZODIAC TACTICAL

Code Name: ARIES

Code Name: VIRGO

Code Name: LIBRA

Code Name: PISCES

Code Name: OUTLAW

Code Name: GEMINI

NEVER TOO LATE FOR LOVE (with Regan Black)

Heartbreak Key Collection

Ellington Cove Collection

Wyoming Cowboys Collection

Holiday Heroes Collection

RESTING WARRIOR RANCH (with Josie Jade)

Montana Sanctuary

Montana Danger

Montana Desire

Montana Mystery

Montana Storm

Montana Freedom

Montana Silence

Montana Rain

LINEAR TACTICAL (series complete)

Cyclone

Eagle

Shamrock

Angel

Ghost

Shadow

Echo

Phoenix

Baby

Storm

Redwood

Scout

Blaze

Hero Forever

INSTINCT SERIES (series complete)

Primal Instinct

Critical Instinct

Survival Instinct

THE RISK SERIES (series complete)

Calculated Risk

Security Risk

Constant Risk

Risk Everything

OMEGA SECTOR (series complete)

Stealth

Covert

Conceal

Secret

OMEGA SECTOR: CRITICAL RESPONSE & UNDER SIEGE (series complete)

Special Forces Savior

Fully Committed

Armored Attraction

Man of Action

Overwhelming Force

Battle Tested

Daddy Defender

Protector's Instinct

Cease Fire

Major Crimes

Armed Response

In the Lawman's Protection

www.ingramcontent.com/pod-product-compliance
Lightning Source LLC
Chambersburg PA
CBHW060852210726
48293CB00006B/1768